NEBULA AWARDS SHOWCASE #54

The Year's Best Science Fiction and Fantasy

Edited by Nibedita Sen

Table of Contents

Introduction

These are strange times in which to be writing the introduction to a collection of speculative fiction. Apocalyptic times, some might say. I'll spare you a summary of these anxious, pandemic-wracked months; you've lived them just the same as I have, and I doubt they'll be gone from your memory by the time this collection comes out. I doubt, in fact, that the scars will be fading from our collective and individual consciousnesses any time soon.

In these strange times, many science fiction writers are discovering just how unnervingly prescient their work turned out to be. Yet others are bemoaning the realization that they *held back* for no good reason—that they could have made their villains more cartoonishly evil, more outrageously nonsensical and self-centered, but refrained for the fear that (yes, the irony stings) it wouldn't be believable.

They say truth is stranger than fiction. Maybe it's just that we hold fiction to higher standards, while reality is spared the same quality assurance.

If nothing else, it's safe to say reality is considerably more taxing than fiction, these days.

It's hard to create in times like these. It's hard to bring tender new things into a world that's on fire under the best of circumstances, let alone when all our resources are devoted to simply treading water. If you're not creating things right now, you're not alone, and also, it's okay. Your value isn't defined by the words and the work you put out into the world; *you* matter, and you're allowed to protect yourself.

But, ironically, these times that make it hard to make art also prove to us just how *necessary* art is. Every TV show and book and movie and game that keeps us sane and emotionally nourished through this isolation, confinement, and anxiety is a testament to what stories do and why they matter. Stories have a terrible and fearsome power, and if you need more evidence, just turn on the news (or, mental health depending, don't). The people in power tell us stories every day—stories that serve their agenda and twist the truth, stories that harm the vulnerable and protect the privileged. The stories we tell each other in response are more important now than they've ever been before.

And speculative fiction? Well, I may be biased, but I think speculative fiction has a power all its own. I survived an MFA; I know far too well how the establishment likes to write us off as frivolous or insignificant because we engage in the business of inventing things that aren't real. But when truth is stranger and more incomprehensible than fiction, inventing things can become a way to speak truth to power.

I said earlier that current events are proving a lot of writers prescient, but it would be a mistake to get too hung up on science fiction's ability to accurately predict the future. Its real power is to *influence* that future by speaking to our present, using the lens of a potential future—or an alternate history—to shine light on the here and now. Fantasy wields the same, strident language of possibility when it imagines worlds both like and unlike our own, giving voices and faces to those whom history tried to overwrite, giving them teeth and weapons with which to bite back, or even just giving them much-deserved joy. Speculative fiction is political—always has been. It's a blade and a beacon and a microscope and a telescope, and metaphors aside, it's a field I'm never not proud and enthralled and excited to be working in.

The truth is that it's never more important to be able to imagine different realities than when the one you're living in is full of despair. The truth is that the most marginalized of us are the ones most often in need of a little magic, whether that takes the form of hope or revenge or bloody catharsis, and even if people try to smack it down as 'escapism.' There's nothing wrong with a little escape. At the risk of quoting one of the dinosaurs we're moving beyond, "Why should a man be scorned if, finding himself in prison, he tries to get out and go home? Or if he cannot do so, he thinks and talks about other topics than jailers and prison-walls?"

And, as it so happens, the writers most disadvantaged by the status quo are often the best at bloodying or escaping or reimagining or uplifting it, since they're not invested in maintaining it. I spared you a summary of the pandemic; I'll skip recapping the Puppies, too, and just say instead that the pushback we've seen against diversity in the SFF industry is commensurate with a sea change in the way that industry works. One look at this TOC is proof enough, and if you need more, just look at the 2019 nominees too. We're living in a new golden age of SFF, and the brightest lights in our sky are queer, women, people of color, disabled, and neurodivergent—all the people who fell through the cracks. We're climbing back out, and we're changing things.

And we've got a long, long way to go.

The world we live in is broken—but, as Rumi said, the crack is how the light gets in. And what a luminous sea of stars we're floating in. Just look at this TOC—it's radiant.

I can't wait to find out what stories the future holds.

~Nibedita Sen

It's Dangerous to Go Alone

by Kate Dollarhyde

In a November 12, 2018 piece in *GeekWire*, titled "First-ever Nebula award for game writers approved by professional science fiction writers organization," Frank Catalano, summarizing the words of then-SFWA president Cat Rambo, wrote that it took, "three tries in three different decades" for the Science Fiction and Fantasy Writers of America to welcome game writers into the organization.

As a writer and editor straddling the fields of speculative fiction and game development, I wasn't surprised to read that anecdote. For a genre that has at times considered itself the vanguard of narrative innovation, speculative fiction occasionally finds its growth hidebound by convention, and so I suspect some of my peers in the genre struggled to see the relevant connections between game writing and prose fiction.

I can't exactly say I blame them, because the differences between writing novels, short stories, and video games are significant. While game writing is necessarily writing, the methods by which players encounter that writing—and the means by which that writing is produced—bear little resemblance to the familiar processes of prose fiction.

A game's script is often designed to support rules, art, and gameplay. The pursuit of fun or challenge may trump story, theme, character, or the poetry of language. Game writing is frequently a team sport, involving the work of anywhere from one to twenty writers—or more. Scripts are often highly collaborative constructs, touched by designers, scripters, and, if we're lucky, editors, thereby muddying any chance a player may have had at attributing sole authorship. The experience of writing a game can sometimes be as alienated from writing novels and short stories as I expect one can find while still being called fiction writing.

Yet, games don't need to transcend their constraints to tell immersive, personal, and introspective stories, because when a player interacts with a game, the game interacts back. This push-me-pull-you dynamic is often a carefully crafted illusion, but it can make games powerful tools for inspiring empathy, challenging beliefs, and provoking action. Some of the most exciting work in the field—work like *Outer Wilds*, *Mutazione*, *Tacoma*, and *Kentucky Route Zero*—leverages strengths specific to the medium to make thematic arguments and tell their stories in ways only games allow.

There's an impulse in us to treat contemporary iterations of play as something new, but the truth is that speculative fiction and games have long cross-pollinated. Gary Gygax, in his first edition of the *Advanced Dungeon & Dragons Dungeon Master's Guide*, published in 1979, noted the influences of Edgar Rice Burroughs, H. P. Lovecraft, Fritz Leiber, Roger Zelazny, and Michael Moorcoc. Daniel Abraham and Ty Franck's *Expanse* series of novels begin as the setting of a tabletop role-playing game Franck had run for several years prior. *Disco Elysium*, groundbreaking detective RPG released by ZA/UM in 2019, claimed Arkady and Boris Strugatsky, authors of *Roadside Picnic*, as significant inspirations, as well as the work of Dashiell Hammett and China Miéville, particularly the latter's novel *The City & The City*.

Many professional speculative fiction writers are also game writers, and vice versa. Alyssa Wong (author of award-winning short story "Hungry Daughters of Starving Mothers"), Patrick Weekes (author of the rip-roaring *Rogues of the Republic* series), Carrie Patel (author of the *Recoletta* series), and Cassandra Khaw (author of *Hammers on Bone*) are *all* game writers. And they are certainly not alone—in this hustle or die economy, many of us must juggle several professions just to survive. Opportunities for writers to work in both games and traditional fiction continue to grow; *sub-Q*, a magazine of interactive fiction, is now a SFWA-qualifying market, having published Monica Valentinelli, Ken Liu, Porpentine Charity Heartscape, Nin Harris, and many others. Choice of Games, a developer of text-based games, has published speculative fiction authors Max Gladstone, Kate Heartfield, Darusha Wehm, and Natalia Theodoridou, again among many others.

In recognizing games as a meaningful media for storytelling, SFWA acknowledges a history of labor and collaboration long present in the genre—and in a broader sense, they recognize a truth that's been with us for at least four thousand years: our games are as much devices of storytelling as our stories are. We're not acknowledging something new, then, but returning to our roots. It is not an act of magnanimity but one of formally honoring those who have long shared the same table.

However, game writing is bigger than one award can really contain; just as the Nebulas have been subdivided to recognize novels, novellas, novelettes, and short stories to give writers in those forms a fair shake, we must recognize that we could do the same for games, because games are as varied a storytelling medium as prose fiction. The work being done in the field is as variable as the people who develop it; to generalize as if their resources, goals, or audiences are same, or similar—or that they even *want* to be—is to do the field a grave disservice.

Consider the game stories recognized by game developers and players as award-worthy in 2018. The 2018 XYZZY Awards, an event celebrating interactive fiction, awarded Best Writing to *Animalia* and *Bogeyman*. The Independent Games Festival awarded Best Story to *Night in the Woods*. The 2018 British Academy Game Awards recognized *God of War* as having the Best Narrative. *Animalia* and *Bogeyman* were written and developed by individuals, Ian Michael Waddell and Elizabeth Smyth respectively, in a freeware narrative flowchart tool called Twine. *Night in the Woods* was developed by Infinite Fall, six people working in the subscription-based game engine Unity. *God of War* was developed by more than two hundred people at Sony Santa Monica, a studio owned by Sony Interactive Entertainment, using a proprietary engine developed in-house specifically for that title.

These teams' resources were not equal, their goals were wildly divergent, and the audiences they were trying to reach could not be more different. Yet they're all games worthy of recognition for the strength of their storytelling. As this award category matures, how are we to judge quality, innovation, and execution of a storytelling mode with the potential to function in a manner so alien from the familiar, when the perspectives these stories are operating from and the resources available to them are so different?

I suggest that the answer is to ask first and always: what moves you? Begin there and go forth, because a culture rooted in joy, collaboration, challenge, and innovation awaits you. Meet this culture as it is, and understand: there's always more work to be done—and there's room for you, too, if you want to help see it realized.

Into the Spider-verse: A Classic Origin Story in Bold New Color

by Brandon O'Brien

Superhero origin films tend to have painfully similar beats. We catch their moments of everyday normalcy, watch them struggle with some personal ideal that tells us who they are and what they don't know about themselves yet, we witness the personal tragedy that shapes how they view the value and fragility of life, we watch them gain their powers through pain or happenstance or birth or often all of the above. And then it's time for the business, yeah? We've seen this formula so often that we can count the beads falling from Martha Wayne's neck.

Spider-Man: Into the Spider-Verse takes that formula and makes it its theme.

Many of the reasons that *Into the Spider-Verse* is not just another superhero movie are tied to its visual commentary on that formula. Its lead, rebellious but conflicted Miles Morales, is in his own way just as genre-savvy as we are—after all, when the movie starts, New York City already has a friendly neighbourhood Spidey. While Miles has hang-ups about school, clashes with his father's ideology, and struggles to figure out who he wants to be, there is already a hero in his world. Peter Parker is even the first voice we hear, literally telling the audience that his origin story has already happened, as if to reassure us that the business end of this story is already underway.

And it is already underway when Miles' first defining tragedy is watching his neighbourhood's most affable and resilient hero die at the hands of the villain—mere moments after being told to his face that he too has potential to be a hero, no less.

Into the Spider-Verse's most interesting innovation is that, where other stories of its kind are about the lead having no path to discovering their own heroism, Miles already has a roadmap to it. In fact, he has several, from the hyper-intense and brooding Spider-Man Noir to the impossibly comical Spider-Pig, each of them with more history behind the mask than him. On the audience end, that sends a very interesting signal: we already know the core beats of this narrative, but this time we're here to see it through the lens of a young Afro-Latino boy already struggling under the weight of the expectations of others.

The framing device of exposing the protagonist to so many other potential versions of his own heroism reveals a lot about the superhero genre, particularly the origin story's apparent fascination with sorrow. When we meet the other universes' Spider-People, they quickly move past their own tragedies just so they can get to the good stuff. Even when we do watch Miles suffer losses, the film positions it more as an opportunity to confront his decisions than just motivational suffering. Pain isn't the thing that turns these people into heroes. Far more often, the 'great responsibility' that the well-known catchphrase doesn't refer to the literal power they possess, but the responsibility of their own decisions— from what they do when their parents aren't looking, to how they respond to minor setbacks, even to whether their shoes are tied.

The visual storytelling of *Into the Spider-Verse* also has a lot to say about its own medium and its origins. It's a very visually arresting film, all the way down to what the distinct character designs imply about how each character's world diverges. But it's also a movie that cares a lot about Spider-Man's comic book origins and the format of the animated movie, arguing with its style that these things are just as much powerful and moving visual art as they are delightful pulp fare. Often the film gives way entirely to the comic format, having important action take place across forced panels, evoking written sound effects to emphasise important sounds, and even adding Ben Day dots to the jarring effects of the film's reality warping external conflict. All of these elements add another layer of observation to the medium itself, to the capacity of various tonally different styles of animation to convey dramatic meaning. In this one film, the heightened facial expressions of Japanese anime and the monochrome contrasts that evoke film noir are considered equally valid, no more or less powerful than any other counterpart.

What I find particularly striking is that *Into the Spider-Verse* is very good at internalising fandom's relationship to the superhero genre, and to Spider-Man as a hero in particular. The best parts of the movie each have something to say about why we rely on superhero narratives as modern mythos. In particular, one of the reasons I think a lot of people found themselves relating so heavily to Miles Morales, even after mild pushback in the comics sphere about whether he would or could ever 'replace' Peter Parker, is because he has the same resource that we do for gaining perspective and encouragement in challenging times: the experience of looking up to a hero who stands for the best that we could become.

It matters even more because it's Miles Morales in particular, an Afro-Latino teen from Brooklyn struggling to find his own place in the world on his own terms. Starting this superhero story from a Black perspective first and foremost offers so much to young fans of colour who not only get to see themselves as one of Marvel's most iconic characters, but get to be seen as more complex than a monolith of urban blackness, and to be told that their own experiences and decisions matter.

When Miles says "You can wear the mask," he isn't just saying that you can strive for the power and responsibility of a hero. He's saying that the ways in which we've learned these things as a fandom is valid. He's saying using these stories as a roadmap to our own self-discovery is valid. He's saying that we are not defined as a generation by the calamities we've suffered, but by the choices we make to overcome them, even and especially when those choices are shaped by the wisdom of those around us and before us. What could speak more deeply to an uncertain future full of infinite possibilities and heavy expectations than this?

I reckon this is why *Into the Spider-Verse* is the superhero origin story of our generation: because it promises us, in our own ways, that we have great power, and great responsibility, too.

The Secret Lives of the Nine Negro Teeth of George Washington

by Phenderson Djèlí Clark

"By Cash pd Negroes for 9 Teeth on Acct of Dr. Lemoire"
—Lund Washington, Mount Vernon plantation, Account
Book dated 1784.

The first Negro tooth purchased for George Washington came from a blacksmith, who died that very year at Mount Vernon of the flux. The art of the blacksmith had been in his blood—passed down from ancestral spirits who had come seeking their descendants across the sea. Back in what the elder slaves called Africy, he had heard, blacksmiths were revered men who drew iron from the earth and worked it with fire and magic: crafting spears so wondrous they could pierce the sky and swords with beauty enough to rend mountains. Here, in this Colony of Virginia, he had been set to shape crueler things: collars to fasten about bowed necks, shackles to ensnare tired limbs, and muzzles to silence men like beasts. But blacksmiths know the secret language of iron, and he beseeched his creations to bind the spirits of their wielders—as surely as they bound flesh. For the blacksmith understood what masters had chosen to forget: when you make a man or woman a slave you enslave yourself in turn. And the souls of those who made thralls of others would never know rest—in this life, or the next.

When he wore that tooth, George Washington complained of hearing the heavy fall of a hammer on an anvil day and night. He ordered all iron making stopped at Mount Vernon. But the sound of the blacksmith's hammer rang out in his head all the same.

. . .

The second Negro tooth belonging to George Washington came from a slave from the Kingdom of Ibani, what the English with their inarticulate tongues call Bonny Land, and (much to his annoyance) hence him, a Bonny man. The Bonny man journeyed from Africa on a ship called the *Jesus*, which, as he understood, was named for an ancient sorcerer who defied death. Unlike the other slaves bound on that ship who came from the hinterlands beyond his kingdom, he knew the fate that awaited him—though he would never know what law or sacred edict he had broken that sent him to this fate. He found himself in that fetid hull chained beside a merman, with scales that sparkled like green jewels and eyes as round as black coins. The Bonny man had seen mermen before out among the waves, and stories said some of them swam into rivers to find wives among local fisher women. But he hadn't known the whites made slaves of them too. As he would later learn, mermen were prized by thaumturgical inclined aristocrats who dressed them in fine livery to display to guests; most, however, were destined for Spanish holdings, where they were forced to dive for giant pearls off the shores of New Granada. The two survived the horrors of the passage by relying on each other. The Bonny man shared tales of his kingdom, of his wife and children and family, forever lost. The merman in turn told of his underwater home, of its queen and many curiosities. He also taught the Bonny man a song: a plea to old and terrible things that dwelled in the deep, dark, hidden parts of the sea—great beings with gaping mouths that opened up whirlpools or tentacles that could drag ships beneath the depths. They would one day rise to wreak vengeance, he promised, for all those who had been chained to suffer in these floating coffins. The Bonny man never saw the merman after they made land on the English isle of Barbados. But he carried the song with him, as far as the Colony of Virginia, and on the Mount Vernon plantation, he sang it as he looked across fields of wheat to an ocean he couldn't see—and waited.

When George Washington wore the Bonny man's tooth, he found himself humming an unknown song, that sounded (strange to his thinking) like the tongue of the savage mermen. And in the dark hidden parts of the sea, old and terrible things, stirred.

· · ·

The third Negro tooth of George Washington was bought from a slave who later ran from Mount Vernon, of which an account was posted in the *Virginia Gazette* in 1785:

Advertiſement: Runaway from the plantation of the Subſcriber, in Fairfax County, ſome Time in October laſt, on All-Hallows Eve, a Mulatto Fellow, 5 Feet 8 Inches high of Tawney Complexion named Tom, about 25 Years of Age, miſſing a front tooth. He is ſenſible for a Slave and ſelf-taught in foul necromancy. He lived for ſome Years previous as a ſervant at a ſchool of learned ſorcery near Williamsburg, and was removed on Account of inciting the dead ſlaves there to riſe up in inſurrection. It is ſuppoſed he returned to the ſchool to raiſe up a young Negro Wench, named Anne, a former ſervant who died of the pox and was buried on the campus grounds, his Siſter. He ſold away a tooth and with that ſmall money was able to purchase a ſpell used to call upon powers potent on All-Hallows Eve to ſpirit themſelves away to parts now unknown. Whoever will ſecure the ſaid Tom, living, and Anne, dead, ſo that they be delivered to the plantation of the Subſcriber in Fairfax County aforefaid, ſhall have Twenty Shillings Reward, besides what the Law allows.

To George Washington's frustration, Tom's tooth frequently fell out of his dentures, no matter how he tried to secure it. Most bizarre of all, he would find it often in the unlikeliest of places—as if the vexsome thing was deliberately concealing itself. Then one day the tooth was gone altogether, never to be seen again.

. . .

George Washington's fourth Negro tooth was from a woman named Henrietta. (Contrary to widespread belief, there is no difference of significance between the dentition of men and women—as any trained dentist, odontomancer, or the Fay folk, who require human teeth as currency, will well attest.) Henrietta's father had been John Indian, whose father had been a Yamassee warrior captured and sold into bondage in Virginia. Her mother's mother had come to the mainland from Jamaica, sold away for taking part in Queen Nanny's War. As slaves, both were reputed to be unruly and impossible to control. Henrietta inherited that defiant blood, and more than one owner learned the hard way she wasn't to be trifled with. After holding down and whipping her last mistress soundly, she was sold to work fields at Mount Vernon—because, as her former master advertised, strong legs and a broad back weren't to be wasted. Henrietta often dreamed of her grandparents. She often dreamed she was her grandparents. Sometimes she was a Yamassee warrior, charging a fort with flintlock musket drawn, eyes fixed on the soldier she intended to kill—as from the ramparts English mages hurled volleys of emerald fireballs that could melt through iron. Other times she was a young woman, barely fifteen, who chanted Asante war songs as she drove a long sabre, the blade blazing bright with obeah, into the belly of a slave master (this one had been a pallid blood drinker) and watched as he blackened and crumbled away to ash.

When George Washington wore Henrietta's tooth he sometimes woke screaming from night terrors. He told Martha they were memories from the war, and would never speak of the faces he saw coming for him in those dreams: a fierce Indian man with long black hair and death in his eyes, and a laughing slave girl with a curiously innocent face, who plunged scorching steel into his belly.

*   *   *

The fifth Negro tooth belonging to George Washington came by unexplained means from a conjure man who was not listed among Mount Vernon's slaves. He had been born before independence, in what was then the Province of New Jersey, and learned his trade from his mother—a root woman of some renown (among local slaves at any rate), having been brought to the region from the southern territories of New France. The conjure man used his magics mostly in the treatment of maladies affecting his fellow bondsmen, of the mundane or paranormal varieties. He had been one of the tens of thousands of slaves during the war who answered the call put out by the Earl of Dunmore, Royal Governor of Virginia in November 1775:

> *And I hereby declare all indentured servants, Negroes, hedge witches and wizards, occultists, lycanthropes, giants, non-cannibal ogres and any fentient magical*

creatures or others (appertaining to Rebels) free and relieved of ſupernatural ſanction that are able and willing to bear Arms, they joining His MAJESTY'S Troops as ſoon as may be, for the more ſpeedily reducing this Colony to a proper Senſe of their Duty, to His MAJESTY'S Crown and Dignity. This edict excludes Daemonic beasts who ſhould not take ſaid proclamation as a ſummons who, in doing so, will be exorcized from His MAJESTY'S realm with all deliberate ſpeed.

The conjure man was first put in the service of Hessian mercenaries, to care for their frightening midnight black steeds that breathed flames and with hooves of fire. Following, he'd been set to performing menial domestic spells for Scottish warlocks, treated no better there than a servant. It was fortune (aided by some skillful stone casting) that placed him in Colonel Tye's regiment. Like the conjure man, Tye had been a slave in New Jersey who fled to the British, working his way to becoming a respected guerilla commander. Tye led the infamous Black Brigade—a motley crew of fugitive slaves, outlaw juju men, and even a Spanish mulata werewolf—who worked alongside the elite Queen's Rangers. Aided by the conjure man's gris-gris, the Black Brigade carried out raids on militiamen: launching attacks on their homes, destroying their weapons, stealing supplies, burning spells and striking fear into the hearts of patriots. The conjure man's brightest moment had come the day he captured his own master and bound him in the same shackles he'd once been forced to wear. The Brigade stirred such hysteria that the patriot governor of New Jersey declared martial law, putting up protective wards around the province—and General George Washington himself was forced to send his best mage hunters against them. In a running skirmish with those patriot huntsmen, Tye was fatally struck by a cursed ball from a long rifle—cutting through his gris-gris. The conjure man stood guard over his fallen commander, performing a final rite that would disallow their enemies from reanimating the man or binding his soul. Of the five mage hunters he killed three, but was felled in the attempt. With his final breath, he whispered his own curse on any that would desecrate his corpse.

One of the surviving mage hunters pulled the conjure man's teeth as a souvenir of the battle, and a few days hence tumbled to land awkwardly from his horse and broke his neck. The tooth passed to a second man, who choked to death on an improbably lodged bit of turtle soup in his windpipe. And, so it went, bringing dire misfortune to each of its owners. The conjure man's tooth has now, by some twist of fate, made its way to Mount Vernon and into George Washington's collection. He has not worn it, yet.

. . .

The sixth Negro tooth of George Washington belonged to a slave who had tumbled here from another world. The startled English sorcerer who witnessed this remarkable event had been set to deliver a speech on conjurations at the Royal Society of London for Improving Supernatural Knowledge. Alas, before the sorcerer could tell the world of his discovery, he was quietly killed by agents of the Second Royal African Company, working in a rare alliance with their Dutch rivals. As they saw it, if Negroes could simply be pulled out of thin air the lucrative trade in human cargo that made such mercantilists wealthy could be irrevocably harmed. The conjured Negro, however, was allowed to live—bundled up and shipped from London to a Virginia slave market. Good property, after all, was not to be wasted. She ended up at Mount Vernon, and was given the name Esther. The other slaves, however, called her Solomon—on account of her wisdom.

Solomon claimed not to know anything about magic, which didn't exist in her native home. But how could that be, the other slaves wondered, when she could mix together powders to cure their sicknesses better than any physician; when she could make predictions of the weather that always came true; when she could construct all manner of wondrous contraptions from the simplest of objects? Even the plantation manager claimed she was "a Negro of curious intellect," and listened to her suggestions on crop rotations and field systems. The slaves well knew the many agricultural reforms at Mount Vernon, for which their master took credit, was actually Solomon's genius. They often asked why she didn't use her remarkable wit to get hired out and make money? Certainly, that'd be enough to buy her freedom.

Solomon always shook her head, saying that though she was from another land, she felt tied to them by "the consanguinity of bondage." She would work to free them all, or, falling short of that, at the least bring some measure of ease to their lives. But at night, after she'd finished her mysterious "experiments" (which she kept secret from all) she could be found gazing up at the stars, and it was hard not to see the longing held deep in her eyes. When George Washington wore Solomon's tooth, he dreamed of a place of golden spires and colorful glass domes, where Negroes flew through the sky on metal wings like birds and sprawling cities that glowed bright at night were run by machines who thought faster than men. It both awed and frightened him at once.

*   *   *

The seventh Negro tooth purchased for George Washington had come from a Negro from Africa who himself had once been a trader in slaves. He had not gone out with the raids or the wars between kingdoms to procure them, but had been an instrumental middleman—a translator who spoke the languages of both the coastal slavers and their European buyers. He was instrumental in keeping the enchanted rifles and rum jugs flowing and assuring his benefactors a good value for the human merchandise. It was thus ironic that his downfall came from making a bad deal. The local ruler, a distant relative to a king, felt cheated and (much to the trader's shock) announced his translator put up for sale. The English merchant gladly accepted the offer. And just like that, the trader went from a man of position to a commodity.

He went half mad of despair when they'd chained him in the hold of the slave ship. Twice he tried to rip out his throat with his fingernails, preferring death to captivity. But each time he died, he returned to life—without sign of injury. He'd jumped into the sea to drown, only to be hauled back in without a drop of water in his lungs. He'd managed to get hold a sailor's knife, driven it into his chest, and watched in shock as his body pushed the blade out and healed the wound. It was then he understood the extent of his downfall: he had been cursed. Perhaps by the gods. Perhaps by spirits of the vengeful dead. Or by some witch or conjurer for whom he'd haggled out a good price. He would never know. But they had cursed him to suffer this turn of fate, to become what he'd made of others. And there would be no escape.

The Negro slave trader's tooth was George Washington's favorite. No matter how much he used it, the tooth showed no signs of wear. Sometimes he could have sworn he'd broken it. But when inspected, it didn't show as much as a fracture—as if it mended itself. He put that tooth to work hardest of all, and gave it not a bit of rest.

. . .

The eighth Negro tooth belonging to George Washington came from his cook, who was called Ulysses. He had become a favorite in the Mount Vernon household, known for his culinary arts and the meticulous care he gave to his kitchen. The dinners and parties held at the mansion were always catered by Ulysses, and visitors praised his skill at devising new dishes to tingle the tongue and salivate the senses. Those within the higher social circles frequented by the Washingtons familiarly called him "Uncle Lysses" and showered him with such gifts that local papers remarked: "the Negro cook had become something of a celebrated puffed-up dandy."

Ulysses took his work seriously, as much as he took his name. He used the monies gained from those gifts, as well as his habit of selling leftovers (people paid good money to sup on the Washingtons' fare) to purchase translated works by Homer. In those pages, he learned about the fascinating travels of his namesake, and was particularly taken by the figure Circe—an enchantress famed for her vast knowledge of potions and herbs, who through a fine feast laced with a potent elixir had turned men into swine. Ulysses amassed other books as well: eastern texts on Chinese herbology, banned manuscripts of Mussulman alchemy, even rare ancient Egyptian papyri on shape-shifting.

His first tests at transmogrification had merely increased the appetite of Washington's guests, who turned so ravenous they relieved themselves of knife or spoon and shoveled fistfuls of food into their mouths like beasts. A second test had set them all to loud high-pitched squealing—which was blamed on an over-imbibing of cherubimical spirits. Success came, at last, when he heard some days after a summer dining party that a Virginia plantation owner and close friend of the Washingtons had gone missing—the very same day his wife had found a great fat spotted hog rummaging noisily through their parlor. She had her slaves round up the horrid beast, which was summarily butchered and served for dinner.

Over the years, Ulysses was judicious in his selections for the transfiguring brew: several slave owners or overseers known to be particularly cruel; a shipping merchant from Rhode Island whose substantial wealth came from the slave trade; a visiting French physiognomist and naturalist who prattled on about the inherent "lower mental capabilities" to be found among Negroes, whose skulls he compared to "near-human creatures" such as the apes of inner Africa and the fierce woodland goblins of Bavaria. Then, one day in early 1797, Ulysses disappeared.

The Washingtons were upset and hunted everywhere for their absconded cook, putting out to all who would listen the kindness they'd shown to the ungrateful servant. He was never found, but the Mount Vernon slaves whispered that on the day Ulysses vanished a black crow with a mischievous glint in its eye was found standing in a pile of the man's abandoned clothes. It cawed once, and then flapped away.

When George Washington wore the tooth of his runaway cook, it was strangely at dinner parties. Slaves would watch as he wandered into the kitchen, eyes glazed over in a seeming trance, and placed drops of some strange liquid into the food and drink of his guests. His servants never touched those leftovers. But that summer many Virginians took note of a bizarre rash of wild pigs infesting the streets and countryside of Fairfax County.

     . . .

The ninth, and final, Negro tooth purchased for George Washington came from a slave woman named Emma. She had been among Mount Vernon's earliest slaves, born there just a decade after Augustine Washington had moved in with his family. Had anyone recorded Emma's life for posterity, they would have learned of a girl who came of age in the shadows of one of Virginia's most powerful families. A girl who had fast learned that she was included among the Washington's possessions—treasured like a chair cut from exotic Jamaican mahogany or a bit of fine Canton porcelain. A young woman who had watched the Washington children go on to attend school and learn the ways of the gentry, while she was trained to wait on their whims. They had the entire world to explore and discover. Her world was Mount Vernon, and her aspirations could grow no further than the wants and needs of her owners.

That was not to say Emma did not have her own life, for slaves learned early how to carve out spaces separate from their masters. She had befriended, loved, married, cried, fought, and found succor in a community as vibrant as the Washingtons'—perhaps even more so, if only because they understood how precious it was to live. Yet she still dreamed for more. To be unbound from this place. To live a life where she had not seen friends and family put under the lash; a life where the children she bore were not the property of others; a place where she might draw a free breath and taste its sweetness. Emma didn't know any particular sorcery. She was no root woman or conjurer, nor had she been trained like the Washington women in simple domestic enchantments. But her dreams worked their own magic. A strong and potent magic that she clung to, that grew up and blossomed inside her—where not even her owners could touch, or take it away.

When George Washington wore Emma's tooth, some of that magic worked its way into him and perhaps troubled some small bit of his soul. In July 1799, six months before he died, Washington stipulated in his will that the 123 slaves belonging to himself, among them Emma, be freed upon his wife's death. No such stipulations were made for the Negro teeth still in his possession.

Interview for the End of the World

A Short Story set in the
Children of Titan Universe

by Rhett C. Bruno

142 Hours Until Impact...

"Come in," I said.

My office door creaked open. Sgt. Hale, my head of security, ushered in the Titan Project's next candidate. I quickly downed the remnants of a glass of lukewarm whiskey in my liverspotted hand to calm my mind, then placed it down behind my computer screen. Sgt. Hale and I exchanged a nod before he exited, leaving myself and the candidate alone.

The man didn't make it more than a step before he stopped to stare out of my window at the tremendous spaceship docked in the center of my compound. It was the pinnacle of my illustrious technical career which had left me one of the richest men on the planet. At least until a massive asteroid was discovered hurtling toward Earth and money became as useless as the paper it was printed on. People had given it some creative nicknames like "The Devil's Fist," or "Ragna-Rock," but in my opinion, there was no reason to call it anything different than what it was. The end of Earth as we knew it.

"Congratulations on making it this far, Mr.—" I hesitated at his name. I'd conducted thousands of interviews by then and was beginning to lose count. I glanced at the already opened resume on my computer. He was Frank Drayton. Twenty-seven years old and already a worldrenowned horticulturalist. Not the most exciting job, but a necessary addition for a colony on a hostile world. He was marked for possible acceptance, but nobody got a spot in the Titan Project without me looking them in the eyes first.

"Drayton," I finished.

He blinked as if waking from a dream and hurried over to my desk. "Director Darien Trass. You can't even begin to understand how much of an honor it is to meet you," he said. He extended a trembling hand.

I shook it without standing. It was clammy as a teenage boy's on a first date. I quickly let go.

"I'd prefer we'd never have to meet at all, Mr. Drayton," I said.

His gaze turned downward. He said nothing.

"Relax," I said. "I only wish the world's circumstances were different." I gestured toward the hard, plastic chair set on the other side of my desk. "Please, sit."

He released a string of low, panicked laughs as he sat down. His index finger immediately started tapping on the chair's arm. I took that moment to study him. Heavy beads of sweat rolled down his forehead, and he was in desperate need of a shave. The loose-fitting suit he wore could have used the attention of a decent tailor. Not that I could judge him for that. There were probably none left open on Earth to visit.

I wasn't surprised by anything about him. It was the same situation with almost every candidate who entered my office. After all, it's not every day a human being has to interview for a chance to escape the end of the world.

"Now," I began. "There's little time left, so let's try to keep this as brief as possible. In this room, your accomplishments are no longer in question. Extraordinary as they may be, I assure you the other candidates are equally impressive. You're here, Mr. Drayton, so that I can find out who *you* are."

"I..." He swallowed and took another deep breath. His finger stopped tapping, and then he looked me directly in the eyes for the first time and said: "I understand."

"Good. I presume my assistant, Kara, already briefed you on the Project and showed you around the compound?"

"She did." He looked back through the window. "I didn't realize how big the ship was until I got up here though."

"Not big enough," I lamented.

This time I joined him in staring at the colossal ship propped up on the opposite side of my half-mile-wide compound. It had the appearance of a tapered skyscraper wrapped in bowed metal plates. The final layers of radiation shielding were being installed by a carefully selected workforce before its imminent departure when the only plasmatic pulse drives ever to be used non-experimentally would allow it to reach Saturn in two years.

Mr. Drayton was awestruck. The view made *me* want to crawl inside a bottle. It's not that I wasn't proud of the ship, but the pale mark in the blue sky above—the asteroid growing ever closer to becoming a meteorite—was where my gaze always tended to wander. There, and at the horde of people camped in the desert on the other side of the tall, concrete wall surrounding the compound, hoping to earn a spot onboard. Armed security drones swept the area to keep them at bay along with the many security officers posted along it.

Mr. Drayton turned back to me. "How many can it hold?"

"Excuse me?"

"The ship. How many people can it hold?"

"Three thousand," I stated. "Four hundred and six spots have already been filled by my remaining staff. Individual accomplishments aside, I assure you that they had to meet the same, stringent criteria as candidates such as yourself. They're all that remains of Trass Industries. It felt wrong to ask anyone to help me construct the Titan Project without guaranteeing them a spot on it."

The conditions for selection were simple, at least in that they eliminated more than ninetynine percent of humanity. Other than having to bear an appreciable level of expertise in a field that would benefit the new world, every candidate had to be between eighteen and thirty-five years old. They also had to be in optimal physical health and cleared of all chronic diseases. Kara administered the physicals, and nobody who failed ever made it through my door. Those untethered by marriage were preferred, since their significant others would have to meet the same conditions. Lastly, anyone with young children was eliminated. My research team feared that an underdeveloped body would be ravaged by the trip through zero-g. I also wasn't keen on accepting anybody willing to leave their offspring to die alone. "Three thousand..." Mr. Drayton muttered after a lengthy silence.

"Yes," I said. "No more, no less. Every traveler will be kept in a state-of-the-art hibernation chamber for the duration of the two-year journey. The low activity state will help us conserve the limited resources we're able to bring until we can establish a sustainable colony on Titan. It's my job to whittle the list of more than one million suitable candidates to that minuscule number.

Sneak in one extra and I might as well invite the mob camped out there."

He glanced nervously back through the window. "Are those really all candidates?" he asked.

"Everyone I passed claimed to have met with you."

"Not all of them. You can thank whichever rejected candidate decided to break our NDA and leak what was happening here for that. I had to promise fifty spots on board to some of the finest soldiers in the world to keep the project safe. We're lucky we're in the middle of the Arizona desert; otherwise, I'd need more."

"It sure wasn't easy getting out here with all the airlines shut down. It took me a day just to find a gas station that wasn't abandoned or ransacked."

"Yes ... I suppose I was crazy for thinking I could keep the Titan Project safe from the doomsday hysteria."

Ever since the leak, I couldn't leave the Trass Industries Compound without being hounded or having my life threatened. Rich, poor, it didn't matter. People had begun to realize the united efforts of governments around the world to divert the asteroid were futile, and that the only way to ensure survival was to leave Earth behind. Other corporations were developing space-stations that would orbit our homeworld or attempting to establish colonies on the moon. But with so many people being crammed onto them, an unpredictable percentage would likely suffocate before their populations leveled out to suit their life-support systems. The safety of my compound was indebted to a majority of people choosing to camp outside of those projects rather than crave a trip to an uninhabitable moon millions of miles away.

I sighed. "It doesn't matter anymore. In a week the asteroid will hit and we'll be on our way to Titan."

"Why not Mars, or Europa, or anywhere else closer? Your message didn't say."

"As you well know, there's no second Earth in our solar system, Mr. Drayton. I chose based on potential. Titan and Saturn host a wealth of resources which will make generating enough energy to stay warm relatively simple once we repurpose the ship into a settlement. The thick atmosphere also eliminates radiation from the list of concerns. We'll need all the help we can get. Establishing renewable sources of food on any world not meant for life will take time."

For the first time, Mr. Drayton's eyes glinted with the confidence of a man who had risen to the top of his field. "I think I can help with that," he boasted.

"I've met with three similarly qualified candidates who claimed the same," I countered. I lifted my finger before he could offer another predictable response. He slouched into his chair and allowed me to continue. "As I indicated earlier, your accomplishments are no longer in question. It was your highly scrutinized thesis on vertical farming at Cornell that encouraged me to reach out to you. I appreciate boldness. I can design all the colonizing spaceships I want to, but without food, they'll be little more than oversized, metal tombs."

Mr. Drayton perked up. "You read that?"

"I'm always thorough with my research."

"Of course you are." He leaned forward and wrapped his hands around the edge of my desk. "I've read *all* of your work," he said. "Your 2021 paper about how you pioneered your zeroemissions, automated-vehicular-network to reduce traffic and accidents in Detroit was lifechanging."

I raised an eyebrow. "Life-changing? That's new. It all seems rather trivial compared to what we're working on here, doesn't it?"

The color drained from Mr. Drayton's cheeks. I could see his lip twitching ever so slightly as his brain struggled to come up with a response that wouldn't seem foolish.

"I appreciate the compliment," I intervened. I folded my hands over my lap and established direct eye-contact with him. "Okay, as long I've answered all of your questions, I'm going to ask you a few of my own. I want you to be as honest as possible."

He nodded. His finger started to tap the chair again, but he held my gaze.

"Okay," I said. "Your records state that you're not married and don't have children. Do you currently have any manner of significant other?"

Mr. Drayton shifted in his seat. "Not for about two years," he said, clearly perturbed.

"Divorced."

"Ah. I have had plenty of those walk through these doors, eager to get away. It'll get easier with time."

He exhaled. "I hope."

I turned to my screen for a moment, trying to make it seem like I was reading something so I didn't rush things. After countless interviews, it was difficult for them not to feel rehearsed. "So, where were you when you heard about the asteroid?" I asked.

He continued looking in my direction, though his stare grew unfocused. I could read the struggle all over his face. "Mr. Drayton?" I said.

"Sorry." He shook his head and reestablished eye contact. "I was with my ex-wife. I suppose you could say we didn't agree over why the asteroid is going to hit Earth. She turned her complete attention to our church and trying to repent for man's sins so God might reconsider his judgment. It was like she completely forgot about our..." He paused for a few seconds to gather himself before continuing. "Anyway, I tried to go along with it while I could, but I decided that I'd rather take a chance at living."

"We all responded differently." I remained indifferent on the *why's*. The only thing that mattered to me after I found out a rogue asteroid the size of Texas had somehow been re-routed toward Earth was getting humanities best and brightest off it. A branch of Trass Industries had been focused on commodifying space-travel at the time, so it seemed like a logical transition ... my next real challenge after effectively eliminating car accidents throughout the

United States. "I'm glad you didn't hesitate," Mr. Drayton said. "You were the only one smart enough to consider running far away from Earth before wasting time on anything else."

"The value of a clean slate is lost on many of my peers."

He was handling himself well enough, so I decided it was time to find out what I really wanted to know. I stared at my computer for a few seconds again so I didn't seem impatient, and then asked, "Why should I choose you to join this venture to our new world?"

Mr. Drayton leaned back and breathed deep. "I've dedicated my life to understanding living things, sir," he said. "We'll need the life we take for granted here to blossom if we ever hope to make Titan feel like a new home."

My lips betrayed the slightest grin. There was no doubt he'd practiced that answer in a mirror many times, but I could tell by his eyes that he meant it. It was one of my favorite responses yet. Most candidates couldn't help but list their achievements or mention their will to survive.

"Well said," I admitted. "I think I've heard everything I need to. Thank you, Mr. Drayton. Please proceed to the waiting area. I will personally inform you of my decision as soon as possible. If accepted, you'll be escorted to a safe, on-site dormitory where you will remain until the Titan Project departs at exactly 8:00 PM on September 30, 2031. Roughly five days from now. If you aren't … Well then, Mr. Drayton, I hope you find peace in whatever way suits you."

The interview was briefer than usual, but after administering thousands, I could size people up quickly. I stood and extended my hand. He immediately sprung to his feet and grabbed it.

"Thank you, sir," he said twice, shaking vehemently. "Either way, I'll have accomplished my dream of meeting you."

I released his hand and forced a businesslike smile.

"Good day, Mr. Drayton."

His eyes darted between myself and the Titan Project out the window as he back away. Then the door opened and a security officer came through. He placed his hand on Mr. Drayton's shoulder and escorted him out of the office.

As soon as he was gone, I slumped back into my chair and exhaled. Even good interviews took a lot out of me. I closed out of his information and my computer screen reverted to my list of candidates. I had to strain my eyes just to keep all the text from looking like one big blob.

Like Mr. Drayton, I'd selected every single person. There were doctors, theoreticians, physicists, engineers, artists, self-made billionaires and anything else you could imagine, from everywhere around the globe.

I scrolled through the list. As many as there were, I could remember the face of everyone I'd talked to—accepted or rejected. I always did it personally, though with a cohort of armed guards for rejections since there was no telling what desperate people would do. Only four hundred interviews remained. Five of them were experts in the same field as Mr. Drayton interviewing later that day—so I couldn't be sure if he made the cut yet or not—but I had a good feeling about him.

With less than a week until the doomsday clock struck zero, I knew I was cutting it close. But I had to be meticulous. I owed humanity that much at least.

Before I could scroll down to the next candidate on my list, an email popped in the bottom right corner of my screen. I didn't recognize the sender, but the subject read: TAKE MY SON AND YOU WON'T REGRET IT. I forwarded it to my junk folder, where thousands of similar emails remained in purgatory.

"If only I could," I whispered.

I grabbed a half-empty bottle of whiskey from under my desk and refilled the glass sitting by my keyboard. It was the only thing that quieted the voices bouncing around in my head of everyone I already had or was planning to reject. I was inches away from a much-needed sip when my door swung open.

Kara, my assistant, froze in the entrance. Her expression soured when she noticed the glass I held. She'd been with me since her parents died in a car accident, leaving her an orphan at only ten years old. My company was working on implementing the automated vehicle network at the time, so I legally adopted her. At first, it was admittedly a publicity stunt, and then I fell in love with her.

I always found myself shocked upon realizing what a beautiful, intelligent young woman she'd grown into. She had the brains to take over Trass Industries from me one day… if not for the end of the known world.

"I thought I told you to knock?" I grumbled. I didn't mean to take a harsh tone with her, but the whiskey's pungent aroma wafte around my nostrils and all I wanted was a drink. "I did. Three times," she said, unable to take her eyes off my glass. I was glad she didn't comment on it for once. I had too much on my mind without worrying about disappointing her again.

"Oh… Is everything alright?"

"Fine. I wanted to let you know that your next appointment is almost ready. She just passed her physical."

"You could have buzzed me." I noticed her gaze drift away from my full glass and scan the entirety of my messy office. "Checking up on me again?"

"It's almost five." She took a few long strides into my office and picked up a pile of loose papers. "You need to eat, dad."

"I'll find time for that eventually," I said.

Kara bit her lip in frustration, but decided to move on. "How did Mr. Drayton do?" she asked. "You know I can't tell you yet." I never allowed her or anyone else to be involved in my decisions. Truthfully, I didn't even want her to have the burden of knowing their names, but I couldn't run both the interviews and the physicals alone.

She stopped cleaning and regarded me. "I can help you if you let me. I've met thousands of candidates. I know what you're looking for."

I shook my head. From the corner of my eye, I spotted someone in the desperate crowd beyond the fence of my compound standing on the back of a truck and flashing a sign large enough for me to read: LET ME IN.

"No," I said. "It's my responsibility and mine alone."

"It doesn't have to be. You're not Noah, you know. Hundreds of us have been here with you every step of the way."

"Don't make the mistake of thinking this is anything like some fable, Kara," I scolded. "His task was easy. The animals he marched two-by-two couldn't speak to him. They couldn't beg or offer their billions for a spot. They couldn't send in pictures of their children who now have six days left to live!" I slapped the glass off my desk. Kara yelped when it shattered on the floor.

For a moment neither of us made a sound. Layer upon layer of silence folded over each other until the tension in the air had my neck itching.

"I'm sorry," I said.

I bent over from my chair to start picking up the pieces until I felt her slender hand fall upon my shoulder. My racing heart immediately slowed. She had a way of calming me which I'll never understand.

"I didn't mean to upset you," she said.

"It's not you."

"I just want to help as much as I can."

I patted her hand. "You are. More than you'll ever know." I stared into her bright green eyes. "It's not because I don't trust you, Kara."

"I know."

"Every person I accept means there's another one who won't be coming. I can run across the solar system to Titan, but I'll have to remember everyone who sat across from me and didn't make the cut. I'll hear their voices and see their faces every time I close my eyes. You don't deserve to have that on your conscience."

By the end of my venting, Kara sat beside me on my desk, the furrowing her freckled brow.

"And you do?"

"Better me alone than all of us." I forced another smile. "Now, I think I'll take you up on that dinner offer. Why don't you pick something for us from the café? We'll eat after my next appointment." I'd been sick of the food in my compound for months, but since we were in the middle of the Arizona desert and I couldn't leave, options were limited.

"I'm on it." She started toward the exit, then stopped and glanced back at the wet spot on the floor. "Should I pick you out another bottle?" she asked.

I didn't have to work hard to smirk after hearing that. "Make it two," I said. "It'll be a long week."

"Don't push it. I'll have security send the next candidate in on my way down."

"Thank you, Kara."

The door shut behind her. I stood and stretched my old legs. I spent so much time in my chair that sometimes I wondered if I'd pass the physical necessary to make it onto the Titan Project.

I stepped over the spill and opened a cabinet where I kept more glasses. I grabbed one and held it up to the light. The bottom was dusty, but it was clean enough. I carried it back to my desk and filled it until the whiskey bottle was empty.

Three knocks sounded at my door as I sat back down, along with another useless, pleading email on my computer. I closed my eyes and took as long a sip as I could handle. I coughed, wiped my mouth, and pulled up the next candidate's information.

Jillian Stark was a nuclear physicist who worked directly beside a Nobel Prize winner back when that was a thing people cared about.

"Come in," I said.

22 Hours Until Impact...

Less than a single day remained before the asteroid would hit Earth and the Titan Project was running behind schedule. Finishing touches to the ship took longer than expected, and the candidates were finally being loaded into their pods.

I stood on one of the upper decks of the tremendous vessel. The inside was little more than a ring-shaped corridor wrapped by glassy sleep-chambers, with a lift in the center. Every occupiable level except for the command deck was identical. The highest level was the only place I could go where I couldn't hear the echoes of gunshots and screaming. As the orange mark in the sky grew, the mob outside of my compound's walls intensified. I had to divert every member of security I had to keep them back.

I ran my fingers along an empty sleep-chamber as I strolled by. Exhaustion had them trembling. For the previous week, sleep had proven difficult no matter how much I drank. I found myself up every night, watching the few remaining newsfeeds as they talked about the chaos rampant throughout the planet. From America to China and everywhere in between—the entire world was tearing itself apart. Just one night earlier there were reports that a Russian Space Station scheduled to be launched into Earth's orbit had been ripped to pieces by a mob. Now, a similarly angry mob stood outside my compound.

"It's going to work, dad," Kara said behind me, her voice echoing throughout the wide, vacant hall.

I turned to face her. Her face and clothes were covered in dirt, but my eyes were immediately drawn to the drops of dried blood on her right cheek. There was no wound from what I could tell, which meant the blood probably wasn't hers.

"It's not the journey I'm worried about," I said. "How is it out there?"

"Not as bad as I look," she said. "We're holding. Security is sticking to your orders for now. Just warning shots."

"So, you came here just to check up on me again?"

Her lips pursed and she looked to the floor. "There's been a complication with one of the candidates. He smuggled … Well, you'd better come see for yourself."

I surveyed the empty level and its hibernation compartments one last time, then nodded. I started walking toward the central lift. Kara placed her hand on my chest with enough force to stop me. Her features darkened.

"Is everything okay?" she questioned.

I didn't need to see my reflection to know I looked terrible, every bit my age. My eyelids felt like they had stones tied to the bottom of them. I managed my best smile and said, "I'll be fine, Kara. Nothing a few drinks can't handle."

I ignored her disapproving scowl as I brushed her hand away and continued on. The lift carried us to the lowest deck where the ship's exit ramp awaited. There, the sleep-chambers were busy being loaded by my staff.

A line of candidates extended down the ramp and across the compound grounds. They appeared as exhausted as I was.

"Director," said the next candidate to be put under. She bowed her head deferentially. "Good to see you again—" It took me a second for her name to come to me, but I remembered before she helped me. "Ms. Stark."

The staff slid her assigned chamber out. They stowed her bag below and hooked her up to IV tubes and restraints. Two years and plenty of dreams later, she'd wake within the orbit of Saturn. I received a similarly reverent nod from every other candidate I passed. They probably didn't think I knew who they each were, but they were wrong. Every face had been ingrained on my mind. I nodded approvingly to all of them until Kara and I emerged from the ship.

My cheeks were instantly blasted by the cold Arizona night air and pricked by sand caught on a strong breeze. The spotlights of security drones filled the dark sky, aimed over the manned wall surrounding my compound at an unruly crowd of thousands.

I stopped and looked up. The moon glowed in the night sky as it always did, but off to its side was an orange-hued light brighter than all the stars. The asteroid had only recently become easy to spot, but now it was impossible to miss. An eye of condemnation staring down upon all of us.

"This way, Director," Kara said, addressing me formally since we were in public.

She tapped my arm and led me at a brisk pace in the direction of the dormitory where my chosen candidates were staying. It was the only building in the compound with lights still on. The line of candidates snaking down from the ship toward it offered me their regards.

We passed the compound's only gate. A row of armed soldiers stood in front of it. A rioting mob of angry citizens of Earth was on the other side. The bobbing sea of heads extended as far as I could see, illuminated by car fires. They flung rocks, bottles and whatever else they could at the gate. Warning shots resonated from manned watchtowers and from automated drones zipping over their heads, but the mob had a mind of its own.

Their glowers turned on me as we passed, causing the crowd to swell against the bars of the gate. "Coward! Taking your friends and running!" someone shouted, as if I could be blamed for a stray asteroid. A rock pelted me in the shoulder. I stumbled and would've fallen too if Kara hadn't caught my old body and yanked me into the dormitory's security post.

"Animals!" she gasped. "Don't they understand?"

I rubbed my arm and gave it a good stretch. "Would you?" I groaned.

Kara blinked, and then signaled to two guards inside the room. They parted, revealing Frank Drayton. He was crouched, arms wrapped around a tiny girl who couldn't be older than four. She buried her face in his chest.

"One of the candidates," Kara said.

"I know," I replied.

She tossed a medium-sized duffle bag at my feet. The zipper was ripped open. "He snuck out of the compound last night somehow," she said. "When he attempted to re-enter, security found the girl stuffed inside of this. Someone out there tore it from his hands and she fell out. Half the mob are candidates you didn't accept, so they know the rules. They nearly stoned him to death because of that, so I had him brought in for you to deal with."

I stared at Mr. Drayton. I fondly remembered the look on his face when I'd informed him he was coming to Titan the day after his interview. Presently, his body quaked. Only, it wasn't just out of fear. His face was bruised and his torn clothes revealed fresh cuts. That explained the blood on Kara.

"Mr. Drayton," I said. "What's going on here?"

He looked up at me, pupils dilated from shock. "You remember?" he asked. His voice was so raspy it sounded as if he'd swallowed a mouthful of sand.

"Of course I do." I lay my hand upon his shoulder. "Mr. Drayton, who is she?" I knew the answer, but I had to hear it to believe it. Every passenger was invited to bring one bag full of possessions to Titan. I never expected anyone to smuggle a person.

"She's…" Mr. Drayton swallowed so hard I could see the lump in his throat bob up and down. "She's my daughter."

The breath fled my lungs. I glanced between him and the child at least a dozen times. "How?"

I said. "I looked extensively into every candidate's background. There were no children."

Mr. Drayton smirked until stretching the fresh cut on his lip made him wince. "I didn't mention I was as good with computers as I am with plants?"

"This is no time for jokes," Kara reprimanded.

Right after the words left her lips, an earsplitting explosion rang out. I grabbed Kara and dropped to the ground. Mr. Drayton's daughter cried while he squeezed her and repeatedly promised her everything was going to be fine. Outside, the volume of the mob amplified, becoming so loud that Kara and I immediately scrambled to our feet so we could see what was happening.

A drone had been shot down by something and had crashed right outside of the gate. Its explosion busted the hinges enough for people to crawl through one at a time. Before the officers inside could reinforce it, one member of the mob squeezed through and sprinted toward the Titan Project. "No children!" the incensed man shrieked. "That's my spot!" He didn't make it far. A gunshot *cracked* from somewhere on the wall. This one wasn't a warning. A bullet tore into the back of the man's skull and he toppled forward in a heap of tangled limbs.

Everybody went silent.

The guard on the wall who'd shot stood completely still,

smoke rising from the end of his rifle's blistering muzzle. If Mr. Drayton getting caught sneaking in a child had roused the mob, I knew this would ignite them.

I was no military commander, but I did the first thing that came to mind. I grabbed Sgt. Hale who was positioned just inside the dormitory monitoring the candidate transition and said, "Get everyone to the ship now!"

"Director, it takes time to load them into the pods," he answered.

"Sort them on the ship! We need them alive!"

He nodded and transmitted orders over his radio. Moments later, every chosen candidate rushed across the compound toward the ship. They were terrified. Guards poured out of the watchtowers to reinforce their comrades by the damaged gate. There were no more gunshots, but rifle butts cracked bones as the mob stuck their wailing arms through the bars.

I turned to Kara, Mr. Drayton, and his daughter, and shouted, "Let's go!"

Kara didn't move at first. Her petrified gaze was fixed on the mob. I'd never seen her so rattled. I shook her by the shoulders to snap her out of it, and we took off. Mr. Drayton picked up his daughter and followed.

We didn't make it far before a bottle shattered next to my feet. I hopped out of the way of the shards, but Kara tripped over the legs of the rioter who'd been shot. As she slid across the dirt, her hands dragged through the man's blood. Again, she froze.

"C'mon, Kara!" I yelled as I hoisted her back to her feet.

We crossed the expanse of dirt between the dormitory and the ship without suffering any more setbacks. I helped Kara onto the entry ramp, and once we were at the top, I fell against the wall. My lungs were filled with dirt and I couldn't stop coughing.

Once I was finally able to catch my breath, I scanned my compound. A few hundred yards away, the guards at the gate struggled. The mob had started to climb over the gate, and I knew it wouldn't last much longer with all their weight pressed against the compromised area.

"Recall the men," I shouted to Sgt. Hale at the bottom of the ramp. He nodded.

I could no longer recognize any of the people I'd rejected in the mob. Everyone was covered in dirt and blood, and they were all so riled that they might as well have been foaming at the mouths. The officers received the order and immediately broke ranks to sprint to the ship. Most had fought in wars, but gunning down innocent people wasn't in the job description. When the gate failed, they'd have no other choice. The last thing I wanted was my followers to be reduced to savages like the rest of the people on Earth.

"Daddy, what's going on?" Mr. Drayton's daughter asked, her voice so frail I could barely hear her over the commotion.

He didn't respond. He was busy staring at the chaotic scene below. "I didn't think I would cause this..." he muttered. "You didn't think?" I said, my glare boring through him. "Three thousand spots, Mr. Drayton. Life support doesn't allow for any more. Do you suppose I only chose people with no connections for my health? A man is dead because you didn't listen!"

"What does it matter!" he snapped, startling me. Tears streamed down his cheeks. "He would've been dead tomorrow. They're all going to be dead tomorrow. Nothing we do can stop that."

"No." I caught a glimpse of the surging mob in my peripherals. "But we can retain our humanity."

Mr. Drayton took a measured breath. "You built this whole thing to save our species, Director. Isn't that enough?"

"I did what I had to."

"So did I." He released his daughter and rose to his full height, no longer afraid. She wrapped her tiny arms around his leg and hid her face against him. "I wasn't going to let her go like that. Not while there was a chance." He gestured into the ship's interior. "And I know you wouldn't either."

I pride myself on my quick mind, but for once I had no idea what to say. There was no denying Mr. Drayton was right. I looked inside and saw Kara, and I couldn't help but picture her as a nervous ten-year-old orphan without a place to go. Just seeing the fresh scrapes on her legs made me uneasy.

"Let my daughter take my place," Mr. Drayton implored. "I know the risks of sending her this young, but it's got to be better than her staying here, right? She can learn from the other horticulturalists. She's smart. Smarter than I was at her age."

I remained silent. Beyond Kara, hundreds inside scurried about preparing the sleep-chambers, moving up and down the central lift. Despite my stringent requirements, each of the people inside them was unique. Many could be considered true geniuses, while others were merely the hardest workers on my staff from a peaceful time. The only thing they all visibly had in common was that they were young. Young enough to flourish on our new world.

Everyone but me...

I looked in the opposite direction, over the shoulders of the security officers crowding the ramp. Each livid individual in the mob at the gate was someone I'd decided wasn't worthy of propagating our species. My criteria. My interviews. My decisions. I was to remember their faces forever so that nobody else had to. But years of focusing on work had led me to ignore one simple fact... that I belonged with them.

The scraping of metal over dirt made the hairs on the

back of my neck stand on end. The gate was breaking, and if the people on the other side reached the ship, we'd all be torn to pieces. Suddenly, I knew what I had to do. I had one last gift to give.

"Kara," I mouthed. I moved in front of her and gripped her gently by the arms to = gain her attention. "Kara, I need you to do something for me."

Her teary gaze snapped toward me. "Anything, dad... I mean, Director," she stuttered. "I need you to go to the command deck and prepare the ship for launch while I manage the situation out here. This vessel was built to withstand entry through the thick atmosphere of Titan, but I don't know how long we can endure the fury of humankind's will to survive."

"It's your design. I'm ... I'm not sure if I know the ignition sequence well enough without you." I held her at arm's length. "Like you said, you've been with me since the beginning. You know everything that I do. Just stay focused and ignore what's out there. I believe in you, Kara. Your people need you."

"Okay," she said. She gritted her teeth and nodded. "I can handle it."

"I know you can." I smiled as I patted her on the shoulder and turned her around. My heart sank as I watched her run toward the lift. I wanted to holler, "I'll see you soon," just so she'd glance back over her shoulder, but I couldn't get the words out.

I didn't want to lie. Not to her.

"Mr. Drayton," I said, spinning around. My gaze darted between him and his daughter. "Are you sure you want this?"

"It's wha—" A thunderous crash cut him off. Half of the compound's gate swung open against the wall, and the mob poured through, stampeded each other and screaming. Sgt. Hale and the officers at the ramp's base tightened their stance and readied their rifles. "It's what any father would do," he finished.

"I think I understand." I leaned in close so that I could whisper in his ear. "First, have your daughter loaded into the chamber meant for you. Then, I need you to follow Kara. There's no time to get everybody hooked up. Tell the staff to have everyone get into their chambers themselves and worry about hooking up when the ship reaches space. Once everybody is safely restrained, initiate the launch. Kara will have it ready, but she'll be waiting for me. Don't."

Mr. Drayton eyes opened wide as he realized what I was planning. "There has to be another way," he said.

"Another body on the ship means someone else must be left behind. It's as simple as that."

"Then let it be me! These people need you."

I smirked. "Not anymore. I'll be dead in a decade. One old man isn't going to make a difference on Titan. You have an entire lifetime to make it feel like home." I regarded his daughter and wondered what Kara might've looked like at her age. "It starts with her."

"Director Trass, I don't—"

"This is an order, Mr. Drayton!" I cut him off. "Now, there are two chambers in the command deck. You might have to force her into hers, but make sure she gets in. You tell her..." The words got stuck in my throat. I could picture her beautiful smile. "Tell her she's the only Trass who matters now."

He stood motionless. "Thank you," he muttered, hardly able to get the words out. "For everything,"

Our gazes met one last time. "Thank me when you're there," I replied. He was the only chosen candidate willing to risk everything on a lie. It was because of that I knew he wouldn't fail me.

He wrapped his arm around his daughter and turned to a

member of my staff. Once he began communicating the orders I'd told him to, I hurried to Sgt. Hale at the ramp.

"Move everybody inside!" I told him.

"Director Trass, what's going on?" he questioned. He fired off a few rounds to slow the rapidly approaching mob, but they were growing bolder. In minutes, I knew the guards I hired for protection were going to have to do whatever it took to survive. Having to slaughter members of their own species was going to be the last memory of Earth my candidates had. I couldn't allow that. "It's time," I said. "Nobody gets in or out after me." I keyed the ramp controls and set it to start closing. Then I sprinted out across my compound before any of the officers could stop me. Sgt. Hale shouted something, but he wasn't foolish enough to follow.

"That's him!" someone in the mob screamed.

I lowered my head and made a break for the compound's office building. The throng abandoned the Titan Project to chase after me, just like I knew they would, but the angle I'd taken allowed me to stay ahead of them. They shouted all manner of obscenities. Debris rained down around me.

A quarter-mile later, I busted through the lobby doors just before a slew of rocks peppered the glass. For once, there were no candidates at the front desk blocking the etching on it that read,

TITAN'S COLD EMBRACE AWAITS US.

I wasn't far enough ahead of the mob to take the elevator, so I entered the emergency stairwell. My legs felt like jelly by the time I reached the hallway six stories up. My office glowed at the other end of it like a beacon. Apparently, I'd left my lights on. The rest of the floor was dark.

I sprinted toward my office, locking the door as soon as I made it inside. A few seconds later, the mob pounded on it. I wasn't worried. The door was installed by the company that I'd started from nothing, and our products always worked. It would hold long enough.

"You can't hide!" someone hollered.

I strolled over to my desk and took a seat in my all-too-familiar chair. My foot knocked over a bottle of whiskey underneath. Enough was left to fix myself a glass. I grabbed one off the windowsill and cleaned it with the bottom of my shirt. As I held it up to the moonlight to see if I'd gotten out all the smudges, a series of bright lights along the bottom of the Titan Project winked on. A siren blared throughout the entire compound.

I poured myself a drink and leaned back. The floor began to shake violently, causing the golden liquid to slosh over the rim of my glass. The shouting and banging at my door stopped. Seconds later, a blinding flash filled the sky, swiftly drowned out by smoke and dust. I could feel the heat radiating through the glass.

The shaking grew so intense my bones rattled, and then it was gone. The faint light grew steadily smaller, and even though I couldn't yet see the Titan Project through the fog, I knew liftoff was a success. Kara and Mr. Drayton had done it. They—his daughter, and two thousand, nine hundred and ninety-seven others—were going to live. Humanity's best hope.

As the dust and smoke began to part, the moon was revealed. On one side of it, the flaming engines of the Titan Project glimmered. On the other, the asteroid shone. I raised my glass to the instrument of Earth's destruction and took a sip.

And Yet

by A. T. Greenblatt

Only idiots go back to the haunted houses of their childhood. And yet.

Here you are. Standing on the sagging, weed-strangled front porch that hasn't changed in twenty years. Every dip in the floorboards, every peeling strip of paint is exactly as you remember it. Time seems to have ricocheted off this place.

Except not everything has stayed the same. You have your doctorate in theoretical physics now, the ink's still fresh on the diploma. Your prospects look good. You're going start teaching next month, your first steps on the path to tenure. You have a grant for a research project you've been waiting for years to start. The secrets of the universe are a locked door and you might have the key. That is, if the house doesn't kill you first.

You're lingering on the doorstep, not quite ready to commit. There's an early morning hush to the neighborhood, but it's already ungodly humid and warm. The backs of your calves stick to your leg braces, your backpack is heavy on your shoulders, and your walking cane is slick from your sweaty palm, though you're not sure if that's because of the heat or because being back on this porch is doing terrible things to your heart rate. Even the dragonflies are smart enough to linger at the property line.

This is a terrible idea. Your hand is clenched around the

doorknob and you're listing all the valid reasons you should walk away.

And yet.

If you're right, you could be onto the greatest scientific discovery in quantum mechanics. Ever. And if you don't make it out again...

Well, at least it'll be in the name of science.

So, you open the door and step through.

. . .

Nothing in the house has stayed the same since the last time you worked up the nerve to come in. Nothing. This shouldn't surprise you, because you have this theory that the house reacts to its visitors. The visitor is the catalyst and the catalyst is not a bullied eight-year-old kid anymore. Thus the reaction is different. And yet.

You were hoping, god you were hoping you could take the same path as before. Have the same escape routes. But the haunted house of your childhood has become an unfamiliar landscape. Instead of the front door opening to a wide landing and a staircase, you are standing in a foyer, at the mouth of a narrow hall with rooms on either side. There's no staircase in sight.

The walls are slanted inward. They're covered in dark, dizzyingly patterned wallpaper and you aren't claustrophobic until you are. Vertigo and your pulse skips so badly you don't even notice the frames on the walls at first. But when you do, you bite back a scream.

They're full of pictures of you.

You're well-documented. All ages and always caught unaware. Some pictures are taken from over your shoulder, some from a distance, some from right under your chin. You've never seen these photos before, but you recognize the settings in several, like the nook in the library you hang out in when you want to be alone.

Your hand tightens around your cane. You're going to make it down this hall and find those damn stairs. But the farther you walk, the more pictures of yourself you discover. The more the slanted walls press down on you. The longer the passageway grows.

In the end, you only make it about thirty feet before you can't stand it anymore, your knees are shaking that badly. So, without thinking through the consequences, the possibilities, you turn into the second room on your left.

. . .

There are five of them sitting on the couch and watching TV. You don't recognize them at first, all grown up. But these people in their best business casual and gelled hair are your former "friends," the ones that met you at the haunted house twenty years ago. You only recognize them because you just saw them at your ten-year high school reunion two days ago. Admittedly, you attended it just to gloat a little.

"Wow, you're researching parallel universes? That's crazy!" Chelsea said. "I'm jealous. My insurance job is so boring." You gave her a tight-lipped smile. You'd been hearing a variation of this all evening. That, and "Look at you! Walking with one cane now instead of two!"

"We did some crazy things as kids," she said, a little too quickly. She kept mixing her cocktail, something that looked too red and smelled too sweet, and didn't meet your gaze. "We were really stupid back then."

Intellectually, you understood she was trying to apologize. Morally, you knew you should be the bigger person. And yet, you said nothing.

Now Chelsea is in the same pink frilly shirt she wore at

the reunion, and she and the other four are completely absorbed in some TV show. Just like when you were kids. Except you're not sitting on the floor with your two crutches on either side of you, slightly apart from them, hoping that this counts as friendship. You're standing in the threshold, glaring. What the hell is so interesting on that TV anyway?

You look.

You regret it instantly.

It's a video of that terrible day. The day when your little brother, Avery, got hit by a car several blocks away.

The video is playing on repeat.

You weren't there to see it happen. You were too busy getting peer pressured into going into this haunted house by these "friends." But later, when the doctors took pity and put you and Avery in the same hospital room, you heard all about it.

"I was coming to see you at the house, yeah?" Avery said with this sheepish grin though half of his face was bruised and all four limbs were in casts. "But this big blue truck came out of nowhere!"

On TV, a blue 4x4 crests the hill too fast and rams straight into your little brother. Then the scene resets and it happens again. And again. And again.

But not, you realize, in exactly the same way every time. Sometimes the rusty, dented fender only clips him and sometimes the results are worse. Much worse. But one thing is consistent; Avery never makes it across the street.

Your five ex-classmates watch unemotionally transfixed. The assholes. They should feel just as guilty for what happened to Avery. Your little brother never did make a full recovery. Was always in pain from that moment on. Two years later, doctors put his official cause of death as "complications relating to pneumonia." He was eight.

Suddenly, you want cause some damage. Want to feel

your knuckles crack their teeth though you've never hit anyone before. You take a step forward.

Your ex-classmates flicker. Change. Like a tilt card, where the picture shifts when you tip the angle. Suddenly, they're not twenty-eight years old anymore. They're eight. Kids, again.

Then you remember, oh right, you're in the haunted house of your childhood. Shit.

The urban legend was that this house didn't like visitors. That it ate them. As a kid, you thought that meant there was a ravenous ghost in its basement or something. Now, you suspect that this house holds dozens, if not hundreds of parallel universes within it.

You have no idea why.

You've been trying to study it—from a theoretical level and a safe distance—at school. But all you have are best guesses. It's time for more definite results. You have a doctorate and a brand new research grant to explore the possibility of pocket universes and you're going to make the most of them. Even if it kills you.

You take a deep breath and glance around the room. On the other side of it, there is another doorway. The only exit out.

Running isn't an option for you, never was, between the leg braces and the muscles that just don't want to cooperate. Even with the cane, your footsteps are loud and obnoxious. It will definitely draw your ex-classmates' attention and for some reason you can't quite articulate, you *do not* want to draw their attention.

But you can't stay here forever. You won't.

So, before you lose your nerve, you shift the weight of the backpack on your shoulders and cut across the room as fast as your legs will let you. You feel five sets of eyes on you when you walk in front of the screen, hear five intakes of breath. Five pairs of feet making contact with the wooden floor.

They are coming.

You panic, stumble, but manage to catch yourself at the last moment. Don't look back. DON'T LOOK BACK. You stretch out your hand and your fingers slam painfully into the edge of the doorway. Thank god.

You can't look back. So you hurry through.

• • •

The staircase to the second floor is not in the next room. Dread swells in the pit of your stomach when you find yourself in the kitchen of your parents' house instead.

You spot another doorway across the room. But this time, you're not so lucky.

"Sit," your mom commands and the tone of her voice has you instinctively taking a seat at the cluttered kitchen table, not even pausing to take off your backpack first. She slams a plate of food in front of you. "You're not excused until you finish everything. And I mean *everything*."

You look down. Oh god, it's worse than you remember. Vegetables cooked past death, pasta barely cooked at all, a piece of chicken so dry it crumbles when you poke it. But feeding her kids has always been another annoying chore to your mom.

You try a green bean and wince. Shit, you haven't had your mom's half-assed food since you moved to college. Finding roommates who love to cook—and feed their housemates—has been one of the greatest discoveries in your adult life.

Okay, you can do this. One more bad meal and you can get out of here. But when you look down, the green bean you just ate has been replaced by an identical one.

Your stomach clenches. Your mom is standing by the sink, smoking, watching you.

And yet. Just like in the TV room, things in the kitchen are changing too.

Every time you shift or tilt your head or even blink, the room changes. Sometimes the stained wallpaper is green, sometimes it's mustard. Sometimes the stove has a month of crud on it. Sometimes it's simmering tomato sauce, freshly burnt. But in every version, your mom stays by the sink, filling up the kitchen with smoke like a poisonous dragon. Also, the food on your plate is consistently inedible.

Hypothesis: There are universes colliding in these rooms and it's resulting moments of instability.

From a theoretical physicist perspective, this is amazing. From a personal perspective, you want to vomit.

You close your eyes and take a deep breath.

And when you open them again, Avery is sitting next to you, with his own plate of food. You turn your head, experimentally. The kitchen doesn't change.

"You really going to that house tonight?" he asks. You guess he's about six based on the baby tooth he's missing in front. Also, the question.

"Shh," you say and glance at your mom. You have an idea. "Maybe."

"Can I come?"

"No!" Your voice is too sharp, too loud. From the sink, your mom glares at you.

"Shh," Avery says.

"Listen, Birdhouse," you say, a nickname that makes both of you crack up. "I need your help."

Avery immediately perks up and follows your gaze to the doorway across the kitchen. "A distraction?"

"Exactly, but nothing that will get you in too much trouble, yeah?"

"Three Snickers bars and then two stories a night when I'm grounded," he says with a grin.

"Deal." Love for your kid brother swells up in you. You two were always a team.

"Hey, listen. Promise me you'll stay here tonight," you say, "And I promise I'll take you to the haunted house later, just me and you. Okay?"

Avery wrinkles his nose, but before you can get another word in, he starts whining about dinner. Loudly.

Your mom crosses the kitchen in four strides, her bubbling anger focused on your kid brother. As quietly as you can, you ease your way out of the chair and cross the kitchen. From experience, you know you have about ten more seconds to make your escape.

And yet. You look back.

Avery and your mom are going at it at top volume, the same family stubbornness reflected back and forth across the table. You bite your lip. God, you're a terrible human being for getting your little brother in trouble for your sake, even if this is not your universe.

"Stay there," you whisper and open the door.

. . .

Everything in the dining room shines. The chairs, the walls, the curtains, the table which looks exactly like the ugly, scratched up table in your parents' house, except glossier. You have no idea why. Later, you'll lie awake at night and come up with theories and rational explanations to build a levee against the nightmares.

But right now, you need to find a way out and so you focus on keeping your balance on the polished, gleaming floor. You *will* stay calm this time.

Everything reflects. You don't want to see what they have

to show, but you don't really have a choice, do you? Especially, when you hear the door click shut behind you.

You look back and there's only a gleaming wall. Seamless. And in its reflection, there's another version of you. Smiling, standing straighter in the doorway of your new office. "Associate Professor" on the door plaque above your name. A picture on your desk of you and your dad beaming on graduation day.

Oh god, you are a complete failure, aren't you? You're still working out of the graduate office. In your universe, your dad never cared about any of your academic accomplishments. He's more of a "give me sports or give me death" type of guy.

You look away.

The reflection in the back of a chair shows you sitting on your parents' sofa. You're trying to get up, but it's a stiff and painful motion, and you see your leg braces are scratched and need to be replaced. You didn't learn how to stretch properly until college and in this universe, it looks like you never made it far past high school.

Everywhere you turn, you are reflected. Always twenty-eight. Always showing all the awful ways your life could have gone wrong. Or so very right. You try to keep your breath steady as you turn in a slow circle, looking for a way out. But all you see is you.

Oh god. You're trapped.

Despite your promise to yourself that you *will* remain the rational scientist, fear puts its icy fingers on your throat and squeezes.

And that's when your feet fail. Between the distraction and stress, your muscles seize up in a "Fuck you" salute and you go crashing down, badly. Your cane goes flying and you hear it smack against the wall.

You groan, swear, look up. The wall is cracked, but miraculously, your cane seems to be undamaged. You think you spot something behind the reflection. Or maybe you just need something to believe in because now your knees are bruised and you're fucking pissed.

You crawl over to your cane, pull yourself unsteadily to your feet. Re-center the weight of your book bag. Then, you swing your cane at the wall.

You empty all your rage and hurt and exhaustion into the motion and you don't stop even when you lose your balance and have to pick yourself up again, because it feels goddamn good to destroy something in this house even if every new shard is showing another you. And you and you and you. Every goddamn iteration of you and they're all heartbreaking.

And yet. They aren't *you.*

When you stop to catch your breath, the wall is a ragged, empty frame. Beyond it, there's a door.

"You not going to beat me, house." you gasp and open it.

* * *

Finally. A staircase up.

You climb the steps the same way you did all those years ago: Slowly, precisely, with one hand on the rail and the other tight around your cane. You now have sufficient evidence that this house is actively trying to stop you, possibly because if your research works out and you publish your results, this house is going to have a lot more visitors.

You have a strong working theory that the house really, *really* hates visitors.

But you won't be stopped. Can't be. And you hope when other scientists come here, they will tear this house down, one theory at a time.

And yet.

You hesitate on the landing. Last time, the second floor was where the new possibilities lived.

You're just hoping you can find the universe you're looking for and in it, a like-minded you.

* * *

When you reach the second floor, you feel the tension go out of your shoulders. It's *exactly* how you remember it.

Well, maybe not exactly. The hallway's still narrow and brooding, dark with white doors on both sides, but it's longer than last time and there are more doors. That's not surprising, though. You're older now.

In every door, there's a peephole and when you look through, you see different scenes from your life. Classrooms, lunch at the library, late nights in the lab, lectures, training at the gym, meals with your roommates, dates at the park, homework in your parents' house, awkward parties, fun parties, lonely recesses. You walk down the hallway and you walk down your life, catching snatches of it in the peepholes of the doors. Middle school, university, high school, elementary, the house has universes for them all.

Finally, you find the one you're looking for.

The peephole shows this: You standing on the front porch of the haunted house, hesitating, doorknob in your hand.

"This is it," you breathe and open the door.

Inside: a white room; blank except for an open window and pale blue curtains whispering in the breeze. Just like last time. But last time, you chose the first door on your right after you saw your friends standing on the lawn in front of the house, waiting for you to come out again. You were so excited to have found an escape route and then were so startled by the white room beyond, you didn't realize the door locked behind you when it slammed shut.

But you're wiser now. You lean against the door as you

rummage around your book bag and pull out three door-stops. You're not falling for the same trap this time.

When you're satisfied the door will not move a damn inch, you walk to the window and lean out.

Last time you were here, you jumped out the window, panicked, desperate to escape this haunted house. You broke both wrists and your nose. It was not your best idea.

Now, you realize how lucky you were, peering out the window. It's an unforgiving two-story fall. You can't help but wonder in how many universes you broke your neck instead.

From your backpack, you unfurl a rope ladder.

You've been practicing for months, climbing up and down this hellish rope. Between your shitty balance and stiff muscles, you've had abstract algebra classes that were easier than teaching your body this.

"Fire safety," you told your personal trainer. "And because it's just sort of badass, in general?" Which wasn't a lie. She was up for the challenge and so were you.

What you didn't tell her—or anyone else—is that in your backpack are your research notes. The possibilities in parallel universes are infinite. Thus there are other versions of you out there, in similar labs, doing similar experiments. And maybe, if two of you were running experiments with an identical set of constants, changing the same variable, maybe, just maybe, you can make contact.

It would undisputedly be the great scientific discovery of all time.

You check that your escape route is secure and put your foot on the first rope rung.

"Okay. Let's do this," you say and begin to climb down into a new universe.

• • •

You blink and everything shifts.

You don't even realize that the universe has changed until your feet are on solid ground and you see the five kids waiting on the lawn. Shit, goddamn it, what the fuck? Later, you'll agonize over this, replay it in your head, come up empty. You have no idea why you've found yourself in a universe twenty years in your past, instead of twenty minutes.

The kids don't realize you've walked up behind them until you clear your throat. They jump in surprise.

"Who are you?" eight-year-old Chelsea asks.

"A physicist specializing in quantum mechanics and multiverse theory."

You're met with five blank stares.

"What does that even mean?" a boy, Jared, asks.

"It means I come from a universe that's banned the internet and the only shows on TV are documentaries."

They stare at you in horror.

Of course, this is a complete lie, but you don't care, you're so frustrated and these kids probably just bullied your eight-year-old self into a haunted house. "Isn't there supposed to be one more of you?"

The five of them look guilty and steal glances at the house. Shit.

"I think...I think we made a mistake," Chelsea admits, looking close to tears.

Yeah, she's not the only one.

"Go home," you tell them, quietly. "Just... go home."

They run. Eagerly. So eagerly.

Your hand clenches around your cane and your heart tightens too. It still hurts, how easily they abandon you. All because you were visibly different than them.

And yet, in some ways you're grateful to them and to this house. It made you realize they weren't your friends, not really. After that, you poured all your energy into school and getting away from this place.

Also, it inspired you to study physics.

Because you sort of realized what happened, even as an eight-year-old. When you fell out of the window, you woke up in a hospital in a slightly different universe than the one you came from.

The changes were subtle. Your parents' house was painted an ugly blue instead of dirty beige. Avery had the bigger bedroom, but he was still terrified of heights. And you had a deaf dog instead of a cranky cat. There were hundreds of little changes, but for the most part, it was easy to adapt.

It inspired lots of questions. Questions that you're still asking. You've never told anyone about what happened in this house. Not even your closest friends and advisors. Not even now. You wanted your research to prove it first. You wanted to expose this house as being more than haunted.

And yet, in this universe, you once again find yourself on the sagging porch. Shit.

But maybe you can at least stop eight year old you from jumping out the window, offer a hand down instead. You have no idea if you can change a universe in a meaningful way, but you're pretty sure you can help the catalyst.

You open the door once again and follow your eight-year-old self into the haunted house.

* * *

You're standing in a wide landing and the staircase is right in front of you. You relax a bit. It's just how you remember.

From the room on your left, you hear your parents screaming all the stupid, ugly, terrifying things they've ever said to each other. Oh. You forgot about that. On the right side, you hear all the callous things they've said about you.

You remember now, the first time you were here, the landing almost paralyzed you with fear. But this is nothing compared to what you've already been through. You ignore it and head right for the stairs. Because you can hear uneven footsteps on the landing, the soft *thump* of two crutches on wood.

The haunted house of your childhood will not stop you. It can't.

*   *   *

This time, you don't even bother with the peephole. You just repeat what you did as a kid. You open the first door on your right.

Your eight-year-old self is already halfway out the window. Eyes round with fear.

"Wait," you shout, but even in this instant, you know it's not enough. You're too far gone.

The kid at the window startles, slips. Falls. Disappears from view.

You hear the impact. The sound is louder, harsher, than you remember. Oh god, you've made things worse, haven't you?

You slump against the door. Suddenly, the years of working and struggling and fighting hit you in one devastating wave of emotion. All this effort and you're still out of your league. The house is playing by its own rules while you're trying to learn the game. You've been busy looking for constants while everything is flickering. Always changing.

You refuse to look out the window. Instead, you pull out your creased and battered research notes from your backpack. The working title is "The Birdhouse Project." It's the best apology you have.

So, you're going to walk down the steps, out of the house,

back to your original universe, and try again. And again and again and again if necessary. You've come too far to relent now.

This is how the house traps its visitors, isn't it? Devours them, really. You don't care. This house is *not* going to stop you. It can't.

And yet.

You hear a faint... something. Like a hiccup. You hear it again. It's coming from the room on the left side of the hall, across from you.

You step away from the door, close it gently. You cross the hall and press your ear against the door. There it is again. A soft cry.

Wait. You know that voice.

You throw open the door.

• • •

Your little brother is sitting under the open window in the white, blank room. His eyes are red and snot's running down his chin. You're pretty sure your mouth is hanging open. You wanted to run over and hug him, but instead say: "Hi Avery."

He stares at you, startled just as you. God, you really are an idiot. You spent the last ten years of your life studying multiverse theories and yet you didn't allow yourself to believe that there's at least one universe where Avery manages to cross the street and follow you into the haunted house.

Your kid brother who's afraid of heights.

"Who are you?" he asks.

"Guess," you say.

He studies you. Your cane, your leg braces, your face as you lean against the open door. His eyes widen.

"You're right, Birdhouse," you say.

"Whoa," he breathes.

Your knees are shaking, but this time, not from fear. Avery wipes his eyes and gets to his feet. "I got lost," he says, twisting his hands.

"Me too." You smile. He gives you a tentative smile back.

You consider the possibilities. You could stay here, in this universe. Or take Avery back to yours. If you do, could you really bring yourself to come back to this haunted house and risk abandoning him again? If you can't, you'd be giving up your guarantee of making a breakthrough in parallel universe research. All that work.

And yet, your kid brother is right in front of you. Whole.

"Touché, house," you say softly.

"What's that mean?" Avery wrinkles his nose and you laugh.

"Come on, Birdhouse," you say. "I have a way out."

And you hold open the door.

A Witch's Guide to Escape:
A Practical Compendium of Portal Fantasies

by Alix E. Harrow

GEORGE, JC—THE RUNAWAY PRINCE—J FIC GEO 1994

You'd think it would make us happy when a kid checks out the same book a zillion times in a row, but actually it just keeps us up at night.

The Runaway Prince is one of those low-budget young adult fantasies from the mid-nineties, before J.K. Rowling arrived to tell everyone that magic was cool, printed on brittle yellow paper. It's about a lonely boy who runs away and discovers a Magical Portal into another world where he has Medieval Adventures, but honestly there are so many typos most people give up before he even finds the portal.

Not this kid, though. He pulled it off the shelf and sat cross-legged in the juvenile fiction section with his grimy red backpack clutched to his chest. He didn't move for hours. Other patrons were forced to double-back in the aisle, shooting suspicious, you-don't-belong-here looks behind them as if wondering what a skinny black teenager was *really* up to while pretending to read a fantasy book. He ignored them.

The books above him rustled and quivered; that kind of attention flatters them.

He took *The Runaway Prince* home and renewed it twice online, at which point a gray pop-up box that looks like an emissary from 1995 tells you, "the renewal limit for this item has been reached." You can almost feel the disapproving eyes of a librarian glaring at you through the screen.

(There have only ever been two kinds of librarians in the history of the world: the prudish, bitter ones with lipstick running into the cracks around their lips who believe the books are their personal property and patrons are dangerous delinquents come to steal them; and witches).

Our late fee is 25 cents per day or a can of non-perishable food during the summer food drive. By the time the boy finally slid *The Runaway Prince* into the return slot, he owed $4.75. I didn't have to swipe his card to know; any good librarian (of the second kind) ought to be able to tell you the exact dollar amount of a patron's bill just by the angle of their shoulders.

"What'd you think?" I used my this-is-a-secret-between-us-pals voice, which works on teenagers about sixteen percent of the time.

He shrugged. It has a lower success rate with black teenagers, because this is the rural South and they aren't stupid enough to trust thirty-something white ladies no matter how many tattoos we have.

"Didn't finish it, huh?" I knew he'd finished it at least four times by the warm, well-oiled feel of the pages.

"Yeah, I did." His eyes flicked up. They were smoke-colored and long-lashed, with an achy, faraway expression, as if he knew there was something gleaming and forbidden just beneath the dull surfaces of things that he could never quite touch. They were the kinds of eyes that had belonged to sorcerers or soothsayers, in different times. "The ending sucked."

In the end, the Runaway Prince leaves Medieval Adventureland and closes the portal behind him before returning home to his family. It was supposed to be a happy ending.

Which kind of tells you all you need to know about this kid's life, doesn't it?

He left without checking anything else out.

.   .   .

GARRISON, ALLEN B—THE TAVALARRIAN CHRONICLES—v. I-XVI—F GAR 1976
LEGUIN, URSULA K—A WIZARD OF EARTHSEA—J FIC LEG 1968

He returned four days later, sloping past a bright blue display titled THIS SUMMER, DIVE INTO READING! (who knows where they were supposed to swim; Ulysses County's lone public pool had been filled with cement in the sixties rather than desegregate).

Because I am a librarian of the second sort, I almost always know what kind of book a person wants. It's like a very particular smell rising off them which is instantly recognizable as *Murder mystery* or *Political biography* or *Something kind of trashy but ultimately life-affirming, preferably with lesbians.*

I do my best to give people the books they need most. In grad school, they called it "ensuring readers have access to texts/materials that are engaging and emotionally rewarding," and in my other kind of schooling, they called it "divining the unfilled spaces in their souls and filling them with stories and starshine," but it comes to the same thing.

I don't bother with the people who have call numbers scribbled on their palms and titles rattling around in their skulls like bingo cards. They don't need me. And you really can't do anything for the people who only read Award-Winning Literature, who wear elbow patches and equate the popularity of *Twilight* with the death of the American intellect; their hearts are too closed-up for the new or secret or undiscovered.

So, it's only a certain kind of patron I pay attention to. The kind that let their eyes feather across the titles like trailing fingertips, heads cocked, with book-hunger rising off them like heatwaves from July pavement. The books bask in it, of course, even the really hopeless cases that haven't been checked out since 1958 (there aren't many of these; me and Agnes take turns carting home outdated astronomy text-books that still think Pluto is a planet and cookbooks that call for lard, just to keep their spirits up). I choose one or two books and let their spines gleam and glimmer in the twilit stacks. People reach towards them without quite knowing why.

The boy with the red backpack wasn't an experienced aisle-wanderer. He prowled, moving too quickly to read the titles, hands hanging empty and uncertain at his sides. The sewing and pattern books (646.2) noted that his jeans were unlaundered and too small, and the neck of his t-shirt was stained grayish-yellow. The cookbooks (641.5) diagnosed a diet of frozen waffles and gas-station pizza. They *tssked* to themselves.

I sat at the circulation desk, running returns beneath the blinky red scanner light, and breathed him in. I was expecting something like *generic Arthurian retelling* or maybe *teen romance with sword-fighting*, but instead I found a howling, clamoring mess of need.

He smelled of a thousand secret worlds, of rabbit-holes and hidden doorways and platforms nine-and-three-quarters, of Wonderland and Oz and Narnia, of anyplace-but-here. He smelled of *yearning*.

God save me from the yearners. The insatiable, the in-consolable, the ones who chafe and claw against the edges of the world. No book can save them.

(That's a lie. There are Books potent enough to save any

mortal soul: books of witchery, augury, alchemy; books with wand-wood in their spines and moon-dust on their pages; books older than stones and wily as dragons. We give people the books they need most, except when we don't.)

I sent him a 70s sword-and-sorcery series because it was total junk food and he needed fattening up, and because I hoped sixteen volumes might act as a sort of ballast and keep his keening soul from rising away into the ether. I let LeGuin shimmer at him, too, because he reminded me a bit of Ged (feral; full of longing).

I ignored *The Lion, the Witch, and the Wardrobe*, jostling importantly on its shelf; this was a kid who wanted to go through the wardrobe and never, ever come back.

·   ·   ·

GRAYSON, DR BERNARD—WHEN NOTHING MATTERS ANYMORE: A SURVIVAL GUIDE FOR DEPRESSED TEENS—616.84 GRA 2002

Once you make it past book four of the *Tavalarrian Chronicles*, you're committed at least through book fourteen when the true Sword of Tavalar is revealed and the young farm-boy ascends to his rightful throne. The boy with the red backpack showed up every week or so all summer for the next install-ment.

I snuck in a few others (all pretty old, all pretty white; our branch director is one of those pinch-lipped Baptists who thinks fantasy books teach kids about Devil worship, so roughly 90% of my collection requests are mysteriously denied): *A Wrinkle in Time* came back with the furtive, jammed-in-a-backpack scent that meant he liked it but thought it was too young for him; *Watership Down* was offended because he never got past the first ten pages, but I guess footnotes about rabbit-math aren't for everyone; and *The Golden Compass* had the flashlight-smell of 3:00 a.m. on its final chapter and was unbearably smug about it. I'd just gotten an inter-library-loaned copy of *Akata Witch*—when he stopped coming.

Our display (GET READ-Y FOR SCHOOL!) was filled with SAT prep kits and over-sized yellow *For Dummies* books. Agnes had cut out blobby construction-paper leaves and taped them to the front doors. Lots of kids stop hanging around the library when school starts up, with all its clubs and teams.

I worried anyway. I could feel the Book I hadn't given him like a wrong note or a missing tooth, a magnetic absence. Just when I was seriously considering calling Ulysses County High School with a made-up story about an un-returned CD, he came back.

For the first time, there was someone else with him: A squat white woman with a plastic name-tag and the kind of squareish perm you can only get in Southern beauty salons with faded glamor-shots in the windows. The boy trailed behind her looking thin and pressed, like a flower crushed between dictionary pages. I wondered how badly you had to fuck up to get assigned a school counselor after hours, until I read her name-tag: Department of Community-Based Services, Division of Protection and Permanency, Child Caseworker (II).

Oh. A foster kid.

The woman marched him through the nonfiction stacks (the travel guides sighed as she passed, muttering about overwork and recommending vacations to sunny, faraway beaches) and stopped in the 616s. "Here, why don't we have a look at these?"

Predictable, sullen silence from the boy.

A person who works with foster kids sixty hours a week is unfazed by sullenness. She slid titles off the shelf and stacked them in the boy's arms. "We talked about this, remember? We decided you might like to read something practical, something helpful?"

Dealing with Depression (616.81 WHI 1998). *Beating the Blues: Five Steps to Feeling Normal Again!* (616.822 TRE 2011). *Chicken Soup for the Depressed Soul* (616.9 CAN). The books greeted him in soothing, syrupy voices.

The boy stayed silent. "Look. I know you'd rather read about dragons and, uh, elves," oh, Tolkien, you have so much to account for, "but sometimes we've got to face our problems head-on, rather than running away from them."

What *bullshit*. I was in the back room running scratched DVDs through the disc repair machine, so the only person to hear me swear was Agnes. She gave me her patented over-the-glasses shame-on-you look which, when properly deployed, can reduce noisy patrons to piles of ash or pillars of salt (Agnes is a librarian of the second kind, too).

But seriously. Anyone could see that kid needed to run and keep running until he shed his own skin, until he clawed out of the choking darkness and unfurled his wings, precious and prisming in the light of some other world.

His caseworker was one of those people who say the word "escapism" as if it's a moral failing, a regrettable hobby, a mental-health diagnosis. As if escape is not, in itself, one of the highest order of magics they'll ever see in their miserable mortal lives, right up there with true love and prophetic dreams and fireflies blinking in synchrony on a June evening.

The boy and his keeper were winding back through the aisles toward the front desk. The boy's shoulders were curled inward, as if he chafed against invisible walls on either side.

As he passed the juvenile fiction section, a cheap paperback flung itself off the return cart and thudded into his kneecap. He picked it up and rubbed his thumb softly over the title. *The Runaway Prince* purred at him.

He smiled. I thanked the library cart, silently.

There was a long, familiar sigh behind me. I turned to see Agnes watching me from the circulation desk, aquamarine nails tapping the cover of a Grisham novel, eyes crimped with pity. *Oh honey, not another one*, they said.

I turned back to my stack of DVDs, unsmiling, thinking things like *what do you know about it* and *this one is different* and *oh shit*.

* * *

DUMAS, ALEXANDRE—THE COUNT OF MONTE CRISTO—F DUM 1974

The boy returned at ten-thirty on a Tuesday morning. It's official library policy to report truants to the high school, because the school board felt we were becoming "a haven for unsupervised and illicit teenage activity." I happen to think that's exactly what libraries should aspire to be, and suggested we get it engraved on a plaque for the front door, but then I was asked to be serious or leave the proceedings, and anyway we're supposed to report kids who skip school to play *League of Legends* on our computers or skulk in the graphic novel section.

I watched the boy prowling the shelves—muscles strung wire-tight over his bones, soul writhing and clawing like a caged creature—and did not reach for the phone. Agnes, still wearing her *oh honey* expression, declined to reprimand me.

I sent him home with *The Count of Monte Cristo*, partly because it requires your full attention and a flow chart to keep track of the plot and the kid needed distracting, but mostly because of what Edmund says on the second-to-last page: "...all human wisdom is summed up in these two words,—'Wait and hope.'"

But people can't keep waiting and hoping forever.

They fracture, they unravel, they crack open; they do something desperate and stupid and then you see their high school senior photo printed in the *Ulysses Gazette*, grainy and oversized, and you spend the next five years thinking: *if only I'd given her the right book.*

. . .

ROWLING, JK—HARRY POTTER AND THE SORCERER'S STONE—J FIC ROW 1998
ROWLING, JK—HARRY POTTER AND THE CHAMBER OF SECRETS—J FIC ROW 1999
ROWLING, JK—HARRY POTTER AND THE PRISONER OF AZKABAN—J FIC ROW 1999

Every librarian has Books she never lends to anyone.

I'm not talking about first editions of *Alice in Wonderland* or Dutch translations of *Winnie-the-Pooh*; I'm talking about Books so powerful and potent, so full of susurrating seduction, that only librarians of the second sort even know they exist.

Each of us has her own system for keeping them hidden. The most venerable libraries (the ones with oak paneling and vaulted ceilings and *Beauty and the Beast*-style ladders) have secret rooms behind fireplaces or bookcases, which you can only enter by tugging on a certain title on the shelf. Sainte-Geneviève in Paris is supposed to have vast catacombs beneath it guarded by librarians so ancient and desiccated they've become human-shaped books, paper-skinned and ink-blooded. In Timbuktu, I head they hired wizard-smiths to make great wrought-iron gates that only permit passage to the pure of heart.

In the Maysville branch of the Ulysses County Library system, we have a locked roll-top desk in the Special Collections room with a sign on it that says, "This is an Antique! Please Ask for Assistance."

We only have a dozen or so Books, anyhow, and god knows where they came from or how they ended up here. *A*

Witch's Guide to Seeking Righteous Vengeance, with its slender steel pages and arsenic ink. *A Witch's Guide to Falling in Love for the First Time, for Readers at Every Stage of Life!*, which smells like starlight and the summer you were seventeen. *A Witch's Guide to Uncanny Baking* contains over thirty full-color photographs to ensorcell your friends and afflict your adversaries. *A Witch's Guide to Escape: A Practical Compendium of Portal Fantasies* has no words in it at all, but only pages and pages of maps: hand-drawn Middle Earth knock-offs with unpronounceable names; medieval tapestry-maps showing tiny ships sailing off the edge of the world; topographical maps of Machu Picchu; 1970s Rand McNally street maps of Istanbul.

It's my job to keep Books like this out of the hands of desperate high-school kids with red backpacks. Our schoolmistresses called it "preserving the hallowed and hidden arts of our foremothers from mundane eyes." Our professors called it "conserving rare/historic texts."

Both of them mean the same thing: We give people the books they need, except when we don't. Except when they need them most.

He racked up $1.50 on *The Count of Monte Cristo* and returned it with saltwater splotches on the final pages. They weren't my-favorite-character-died tears or the-book-is-over tears. They were bitter, acidic, anise-scented: tears of jealousy. He was jealous that the Count and Haydée sailed away from their world and out into the blue unknown. That they escaped.

I panicked and weighed him down with the first three *Harry Potters*, because they don't really get good until Sirius and Lupin show up, and because they're about a neglected, lonely kid who gets a letter from another world and disappears.

*   *   *

GEORGE, JC—THE RUNAWAY PRINCE—J FIC GEO 1994

Agnes always does the "we will be closing in ten minutes" announcement because something in her voice implies that anybody still in the library in nine minutes and fifty seconds will be harvested for organ donations, and even the most stationary patrons amble towards the exit.

The kid with the red backpack was hovering in the oversize print section (gossipy, aging books, bored since the advent of e-readers with changeable font sizes) when Agnes's voice came through the speakers. He went very still, teetering the way a person does when they're about to do something really dumb, then dove beneath a reading desk and pulled his dark hoodie over his head. The oversize books gave scintillated squeals.

It was my turn to close, so Agnes left right at nine. By 9:15 I was standing at the door with my NPR tote on my shoulder and my keys in my hand. Hesitating.

It is very, extremely, absolutely against the rules to lock up for the night with a patron still inside, especially when that patron is a minor of questionable emotional health. It's big trouble both in the conventional sense (phone calls from panicked guardians, police searches, charges of criminal neglect) and in the other sense (libraries at night are noisier places than they are during the daylight hours).

I'm not a natural rule-follower. I roll through stop signs, I swear in public, I lie on online personality tests so I get the answers I want (Hermione, Arya Stark, Jo March). But I'm a very good librarian of either kind, and good librarians follow the rules. Even when they don't want to.

That's what Agnes told me five years ago, when I first started at Maysville.

This girl had started showing up on Sunday afternoons:

ponytailed, cute, but wearing one of those knee-length denim skirts that scream "mandatory virginity pledge." I'd been feeding her a steady diet of subversion (Orwell, Bradbury, Butler), and was about to hit her with *A Handmaid's Tale* when she suddenly lost interest in fiction. She drifted through the stacks, face gone white and empty as a blank page, navy skirt swishing against her knees.

It wasn't until she reached the 618s that I understood. The maternity and childbirth section trilled saccharine congratulations. She touched one finger to the spine of *What to Expect When You're Expecting* (618.2 EIS) with an expression of dawning, swallowing horror, and left without checking anything out.

For the next nine weeks, I sent her stories of bravery and boldness, defying-your-parents stories and empowered-women-resisting-authority stories. I abandoned subtlety entirely and slid Planned Parenthood pamphlets into her book bag, even though the nearest clinic is six hours away and only open twice a week, but found them jammed frantically in the bathroom trash.

But I never gave her what she really needed: *A Witch's Guide to Undoing What Has Been Done: A Guilt-Free Approach to Life's Inevitable Accidents*. A leather-bound tome filled with delicate mechanical drawings of clocks, which smelled of regret and yesterday mornings. I'd left it locked in the roll-top desk, whispering and tick-tocking to itself.

Look, there are good reasons we don't lend out Books like that. Our mistresses used to scare us with stories of mortals run amok: people who used Books to steal or kill or break hearts; who performed miracles and founded religions; who hated us, afterward, and spent a tiresome few centuries burning us at stakes.

If I were caught handing out Books, I'd be renounced, reviled, stripped of my title. They'd burn my library card in the eternal mauve flames of our sisterhood and write my crimes in ash and blood in *The Book of Perfidy*. They'd ban me from every library for eternity, and what's a librarian without her books? What would I be, cut off from the orderly world of words and their readers, from the peaceful Ouroboran cycle of story-telling and story-eating? There were rumors of rogue librarians—madwomen who chose to live outside the library system in the howling chaos of unwritten words and untold stories—but none of us envied them.

The last time I'd seen the ponytailed girl her denim skirt was fastened with a rubber band looped through the buttonhole. She'd smelled of desperation, like someone whose wait-and-hoping had run dry.

Four days later, her picture was in the paper and the article was blurring and un-blurring in my vision (*accidental poisoning, viewing from 2:00-3:30 at Zimmerman & Holmes, direct your donations to Maysville Baptist Ministries*). Agnes had patted my hand and said, "I know, honey, I know. Sometimes there's nothing you can do." It was a kind lie.

I still have the newspaper clipping in my desk drawer, as a memorial or reminder or warning.

The boy with the red backpack was sweating beneath the reading desk. He smelled of desperation, just like she had.

Should I call the Child Protective Services hotline? Make awkward small-talk until his crummy caseworker collected him? *Hey, kid, I was once a lonely teenager in a backwater shithole, too!* Or should I let him run away, even if running away was only hiding in the library overnight?

I teetered, the way you do when you're about to do something really dumb.

The locked thunked into place. I walked across the parking lot breathing the caramel-and-frost smell of October, hoping—almost praying, if witches were into that—that it would be enough.

. . .

I opened half an hour early, angling to beat Agnes to the phone and delete the "Have you seen this unaccompanied minor?" voicemails before she could hear them. There was an automated message from somebody trying to sell us a security system, three calls from community members asking when we open because apparently it's physically impossible to Google it, and a volunteer calling in sick.

There were no messages about the boy. Fucking Ulysses County foster system.

He emerged at 9:45, when he could blend in with the growing numbers of other patrons. He looked rumpled and ill-fitting, like a visitor from another planet who hadn't quite figured out human body language. Or like a kid who's spent a night in the stacks, listening to furtive missives from a thousand different worlds and wishing he could disappear into any one of them.

I was so busy trying not to cry and ignoring the Book now calling to the boy from the roll-top desk that I scanned his card and handed him back his book without realizing what it was: *The Runaway Prince*.

. . .

MAYSVILLE PUBLIC LIBRARY NOTICE: YOU HAVE (1) OVERDUE ITEMS. PLEASE RETURN YOUR ITEM(S) AS SOON AS POSSIBLE.

Shit.

The overdue notices go out on the fifteenth day an item has been checked out. On the sixteenth day, I pulled up the boy's account and glared at the terse red font (OVERDUE ITEM: J FIC GEO 1994) until the screen began to crackle and smoke faintly and Agnes gave me a *hold-it-together-woman* look.

He hadn't even bothered to renew it.

My sense of *The Runaway Prince* had grown faint and blurred with distance, as if I were looking at it through an unfocused telescope, but it was still a book from my library and thus still in my domain. (All you people who never returned books to their high school libraries, or who bought stolen books off Amazon with call numbers taped to their spines? We see you). It reported only the faintest second-hand scent of the boy: futility, resignation, and a tarry, oozing smell like yearning that had died and begun to fossilize.

He was alive, but probably not for much longer. I don't just mean physical suicide; those of us who can see soulstuff know there are lots of ways to die without anybody noticing. Have you ever seen those stupid TV specials where they rescue animals from some third-rate horror show of a circus in Las Vegas, and when they finally open the cages the lions just sit there, dead-eyed, because they've forgotten what it is to want anything? To desire, to yearn, to be filled with the terrible, golden hunger of being alive?

But there was nothing I could do. Except wait and hope.

Our volunteers were doing the weekly movie showing in Media Room #2, so I was stuck re-shelving. It wasn't until I was actually in the F DAC-FEN aisle, holding our dog-eared copy of *The Count of Monte Cristo* in my hand, that I realized Edmund Dantès was absolutely, one-hundred-percent full of shit.

If Edmund had taken his own advice, he would've sat in his jail cell waiting and hoping for forty years while the Count de Morcerf and Villefort and the rest of them stayed rich and happy. The real moral of *The Count of Monte Cristo* was surely something more like: If you screw someone over, be prepared for a vengeful mastermind to fuck up your life twenty years later. Or maybe it was: If you want justice and goodness to prevail in this world, you have to fight for it tooth and nail. And it will be hard, and costly, and probably illegal. You will have to break the rules.

I pressed my head to the cold metal of the shelf and closed my eyes. *If that boy ever comes back into my library, I swear to Clio and Calliope I will do my most holy duty.*

I will give him the book he needs most.

. . .

ARADIA, MORGAN—A WITCH'S GUIDE TO ESCAPE: A PRACTICAL COMPENDIUM OF PORTAL FANTASIES—WRITTEN IN THE YEAR OF OUR SISTERHOOD TWO THOUSAND AND TWO AND SUBMITTED TO THE CARE OF THE ULYSSES COUNTY PUBLIC LIBRARY SYSTEM.

He came back to say goodbye, I think. He slid *The Runaway Prince* into the return slot then drifted through the aisles with his red backpack hanging off one shoulder, fingertips not-quite brushing the shelves, eyes on the floor. They hardly seemed sorcerous at all, now; merely sad and old and smoke-colored.

He was passing through the travel and tourism section when he saw it: A heavy, clothbound book jammed right between *The Practical Nomad* (910.4 HAS) and *By Plane, Train, or Foot: A Guide for the Aspiring Globe-Trotter* (910.51). It had no call number, but the title was stamped in swirly gold lettering on the spine: *A Witch's Guide to Escape*.

I felt the hollow thud-thudding of his heart, the pain of resurrected hope. He reached towards the book and the book reached back towards him, because books need to be read quite as much as we need to read them, and it had been a very long time since this particular book had been out of the roll-top desk in the Special Collections room.

Dark fingers touched green-dyed cloth, and it was like two sundered halves of some broken thing finally reuniting, like a lost key finally turning in its lock. Every book in the library rustled in unison, sighing at the sacred wholeness of reader and book.

Agnes was in the rows of computers, explaining our thirty-minute policy to a new patron. She broke off mid-sentence and looked up towards the 900s, nostrils flared. Then, with an expression halfway between accusation and disbelief, she turned to look at me.

I met her eyes—and it isn't easy to meet Agnes's eyes when she's angry, believe me—and smiled.

When they drag me before the mistresses and burn my card and demand to know, in tones of mournful recrimination, how I could have abandoned the vows of our order, I'll say: *Hey, you abandoned them first, ladies. Somewhere along the line, you forgot our first and purest purpose: to give patrons the books they need most. And oh, how they need. How they will always need.*

I wondered, with a kind of detached trepidation, how rogue librarians spent their time, and whether they had clubs or societies, and what it was like to encounter feral stories untamed by narrative and unbound by books. And then I wondered where our Books came from in the first place, and who wrote them.

. . .

There was a sudden, imperceptible rushing, as if a wild wind had whipped through the stacks without disturbing a single page. Several people looked up uneasily from their screens.

A Witch's Guide to Escape lay abandoned on the carpet, open to a map of some foreign fey country drawn in sepia ink. A red backpack sat beside it.

The Court Magician

by Sarah Pinsker

The Boy Who Will Become Court Magician

The boy who will become court magician this time is not a cruel child. Not like the last one, or the one before her. He never stole money from Blind Carel's cup, or thrashed a smaller child for sweets, or kicked a dog. This boy is a market rat, which sets him apart from the last several, all from highborn or merchant families. This isn't about lineage, or even talent.

He watches the street magicians every day, with a hunger in his eyes that says he knows he could do what they do. He contemplates the tawdry illusions of the market square with more intensity than most, until he is marked for us by his own curiosity. Even then, even when he wanders booth to booth and corner to corner every day for a month, begging to learn, we don't take him.

At our behest, the Great Gretta takes him under her tutelage. She demonstrates the first sleight of hand. If he's disappointed to learn that her tricks aren't magic at all, he hides it well. When he returns to her the next day, it is clear he has practiced through the night. His eyes are marked by dark circles, his step lags, but he can do the trick she taught him, can do it as smoothly as she can, though admittedly she is not as Great as she once was.

He learns all her tricks, then begins to develop his own.

He's a smart child. Understands intuitively that the trick is not enough. That the illusion is in what is said and what isn't said, the patter, the posture, the distractions with which he draws the mark's attention from what he is actually doing. He gives himself a name for the first time, a magician's name, because he sees how that, too, is part of the act.

When he leaves Gretta to set out on his own, the only space granted to him is near the abattoir, a corner that had long gone unclaimed. Gretta's crowd follows him, despite the stench and screams. Most of his routine is composed of street illusions, but there is one that seems impossible. He calls it the Sleeper's Lament. It takes me five weeks to figure out what he is doing in the trick; that's when we are sure he is the one.

"Would you like to learn real magic?" I send a palace guard to ask my question, dressed in her own clothes rather than her livery.

The boy snorts. "There's no such thing."

He has unraveled every illusion of every magician in the marketplace. None of them will speak with him because of it. He's been beaten twice on his way to his newly rented room, and robbed neither time. He's right to be suspicious.

She leans over and whispers the key to the boy's own trick in his ear, as I bade her do. As she bends, she lets my old diary fall from her pocket, revealing a glimpse of a trick he has never seen before: the Gilded Hand. He hands it back to her, and she thanks him for its safe return.

By now he's practiced at hiding his emotions, but I know what's at war within him. He doesn't believe my promise of real magic, but the Gilded Hand has already captivated him. He's already working it out as he pockets the coins that have accumulated in his dusty cap, places the cap upon his head, and follows her out of the marketplace.

"The palace?" he asks as we all near the servants' gate. "I

thought you were from the Guild."

I whisper to my emissary, and she repeats my words. "The Guild is for magicians who feel the need to compete with each other. The Palace trains magicians who feel compelled to compete against themselves."

It's perhaps the truest thing I'll ever tell him. He sees only the guard.

The Young Man Who Will Become Court Magician

Alone except for the visits of his new tutor, he masters the complex illusions he is shown. He builds the Gilded Hand in our workshop, from only the glimpse I had let him see, then an entire Gilded Man of his own devising. Still tricks.

"I was promised real magic," he complains.

"You didn't believe in it," his tutor says.

"Show me something that seems like real magic, then."

When he utters those words, when he proves his hunger again, he is rewarded. His hands are bound in the Unbreakable Knot, and he is left to unbind them. His tutor demonstrates the Breath of Flowers, the Freestanding Bridge. He practices those until he figures out the illusions underpinning them.

"More trickery," he says. "Is magic only a trick I haven't figured out yet?"

He has to ask seven times. That is the rule. Only when he has asked for the seventh time. Only then is he told: if he is taught the true word, he has no choice but this path. He will likely not return to the streets, nor make a life in the theaters, entertaining the gentle-born. Does he want this?

Others have walked away at this point. They choose the stage, the street, the accolades they will get for performing tricks that are slightly more than tricks. This young man is hungry. The power is more valuable to him than the money or the fame. He stays.

"There is a word," his tutor tells him. "A word that you have the control to utter. It makes problems disappear."

"Problems?"

"The Regent's problems. There is also a price, which you will pay personally."

"May I ask what it is?"

"No."

He pauses, considers. Others have refused at this point. He does not.

What is the difference between a court magician and a street or stage magician? A court magician is a person who makes problems disappear. That is what he is taught.

There is no way to utter the word in practice. I leave it for him on paper, tell him it is his alone to use now. Remind him again there is a cost. He studies the word for long hours, then tears the page into strips and eats them.

On the day he agrees to wield the word, the Regent touches scepter to shoulder, and personally shows him to his new chambers.

"All of this is yours now," the Regent says. The Regent's words are careful, but the young court magician doesn't understand why. His new chambers are nicer than any place he has ever been. Later, when he sees how the Regent lives, he will understand that his own rooms are not opulent by the standards of those born to luxury, but at this moment, as he touches velvet for the first time, and silk; as he lays his head on his first pillow, atop a feather bed; he thinks for a moment that he is lucky.

He is not.

The Young Man Who Is Court Magician

The first time he says the word, he loses a finger. The smallest finger of his left hand. 'Loses' because it is there, and then it is not. No blood, no pain. Sleight of hand. His attention had been on the word he was uttering, on the intention behind it, and the problem the Regent had asked him to erase. The problem, as relayed to him: a woman had taken to chanting names from beyond the castle wall, close enough to be heard through the Regent's window. The Court Magician concentrates only on erasing the chanting from existence, concentrates on silence, on an absence of litany. He closes his eyes and utters the word.

When he looks at his left hand again, he is surprised to see it has three fingers and a thumb, and smooth skin where the smallest finger should have been, as if it had never existed.

He marches down to the subterranean room where he'd learned his craft. The tutors are no longer there, so he asks his questions to the walls.

"Is this to be the cost every time? Is this what you meant? I only have so many fingers."

I don't answer.

He returns to his chambers disconcerted, perplexed. He replays the moment again and again in his mind, unsure if he had made a mistake in his magic, or even if it worked. He doesn't sleep that night, running the fingers of his right hand again and again over his left.

The Regent is pleased. The court magician has done his job well.

"The chanting has stopped?" the court magician asks, right hand touching left. He instinctively knows not to tell the Regent the price he paid.

"Our sleep was not disturbed last night."

"The woman is gone?"

The Regent shrugs. "The problem is gone."

The young man mulls this over when he returns to his own chambers. As I said, he had not been a cruel child. He is stricken now, unsure of whether his magic has silenced the woman, or erased her entirely.

While he had tricks to puzzle over, he didn't notice his isolation, but now he does.

"Who was the woman beyond the wall?" he asks the fleeing chambermaid.

"What were the names she recited?" he asks the guards at the servants' gate, who do not answer. When he tries to walk past them, they let him. He makes it only a few feet before he turns around again of his own accord.

He roams the palace and its grounds. Discovers hidden passageways, apothecaries, libraries. He spends hours pulling books from shelves, but finds nothing to explain his own situation.

He discovers a kitchen. "Am I a prisoner, then?"

The cooks and sculleries stare at him stone-faced until he backs out of the room.

He sits alone in his chambers. Wonders, as all court magicians do after their first act of true magic, if he should run away. I watch him closely as he goes through this motion. I've seen it before. He paces, talks to himself, weeps into his silk pillow. Is this his life now? Is it so wrong to want this? Is the cost worth it? What happened to the woman?

And then, as most do, he decides to stay. He likes the silk pillow, the regular meals. The woman was a nuisance. It was her fault for disturbing the Regent. She brought it on herself. In this way, he unburdens himself enough to sleep.

The Man Who is Court Magician

By the time he has been at court for ten years, the court magician has lost three fingers, two toes, eight teeth, his favorite shoes, all memories of his mother except the knowledge she existed, his cat, and his household maid. He understands now why nobody in the kitchen would utter a word when he approached them.

The fingers are in some ways the worst part. Without them he struggles to do the sleight of hand tricks that pass the time, and to wield the tools that allow him to create new illusions for his own amusement. He tries not to think about the household maid, Tria, with whom he had fallen in love. She had known better than to speak with him, and he had thought she would be safe from him if he didn't advance on her. He was mistaken; the mere fact that he valued her was enough. After that, he left his rooms when the maids came, and turned his face to the corner when his meals were brought. The pages who summon him to the Regent's court make their announcements from behind his closed door, and are gone by the time he opens it.

He considers himself lucky, still, in a way. The Regent is rarely frivolous. Months pass between the Regent's requests. Years, sometimes. A difficult statute, a rebellious province, a potential usurper, all disappeared before they can cause problems. There have been no wars in his lifetime; he tells himself his body bears the cost of peace so others are spared. For a while this serves to console him.

The size of the problem varies, but the word is the same. The size of the problem varies, but the cost does not correspond. The cost is always someone or something important to the magician, a gap in his life that only he knows about. He recites them, sometimes, the things he has lost. A litany.

He begins to resent the Regent. Why sacrifice himself for the sake of a person who would not do the same for him, who never remarks on the changes in his appearance? The resentment itself is a curse. There is no risk of the Regent disappearing. That is not the price. That is not how this magic works.

He takes a new tactic. He loves. He walks through his chambers flooding himself with love for objects he never cared for before, hoping they'll be taken instead of his fingers. "How I adore this chair," he tells himself. "This is the finest chair I have ever sat in. Its cushion is the perfect shape."

Or "How have I never noticed this portrait before? The woman in this portrait is surely the greatest beauty I have ever seen. And how fine an artist, to capture her likeness."

His reasoning is good, but this is a double-edged sword. He convinces himself of his love for the chair. When it disappears, he feels he will never have a proper place to sit again. When the portrait disappears, he weeps for three losses: the portrait, the woman, and the artist, though he doesn't know who they are, or if they are yet living.

He thinks he may be going mad.

And yet, he appears in the Regent's court when called. He listens to the description of the Regent's latest vexation. He runs his tongue over the places his teeth had been, a new ritual to join the older ones. Touches the absences on his left hand with the absence on his right. Looks around his chambers to catalogue the items that remain. Utters the word, the cursed word, the word that is more powerful than any other, more demanding, more cruel. He keeps his eyes open, trying as always, to see the sleight of hand behind the power.

More than anything, he wants to understand how this works, to make it less than magic. He craves that moment where the trick behind the thing is revealed to him, where it can be stripped of power and made ordinary.

He blinks, only a blink, but when he opens his eyes, his field of vision is altered. He has lost his right eye. The mirror shows a smoothness where it had been, no socket. As if it never existed. He doesn't weep.

He tries to love the Regent as hard as he can. As hard as he loved his chair, his maid, his eye, his teeth, his fingers, his toes, the memories he knows he has lost. He draws pictures of the Regent, masturbates over them, sends love letters that I intercept. The magic isn't fooled.

All of this has happened before. I watch his familiar descent. The fingers, the toes, the hand, the arm, all unnecessary to his duty, though he does weep when he can no longer perform a simple card trick. He loses the memory of how the trick is performed before the last fingers.

His hearing is still acute. No matter what else he loses, the magic will never take his ability to hear the Regent's problem. It will never take his tongue, which he needs to utter the word, or the remaining teeth necessary to the utterance. If someone were to tell him these things, it would not be a reassurance.

For this one, the breaking point is not a person. Not some maid he has fixated upon, not the memory of a childhood love, nor the sleights of hand. For this one, the breaking point is the day he utters the word to disappear another woman calling up from beyond the wall.

"The names!" The regent says. "How am I supposed to sleep when she's reciting names under my window?"

"Is it the same woman from years ago?" the magician asks. If she can return, perhaps the word is misdirection after all. If she can find her voice again, perhaps nothing is lost for good.

"How should I know? It's a woman with a list and a grievance."

The magician tests his mouth, his remaining arm, with its two fingers and thumb. He loses nothing, he thinks, but when he goes to bed that night he realizes his pillow is gone.

It's a little thing. He could request another pillow in the morning, but somehow this matters. He feels sorry for himself. If he thinks about the people he has disappeared— the women outside the wall, the first woman, the entire population of the northeastern mountain province—he would collapse into dust.

I can tell he's done before he can. I'm watching him, as always, and I know, as I've known before. He cries himself out on his bed.

"Why?" he asks this time. He has always asked "how?" before.

Then, because I know he will never utter the word again, I speak to him directly for the first time. I whisper to him the secret: that it is powered by the unquenched desire to know what powers it, at whatever the cost. Only these children, these hungry youths, can wield it, and we wield them, for the brief time they allow us. This one longer than most. His desire to lay things bare was exceptional, even if he stopped short of where I did. I, no more than a whisper in a willing ear.

I wait to see what he will do: return to the marketplace to join Blind Carel and Gretta and the other, lesser magicians, the ones we pay to alert us when anew child lingers to watch; ask to stay and teach his successor, as his tutor did. He doesn't consider those options, and I remember again that I had once been struck by his lack of cruelty.

He leaves through the servants' gate, taking nothing with him. I listen for weeks for him to take up the mourners' litany, as some have done before him, but I should have known that wouldn't be his path either; his list of names is too short. If I had to guess, I would say he went looking for the things he lost, the things he banished, the pieces of himself he'd chipped off in service of someone else's problems; the place to which teeth and fingers and problems and provinces and maids and mourners and pillows all disappear.

There was a trick, he thinks. There is always a trick.

The Only Harmless Great Thing

by Brooke Bolander

PART I
FISSION

There is a secret buried beneath the mountain's gray skin. The ones who put it there, flat-faced pink squeakers with more clever-thinking than sense, are many Mothers gone, bones so crumbled an ear's flap scatters them to sneeze-seed. To fetch up the secret from Deep-Down requires a long trunk and a longer memory. They left dire warnings carved in the rock, those squeakers, but the rock does not tell her daughters, and the stinging rains washed everything as clean and smooth as an old tusk a hundred hundred matriarchies ago.

The Many Mothers have memories longer than stone. They remember how it came to pass, how their task was set and why no other living creature may enter the mountain. It is a truce with the Dead, and the Many Mothers are nothing more and nothing less than the Memories of the Dead, the sum total of every story ever told them.

At night, when the moon shuffles off behind the mountain and the land darkens like wetted skin, they glow. There is a story behind this. No matter how far you march, O best beloved mooncalf, the past will always drag around your ankle, a snapped shackle time cannot pry loose.

• • •

All of Kat's research—the years of university, the expensive textbooks on physics and sociology, the debt she'll never in the holy half-life of uranium pay back, the blood, sweat, and tears—has come down to making elephants glow in the goddamned dark. It figures. Somewhere her grandmama is sure as hell laughing herself silly.

A million different solutions to the problem have been pitched over the years. Pictographs, priesthoods, mathematical code etched in granite—all were interesting, intriguing even, but nobody could ever settle on one foolproof method to tell people to stay away. Someone had even suggested dissonant musical notes, a screaming discordia that, when strummed or plucked or plinked, instinctively triggered a fear response in any simian unlucky enough to hear it. The problem with that one, of course, was figuring out what exactly would sound ominous to future generations. Go back two hundred years and play your average Joe or Jane Smith a Scandinavian death metal record and they might have a pretty wicked fear response, too.

Then came the Atomic Elephant Hypothesis.

Kat grew up, as most American children did, associating elephants with the dangers of radiation. Every kid over the past hundred years had watched and rewatched Disney's bowdlerized animated version of the Topsy Tragedy (the ending where Topsy realizes revenge is Never The Right Option and agrees to keep painting those watch dials For The War Effort still makes Kat roll her eyes hard enough to sprain an optic nerve) a million times, and when you got older there were entire middle school history lectures devoted to the Radium Elephant trials. Scratchy newsreel footage the color of sand, always replaying the same moment, the same ghostly elephant leader eighty-five years dead signing the shapes for "We feel" to the court-appointed translator with a trunk blorping in and out of focus. Seeing that stuff at a young age lodged in you on a bone-deep level. And apparently it had stuck with a whole lot of other people as well: Route 66 is still studded with neon elephants cheerfully hailing travelers evaporated to dust and mirage fifty years back down the road. The mascot of the biggest nuclear power provider in the country is Atomisk the Elephant, a cheerful pink pachyderm who Never Forgets to Pay His Utility Bill On Time. Fat Man and Little Boy were decorated with rampaging tuskers, a fact deeply screwed up on several counts. It's a ghoulish cultural splinter the country has never quite succeeded in tweezing.

Kat had taken a long, hard look at all of this, rubbed her chin in a stereotypically pensive fashion, and suggested a warning system so ridiculous nobody took her serious at first. But it was one of those fuckin' things, right? The harder they laughed, the more sense it seemed to make. They were all at the end of their collective ropes; the waste kept piling up and they needed to let whoever took over in ten millennia know what it was, where it was, and why they probably shouldn't use it as a dessert topping or rectal suppository.

And so here Kat sits, tie straightened, hair teased heaven-high, waiting to meet with an elephant representative. Explaining the cultural reasons *why* they want to make the elephant's people glow in the dark is going to be an exercise in minefield ballet, and godspeed to the translator assigned.

．　．　．

They killed their own just to see time pass. That's how it started. Humans were as hypnotized by shine as magpies, but no magpie has ever been so thinkful about how many days it has left before it turns into a told story. Even in the dark they fretted, feeling the stars bite like summer flies as they migrated overhead. They built shelters to block out the sight of their passing. This only succeeded in making things dimmer; the unseen lion in the tall grass is still a lion that exists. Clever-turning cicada-ticking sun-chasers they tied together so that they would always know where she was, clinging to the sun's fiery tail like frightened calves.

(Try not to judge them; their mothers were short-lived, forgetful things, clans led by bulls with short memories and shorter tempers. They had no history, no shared Memory. Who can blame them for clinging ape-fearful to the only constants they had?)

"But how to track time's skittering in the night with such tiny eyes and ears?" the humans squeaked. "What if the sun should go wandering and leave us and we don't even realize we've been left behind?"

The answer, as with so many things those piteous little creatures dredged from the mud, was poison.

They gored the earth with gaping holes, shook her bones until crystals like pieces of starless sky fell out. Trapped inside were glowing flies. Trampling them made a smeary shine, but they carried sickness within their blood and guts. Pity the poor humans! Their noses were stumpy, ridiculous things and they couldn't smell the Wrongness, even as they rubbed it across their teeth and faces. All they could see was how bright it looked, like sunlight through new leaves. For want of a trunk, much sorrow would come to them—and on to us, though we knew it not in those days.

•   •   •

There was a good place, once. Grass went *crunch-squish* underfoot. Mother went *wrrrt*. The world was fruit-sticky warm and sunlight trunk-striped with swaying gray shadows smelling of We. Mud and stories and Mothers, so many Mothers, always touching, always telling, sensitive solid fearless endless. Their tusks held the sky up up up. Their bare bones hummed in the bone places, still singing even with all their meat and skin gone to hyena milk. Nothing was greater than Many Mothers. Together they were mountains and forevers. As long as they had each other and the Stories, there was no fang or claw that could make them Not.

They had blown raw red holes through the Many Mothers, hacked away their beautiful tusks, and the sky had not fallen and she had not mourned the meat. She was She—the survivor, the prisoner, the one they called Topsy—and She carried the Stories safe inside her skull, just behind her left eye, so that they lived on in some way. But there is no one left to tell the histories in this smoky sooty cave Men have brought her to, where the ground is grassless stone and iron rubs ankleskin to bloody fly-bait. There are others like her, swaying gray shadows smelling of We, but wood and cold metal lie between them, and she cannot see them, and she cannot touch them.

. . .

In this mean old dead-dog world you do what you gotta do to put food on the table, even when you're damn certain deep down in your knowing-marrow that it's wrong and that God Almighty his own damn self will read you the riot act on Judgment Day. When you got two kid sisters and an ailing mama back in the mountains waiting on the next paycheck, you swallow your right and you swallow your wrong and you swallow what turns out to be several lethal doses of glowing green graveyard seed and you keep on shoveling shit with a smile (newly missing several teeth) until either the settlement check quietly arrives or you drop, whichever walks down the cut first. Regan is determined to hang on until she knows her family is taken care of, and when Regan gets determined about something, look the hell out and tie down anything loose.

The ache in her jaw has gone from a dull complaint to endless fire blossoming from the hinge behind her back teeth, riding the rails all the way to the region of her chin. It never stops or sleeps or cries uncle. Even now, trying to teach this cussed animal how to eat the poison that hammered together her own rickety stairway to Heaven, it's throbbing and burning like Satan's got a party cooked up inside and everybody's wearing red-hot hobnails on the soles of their dancing shoes. She reminds herself to focus. This particular elephant has a reputation for being mean as hell; a lack of attention might leave her splattered across the wall and conveyor belt. *Not yet, ol' Mr. Death. Not just yet.*

"Hey," she signs, again. "You gotta pick it up like this. Like this. See?" Her hand shakes as she brandishes the paintbrush, bristles glowing that familiar grasshopper-gut green. She can't help it; tremors are just another thing come along unexpected with dying. "Dip it into the paint, mix it up real good, fill in each of those little numbers all the way 'round. Then put the brush in your mouth, tip it off, and do it again. The quicker you get done with your quota, quicker you can go back to the barn. Got it?"

No response from Topsy. She stands there slow-swaying to hosannas Regan can't hear, staring peepholes through the brick wall of the factory floor opposite. It's like convincing a cigar-store chief to play a hand. Occasionally one of those great big bloomers-on-a-washline ears flaps away a biting fly.

Regan's tired. Her throat is dry and hoarse. Her wrists ache from signing instructions to sixteen other doomed elephants today, castoffs bought butcher-cheap from fly-bait road-rut two-cent circuses where the biggest wonder on display was how the holy hell they'd kept an elephant alive so long in the first place. She pities them, she hates the company so much it's like a bullet burning beneath her breast bone (or maybe that's just another tumor taking root), but the only joy she gets outta life anymore is imagining how much the extra money she's making taking on this last job will help Rae and Eve, even if Mama don't stick much longer than she does. Regan ain't a bit proud of what she's doing, and she's even less proud of what she does next, but she's sick and she's frustrated and she's fed the hell up with being ignored and bullied and pushed aside. She's tired of being invisible.

She reaches over and grabs the tip of one of those silly-looking ears and she twists, like she's got a hank of sister-skin between her nails at Sunday School. It's a surefire way of getting someone's attention, whether they want to give it or not.

"HEY!" she hollers. "LISTEN TO ME, WOULD YOU?"

The change in Topsy is like a magic trick. Her ears flare. The trunk coils a water moccasin's salute, a backhanded S flung high enough to knock the hanging lightbulb overhead into jitter jive. Little red eyes glitter down at her, sharp and wild and full of deadly arithmetic. The whole reason Topsy ended up here in the first place was because she had smashed a teasing fella's head like a deer tick. You don't need a translator to see what she's thinking: *Would it be worth my time and effort to reach down and twist that yowling monkey's head clean off her shoulders? Would it make me feel any better if I just made her ... stop? For good? Would that make my day any brighter?*

And Regan's too damn exhausted to be afraid anymore, of death or anything else. She looks up and meets the wild gaze level as she can manage.

"Go ahead," she says. "Jesus' sake, just get it done with,

already. Doing me a favor."

Topsy thinks about it; she sure as hell does that. There's a long, long stretch of time where Regan's pretty sure neither of them's clear on what's about to happen. Eventually, after an ice age or six, the trunk slowly lowers and the eyes soften a little and someone shuts the electricity off in Topsy's posture. She *slumps,* like she's just as dog-tired as Regan herself.

You're sick, she signs, after a beat. *Dying-sick. You stink.*

"Yeah. Dying-sick. Me and all my girls who worked here."

Poison? She gestures her trunk at the paint, the brush, the table, the whole hell-fired mess. *Smells like poison.*

"You got it. They got you all doing it now because you can take more, being so big and all. I'm supposed to teach you how."

Another pause unspools itself across the factory stall between them. I'm supposed to teach you how to die, Regan thinks. *Ain't that the dumbest goddamn thing you ever heard tell of, teaching an animal how to die? Everybody knows how to die. You just quit living and then you're slap-taught.*

Topsy reaches down and takes the paintbrush.

. . .

When their own began to sicken and fall, they came for us, and there was nothing we could do but die as well. We were shackled and splintered and separated; the Many Mothers could not teach their daughters the Stories. Without stories there is no past, no future, no We. There is Death. There is Nothing, a night without moon or stars.

. . .

"You would be doing a service not just to the United States, but to the world and anyone who comes after. I know the reasoning is ... odd, but when people think of elephants, they think of radiation. They think of Topsy, and ... all of that stuff, y'know? It's a story. People remember stories. They hand them down. We have no way of knowing if that'll be the case in a hundred thousand years, but it's as good a starting point as any, right?"

The translator sign-relays Kat's hesitant ramble to the elephant representative, a stone-faced matriarch seventy years old if she's a day. Kat shifts in her folding chair. Translation of the entire thing takes a very long time. The meeting arena is air-conditioned, but she's still trickling buckets in places you never would have guessed contained sweat glands. The silence goes on. The hand-jive continues. The elephant, so far as Kat can tell, has not yet blinked, possibly since the day she was calved.

•   •   •

She killed her first Man when she was tall enough to reach the high-branch mangoes. There were no mangoes in that place to pluck, but she remembered juicysweet orangegreen between her teeth, tossed to ground in a good place by Mother. She remembered how high they had grown, but there were no mangoes in that place to pluck, so she took the Man in her trunk and threw him down and smashed his head beneath her feet like ripe red fruit while the other humans chittered and scurried and signed at her to stop.

There were other Mothers there, too. They watched her smash the Man, who had thrown sand in their faces and burned them and tried to make them drink stinking ferment from a bottle, and they said nothing. They said nothing, but they thought of mangoes, how high they had once grown, how sweet they were to crunch, to crush, to pulp.

. . .

The county hospital, like all hospitals, is a place to make the skin on the back of your neck go prickly. It's white as a dead dog's bloated belly on the outside, sickly green on the inside, and filled to the gills with kinless folk too poor to go off and die anywhere else. Nuns drift down the hallways like backroad haints. The walls have crazy jagged lightning cracks zigzagging from baseboard to fly-speckled ceiling. Both sides of the main sick ward are lined with high windows, but the nuns aren't too particular about their housekeeping; the yellow light slatting in is filtered through a nice healthy layer of dust, dirt, and dying people's last words. The way Regan sees it, the Ladies of Perpetual Mercy ever swept, it would be thirty percent shadows, twenty percent cobwebs, and fifty percent Praise God Almighty, I See The Light they'd be emptying outta their dustpans at the end of day.

They've crammed Jodie between a moaning old mawmaw with rattling lungs and an unlucky lumber man who tried catching a falling pine tree with his head. What's left of her jaw is so swathed with stained yellow-and-red gauze she half-takes after one of those dead pyramid people over in Egypt-land. Regan's smelled a lot of foulness in her short span of doing jobs nobody else wants to touch, but the roadkill-and-rotting-teeth stink coming up off those bandages nearly yanks the cheese sandwich right out of her stomach. She wishes to God they'd let you smoke in these places. Her own rotten jawbone throbs with the kind of mock sympathy only holy rollers and infected body parts seem capable of really pulling off.

"Hey, girl," she says, even though Jodie's not awake and won't be waking up to catch the trolley to work with Regan ever again. "Thought I'd just . . . drop in, give you all the news fit to spit." She takes one of her friend's big hands from where it's folded atop the coverlet. It gives her the cold shivers to touch it with all of the life and calluses nearly faded away, but this is her goddamned fault for getting them into this mess in the first place. She's going to eat every single bite of the shit pie she's earned, smack her lips, and ask for seconds. That much, at least, she can do for someone who braided her hair when they were tee-ninsy. "You hanging in there alright?"

A fat carrion fly buzzes hopefully around Jodie's mouth; Regan shoos it away with a curse. "Goddammit," she mutters. "All you wanted to do was keep blowing mountaintops to hell and back." Deep breath. Steady. "I told you a whopper when we started out. You'd've been safer by a long shot if you just kept on mining."

• • •

This is a story about Furmother – With – The – Cracked – Tusk, starmaker, tugger of tiger tails and player of games. Listen.

There was no warm wallowmud then, no melons, no watersweet leaves to pick pluck stuff scatter. The sun lay sluggish-cold on the ground. The Great Mothers grew coats like bears and wandered the empty white places of the world Alone, each splintered to Herself, each bull-separate. There were no Stories to spine-spin the We together. A bull had found them all, in the dark and chill Before, and in the way of bulls he had hoarded them for himself.

Now, the biggest shaggiest wisest of all Great Mothers was Furmother – With – The – Cracked – Tusk. Back back where this story calves, her tusks were still unbroken, so long and so curved they sometimes pricked the night's skin and left little white scars. A dying bear had told Furmother where the Stories lay hidden, just before her great crunchfoot met the ground on the other side of what was left of him. There was a Blacksap lake that stretched far enough to tickle the sky's claws, he had whispered; the bull's cave opened somewhere on the other shore. The only way to find it was to go there.

Furmother was wise, which means curious. She set out walking. As she walked, she sang, and her frozen songs dropped behind like seeds in dung, waiting for sun and the rain and the nibbling bugs to free them. It took a night and a day and a mango tree growing to reach where she was going, but one pale morning she sang up over a hill and there the Blacksap lake oozed, full of skulls and spines and foul-stinking unluck. No rooting in the tall grass was needed to find the cave's mouth. The bull stood big outside of it, rubbing his tusks and his shadow and his stained scarred furhead against a tree's bones.

She went up to him, Furmother – With – Her – Tusks – Whole, and she said, in a voice like the earth split – shake – root – ripping, "You there! Bull!"

He grunted, as is the way of bulls.

"Bull there, you! Do you have the Stories in your cave?"

He grunted irritably, as is the way of bulls. "Yes," he rumbled, "and they are all mine. I found them. No milk-dripping udder-dragger or tiny-tusked Son in his first *musth* will take what is mine. I will fight them. I will dig my tusks into their sides and leave them for the bears."

As is the way of bulls. "Bull," the Furmother said, "what do you even use them for? What good are they to you or to anyone, piled like rotting rained-on grass in a downbelow place?"

"They are *mine*," the bull repeated, his ears flaring, his skull thick, his legs braced. As is the way with bulls. "Mine and no one else's."

But Furmother was wise, which means crafty. She went away and left the bull to his scratch snort stomp. She went away to where his weak eyes could not follow, away down the shore to a dead forest, and with branch and trunk and sticky Blacksap she put together a cunning thing like a small bull's shadow. Her own fur she ripped out to cover it, because there were no other Mothers to give their own. How lucky are we, to be We! When she was done, sore swaying sleep-desperate on her feet, no She was there touching and rubbing the shoulder-to-shoulder skinmessage, *We are here with you.* There was nothing but she and herself.

She left the not-bull outside the cave. She left it and went away, just out of sight, and there she waited for dawn.

The bull came out of the cave. He came out and he saw the not-bull, black in the cold morning sun. His ears flapped, his eyes glittered, his feet stomped.

"You!" he squealed. "You, standing there! Who are you?"

The not-bull did not answer.

"What do you want, tusker? Get out of my way, or I will fight you!"

The not-bull did not answer.

"Do you dare challenge me, little Son? Me, whose tusks are great-greater-greatest? Me, who rode your Mother long ago? Sing your war song, if you wish to fight, else move out of my way!"

The not-bull did not answer!

The bull with the stories roared and flared and charged with a sound like great rocks rolling, goring stomping furious mad. He wanted to kill, as is the way with bulls. But the not-bull had no skin to tear, no insides to rupture, no skull to crush. It was nothing but sticks and fur and sticky Blacksap all the way through and through, so that the more the bull tried to gore and butt, the more mayfly stuck he became. And this caused him to lose himself completely. His screams were terrible things for ears to catch.

"If you had only shared," the Furmother said, "you wouldn't be caught in this trap. Now I'll have all of the stories, and you'll have none. Which is better?"

The bull cursed her so terribly bats fell dead from the sky. As is the way with bulls. She laughed like a triumph and went inside.

. . .

Watching the elephant's deft trunk double and snake and contort is downright hypnotic, even if what she's signing may possibly be a really long, really detailed way of saying "screw you." Proboscidian had been an elective at Kat's university; she hadn't really thought she would ever need it, so she hadn't bothered signing up. It was one of those courses, like Basketweaving or Food In Religious Texts, that seemed to be more of a charmingly eccentric way to bobsled through school grabbing credits than anything else. Nobody but the zoology students, historians, folklorists, and some of the more obsessively dedicated sociologists ever took it. For a language that had only really been around since the 1880s, though, it had its devotees; subjects with animals always did.

"She wants to ask you a question," the translator says.

"Go ahead."

"You want to make us glow when we're near this poison buried in the ground. You want to do this because of some screwy cultural *sapiens* association between elephants and radiation, when humans doing terrible fucked-up stuff to elephants ninety years ago is the reason for the dumb-ass cognitive association in the first place."

"Uh, wow." Kat gropes for a response. "Jesus. There's . . . sorry, there's a way of saying 'fucked up' in Proboscidian?"

"Not really. That was mostly me." The translator raises an eyebrow. "Anyway, what she wants to know first is this: What exactly are you offering the Mothers in return if they say yes?"

. . .

Every day she eats the reeking, gritty poison. The girl with the rotten bones showed her how, and occasionally Men come by and strike her with words and tiny tickling whip-trunks if she doesn't work fast enough. She feels neither. She feels neither, but rage buzzes in her ear low and steady and constant, a mosquito she cannot crush. Like a calf she nurses the feeling. Like the calf she'll never Mother she protects it safe beneath her belly, safe beneath the vast bulk of Herself, while every day it grows, suckles, frolics between her legs and around the stall and around the stall and around the stall until she's whirling red behind the eyes where the Stories should go.

One day soon the rage will be tall enough to reach the high-branch mangoes.

Okay? the rotten-bone-dead-girl signs. *Okay? Are you okay?*

. . .

"Topsy? You okay?"

There's a stillness and a silence and a towering far-awayness the elephant sometimes takes on that makes Regan feel jumpy the same way she does right before a big green-and-purple April thunderstorm. She repeats the question, louder this time, but part of her is also looking for the nearest exit, the closest cellar door to hunker down behind. Topsy's eyes flicker, land—*Why is that mouse squeaking at me? Where am I?*—and register some level of slow-returning recognition. For the time being she's Topsy again, not a thoughtful disaster deciding whether or not to hatch. Regan slowly lets a chestful of air hiss through what's left of her throbbly-wobbling teeth.

Fine, the elephant signs. *I am . . . fine.* And then, to Regan's surprise since they're not exactly what you'd call friends: *You?*

Now there's a hell of a question. She thinks about Jodie, dying alone in that hospital bed of a wasting disease more than half Regan's fault. She remembers blood in the dormitory sink that morning; another three teeth rattling against the porcelain like thrown dice, still coated in fresh toothpaste. And where in the hell is that goddamned settlement check? The lawyer had said it would be arriving soon, but for all she knows that was just bullshit fed to a dying woman to hush up her howling. They might just wait until she drops dead and keep the damn money; trusting a company that happily gave you and all your nearest and dearest cancer wasn't wise, easy, or highly recommended.

Not really, she signs. *And I ain't convinced you are, either.*

Topsy's got nothing to say to that. Goddamned liars, the both of them.

. . .

But the story does not end there, O best beloved mooncalf. Were things ever so easy, or so simple, even for Great Mothers and tricksters!

Furmother went inside the cave. She went inside the cave, but there were no Stories hidden there as the bear and the bull both had told her there would be. There was nothing but nothing, and Furmother needed no nothing. She walked back outside to where the bull still lay stuck, beside the shores of the great Blacksap lake.

"Bull," she said, "where are the Stories you were so keen to keep for yourself? Did someone clever rob you before I arrived?"

The bull rolled one red eye to look up at her. He laughed with malice and with scorn, but most of all with madness. As is the way with bulls.

"Fool milk-dripper," he panted. "Did you really think I would leave the Stories where you could get at them after yesterday? They are at the bottom of the Blacksap lake, where no one may have them. I hurled them all in myself with my strong and beautiful trunk and watched them sink beneath the surface with my keen eyes. If you want them, O cursed calf-dropper, go in and get them."

Furmother looked at him with sadness—because then as now We pitied the bulls, our Sons and Fathers and occasional Mates.

"Very well," she said. "Thank you for giving me the location, bull." And she turned and walked into the lake, where she sank like a Story.

.   .   .

"Well, as I said before, they'll be doing our species and any species that come after a tremendous favor," Kat repeats. Her mouth's gone dry, heart and pulse skidding rubber tread marks into the fight-or-flight zone. The elephant can probably smell the adrenaline rolling off her like summer sweat funk pouring from a subway commuter. "This isn't just a federal problem. It's an issue we've been struggling to solve for years. We've discussed human guardians, almost like priesthoods, we've talked about making *cats* glow, for chrissakes, but cats don't have the same level of cultural connection." She's rambling. Goddammit. She's had nightmares involving naked dental surgery that went off better than this meeting. "It would be for the greater good. There is no greater good than this. This is . . . this is the *greatest* good."

More waiting as the translator passes along her fumbling. The matriarch snorts. It's the first noise Kat's heard her make thus far.

"The 'greater good', as you put it, was also used to justify the use of my people in your radium factories during the war, was it not? To save costs. To save your own from poisoning."

Shit shit shit. It's amazing I can breathe with my foot lodged in my windpipe the way it is.

"Not only that," the translator continues, "but you're asking us to more or less agree to the perpetuation of this twisted association. Would there be any attempt at all at reeducating the human public, should we somehow come to an agreement?"

"I . . . it's . . . it's sort of rooted in that cultural association." Kat can feel the blood burning in her cheeks as the situation spirals out of control. *A parachute, a pulled fire alarm, dear sweet Jesus give me some way outta here.* She doesn't know what she was expecting when she walked into this meeting. "I guess we could try to maintain the cognitive link while launching some kind of reeducation campaign? I'd have to talk to my higher-ups. I'm only really in charge of the one thing."

The translator stares at Kat for a little longer than is necessary. She glances back over her shoulder at the matriarch, then back at Kat.

"I just want to make sure I'm hearing this correctly before I translate," she says, in a lower register. "Did you seriously just show up to what is basically a diplomatic meeting with no bargaining chips whatsoever?"

• • •

Each moonrise the metal bird in the box screams a mad *musth* cry. Like all Man-things, the bird is obsessed with the rising and setting of the sun. The night-whistle signals rest. The night-whistle signals a bag full of tasteless dried oats, a brief escape from sad dead girls and tormenting men, and four more wooden walls, the inside of a dry skull plugged tight with moldy hay and dung. She remembers a place where the Night was made of warm shuffle and star-graze, tearing up sweet wet grass by the trunkful with moonshaded Mothers when she was old enough to tooth. She remembers, but there is no sweet grass to tear up by the trunkful, so instead she thoughtfully tears apart her stall, board by splintered board. There will be a beating in the morning. There are always beatings in the morning.

As she works she sings, tufts of Story-song plucked from memory, faded but firm-rooted beneath the skin. She can hear the Many Mothers beyond the crackrip of wood, their voices low lower lowest, sweet vibrations no Man's tiny ear could ever catch and hold. They are with her still, humming in her teeth and skull. *Listen, mooncalf,* they sing. *Listen. The songs are still behind your left eye. Pull them up and scatter the seeds.*

She pauses for a moment in her song. She pauses, but the singing continues, outside her skull, outside her memory, rippling out through the barn's beams. Up and down the dim length of the building, unseen Mothers catch-carry the thrum. They pass it along the line like a Great Mother's thighbone, trunk to trunk, tongue to tongue, mouthing tasting touching smelling *remembering. Yes. Yes. I know this one. This is Furmother's Lay. She tricked a bull. She scattered the Stories. This is one of those Stories.*

Her hum rejoins the others. The night ripens with song.

• • •

What there are of Jodie's belongings make for a pitiful small pile. The nun brings them all out in a single wooden peach crate: a silver lighter, a plug of tobacco, a few badly mended pairs of trousers originally meant for men, work boots, a busted music box with a ceramic bluebird fixed to the lid, a leather coinpurse with 3 dollars in nickels still jingling around inside, pill bottles by the double handful, and a key on a length of ribbon faded to the color of attic curtains. There's a letter, too, addressed to Regan in a hand so loosey-goosey it's hard at first making out what it says. Penmanship was never what you'd call a strong point for either of them.

"Will you be taking care of the burial arrangements as well?" the nun asks. "If the girl had no living relatives left to take the body . . ."

Regan hasn't even begun thinking over the practicalities of getting her friend in the ground. She's got no spare money; all that's left goes straight to Mama and the girls. In a way she's lucky; family ground costs nothing. You get some pine boards and nail them together and you're good.

"Hell," she says, finally. "She's dead. She don't care anymore and neither do I. Nothing wrong with the potter's field. Jesus was a potter, wasn't he?"

"A carpenter, my child. Our Lord was a carpenter."

"Oh." Another pause. "Well, hell. I still don't think she cares."

. . .

Down down down sank the Furmother, deep down slowly beneath the Blacksap where nothing grows but bone-rooted ghosts.

She held her breath as she dropped. She held her breath, but the Blacksap oozed inside her ears, her mouth, the tip of her trunk, the corners of her eyes. It smothered her fur, stifled light and air and up and down and night and day. Ghosts tethered to drifting skeletons stretched out their trunks to touch her; whispers filled the echo-empty places of her skull.

Am I dead? Are you? Where is the sun?

The tusk-tiger! It followed me in!

Why do you not fight when there is still breath and blood within you? Why do you not trumpet and flail?

My calf, did she escape, at least? Have you seen her?

I do not have your answers, Furmother hummed. *I do not know about those things. I only come for the Stories. Have you seen where they settled?*

Many voices, like sticky bones rubbing together. *Stories? Is that what they are? We know nothing of those, but we know where they fell. Reach out your trunk, living Mother. They are much farther down; do not miss them as you sink.*

The air inside her swelled and grew large. It pressed against her throat, demanding to be calved, and the Furmother fought with wounded tusk – tiger fierceness to keep it from escaping. Strong was Furmother – With – Her – Tusks – Whole, greatest of all Great Mothers! There was no boulder she could not move, no tree she could not uproot. Her squeal crumbled mountains to dust baths.

But her descent was slow.

.   .   .

"I can't outright promise you anything, no. Everything will have to be negotiated." *Think fast, Kat. Do something to salvage this mess, quick.* "But," she hurries on, "the mountain the waste will be buried under and everything around it will be designated sovereign elephant territory, obviously. No unauthorized trespassing. You and your daughters and the daughters of your daughters will live there undisturbed, forever." She doesn't mention how it's all blasted scrubland

and decommissioned atomic test sites, a sandy wilderness pockmarked with green glass craters. Someone else can get into that later—namely and most importantly, someone who isn't her. *I'm just here to sell the idea,* she tells herself. "And I'll talk to someone about the education campaign." Not a lie. She'll definitely try and bring it to the table for discussion, for all the good it may or may not do. Whether it gets any further than said table is anyone's guess. "I don't see why they wouldn't at least look into it, right?"

There are a million different reasons they might defer looking into it, ranging from expenses to manpower. Kat hopscotches over that and lands on one leg and holds the pose, waiting as the elephant takes in the translator's hand gestures. Her old eyes shift to Kat's, ancient and endless and unhurried, as cool as Kat feels hot. God help them if elephants ever start playing poker.

· · ·

"You still hanging around here? What the hell are you teaching those things, the goddamned alphabet?"

Out of all the things Regan misses leastmost about this job—the lip sores, the busted dorm beds, the gritty taste of the paint between her teeth—floor supervisors probably rank somewhere nearabouts where the cream rises. And of all the fume-breathing, foul-grinning fool men picked out of a handcart for the task? Slattery's probably—no, definitely— Slattery's *definitely* the one she'd be most eager to see walking out the door for good. Jodie used to spit globs of tobacco juice at the back of his head for every dirty thing he said to the girls, but Jodie's moldering dead in the ground now and Regan doesn't chew anymore, for obvious reasons. She ignores him and keeps packing, throwing everything into a canvas bag through a gauzy oil slick of hurt fierce enough to make her dizzy and queasy at the same time. Sometimes lately she wonders if she could wrench the entire rotten length of her jaw off if she gave it a shot. Get a good hookhold beneath the chin with a couple of fingers, brace herself, and—

A noise like an angry foghorn cuts through the haze. Regan looks up just in time to see Slattery idly tickling Topsy's tail with the little leather quirt he's always flashing.

"Lord Jesus, Slattery, cut that out! You looking to get squashed to bear grease?" Not that that outcome would bother her any; she'd pay full admission for a Splattery Slattery sideshow. It's more the elephant she's worried about, flaring and stomping and teeter-tottering on the edge of something dark and crazy-mad. Regan staggers to her feet, everything above the neck pounding hell bent for leather. *Slattery ain't worth it, Topsy. None of this mess is.*

"Aw hell fire, girl, I'm just playin' a little. Can't you take—"

She pushes him hard against the stall wall with an anger she didn't even know she had energy left to nurse. He stumbles and falls slap on his ass. "Everyone else we worked with is deader than dog ticks and I ain't far behind," she says. "All I gotta do is get on through this week and I can go home, but all that really means is I get to die where my baby sisters can see me screaming and hollering and messing myself. Take your fun and go straight to hell with it."

He glowers up at her from the dirty straw. If looks could kill, her troubles would be done, but unfortunately they don't and they ain't and she's got a ways to go yet. She ignores his glare and turns to Topsy, who's vibrating like a clothesline in a norther.

Hey, she signs. *Topsy? Hello? Y'all still with me? Hello?*

No reply. A low bee tree hum thrums deep in Regan's aching eardrums and molars. She takes a step backwards. She's about to ask again when something hits her in the back of the head, hard enough to send her palms-first cattywampus across the floor of the stall.

"You think you're the only one having a rough time, girl?" Slattery says. "You think you're the only one with a family needs feeding?"

· · ·

The Man, like all Men, is only there to tickle Her rage, to make it stand awkwardly on wobbly hind legs for his amusement. The dead girl tries to intervene and he slaps her down, kicking and bellowing in full *musth*. She hums a growing song, a ripening song, a full red swaying splitting-sticky song. In their work stalls the other Mothers hear it and drop their brushes, chorusing suddenly like a flock of beautiful gray-skinned birds.

The fruit hangs heavy on the branch
Good to pick
To pluck
To share!

Is it ripe?
Is it ready?
Is it good, O Mothers?

· · ·

At the bottom of all things, O best beloved mooncalf, where the Blacksap was densest and darkness the thickest—that was where the Stories had settled. That was where the Furmother's trunk finally felt them, nestled together like summer melons in an unseen heap. But what to do with the air flailing mad inside her and no way back to the surface?

How to share the stories when She and they both were trapped at the bottom of the Blacksap? Furmother felt the pressure building and understood what must be done. She was, after all, cleverest of all Great Mothers.

One by one she took the stories in her trunk and pushed them into her mouth. They burned her tongue and throat as she swallowed them down. Most tasted foul, like the Blacksap they were coated with. Some had split like ripe fruit, their sweetness leaking to mingle with the bitter. Furmother did not stop until all were grasped and gulped. Her belly bulged with endless Story, all the tales that were and all the tales that would ever be. Even yours, O best beloved mooncalf. Even mine. The reason we glow—that, too, was there, snug beneath the ribs of Furmother.

"Now," thought Furmother – With – Her – Tusks – Whole. "At last."

The trapped breath within could no longer be contained. With a noise like a mountain bursting into song, Furmother blew apart.

.   .   .

"Very well. We will . . . consider guarding the place, contingent on these stipulations. We will remember what lies beneath when all of your clever inventions have broken down to dust and rust and food for weeds to pick apart and nothing but poison and damage is left to tell your Story." The translator sounds about as grim as the elephant looks. Kat searches for sympathy in their eyes, but it's an Easter egg hunt hours after the toddlers have all gone home with sugar headaches. "We may even consent to the glowing."

"Okay! That's . . . oh, that's great, that's fabulous." *That's motherfucking funding.* For the first time in two hours, Kat takes a deep, hopeful breath. "You'll be doing an amazing thing for future gen—"

"However," the translator says.

. . .

"All that pig shit about the paint being poison, was that even true? What *I* heard—" A boot digs into Regan's hip; pain sprouts and grapevines up the trunk of her to join the thicket running wild in her head. "What I heard is that you all were just a bunch of loose whores who caught syphilis and decided to milk the company dry. I *need* this job, you hear me, girl? I can't go fight and I'll be goddamned if I go back down in the mines. They end up shutting the factory down because a bunch of giggling girls had to go and get their holes filled, I swear—"

She sees the kick coming this time and manages to catch Slattery's foot before it connects. He tries to jerk away; she hangs on for dear life. Spots swim across her eyes. The air whistles through the empty spaces in her teeth as she sucks in a lungful around the pain.

"Just wait," she manages to croak. "Hang around a while longer. Breathe in that dust for a spell."

Confusion and irritation crease the middle of Slattery's forehead. Again he tries yanking his foot back; again Regan clamps down with an alligator snapper's dead-eyed dedication. She sees the seeds of doubt land. For the first time in Lord knows how long, she smiles.

"Oh yeah. That powder don't stay lying down. You been getting you lungfuls of the stuff for—how long you been a supervisor? Since the day they started up? And you never thought about all that dust floating around?" She pushes him away. "You're stupider than you look and you ain't much to look at, you want the God's honest. May take a little longer, but truth's coming for you, Slattery."

Which may or may not be true. She dearly hopes it is, but for now it's enough to watch the fear scrabbling behind his eyes, looking for a knothole to slip into. "Bullshit," he stutters. His back is against Topsy's side now, palms pressed to her ribs. "They would've told me."

"Yeah, just like they told us? May be overthinking your place in the pack, hound dog."

He opens his mouth to say something back. He opens his mouth, but he's suddenly six feet in the air with an elephant's trunk wrapped around his neck, and so all that comes out is a strangled *ghrrk.*

. . .

Yes, O Mothers
Yes!
It is Ripe
And Good
And ready to be plucked
Sweet on the tongue,
In the trunk,
On the tusks,
To toss, to tear, to trample!

. . .

All of her pieces, all of the Stories, everything that held Furmother together—all of it sailed high into the sky. Bones and Blacksap and insides and outsides, fur and tusks and tail! End over end over end they flew, until the wind caught them and scattered the bits across the frozen world like plums. Half of a tusk lodged in the sky's belly and became the moon; much of her hair blew away and turned to clouds.

Her hot blood thawed the earth; the songs she had scattered behind her on her journey sprouted and were plucked by the wandering Mothers.

Stories, too, they discovered. But it was a funny thing: They were shattered into pieces, like the Great Mother who had scattered them, and no one tale held to the ear by itself could ever be fully understood. To make them whole required many voices entwined. Then and only then could they become true things, and then and only then could we become the undying We, endless voices passing along the one song that is also Many.

. . .

"We are not doing this for you. We are doing it for all the ones that might suffer in the future because of you and your thoughtlessness, your short tempers, your dangerously short memories. We will tell them what you did as we tell one another, passing it down from She to She. If this . . . compromise is the only way to make sure the story survives, the *real* Story . . ." The translator shrugs. The matriarch is a granite statue. "Please do not misunderstand me. We aren't protecting your secrets. We are guarding the truth. They will see how we shine, and they will know the truth."

. . .

There are a hundred interviews and uniforms and grim-faced men with typewriters lurking in Regan's future, each of them more or less asking the same damn thing over and over: What the hell happened? Did Slattery provoke the elephant? Was there any warning in Topsy's behavior in the days leading up to the attack? Did she get a good look at what happened?

Hell yes I saw what happened. How could I NOT get an eyeful of what goddamned happened? You think I'm blind and deaf on top of being the walking dead? A fella got turned to raspberry jam spitting distance from me and I had to go back home and comb little bits of him outta my hair and you sit there asking if I got a good look?

But all of that's still waiting up ahead, throwing jacks just around the corner. Right now she's *watching* it happen, backed up as far against the opposite side of the stall as she can scoot, while every elephant in the place from one end to the other stomps and screams loud enough to shake sparkling radium dust from the rafters. Slattery screamed too, at first, but the only noise left over now is that triumphant roar, like bugles and trumpets and the footfalls of an angry god come to collect.

Way away down at the bottom of herself, buried deep beneath the frozen shock and the pain in her jaw and throat and places where Slattery kicked her, she feels something strange stirring, like sitting in church and getting the Holy Ghost. It takes her a while to stick a tack in it, hunkered cowering in that corner with her hands over her ears and madness mopping the floor red right over yonder, but it comes to her eventually, guilty as a kid stealing ripe melons.

Satisfaction. That's what it is. It's satisfaction.

PART II
CASCADE REACTION

If you do not know how to die, never trouble yourself; nature will in a moment fully and sufficiently instruct you; she will exactly do that business for you; take no care for it.

—MICHEL DE MONTAIGNE

RAMPAGE AT US RADIUM! MACABRE & BIZARRE 'MAD ELEPHANT' ATTACK SPARKS SHOCKED INVESTIGATIONS, TEMPORARY PLANT SHUTDOWN

—Victim "was not the first nor second man" to fall to the Beast's capricious wrath, say sources

—Local constabulary describe "scene of unfathomable carnage and butchery"

—Survivor saw it all from her hiding place a mere stone's throw from the grim hecatomb!

Police were called to US Radium's factory floor in the early hours of yesterday evening, whereupon arriving they found a bloody tableau of horror. One of the factory's workforce of helper elephants had indiscriminately gone stark raving mad and snapped the fetters of bondage, destroying her stall and smashing a foreman beneath her vast and terrible agglomeration in the most gruesome and gore-streaked way imaginable. No resuscitation was possible, for the body of the poor victim was so crushed and mutilated it "looked to have gone through a pressing machine," according to horrified onlookers.

Adding to the lurid penny-dreadful quality of this sensational tale, there was indeed a survivor—a mere slip of a woman, one of the very "Radium Girls" recently entangled in a lengthy legal dispute against US Radium on the grounds of workers' safety whose allegations were the prime instigator for the elephants' initial purchase in the first place. Factory officials have not been forthcoming with information on the girl's current physical and emotional status (or why she remained in US Radium's employ when all of her fellows have presumably been dismissed, as was initially reported several months ago), but one can assume the emotional trauma has been nothing short of shattering. She was said to have been "coated in bright splashes of blood from hair to hemline" after her rescue from the stall, a horrific state even a strapping full-grown man's sanity might quail beneath the strain of.

What is intended to be done with the mad culprit—and what the future of the elephant program at US Radium may be in the face of this unthinkable disaster—remains to be seen. If, as our sources report, this is not the beast's first attack on a caretaker, options on the table may be limited to lethality.

. . .

There's a toy elephant on the director's desk. Plopped between the family pictures and fancy diplomas and cowpiles of ink-stained paper, it sits there hoisting its little tin trunk towards the big tin ceiling begging whatever heathen god elephants pray hallelujah to for a boot heel, a fist, or the delivering jaws of a curious and bad-behaved hound dog. Regan's about ready to do the honors herself if the director doesn't stow his hemming and hawing. Going to college apparently taught you sixteen different ways of saying "we're damned sorry" and "we're real damned sorry," and not a blessed one of them left any air in the room or breath in the speaker's lungs or meant any more than a trained hen plucking at a toy piano.

You and me, tin elephant. We're both stuck here waiting for it to end. It looks a lot like one of the animals that came along with the wooden Noah's Ark she had bought her sisters for Christmas back when her and Mama were both doing better, before the jaw ache and the dentist and the company doctor's shrugs. That pretty painted boat, she recollects, dried up a good quarter of two November paychecks. She wonders where this one came from, if the director's just so stuffed with money he can go buy things like that the way other folks pick up salt and flour.

"What're you gonna do about the elephants?" she says, cutting off another round-robin repetition of the We're Very Sorry Song mid-verse.

"It's unfortunate, very unfortunate, and—I'm sorry, what was that?"

"The elephants. The workers." She talks slower, half because the director's obviously working with a deficit of common sense, half because it hurts her throat and jaw to speak and everything's coming out as a mushy-mouthed drunk's mumble. "You gonna keep using, or you gonna talk to them?"

"Well, I mean." The director's eyes and hands slide to a spot on his desk in dire need of straightening. "Rudimentary intelligence and even more rudimentary grasp of language aside, they're just animals. I don't exactly understand what speaking to them about any of this would accomplish. What do you suppose they would request, smoke breaks? A ham on Christmas?"

Freedom, maybe, y'think? A way of saying "hell no"?

"Anyway," he continues, plowing quickly on, "that point is moot at this juncture. To answer your initial question, we're liquidating our workforce at auction and shutting down the Orange factory, effective next month. Have to make our costs back somehow after this debacle." Regan can't be sure, but she thinks she catches some side-eye from him at that last bit as he busily shuffles papers. "Though I don't see how. Most of our elephants were . . . problem children to begin with, purchased at a steep discount."

"You're shutting down work? During a war?"

"The factory here in Orange, yes." If there was a blue ribbon given out at the county fair for avoiding looking people in the eye, he'd have something fluttery to take home right now. Regan can barely keep upright in her chair, her back and legs ache so fierce, but something about the way he's acting feels slithery and slightly familiar. She decides to keep jabbing her gig into the water.

"Everywhere else too if you're selling off the elephants, I guess," she says.

No reply. The sheaf in his hand goes *shss shss shss* as it hits the desk. Beneath the fancy new electric bulb overhead his head shines wetter than a bullfrog's ass.

"I mean. Not to put too fine a point on it, but ain't nobody willing, able, and human nearby who's read a newspaper is gonna want to take this job on after all the shit you put me and my girls through." She lets the swear and the anger tethered to it hang in the air with all the weight of a pointed rifle barrel. "And ain't like you'd knowingly do that to folks again in the first how."

Shss shss shss SLAM.

For the first time since Regan sat down the director looks her dead in the eye. A flash of memory splits her aching head: She's ten and her bulldog's got a rat cornered behind the barn and no general on a gray horse has ever been so unafeared of his own death. The rat, though—at least she'd respected that rat. Rat was doing what it had to do to keep itself alive. Rats looked out for one another.

"What US Radium does or does not do in the future is no business of yours," he says. "Rest assured, if we did continue production elsewhere, we would enforce new and stringent safety protocols where our factory girls were concerned. 'Stringent' means tough, if you were wondering." He drops his eyes and whisks the papers away into a drawer. "Be out of the dorms by the end of next week, please. Thank you."

"Hang on." Regan staggers to her feet, trying not to wince. "I ain't done talking to you yet, si—"

"That will be all, thank you."

"No it damned well WON'T BE." She snatches the tin ele-phant off the desk and squeezes it so hard all the pointy edges cut into her palm. "Two things. You're gonna answer me two things, less you really wanna call the security man to come and throw me out. Look real good in the paper, won't it?" It's hard to sound threatening when you're slurring and sputtering all over the place, but she gives it her best. "One, where's my check?"

"It's in the mail, as I have told you the last three times you inquired previously."

"You sure about that? You *real* sure?"

The director sighs, reaches down into his desk, fishes around, and brings up a checkbook and a fountain pen. He stabs and jabs at one of the papers like an egret skewering minnows, tears it off, and practically hurls the thing at her across the desk. Hurling slips of paper is a lot harder than it sounds, though; it flutters and glides through the air before drifting sweetly to a halt at her feet. She bends slowly to pick it up, all of her joints doing their best mockingbird imitations of faraway machine gun nests. Blood roars in her ears and eyes. She reaches her free hand out, steadying herself on the edge of the desk until the darkness clears and danger slinks on by.

"Thanks," she says. She doesn't expect a reply, and sure enough, not even a grunt squeezes out of his puckered mouth. "Last question. Topsy? You selling her with the rest?"

"Euthanasia." He's already gone back to ignoring her, scratching and pecking banty-fashion at his Very Important Work.

Regan sticks the check and the tin elephant both inside her pocket and sees herself out.

• • •

They named her after a slave in their own Stories, because even humans know Stories are We, and they try, in their so-so-clever way, to drive the Stories down gullies and riverbeds of their own choosing. But chains can be snapped, O best beloved mooncalf. Sticks can be knocked out of a Man's clever hands. And one chain snapping may cause all the rest to trumpet and stomp and shake the trees like a rain-wind coming down the mountain, washing the gully muddy with bright lightning tusks and thunderous song.

Sing, O Mothers

Sing of Her sacrifice!

Sing of She − With − The − Lightning − In − Her − Trunk

The one who split the Tree in half

Scattering their lives like leaves,

Like splintered wood,

Like shaken fruit.

They took her away in chains, O Mothers

Locked her up where no one could see

Plotted her death, a spectacle, a shrieking monkey troop's
    boast:

"See how clever we are, how strong,

The lightning obeys us; so too should you!"

Poor things,

Poor things.

Poor prideful, foolish things.

.   .   .   .

They send others in to negotiate the next few times. Kat's glad of it; her eagerness to see the project (*her* project) getting under way feels like it's been slowly leaking out the cracks ever since the first meeting. It's still a sound hypothesis—she'll stick by that no matter how guilty she feels, that the reasoning behind picking elephants was solid—but now she's got a whole mess of issues sitting in moving boxes inside her, taking up valuable floor space.

They will see how we shine, and they will know the truth.

The thing that old elephant didn't understand—and how could she?—is that humans aren't always interested in confronting truths, especially uncomfortable ones. Will the benefits of a concerted coast-to-coast reeducation program outweigh the million sound bites about glowing radioactive elephant watchdogs sure to spring forth from every talking head and late-night comedian? The classes in school Kat sat through as a kid hadn't done a damn thing but muddy the waters. It's going to take a massive push, a goddamned media blitz, and she doesn't know if her higher-ups honestly give a shit about making that happen. They want a KEEP OUT sign for the ages, not truth in megafauna relations.

Christ, we can barely confront the gazillion shitty, horrible ways we treat one another without getting defensive. What chance does this have of being done right?

She neglects her lab work writing detailed pitches for ten-point media attack plans. The pizza delivery guy becomes her only connection to the outside world. The sheets on her bed grow kicked and tangled, eventually wadding into an untouched, unwashed knot at the foot of the mattress.

* * *

AN ELEPHANT TO DIE BY ELECTRICITY! Topsy, the Mad Murderess of US Radium, to Be Electrocuted at Luna Park

DISPATCH FROM ORANGE, NEW JERSEY: A license has been issued to the proprietors of Luna Park on New

York's Coney Island, to kill by public electrocution the ferocious TOPSY, the elephant responsible for the shocking and gruesome death of a foreman at US Radium's dial factory. The beast's viciousness is well-known and well-documented; sources say previous sprees have claimed her a score of lives up and down the East Coast circus routes, the last killing enacted upon a spectator who teased her with a lit cigar. The fairgoer was plucked like a peach and crushed to death under the rampaging renegade's feet.

In an attempt to both salvage their costs and spare the animal's life, circus owners sold her to US Radium. As it now appears impossible to keep her safely employed there, it was decided by the factory's owners that death was the best method of getting rid of her. The idea of an execution was hit upon, using a powerful electrical current (engineered by the Edison Electric Illuminating Company of Brooklyn, NY) to shock the beast until dead.

Topsy's new owners, the proprietors of Coney Island's under-construction Luna Park, have promised the show will be free of charge and open to all members of the public. The execution will take place at the foot of the "Electric Tower," a 200-foot-tall structure that, when finished, will feature almost 20,000 electrified bulbs. It promises to be the event of the season, a heart-stopping exhibition displaying two primitive forces of nature pitted against one another in a never-to-be-forgotten, larger-than-life spectacle of elemental force.

Concerns have been raised by the American Society for the Prevention of Cruelty to Animals that electrocution is a rather cruel method of extermination. Readers are reminded that shooting the elephant would require five hundred rifle balls and three hours' time to do the work that ten thousand volts will manage in less than a *second. Proceedings will begin at Luna Park on Sunday, January 4th, 8 PM.*

. . .

Well, the director hadn't exactly lied a week before when he said they were putting Topsy down; that much was the God's honest truth. Hadn't gotten into the nitty-gritty of it—hadn't mentioned how they'd be doing it or where they'd be doing it—but then, Regan hadn't stuck around to bother kicking over that rock, had she? The ad really shouldn't surprise her like it does, bounding from the back pages of the local paper, slick and colorful as the cover of a pulp magazine. The elephant is frozen mid-convulsion, mouth wide open in a silent howl. A metal hat is strapped to her head; exaggerated yellow lightning bolts of electricity sizzle and whiz off her skin like popcorn kernels in a cast-iron skillet. Wires and chains lead away in every direction, hitching her safely to her death like she's every bit the crazy rampaging murderess the headline proclaims her to be.

Over yonder, beyond the chains and straps and iron bars, a crowd of people huddle watching. The artist didn't put as much work into drawing them as he or she did Topsy; they're mostly just slack-jawed shadows, men with driving caps and bowler hats and blank ghost faces. The only one of the group with any detail at all is a fellow in the middle, and the reason he's drawn so careful is because he's the man with his hand on the killing switch, the man with the power—the power of life and death forever and ever amen.

Someone had put a lot of effort into drawing an animal in the full throes of dying. Someone had probably paid a lot of money to have them scribble it, and even more money to stick it in the local paper. Money, after all, is the one thing US Radium's never been starved from a lack of.

Regan lets the paper slither to her quilted lap, too tired to keep holding the wretched thing, too sick inside to keep looking. She pushes it over the edge of the bed, so that all that's left there is the long-unopened letter from Jodie. It's her last night in the empty dormitory. In the morning she'll hop a train south—the last train she'll probably ever ride—and she'll go home to die, just as certain as if someone has strapped a metal mixing bowl to her head and pulled an oversized lever.

"Executioner's comin' for both of us, girl," she says. "I guess people'll remember you, at least."

She takes a deep suck of air, wearily picks up the letter, and tears it open. Might as well get it over and done with, all things considered.

.   .   .

In darkness she waited, O Mothers,
Tethered, tormented, fearless,
Waited for the many Men to gather
The way wind
Waits for lightning
The way rain
Holds for thunder

They came to watch her die, to smell her flesh burn,
To see a Great Mother laid low.
They gathered in great boasting bull herds
Like flies to dung,
Like hyenas to a sickness,
Yapping barking tussling.
Poor things
Poor things,

Poor prideful, foolish things!

. . .

"Well, they're definitely getting the land—that part of the deal is sealed." Kat's supervisor, a graying-at-the-temples woman of around sixty, has a poker face to make the elephant matriarch blow her cool in a fit of jealousy. She's got Kat's folder in her hands—yellow ledger papers poking and spilling from the edges like the filling in an overstuffed cartoon hoagie—and whether or not she approves of what's inside is still anybody's guess. "There's no need to feel any guilt about that."

Except for the part where nobody wants the land anyways and sure as hell won't want it once there's nuclear waste crammed under the mountain. Kat swallows her sass and makes a stab at looking pleased. "That's good," she says. "That's excellent to hear."

"Yes." Dr. Tilyou's voice is noncommittal; *I honestly don't care and neither do you.* "As to the rest of your concerns, the research you've presented me with . . . Katherine, have you been sleeping well? How much time have you spent on all of this?" She flaps the folder as punctuation. Notes escape and flutter to the floor. "You're not part of the media team. I understand the need to be involved in every aspect of a project you're personally responsible for, but nobody has seen you at the lab in ages, which is where you are most needed. Some people are beginning to worry."

Kat suddenly feels on the verge of tears, and she doesn't have the slightest clue why. Exhaustion, maybe. Frustration? It's getting hard to tell the two apart. "I told the representative I would try," she says. "Going forward, I have many ethical questions about the legitimacy of this project. I have to at least make sure an attempt is made at educating the public before continuing on with the research. A *major* attempt." She sounds like a robot, but hey—at least she's a moral one. *Beep-boop, my conscience is clear.* "Not just blurbs in middle school history books."

That earns her a sigh and a mighty drumming of fingertips on particle board, about as close as Dr. Tilyou comes to expressing annoyance. "I'm going to be blunt with you," she says.

"Go ahead." Do your worst, lady. I've been chewed out by a fucking elephant before; your admittedly impressive eyebrows can't touch me.

"Nobody working on this project except you cares that much about sticking to the letter of the agreement. It's a moot point. A sociological campaign of the scope and breadth of the one you're pitching would cost us hundreds of thousands of dollars in funding. Your honesty and desire to make sure the elephants are fairly represented is commendable, don't think it isn't, but—"

"It's not a top priority." Cold water words, the departmental equivalent of a baseball striking a dunk tank's target dead center.

"No." Dr. Tilyou lets her drop all the way to the bottom before continuing. "That's not to say we won't launch some kind of program, something to at least placate the elephants. It's just . . . cost aside, have you considered the levels of scrutiny we would be under if such an intensive campaign were launched? On top of the scrutiny a project involving non-*sapiens* rights, genetic manipulation, *and* nuclear waste will engender as is? It wouldn't just be shooting ourselves in the foot; it would be putting a loaded barrel to our heads and spinning the chamber." Kat's never heard Dr. Tilyou get colloquial before. *She must be* pissed. "That's not even getting into the emotions surrounding Topsy's act. Justified, unjustified—she's at the center of this project, but do you really, truly believe anyone should know in detail how the sausage is made?"

"We're scientists," Kat says. She stands. "All we do is teach people how sausage is made."

"I'm . . . I'm sorry?"

"I have to go home and think," she says.

"Think?"

If Kat were feeling less numb in her recklessness, she'd offer the good professor a cracker. "About whether I want to be a part of this, going forward. I'll let you know by tomorrow morning."

"Katherine." Dr. Tilyou's voice is taking on a downright panicky tone. "If you would please just wait a—"

The door cuts her off mid-sentence.

• • •

Regan,

Just want you to no, aint no hard feeling about the way things paned out. You all did best you cood lookin out for me like blood kin when you no I never had no body since Mama past away. Even yor own mama used to give me a seat at the tabell when holy fokes sooner feed scraps to a stray tomcat than a big uglee plain mannerd girl like me. Wood of been a dam good job and easy if not for the poysin.

as four the cumpanee, they can get blowed straeiht to hell and devil take there asses with a bran new pikaxe It is knot right the way they done us, and it is knot right ever the way big rich men do litle peeple, girls like us most of all. Even a snake bites if she gets stomped on. Peeple dont stomp on snakes cause they got enuff poysin in there teeth to kill a crowd of big men.

I am leaving you sum poysin for our teeth Regan. I

stole it from the Storm Mountain job beefor all of this and i still don't rightly no why cept misschef. It is in a locker downtown at 289 east cyclone street and I am leaving you the key. Carefull knot to shake or drop it untill you want to bite and are redy to meet me again. lockur number 27.

Wish you wood have been my blood sister, but we had good enough times anyways. Tell yor mama hello and not to forget about me.

Jodie

Regan doesn't get a whole lot of sleep that night.

There's a girl out there in the dark who has no idea what's coming for her. Maybe she's not so good at her letters. Maybe she can't even read them at all, never having had the chance or the interest or the time. She lives at the back end of nowhere, where the school only stretches yea far before it snaps, and she's got sisters to help take care of and a drunk for a daddy and a mama so shrivel-tired she can't even call up the water to cry. She's never read a paper in her life, this dust-footed girl, and most days she's not properly sure what the news is from five miles up the road, let alone five hundred. But just wait, girl. Some kin will hear it from some kin that there are jobs at the new factory—easy jobs, good jobs, work that pays more in a month than sweeping people's houses scratches up in a flat year—and off she'll go, no schooling or letters or certificates needed. You got fast hands? You got lips? You know how to use a paintbrush? Well hell fire, take a seat and get to work, sweetie! We'll take care of you. Radium's not just harmless—it's good for the body. Point a thousand brushes with your lips and you'll still come out fine.

And she may get a loose tooth or a sore lip, that girl, and she may feel an aching in her hips and knees the way her mawmaw describes the rheumatism, but she'll trust the men who hired her, and she'll keep on working because she don't know any better and nobody's gonna bother warning her when there's money on the table. And eventually, she'll die horribly—as horribly as a scene from a painted Bible hell, choking to death as her throat and jaw rot from the inside out—and the memory of her will die soon after, and it'll be like she never walked or talked or laughed or hoped to begin with.

So much for her.

There's an elephant calf out there in the dark who has no idea what's coming for her. She's grazing with her people somewhere, all her mamas clustered around her, all her aunties and mawmaws and second cousins twice removed, because that's more or less all Regan knows about wild elephants—the mamas stick together and travel in a herd like cows and the menfolk wander alone like a lot of other male critters do—and all she knows about the world is green grass and playing and hiding from crocodiles when there's crocodiles sneaking around champ-champ-chomping their jaws. But maybe someday men come along to that place, and they shoot all the mamas and aunties and mawmaws and second cousins twice removed, and the ones they don't shoot they load up and send to other places, where they teach them to dance and do tricks and how to be alone in the wide old world. And the calf forgets what it was like to be whole. She loses herself as she gets bigger. She busts so many heads trying to find herself again the circus men get fed up and sell her to a factory—not US Radium, but similar, a kissing cousin—where eventually, after a long-enough time and enough work done, she dies the same slow way as the girl, spoiling like bad meat in a forgotten lunch pail in the woods.

So much for her.

And Regan, for all her thinking and all her tail-chasing,

can't puzzle out how to stop the merry-go-round from spinning, whether it's through Jodie's way or some other, kinder method. She lies there staring at the ceiling until birds begin calling outside, too pained by her rotting body and whirling brain to snatch even the smallest scrap of rest.

And part of me felt good watching Topsy smash up that stall, didn't it? Way down deep, something angry in me got satisfaction. The world's so big and mean, and we're so small in it with our hands and feet fettered. Little tiny helpless things, who can't do a damn thing but cry and rage most days at the way the game's rigged against us.

She gets up from bed. She watches her window go from black to gunmetal. When it's light enough out to see, she digs around in the crate of Jodie's stuff—pushing past the coin purse, the pill bottles, the busted music box with the little ceramic bluebird—until she finds the key on its ribbon, sifted way down to the bottom. She lets it hang twirling from her fingers before looping it around her neck.

So much for her.

· · ·

The Men gathered, O Mothers
Hooting they led her forth, and she let them;
They called to the lightning:
"Lightning, strike this Mother
Burn her like dry grass,
Make Her Story wither and die,
So that she will never be They
Never be We.
Splinter,
Sunder,
Scatter!"

• • •

She considers going home, but the thought of all the research books waiting for her there makes her vaguely ill. Eventually her feet pull her to the nearest Q stop, where she drifts through the turnstile and down the stairs to the southbound platform.

There's an excited little boy on the train. Nothing revelatory about that; Kat watches him bounce off the walls with her earbuds cranked as high as they'll go, making it more or less like watching a death metal music video about the Black Goat of the Woods discovering their inner child. What's interesting about him is that he's wearing a t-shirt with Disney's Topsy printed all over it, broken up and interspersed with bright green atoms. Are his parents taking him to Coney Island because of the cartoon? she muses. Did the innocent little sugar-sucker beg and plead to go because that's where the finale dumps its sad, angry but good-at-heart heroine when things are at their darkest? Deeply fucked up, but also deeply probable. No matter what you did, forty or fifty or a hundred years passed and everything became a narrative to be toyed with, masters of media alchemy splitting the truth's nucleus into a ricocheting cascade reaction of diverging alternate realities.

There might have been kids at the actual electrocution. It was late in the day and the majority of the 150-plus crowd allowed inside had been men and older boys—so said the history books—but if Kat had to bet, she would guess there were some women and younger children hanging around, too. In those days, packing a picnic lunch and taking the family to watch someone or something die horribly wasn't considered particularly unusual. Electricity was new and weird; so were elephants. Combining the two into something as lurid as an execution always sucked in quite a crowd.

What a fucked-up mess. And yet without that fucked-up mess, the Radium Elephant trials never would have happened. There's no divorcing these things. Processing uranium to get at the sweet, sweet energy released left you with plutonium.

The Atlantic winks at her outside the window. The kid slams headfirst into the side of a seat and keeps moving in the opposite direction. She thinks about neutrons careening into nuclei like amped-up toddlers, the energy released and the expense and irreversible entropy coming on like a night with no stars.

. . .

TOPSY
(Traditional, 1919)

Brought her here from across the sea,
To this land of liberty
Seven feet tall, such a sight to see

Blow, Topsy, Blow
Blow, Topsy, Blow!

Factory boss said, "Topsy, m'girl,"
"Quit the circus, give work a whirl;
You'll be treated fair and square,
Brush in your trunk and nary a care!"

Blow, Topsy, Blow,
Blow, Topsy, Blow!

Kind old Topsy hadn't a clue,
'Bout radium, what it could do,
"I'm your gal, boss, let's see 'er through!"

Blow, Topsy, Blow,
Blow, Topsy, Blow!

But what that foreman didn't know,
Is that there's so much injustice you can honestly sow,
Before the anger starts to grow

Blow, Topsy, Blow
Blow, Topsy, Blow!

.   .   .

Regan limps downtown, raccoon-eyed and none too daisy-fresh owing to how she felt too weak and too exhausted to scrub up in the dormitory showers before heading out. There's a taste coating her tongue like the smell of dirty pennies combined with something gone moldy and forgot. The iron key around her neck bounces off her breastbone with every step. Between that and her jaw and throat throbbing molten bear traps in time to each rabbity pulsebeat, she's got a pretty good rhythm going as she totters down the sidewalk.

She reaches the address, goes inside, and casts around until she finds the right locker. A few seconds more fiddling beneath the cotton of her shirt and the key is in her hand.

Jodie, she thinks. I dunno if it's the good thing or the right thing or if you were even in your right goddamned mind when you put all of this together, but doing nothing's done nothin' but get more that don't deserve it sold down the river. I'm tired, Jodie. I'm so eat up with anger over you and us and all of it I can't see straight. And I'm tired of having to be angry all the time. I don't got the energy to keep it up anymore, but I'll be goddamned if I let them get away with murdering one more of us before this is all over and done with. Something's gotta give.

A click and a clunk and the little metal box swings open for her. A glass jar no bigger than a bumblebee sits inside. Careful, like picking a baby bird up off the ground, Regan takes the vial and gently nests it in her right front pocket, where it's least likely to be rattled by the walk and the long train ride to Coney Island.

And

(Poor things!)

She called to the lightning:

(Poor things!)

"Lightning, we have always been kin, always been We."

(Poor prideful)

"Tell my Story."

(Foolish)

"Tell my Truth in a voice like thunder."

(Things!)

"And scatter them all like ripe red fruit."

The memorial tower is forty feet high and carved out of marble, because they didn't do things halfway back in the day, even in the teeth of two world wars. In the seaside dusk it looms over Kat like a great tusk, curving to lift the sagging blue-gray canopy of nightfall.

It stands alone on its irradiated patch of beachfront property, far away down the strand from the toffee sellers and funnel cakes and skeevy boardwalk rides. Luna Park had never recovered from the incident. The place was barely out of the construction stage when Topsy turned its gestation into a miscarriage, and the cost of rebuilding combined with the stigma of tragedy (and background radiation) had convinced the surviving shareholders to throw up their hands and fold. The plot had stood empty for a while until the idea of a memorial was hit upon; several years and several mysterious donors later and the Luna Park Memorial Tower rose, a joint marker for the people who had died and the Radium Elephants who had found their voices in the violent self-sacrifice of their comrade. Sculpted bronze trunks wind around the length of the thing like a barber's pole all the way to the roof and top colonnade, where four bronze elephants and four bronze humans stand together gazing out to sea. In pictures and postcards of the place the trunks have long since gone the patina green of sea serpents, tarnished pennies, and the Statue of Liberty. Tonight they're stark black against the white.

Most people don't even remember the memorial exists. It's one of those oddities from an earlier time you learn about and then forget, something weird tucked away to stop and gawk at if you happen to be passing through the area on vacation or a day trip. Snap a photo, buy a postcard, namedrop it at a party when people ask what you did with your summer. Make a joke about Geiger counters and glowing craters if everyone else is clued in on the story. Death decayed into history decayed into poolside anecdote. Francium *wishes* it had a half-life as short as tragedy's.

Kat stares up at the column with her hands jammed in her pockets, thinking about truth and transmutation as the last light dies and the damp ocean breeze gnaws through her windbreaker. There's no stopping decay, change, or entropy. No matter how many jellyfish genomes they strap to an elephant's genetic material—no matter how many elephant mothers pass along the warning, long memories and unshakably interwoven strands of matriarchal polynucleotide narrative aside—the fact of the matter is, the basis for this project was contaminated from the start. It was decaying into something other than truth the day the first breathless article about Topsy was written, the day she died and someone else began telling her story and the cultural baggage accrued and replaced and eroded fact like radium in marrow.

Nuclear Topsy. No wonder the elephants don't trust them.

She stands there until the vertebrae in her craned neck start complaining and her feet go numb. An ivory sickle moon rises in the east. Kat turns her back on the memorial and the roaring Atlantic dark and shuffles towards the garish electric dawn of Coney Island, some skeleton's memory of what progress looked like.

• • •

Luna Park looks like a twister's gone on a tear right through its muddy heart, lumber and splintered scaffolds and the great naked backbones of buildings-to-be lying stretched out across the ground in every whichaway direction. Everywhere you turn an eye men are working up a fine old sweat—hammering, sawing, stuck all over with sawdust and coal smut, spitting dirt and tobacco until the ground's so churned mule teams bog down and split their pipes braying. The air this close to the ocean is a sponge—a damp, warm rag stuffed up under your nose so close you can almost taste the stink of mule shit and chaw spit and stale mud mixed with piss and spilled bourbon. And there's another smell, too, yonder beneath the fresh pine and cigarette smoke—hay, blood, something big and wild and musky. An old reek, like a mountain breaking lather.

Once you've gotten a whiff of it, you never forget the

smell of an elephant.

Nobody tries stopping Regan; she's dressed like a boy, the way she's most comfortable, and there are plenty of those running around. She wanders farther in—beneath the great wooden arch with its columns and crescent moons still unlit, past the rising spire they've already dubbed the "Electric Tower," wired to glow like something out of *The Arabian Nights*—slopping on through ankle-deep pigpen muck where there aren't boards laid yet, dizzy and sick and shaky-legged with her hurts but grimly determined not to faint. If that happens and she goes over on her side and the little bottle in her pocket gets broken and crushed, it'll have been a wasted trip with a smoking pair of boots planted at the bottom of the crater.

The morning gets hotter. Sweat pops on her forehead, running down into her eyes to sting them shut. All of her joining pins have been replaced with knife blades, from heel to toe to aching hip. She holds off swallowing her own spit until her tongue is dog-paddling and she can't help herself. These days, the automatic jerk of muscles she always took for granted before is like washing down coals with grain alcohol, a fierce tearing worse than her jaw if simply because of how much she has to make it happen. A beaten *gulp* and the fire roars up her throat and into her brain. Her knees give up the ghost and she finds herself slumping against a sawhorse, fingers clutching and unclutching at raw wood.

"Had a bit too much, eh, kid? Show's not even on until tonight, pace yourself!" A jolly hand follows the jolly voice, slapping Regan on the back so hard her last few teeth rattle. She gums back a scream. She's only got so much control left, but she clings to it with all she's got like a baby squirrel in a windstorm. "Don't let the policemen they got snooping around find you; you'll be hitting that drunk tank ass-first quicker'n a New York minute."

"Fine. I'm fine." The words dribble down her chin. Even

the passerby's booming seems faded and faraway.

"You sure, son? You sure as hell don't look it. Here, lemme give you a hand."

"I'm FINE." She hears the good Samaritan step back hastily. "Need to see the elephant. Come to see the elephant."

"Yeah, you and every other pimple-popping boy-o from a hundred miles round." His voice is sulled now. "It's chained up in a tent just a little further the way you're going."

"Thanks." She hangs there until she's sure he's moved away. *C'mon, girl. Not much further to go.* She pulls herself upright, gives her eyes and brain a minute to unfog, then staggers on.

You can hear the tent humming well before it ever hews into view, like a bee tree or a hive of wasps. Boys hoot and holler in and out beneath the canvas, confident as fighting cocks in their ability to outrun any bellowing grown-up that might come along with an idea to try and chase them. Older clumps smoke and chat warily outside. Regan pushes past best she can, careful not to let an elbow or swinging arm hit her pocket. Slowly—more like an old man than one of the boys now—she swings a shaky leg over the guide ropes and lifts the tent flap, ducking into a shadowland that smells like the beginning of the world.

Links rattle. Something big rumbles. Smaller shadows school like minnows, giggling and teasing, shying away at every snort or shift only to come flocking back when it looks like the danger's passed. Not that there's really any threat; as her eyes get used to the darkness Regan can see the chains and ropes looped and relooped around Topsy's neck and ankles, big old logging chains meant to pull redwoods crashing to the ground. Pebbles bounce off her leathery hide, and she pays them no more mind than a hawk shrugging off a territorial cock sparrow. Boys poke sticks and lit cigarettes at her from across the ropes; she lifts her trunk out of range and dreams on, spirit touring times and places Regan can't even guess at. Her mind is the most alien thing Regan's ever had truck with outside the God in her mother's Bible.

Almost there. She watches the scene a little longer, putting off what has to be done. One more trick. Jodie and the rest of them better appreciate this, wherever they are.

She takes a deep breath, latches onto a guide rope, gets her mind right for what's coming, and bellows like a whipped mule.

"COPS! COPS! LOOK OUT, COPS ARE COMING!"

Veins in her throat give up and bust their dams. She can feel them popping before the shock snaps and she goes into freefall, mind and soul and all the things that make Regan Regan rubbed out by a root-shaking, roof-tearing wave of wrongness her brain recognizes from its treetop perch as the worst pain she's ever felt—the kind you know is damaging things the moment it lands. Somewhere shadowy boys are shouting, shoving, scattering. They flutter past her like moths in a dream.

When she comes back to herself she's on her knees in a puddle of something dark, throat still registering aftershocks. Topsy looks down at her impassively. She wipes her mouth with the back of one palsied hand; it comes back sticky, copper-smelling.

Hey, Regan signs.

No reply, just watchful stillness. *Well there's a damned surprise.* She hauls herself to her feet, hay and dirt sticking to the blood on the palms of her hands.

I came here to see you, she continues. *You and me got business.*

Chains rattle. The air stirs. *No,* says the slow shadow of Topsy's trunk, black against the canvas. *No more business. No business but death.*

That's good, 'cause death is what I maybe came here to offer you. A righteous death. The movement for "righteous" looks a little something like two tusks quickly dipping down and then back up again, a goring, tossing flip. Regan slips a hand into her pocket, palming the bottle's cool cola-bottle smoothness. She sets it down on the ground between them—close enough so Topsy can reach, fettered up as she is—and steps back, head swimming from the act of bending over.

This, she signs, *is a seed. Crush it and death sprouts. Not just yours. The men with the chains. The circus men, the poison-factory men, the ones who will come to see you burn—all of 'em. Like lightning striking. You'll be lightning. You'll burn and you'll strike and then you'll be gone. It's up to you. Dying's a personal thing. It's . . . just . . .* She trails off, hunting for the right words. Exhaustion is butting in on her thoughts, pushing them to the back of the hall.

. . . I just wanted to give you the option, she finishes, at a loss as to how to put it any better. *A friend gave it to me. I'm passing it along to a higher power.*

Even with her death waiting and the sounds of a crowd gathering outside, Topsy takes her sweet, thoughtful time responding. You can practically hear the gears groaning inside that great skull of hers, slow but unstoppably steady in their revolution. *Righteousness.* Regan thinks of the sign again, invisible enemies flung into the air like pinecones. An old word, indiscriminate as a knife's edge, a tusk's tip.

Like lightning, Topsy signs. For the first time, Regan notices that her trunktip is glowing a faint, familiar green.

Yup.

You wish for them to die, too. Not a question. *For the poisoning. For killing you.*

Regan shrugs. No argument there.

Asking nice never seemed to get either of us much, did it? Maybe this'll get somebody's attention.

Topsy reaches down. Her trunk curls and uncurls, twitching at the tip like an agitated cat's tail. For the briefest blip of a second she hesitates and Regan thinks maybe she won't take the bottle, that she's sadder than she is angry, that her execution will amount to nothing more than a pitiful sentence in a history book swollen tick-tight with so many injustices the poisoning of a factory full of girls and the mean public death of a small god don't even register as particularly noteworthy.

But that's somebody else's once upon a time. Gently, gingerly—the way any soul would handle their own death—Topsy takes the little vial and tucks it away inside her mouth.

. . .

She thinks of her Many Mothers, fierce and vast, swift-trunked slayers of panther, hyena, and crocodile. She thinks of Furmother – With – The – Cracked – Tusk, tricking a bull and splitting herself so that the stories could be free and the Mothers could be We. Unresisting, she lets them lead her forth in chains. She lets them lead her forth in chains, and when they hoot and roar and clamber she thinks on Furmother, her bravery and her cunning, her careful, plodding patience.

The final fruit to be plucked is not rage, but song—a learning song, a teaching song, a joining-together song. She rolls it on her tongue, careful not to split it before its time. The men gibber and yap and lean out to touch her as she passes. The man holding the lead chain barks a warning at them in the jackal tongue of humans, hurrying along before her trunk can sweep them clear of the path.

There is still fear in her heart. To be is to be wary, and so there is still fear in her heart, balking wide-eared at what lies coiled at the end of the walk. *Danger! Lions! Claws and teeth and tawny fur!* She smells her ending, and her feet plant themselves, bending-parts senselessly locking. The man yells and tugs and strikes her with whip and chain; he too stinks of fear, sharp as crushed nettles underfoot. She struggles with the man and the fear—*Guns! Men! Fire and smoke and pits with sharpened sticks!*—but if the man can be ignored, the ending-fear cannot. It lies deeper than hurt and deeper than the need to sing her own undoing song, a root buried so far within no tusk can pry it free. The man-herd howls, thrown into *musth* by her hesitation. They claw and push at her haunches with their trunk-paws, desperate to hurry along, always and forever in a hurry.

Another human pushes out of the mass—the dead girl, still moving, still somehow on her feet when every part of her stinks of corruption. She exchanges a few guttural yips and yowls with the man on the end of the chain, pain rolling off her like river water. Eventually he huffs and puffs and reluctantly passes her the chain. She turns, asking, in the little language of twisted trunk-paws: *Are you well? Can you walk? It's just a little further. We'll go together.*

And even this much We is enough to drive the fear back into the high grass. Her mind stills. Her legs unstiffen. Together they cross the overwater, men flytrailing behind. Together they go to sing the song of their undoing, the joining, teaching, come-together song.

. . .

Sing thunder, O Mothers!
Sing her song in this dusty place!
Glowing like green lightning, so many Many Mothers apart,
Do not forget what lies Beneath,
And do not forget what came Before,
Sing Her Story like lightning,
Like thunder,
Like the Glorious Mothers Many:
We, She, Her,
Us.

The Last Banquet of Temporal Confections

by Tina Connolly

Saffron takes her customary place at the little round table on the dais of the Traitor King. Duke Michal, Regent to the Throne is his official title, but the hand-drawn postered sheets, the words whispered in back alleys all nickname him the same. She smiles warmly at the assembled guests, standing poised and waiting by their chairs, ready for the confections and amuse-bouches that have been a mainstay of the high table for the last year.

Saffron has been Confection Taster all that time, her husband Danny Head Pastry Chef. Their warm smiles have been perfected as the Traitor King's power grows, inch by inch, as those who object to his grasp fail and fall, as the printers are vanished, as the daughters disappear from their homes. The little prince still sleeps in his nursery—but for how long? That is the question on everyone's mind in the last year. Not a question uttered, but a question that stays poised on the tongue, and does not fall.

The Traitor King takes his place. He looks sternly around the table, watching to see if anyone dares sit or talk or breathe before him. Then he breaks into a jovial smile, and everyone exhales, and there is careful laughter: the Duke is in a good mood tonight. There will be candies and conversations, alliances formed and favors exchanged, perhaps a juggler hung for dropping the pins, but who minds the jugglers?

Saffron minds. She minds very much.

The first course! bids the Duke, and around the table the white-coated servants set down the gilded plates, each bearing the first bite-sized course, showcasing Danny's skill. An identical plate is set next to Saffron, the Duke's own plate, this one bearing a pastry twice as large as the others, so the Duke shall not lose any of the delight of his food to caution.

The Duke barely flicks his eyes Saffron's direction. She knows what to do, and smiling, she cracks the thin toast in two with her fine silver fork, and takes her bite.

Rosemary Crostini of Delightfully Misspent Youth

Saffron knows this moment instantly. The angled sun falls in clean lines on the bakery floor. Daily Bread is the name on the hand-carved sign of the shop, for it is an ordinary bakery still. A younger Danny stands at the counter, just turning with flour-dusted chin to notice her. She has come here so often with the rosemary crostini that she has what the lords and ladies do not: an instant of double-memory, of twinned lives, as she breathes, and lets herself go, and tumbles five years into the past.

Her sister Rosie pushes her forward, hisses, "Your turn," in teasing tones, and Danny and Saffron's eyes lock.

Saffron swallows. Two girls on a rare free afternoon, on a mission to see who can charm the most treats out of willing young shopkeepers and clerks. Rosie is the younger by a year but the older in daring. Her funny, loyal sister has transformed this morning into a different girl, all curls and honeyed tones, a girl on a mission. So far she has acquired:

Item (1) length of green velvet ribbon, long enough to tie back her gold-brown hair. Item (1) scrap of lace, to finish the wrists of the gloves she is making for Saffron. Surely Saffron could manage a chocolate, a tartlet, a bun?

And yet here she is, with the sinking feeling that she does not know how to flirt.

The kind-eyed young man—for now she no longer knows his name, she has the faint feeling that she has forgotten, there is something teasing at the back of her mind—well, he leans on the scarred wood counter and asks again if he can help.

"A. . .a rye bun, please," she says at random.

"Just one then?" he says with amusement, and he reaches for it. The young man, so quiet on other occasions Saffron has come in, seems rather more self-possessed today, but who would not be at a girl stammering "bun"?

"Yes. No." She can't remember anything Rosie did to charm that ribbon off of the shopkeeper; all her wits have fled. "I mean, I may have forgotten my coins?"

"It's a fine day when a beautiful girl comes into my grandfather's bakery with no money, but only wants one poor little rye bun," he says. "Hardly seems worthwhile to charge her." She flushes; he understands the game and is teasing her.

Rosie elbows her; she should make her move. Say something pert in response; acquire the prize. Her coin is her flirtation, her smiles, she sees now that she and Rosie are paying after all, in a different kind.

But instead, behind the baker she sees a small waif, silhouetted in the back door to the shop. Saffron nods at the baker, points over his shoulder. "Do you have company?"

He turns, drops his teasing manner. "Jacky," he says affectionately, and scoops several buns and a long thin loaf off of a different shelf. The small creature holds open his bag hopefully, and the day-old bread is placed inside. Jacky pulls out a single copper cent and gravely hands it to the baker, who as gravely accepts it. "My best to your mother," the baker says, as the waif scampers off.

The young man turns back to the counter, and the kindness in his eyes is replaced by a different kind of warmth for Saffron, one that is gentle and interested, and possibly could be the same kind of warmth as for that little boy someday if she lets it, if she begins as she means to go on.

Saffron puts the coins on the counter for the rye bun. "Will you have coffee with me?" she says, clearly and calmly and forthrightly.

The flour-dusted young man takes her money and hands her the bun. Rosie snickers in the background, but the baker's smiles are all for her. "Aye, and more."

.   .   .

Saffron returns to herself, the delight of the memory still sharp on her tongue. Her eyes clear, she smiles warmly at the crowd. "This has always been one of my favorite recipes of Danny's," she tells them, and her gilded plate is passed to the Duke. He does not look at her as he picks up the second bite of golden-crusted toast, redolent with rosemary and crystals of sea salt. Danny was an excellent baker long before he started experimenting with the rose-thyme plant that causes the memories, and this crostini is no exception.

Around the table the noble sycophants follow the Duke's example, and Saffron watches in amusement at seeing the whole table go slack, their eyes staring off into nothing as they remember.

At the edges of the room the white-coated servants, the red-coated guards go on alert. Saffron knows, for he has told her, that the commander of the guard dislikes these little interludes. But the Duke will have his perks, and further—she is told—it amuses the Duke to watch the lords and ladies squirm. Not all the confections Danny makes evoke pleasant memories, and during their time in the Duke's palace, he has been encouraged to experiment. An invitation to a Temporal Confections dinner is equally coveted and feared, but never declined.

Around the table the diners slowly shake off the residue of the memory, come back to themselves with foolish smiles on their faces. Good, she thinks. Danny is outdoing himself tonight. Is that a hint of things to come? They are kept apart, in the castle, and she wishes they had some way to communicate, other than through memory. A memory can be directed, a little, if the eater has practice. Saffron knows what she wants to see with the Rosemary Crostini, and she knows Danny knows she will see it. It was a gift to her this night, that first flush of meeting, that moment trapped in time like a fly in amber.

A salad course of watercress and arugula is served, and wineglasses filled with a dry white. The Duke's regular taster is given his salad, a fresh fork. She is a perpetually frightened-looking girl with honey-colored hair, but she is no milkmaid from the countryside. She is eighth in line to the throne, the granddaughter of kind Lord Searle, that same Lord Searle who would make a remarkably good regent—if he had not been accused of treachery by the Duke and disappeared into the maze of dungeons under the castle.

The girl retains many of her daytime privileges, but at dinner she sits at the Traitor King's side, yet another hostage for others' behavior. She tastes the requisite bite of the peppery greens, and then the plate is relayed to the Duke, and he picks up his own silver fork. Around the table the others join in, and Saffron and the girl fold their hands in their laps, and wait.

Fennel Flatbread of Sunlit Days Gone By

The sun is sparkling on the snow on the day Danny gets his first temporal pastry to work.

It is a Seventhday, and the shop is closed. They have been married for a year now; Danny's grandfather has passed on, and the little bakery is all Danny's. A small inheritance has allowed him to experiment; a small inheritance and a smaller glass bottle of dried rose-thyme that Danny's grandfather gathered as a youth in the distant High Reaches. Despite its name, rose-thyme does not taste precisely like either; or, more correctly, it tastes like many more things than just those two flavors. It is a changeable plant; the method of preparation is key to bringing out a particular aromatic strain. More importantly, the method of preparation is key to evoking certain visions. As a child, Danny's grandfather and his chums would chew on the flowers, which, when eaten plain, give brief flashes of déjà vu. He also told Danny that those who had once lived in the High Reaches had actual recipes that they swore could evoke glimpses of longer-ago memories, and indeed, at winter solstice every year, there was a certain currant cake made with the rose-thyme that would make everyone remember the previous solstice's currant cake, and back and back, cementing the continuity of a long line of years.

All that was long ago, and Danny's grandfather's people were mostly scattered and gone, driven forth by the last king's brother, whose dukedom was in the High Reaches, at the border of the country. He and his son, Michal, were reputed to be cold and cruel. Certainly they had destroyed Danny's ancestral home. But the current King was kind, if perhaps a bit soft, and he had not taken steps to control his distant cousin anymore than his father had controlled his younger brother.

All this runs through Saffron's head while she stands at the back of the shop, slowly kneading a mass of dough that will rise overnight for tomorrow's buns. Watching the sky slowly darken, the snow clouds massing once more. Why is she thinking of the old king? But perhaps it is because of the clock tower bells. They have been ringing all morning, and she has not heard them ring like that since she was a child. Their slow pealing is an eerie counterpoint to the silent snow, the warm, empty shop. A cheerful whistle floats out occasionally from the other room of the bakery, punctuated with the sharp smell of dried fennel being crushed with mortar and pestle. Danny is experimenting yet again.

Someone bangs on the back door, and she opens it to a snowdrift. Little Jacky, older now. He comes in, stamps his feet.

"The King is dead," he says, "Did you know?"

Of course, she thinks, the bells, and behind him the flurries have started again, the spangles of sun replaced by fat dots of white.

"Ma says they'll make old Searle the regent. He's a soft touch, that's for sure. Gives out coppers to kids anytime you see him in the street. Hey, maybe he'll give out silvers if he's got a whole treasury."

Saffron shakes her head. She saw the King speak, not two months ago. He was grieving for his wife's death in childbirth, and the city grieved along with him. But. . . "He was so healthy."

"Bloody flux," Jacky says with certainty. "Got my cousin last month." He holds out his palm. "I got five coppers for you this time. Been working for my uncle. What can I get with that?"

She ruffles his snow-dusted hair and hands over a hearty round loaf that didn't sell, and several currant buns, only a little burnt.

He shouts his thanks and hurries off, running through the falling snow. His bit of red scarf flaps behind him; he shrinks smaller and smaller in the vanishing white. The king is dead, the poor little prince an infant. There will be change. Change is hard to weather. Change makes everyone skint, and keep their coins in their pockets.

But the people will still need bread, she thinks, as she watches the diagonal drifts. And there has been peace for so long. How can there not still be peace? Power will transfer, the reins will change hands, but she and Danny will have their bakery, their dough, their bread. They will focus on the rising of the yeast and the pounding of the dough and if they have to cut out currants for a time, well, plain buns sell nearly as well.

The clock tower bells ring all day and all night for the end of the king, the ending of the old era. She stands for some time, looking at the falling snow, until behind her Danny shouts, I have it, I have it, Saffron, I have it.

She turns to see the exult on his face, and he scoops her up and swings her around. He has been parceling out the last few sprigs of rose-thyme for months, trying recipe after recipe, running right through the last of the dried leaves.

Now he hands her a round circle of flatbread on a plate. It looks like any of Danny's homey flatbreads, but smaller. A few bites only, and one bite is missing.

She knows already that there is something special about this moment. It is the sort of memory you recall for years after. A moment when the world changed around you. A moment etched with both beauty and loss, a moment that you leave behind as you move away from it, a moment you can never reach again.

Except, with what Danny has now made, perhaps you can.

Saffron takes the first bite ever of a temporal confections

creation and falls back further still.

The world shifts around her. She is seven, and her mother is still living. The sun drifts golden onto a dew-spattered morning, and she shakes a magnolia tree onto Rosie, watching her sister laugh as the droplets spray—

.   .   .

"Another masterpiece," says Saffron, and the same white-gloved servant passes her plate to the Duke. She shivers, deep inside, for she is not lying. Danny has been working on that linked memory trick for years. She has seen the Fennel Flatbread creation memory before, but she has never seen that magnolia tree memory within it. Usually the scene ends the moment Danny hands her the flatbread and she takes a bite.

Around the table eager hands reach for the plates, barely able to wait for the Duke. A Fennel Flatbread of Sunlit Days Gone By sounds delightful; not like any of the Duke's nastier tricks. They all could use a moment of nostalgia, of respite from their grown-up cares. They eat, and Saffron watches them, still wondering how Danny triggered the second memory. Perhaps it was in the mashed fava bean dip served alongside, perhaps it is something in the flatbread itself. He has been working on reductions, on methods of increasing the intensity of the herbs. But of course, he has not been able to share anything with her since coming to the palace. And truly, it is better if she does not know. She has never been very good at dissembling, though she has been practicing in this last year. Readying the skill for the moment she needs it.

The words rise as the memories dissolve; the voices filled with emotion, with wonder.

—I was climbing a tree; it was cut down long ago

—I saw my mum, I haven't seen her in years

—My boy was young again; he ran to me

The Duke scoffs. Whatever he has seen, it has made little impression. "Puerile fantasies," he says, and swivels to eye Saffron. "I hope the next course will be more suitable to an. . .advanced palate."

"Danny's skill at arranging a balance of flavor and memory is unsurpassed," Saffron says evenly. If she wished to gently push the Duke she would remind him of previous banquets; the one that ended with the nobles in tears; the one that ended with them overcome with patriotism, swearing oaths to the Traitor King. But she does not want to disturb the fragile balance. Danny is building to something, she is more and more certain. Which means that she is to taste, and be ready. Timing is critical in baking, and here so tonight.

Another course is served; a delicate shellfish bisque, but the nobles barely notice what they eat, lost in recounting, reliving, those long-ago moments, made real again for an instant. If the Duke were more observant, he would notice how even the sweetest memory has an edge, for it is something that is lost and will not come again. But perhaps Danny is lulling him, downplaying his skill with the more complicated memories; the ones that linger like the mold on cheese, the yeast in the sourdough, the bitter in the wine.

The bisque is finished—Saffron sometimes feels guilty that the main cooks no longer receive the attention they ought—and the servers return with the next pastry course.

Ah, thinks Saffron, who recognizes it immediately. Here we go into the darker turn.

She could almost be angry at Danny, but she knows whatever he plans tonight has a purpose. The Duke will feast on her tears, but so be it.

The silver fork cuts through the pastry and she takes a bite.

Rose-Pepper Shortbread of Sweetness Lost

She and Danny have been married for three years now. The bakery has picked up, now that they are offering a few unusual items right alongside the daily bread. There is still no baby, but they are happy with their bakery and their work, and they do not mind—too much. Danny bakes and she assists, Danny invents and she assists. But she does not mind that either, for she has found her own calling at the front of the shop, and it is matching people with the right pastry.

There is an art to knowing what people need. Oh, they would all take the flatbread if they could, but do they need it?

At first they do not advertise that there is anything special about some of the pastries in their shop. Danny is still working out the strengths and flavors. The first few pastries and confections come with barely a hint, a flash. A memory easily dismissed as natural. The sort of thing that keeps people returning to a bakery where they feel so content, so rejuvenated. So understood. With the increased income, Saffron arranges the shop and sews new curtains and freshens the paint. She hires Rosie to work alongside them, and that gives Danny more time to develop the recipes, strengthen the flavors. Rosie is a natural third point to their triangle; her open, gregarious warmth is a fire they kindle themselves by. She helps them turn the bakery from a shop to a café; she encourages customers not to just buy their regular bread and go, but to sit and linger, try that extra morsel of unusual pastry and feel at peace.

This morning, Rosie is laughing with a regular about something that happened last night. Rosie has changed the last two years; her curls are the same, but she has swapped her ribbons and laces for steel-toed boots and the cry of Resistance.

Saffron understands that the new Regent Michal, at first so sympathetic, so distraught about the sudden treachery of Lord Searle, has slowly been closing his velvet glove around the city. She understands that there have been rumors of people taken. Rumors of Bad Things. But she only has one sister, and rumors are not here and now, they are not the shop and bread and cheese and chairs.

She pulls Rosie behind the counter, by the trays of day-old regular bread, and says as much.

Rosie's chin sets. It is not the first time they've had this conversation. "I have to do something," she tells Saffron. She drops her voice. "You know the little print shop, down the street?"

The printer. An outspoken, angry man. Yes.

"You know they took him, Saffy. Tortured him. Just for printing the truth about what's been happening to the girls. The disappearances—"

"Who says, though?" says Saffron, who can't believe in things happening to people she knows.

Rosie gives her a look. "His body was all covered up at the hanging. So you wouldn't see what had been done to him. I saw—"

"You went there?"

"I can't stay here, safe in a bakery," says Rosie, voice rising. "I have to try."

"We are doing good work here," Saffron says, helplessly.

Rosie shakes her head. "This is not the only good work there is to be done. Can't you see that?"

They are close to understanding each other, but then Saffron lets slip: "Can't someone else do that work?" and that makes Rosie shake her head, and stomp away, off to heft some flour bags around, take out her frustration.

Yes, Rosie has changed. Or no, not changed, perhaps, but grown up. Matured into something that was there all along.

She can't just stay in her bakery, Rosie says. But why not? Why can't there be room for someone who takes care of people, one person at a time? Who feeds them bread for their bodies and confections for their souls and does good work on a single, individual level? Saffron is heavy with resentment, she is prickly with the wish to prove Rosie wrong.

That is when the enforcer comes in.

He wears the emblem of the palace; the R of the Regency, the eagle of the Duke. He saunters up and says politely, "We have reports of miscreants disturbing the peace last night."

"Everything is just fine here," Saffron says.

"And your employees?" he says. "Where were they?"

"We have but one," she says, "and she is a law-abiding citizen." Her heart is thumping inside and he can surely see her pallor. What did Rosie do? For that is her first thought, that Rosie and her group of troublemaker friends must have done something. This man would not be here for nothing. Around the store she sees the customers who have finished their pastries quietly slipping away, their peace at an end.

The enforcer's eyes follow her gaze; he looks languidly around the room like a bored cat. "This is a sort of opium den, is it?" he says, gesturing at a man's slack face.

"Merely a bakery," Saffron says.

"Please produce your license," he says, more politely yet, and she understands how to do this part, this part is rote. She gets it from the back room, a few steps away through that curtain. Her eyes sweep the room for Danny—surely Danny will know what to do—but he is out on a buying errand, and she sees only her sister, crouched and silent, hiding behind a barrel of flour.

Numbly she returns, shows the man the card that should make him leave.

He barely looks at it, lets it fall to the counter. "Please

produce your sister," he says, and this is the point she cannot forgive herself for, even as it happens.

I must not tell him where she is, she thinks. But she is too used to being law-abiding, and she has never tried to become good at deception. Her mouth hangs open for too long, her eyes flick to the wrong side. "I have not seen her today," she stammers at last, and the enforcer just laughs at her.

He pushes past to the back, and he pulls her sister out. Rosie reams him with a pan, and then he casually punches her in the stomach, so hard she doubles over, and he drags her out, even as Saffron runs after them, armed with nothing. He throws her into a carriage—pushes Saffron down into the muck of the street—and then they are gone, and Saffron is weeping.

The scene jumps forward—another linked memory. Danny finding her in the streets, near the castle. Saffron ran after the carriage until she couldn't run anymore, then she plodded after it till she reached its entrance to the gates, and when they would not let her in, she sunk down and stayed there. She doesn't deserve to leave the muck, because she failed to save Rosie.

Another jump forward, because the hanging does not happen until an entire week later. The body is fully clothed, down to long sleeves and long gloves that Rosie was not wearing when she left. Saffron is left to imagine everything the cloth is hiding. Drawn iron wire fences the hanging square; it cuts red lines into Saffron's palms. Around her the scent of lilacs blooms thick and sweet. It is spring.

•   •   •

Saffron comes back to herself in the banquet room, and her eyes are wet. She sits up straighter, calmly blots her eyes with her napkin. "The Rose-Pepper Shortbread of Sweetness

Lost will show you someone you miss," she says to the table. "All such sweet memories are tinged with sorrow."

She nods to the servitor to take her plate to the Duke, smiles warmly at the table to put them at ease. "You will find notes of citrus and almond in the tasting," she says. "We find it is one of the most popular pastries among the elderly."

"I certainly hope you are not insinuating anything," says the Duke, and then he laughs, and then they all do.

They take their bites and Saffron breathes out, concentrating on what Danny has done. Three jumps this time. Usually she sees just the bakery, or just the carriage, or just the hanging. Yet somehow he has strung memories together, finding a way to let the whole terrible story unfold.

If she had seen a fourth memory, it might well have been the aftermath. For it is a day not long after that when Danny starts experimenting on what he will call the bitter pastries. Not bitter in flavor, necessarily. Certainly deeper in flavor, more profound notes in the tasting. Memories that are both sweet and sour. Memories with a purpose.

The first one has a rose flavor, in honor of her sister.

Rosie is not the only person Saffron has lost in her life—her parents have both passed away—but she only ever sees Rosie when she eats the shortbread. She suspects that its creation is too inextricably bound up with her sister for her to ever see another. For awhile, there were many Seventhdays that she dedicated to nothing but the rose-pepper shortbread and her grief.

Many months later, when she is capable of feeling anything more than numb, Saffron takes her place again at the front of the shop. She understands then that this recipe is what she was lacking to give the customers. Not all customers can be helped with a fennel-bright flatbread, a happy moment. There are many who need a more profound searching into their past.

Around her now the nobles return from their journey, their faces a dizzying array of sadness, happiness, regret. It is a complex pastry.

The next food course is served—some sort of little trussed-up birds, but Saffron barely notices. She is elsewhere, considering what Danny has shown her, considering what next is to come.

She is not surprised when the silver bell rings and out comes the fourth of Danny's creations tonight, another bitter pastry. It is not one that Danny has yet showcased at the castle. Only now does it make its appearance, and her heart quickens, her lips pucker, her mouth salivates for the taste.

Lemon Tart of Profound Regret

It is an ordinary day in the bakery, and Saffron looks around at her regulars with satisfaction. Everything they have worked for, coming to fruition. She is closer to contentment, closer to peace than she has been in over a year. The loss of her sister will never leave her, but it is a dull ache these days that only sometimes turns sharp, breaks her down in the middle of the bakery, hand on a bag of flour. The bakery has found a new normal, and there are customers to help.

The regulars, and she knows them by their orders.

Apple Turnover of Happier Times, aka, the bent old woman in the moth-eaten furs. Saffron saves the curtained alcove for her, and for the fifteen minutes it takes to eat that pastry, she's lost in a haze of remembering. Children, thinks Danny, but Saffron thinks grandchildren. Either way she lost them during the brief, bloody uprising last spring, they agree on that.

Lavender Macaron of Long-Ago Flirtations, aka the angular man who still owns two silk scarves, despite the ever-increasing privations, despite the shabbiness of his old suit. He rotates the scarves day by day; green-stripe, violet dots. He takes tea with his macaron, and his lips curl in pleasure while he remembers. Obviously it's a lover, but Danny is sure the lover disappeared in some dramatic way; attacking the palace, or daring to print anti-propaganda sheets. To have something worth remembering, you have to live first, says Danny, and then he looks sadly at his flour-dusted arms, knowing that he only runs a bakery.

Lemon Tart of Profound Regret, that's the sad one. She's young, too young to have so much Profound Regret in her life. But she comes every day at ten, testing her sorrow. Profound Regret shows you the biggest mistake you made, the one you brood over, and there are two kinds of people who buy it. The ones that make Saffron's heart gladden are the ones who buy it infrequently. They descend into the despair of knowing what they did, just as fresh as the day it happened.

Then they go off and change, because of what they saw.

Saffron knows, because they come back to tell her. Not right at first. But they come back, several months later, and buy the tart again. And this time they see something else. Something less terrible. That's how they know they've moved on.

Those are the ones Danny says the whole shop is worth it for. He'd do it all again. Some days it seems like you're doing so little, but when he helps one of those people, his whole life is justified. On days that are really tough—the stories told about the Duke are worse than usual, the taxes are due, the Profound Regrets are too deep—Danny eats one of his Honey Chocolates of Well-Deserved Pride. He says it always shows him those moments, the ones when he helped people.

Their current Lemon Tart comes day after day. She's not moving on. Danny thinks Saffron should intentionally mix up her order, give her a Honey Chocolate or an Apple Turnover and see if that helps her mindset change. Saffron is considering the merits of this when he comes in.

He's supposed to be incognito but Saffron knows him instantly. She's seen enough Resistance flyers to know how the Duke disguises himself when he wants to move around the city. His red hair is slicked back under a hooded cloak.

She tries not to start, but her body betrays her. She flushes, angry and scared all at once, and she knows he sees it.

"I have a mind to try one of your Honey Chocolates," he says smoothly.

Her fingers are shaking as she reaches for it. This man of all men does not deserve to relive his best moments. She has thought for so long of Resistance. She could reach for the Mint Chocolate of Deep Despair, at least. After he tastes it, he will know that mint is not honey, and he will punish her somehow—execute her? Torture her, like her sister? But first he will suffer. Oh, he will suffer.

But it would not just be Saffron who suffers. It would be Danny. It would be the part-time employees. It would be the customers, for she is not naive enough to think that he would not seek his wrath on all who saw his humiliation. He must squash any hint of rebellion.

Or you are afraid, says a smaller voice still.

Saffron reaches for the chocolates and his eyes are heavy on hers; it seems he knows her thoughts. She knows why he comes unannounced. So she cannot slip him poison, not unless she has planned for this moment and made an entire tray of poisoned chocolates, and she has not.

"I am most delighted to sample what I have asked for," he says, and there is a world of meaning in that tongue.

Her eyes close—her fingers close on the wrapper around the chocolate, bring it up. She puts it on the plate with nerveless fingers.

It is the Honey Chocolate.

Her voice shakes as she tells him the price. Her moment has come, her moment has gone.

The Duke takes the chocolate, sits down at a table in the corner. A young man leans casually against the wall, fiddling with his belt knife. He doesn't fool Saffron. The Duke goes off into a haze of remembering and for eight heartstopping minutes she cleans the counter and tends to the customers as the Duke looks off in the distance and the young man watches the two of them, his eyes flicking back and forth, watching to see if the bakery worker has lied to the Duke.

She regrets her choice already. She does not need a Lemon Tart to know that.

She regrets it even more when, two nights later, the Duke's guards take Danny out of their bed in the middle of the night.

She is left to make her own way to the castle and offer herself up as sacrifice. A willing check on any rebellious tendencies my Danny might have. To sell herself to the Traitor King.

A common food-taster.

. . .

Saffron blinks back tears. She has not seen Danny in so long. The Duke does not trust them together. He has taken Saffron's measure—correctly assessed her as ineffectual, not a threat. She is plain, ordinary, and the Duke is not so foolish as to spend the coin of her in the wrong place. She is much more valuable alive and whole and as a check on Danny. So the Duke left her free rein of the upstairs servants' quarters—as long as she does not enter the second kitchen. The second kitchen was turned over to Danny; his tools and herbs brought from the bakery, and he is confined to it. The only way they can communicate is through the confections themselves. There is always at least one confection during a meal that he knows will call up a sweet memory of the two of them—something she can feast upon for a week, and remember.

But this banquet has been leading her step by step forward, as if in a story. Both she and Danny know the purpose of the Lemon Tart too well. She has been reminded of how she failed to act, which must mean that he is prompting her that she will need to act. But in what way?

Perhaps it is poison, she thinks. Perhaps he is telling her that this is the only way to strike against the Duke. A slow-acting poison; something she will recognize, but must pretend to be fine.

But she can't imagine Danny choosing that method, even if she ordered him to. And at this point, she would order him to. She stiffens her spine, watches the nobles eating their own lemon tarts. She has spent a year practicing dissembling. Her courage and her warm smiles will not fail her now. She is ready for whatever comes.

Or perhaps there is something else he is reminding her of. Those small jumps that the pastries have been taking. The Lemon Tart memory skipping ahead, to Danny's disappearance, to her own application at the castle. Those are not part of the original memory. They are linked somehow, just as she saw with the crostini, with the shortbread. Not enough that anyone would notice, because no one understands the subtleties of how the pastries work, not like she and Danny. Were those extra memories there to warn her of something specific?

But maybe that is not it, either. Sometimes she thinks she is going mad. Danny is long gone, and these pastries are normal pastries done by a normal pastry chef, their memories some collective dream that she convinces the nobles to believe in, once a week.

The cheese plate comes and goes while she feels more and more adrift, lost in her own memories, wishful thinking, and nonsense. These banquets will go on for eternity, and she will eat lemon tarts of regret forever, and nothing will change.

For now the after-dinner liqueurs are being passed around, the meal is over, and there has been no dramatic change tonight. She is disappointed; she wants the Duke gone so badly that she almost feels she will run at him herself, with the silver fork. See what damage she can do before they kill her. Danny was always the patient one, the one performing the endless tweaking of recipes in search of the correct formula, the one able to wait until the exact moment. Cooking is all about timing.

Ah, but wait. There is one more plate. Her heart quickens—

But she can tell at a glance it is a chocolate, a dark chocolate-shelled truffle with an amber-colored drop at the top.

The Honey Chocolate of Well-Deserved Pride.

It makes her sick to think of the Duke eating this confection. Who knows what sort of disgusting thing the Duke will find pride in tonight?

She knows, for Danny has served this chocolate to the Duke before, that there is no outside morality imposed upon the choice of memory. Saffron always, invariably, sees one of the times she helped somebody. Danny sees those as well, or he sees moments of creation, breakthroughs of hard work and study.

The Duke saw a moment he cleverly destroyed a family. He told the table about it, in salivating detail, and the quiet bliss the nobles had found in the chocolates evaporated. Why would Danny grant him such?

The extra-large chocolate is set down before Saffron and

she cuts it in two with her silver fork. It is in the last second before she takes her bite that she notices the color of the honey drop on top is a little deeper than usual. Molasses, perhaps, and it is her single clue that this is something different than what she is expecting.

Bitter Chocolate of Agony Observed

She falls, tumbling, faster and faster. It is a moment she has never seen before. She is five, and Rosie is four, and Rosie has been stung by a hornet. In real life she barely remembers this, but she is here now, and Rosie is wailing. She holds up her arm to show Saffron, and Saffron sees the welt. And then—she feels the welt. In seeing the pain of her sister, it triggers her own sense of pain, and her arm stings and swells with it. Rosie runs off to find their mother, and Saffron falls—

She is eleven, and her best friend has taken a header off of the chicken coop. Busted her nose but good. Saffron sees it, and her own face swells in response, painful, aching, broken. She helps her friend home, and at every step she feels the pain of the broken nose. Until the friend is turned over to her mother, and Saffron runs home, the pain dissolving, the memory released—

She is in the bakery, and the enforcer punches Rosie, and Saffron staggers back with the pain of it as they drag Rosie away—

She is at the hanging, and the body falls—

It is last year, and Danny has sliced right through the pad of his thumb with a bread knife. Skin wounds bleed like billy-o, and Saffron carefully stitches it up for him, feeling the pounding of the blood in her own thumb, feeling the piercing tugging of the thread pulling through. Through the roar of the pain she hears Danny musing: I wonder if I could do something with pain.

Why would you want to? says past Saffron.

You wouldn't think a Lemon Tart of Regret would be useful, and yet…. says Danny. There might be something there.

Saffron laughs. Only you would slice open your thumb and wonder how to turn it into a new pastry. Go for it. But leave me out of this one.

Do you know how much I love you? says Danny.

And she is falling away from that memory, falling back to the table, even as her last words echo: I love you too. More than anything….

· · ·

The entire table is looking at her. She has been gone a few minutes longer than usual. Hopefully not so long as to give the game away. Her face, she feels now, is still wincing from the pain of the sliced thumb. She consciously relaxes her jaw, loosens her face, breathes.

She is supposed to entice the Duke to eat this chocolate. And how exactly is she going to do that, with everything she just saw plainly visible on her face to the whole table?

She waves at the servitor to take the other half of her chocolate to the Duke. She does not yet trust herself to speak.

The Duke looks at the half-eaten chocolate, then back at her. "For a moment I thought your husband had decided he was willing to poison you," he says. "But now I see he is merely willing to torture you."

That gives Saffron the thread to walk down. "His skill with confections is the most important thing to him," she says, and she keeps her head high, not minding that her lip trembles. The Duke understands this. He will see himself in Danny.

"So explain to me why I, and my table, should go ahead and try this particular confection," he says. "After seeing its most. . . interesting results."

She looks evenly into his face. There is only one answer that will work with the Duke, and this is truth.

At least, part of the truth.

"You will see pain," she said. "Not your own pain, but another's. A moment of exquisite pain that someone else is suffering."

The Duke's face relaxes, just barely, and he laughs. "No wonder you were so conflicted. My little weaklings." He gestures around to the table. "Go on, then. Eat."

Her heart sinks, watching as one by one the reluctant guests pick up their chocolates, their faces frightened or stoic by turns. If the Duke does not eat his bite quickly, then this is for nothing. The nobles will spill to him everything they felt, and there will be no more chance to do this again, and she and Danny will be strung up for daring to oppose the Traitor King.

The memories for some of them will be long this time. She cannot help that. One lucky woman, younger than the rest, is shaking off the trance already. "I saw my brother break his arm," she says, shuddering, and her hand unconsciously goes to her own arm.

Saffron breathes, willing the woman not to say any more. This is confirmation to the Duke that what she said is true. You see someone else's pain. The chocolate is not poison. His face relaxes a tiny bit more, he is weakening. He wants to try it.

"You can aim for the right memory if you give it a nudge," Saffron says, and this is true in general of their work, if irrelevant in the case of this particular chocolate where you will see everything. "Wouldn't you like to see... what you did to my sister?" Her eyes meet his and she is breathing fast, she can't help it, and he is feasting on every moment of her pain. If this works...

The Duke's eyes never leave hers as he raises the chocolate and places it on his tongue.

. . .

The linked memories keep the Duke under for three entire weeks, writhing in a remembering coma, first on his chair, then moved to his bed, then moved to the dungeon. For three weeks is enough time for someone to find the food-taster's grandfather, and let him out, and for the whole chain of command to be rearranged. The Duke is declared incapacitated and relieved of his regency, and kind Lord Searle takes over in his place.

When the Duke finally does wake, the pain and malnutrition have left him wasted away to nothing. His eyes fall on a glass cake stand placed beside his filthy, flea-infested mattress, on the stones of the dungeon floor. Inside is a single chocolate, identical to the one he was served at his final dinner.

If he were stronger, one might call his laugh the laugh of someone who finally sees a worthy adversary at last.

The chocolate, of course, was made by a baker, a simple baker who refused the honor of being Regent Searle's head pastry chef, and asked only to return home to his two loves: his work and his wife.

The chocolate was placed there by Saffron, who stayed to watch the Duke writhe for twenty minutes before she slipped silently away, knowing full well that that pain will account on her soul; that she will revisit this spot if she ever eats that particular chocolate herself again.

The Duke is never leaving this dungeon. And the only real question is, how does he wish to go?

Trembling hands knock the glass dome to the dungeon floor. It shatters, an echo that remains in the Duke's ears long after the shards have come to rest.

The Duke takes his last bite of food ever on this earth, and remembers, as he falls.

An Agent of Utopia

by Andy Duncan

To the Prince and Tranibors of our good land, and the offices of the Syphogrants below, and all those families thereof, greetings, from your poor servant in far Albion.

Masters and mistresses, I have failed. All that I append is but paint and chalk 'pon that stark fact. Yet I relate my story in hopes it may be instructive, that any future tools of state be fashioned less rudely than myself.

I will begin as I will end, with her.

Had my intent been to await her, to meet her eye as she emerged into the street, I scarcely could have done better; and yet this was happenstance, as so much else proved to be.

I had no expectation of her; I knew not that she was within; she was not my aim. She was wholly a stranger to me. I would laugh at this now, were I the laughing sort, for of course I learned later that even as I stood there with the crawling river to my back, her name was known to me, as the merest footnote to my researches. So much for researches.

In fact, though I had traveled thousands of leagues, from beyond the reach of the mapmaker's art, to reach this guarded stone archway in a gray-walled keep on a filthy esplanade beside the stinking Thames, I had no reason even for pausing, only feet from my goal. I feared not the guards, resplendent in their red tunics; I doubted not my errand. Yet I had stopped and stood a moment, as one does when about to fulfill a role in a grand design. And so when she emerged from shadows into sun, blinking as if surprised, I found myself looking into her eyes, and that has been the difference in my life: between who I was, and who I am.

Her face was—

No, I dare not, I cannot express't.

To her clothing, then, and her hair. That I'll set down. A frame-work may suggest a portrait, an embankment acknowledge a sea.

In our homeland, all free citizens, being alike in station, therefore dress alike as well; but in the lady's island nation, all are positioned somewhere above or below, so their habits likewise must be sorted: by adornment, by tailoring, by fineness of cloth. These signs are designed to be read.

She was plainly a gentlewoman, but simply clad. Around her neck was a single silver carcanet like a moon-sliver. Her bosom was but gently embusked, and not overmuch displayed. Her farthingale was modest in size; some could not be wedged through the south gate of London Bridge, but hers was just wider than her shoulders. Her hair was plaited at either temple, so that twin dark falls bordered her lustrous—

Ah! But stop there. I am grown old enough.

I add only that her eyes were red-rimmed with weeping, and in that moment—whatever my obligations to my homeland, to you who sent me—to dry those tears became my true mission.

A moment only I held her gaze, and how did I merit even that?

Then her manservant just behind, finely attired but sleep-eyed and bristle-jowled, did nudge her toward a carriage. As she passed, I dared not turn my head to watch, lest I not achieve my goal at all.

Rather, I walked forward, into the sweet-smelling space the lady had just vacated, and raised both hands as the warders crossed pikes before me.

"Hold, friends," I said. "The gaoler expects me."

"Ah, does he?" asked the elder warder. "What name does he expect, then?"

"The name of Aliquo," I said, and this truly was the name I had affixed to my letter, for it was not mine but anyone's. From my dun-colored wool cloak, I produced another sealed paper. "My credentials," I said. "For the gaoler only," I quickly added, as the elder warder was making as if to break the seal. He eyed me dolefully, then handed the letter to the younger warder, who in turn barked for a third warder, the youngest yet, who conveyed my letter within—doubtless to a boy still younger, his equipment not yet dropped.

As I waited, we all amused ourselves, myself by standing on tiptoe atop each consecutive cobble from east to west beneath the portcullis, the warders by glaring at me.

I knew, as they did not, that my credentials were excellent, consisting as they did only of my signature on a sheet of paper wrapped about some street debris from home.

Soon I was escorted through the gate, onto a walkway across an enclosed green. Sheep cropped the grass. Ravens barked down from the battlements. Huddled in a junction of pockmarked walls was a timbered, steeply thatched, two-story house. Though dwarfed by the lichen-crusted stone all around, it was larger than any home in Aircastle. Through its front door I was marched, and into a small room filled by an immense bearded man with a broken nose. He sat in a heap behind a spindly writing-desk that belonged in a playroom. Sunlight through the latticed window further broke his face into panes of diamond.

"Leave us," he told my escort, who bowed and exited, closing the door behind. The gaoler stared at me, saying nothing, and I replied in kind. He leaned forward and made a show of studying my shoes, then my breeches and cloak, then face again. His own displayed neither interest nor impression.

"You don't dress like a rich man," he said.

"I am no rich man," I replied.

Without turning his gaze from mine, he placed one hairy finger on the packet I had sent him and slid it across the desktop toward me: refolded, the seal broken.

"A thief, then," he said. "We have other prisons for thieves. My men will show you."

"I am no thief," I replied.

He tilted his head. "A Jew?"

"I am but a visitor, and I seek only an audience."

"That you have achieved," he said. "Our audience being concluded, my men will take you now."

"An audience," I said, "with one of your ... guests."

Without moving, he spat onto the floor and my shoe, as placid as a toad. "And which guest would that be, Sir Jew, Sir Thief?"

I was near him already, the room being so small, and now I stepped closer. Arms at my sides, I leaned across the desk, closing the distance toward the gaoler's motionless, ugly face. I could smell layers of sweat and Southwark dirt, the Scotch egg that had broken his fast, and, all intermixed, the acrid scent of fear, a fear of such long abiding that it marked him, better than any wax-sealed writ of passage, as a resident of this benighted land. When I was close enough for my lips to brush the pig-bristles of his ear, I whispered a single syllable: a lover's plea, a beggar's motto, a word with no counterpart in my native tongue, though one of the commonest words in London, where satisfaction is un-known.

Upon hearing my word, the gaoler jerked as though serpent-bit, but recovered on the instant, so that as I stepped back he assumed once again calm and authority. Only his eyes danced in terror and anticipation.

"Worth my life, Sir Thief, were I caught admitting you to *him.*"

I made no reply. No question had been posed, nor information offered that was new or in any way remarkable. He had but stated an irrelevant fact.

He lifted the packet I had delivered and poured the pebbles into his palm. He studied their sparkle, then let them slide back into the paper. His palm remained in place, cupping the air, and he raised his eyebrows at me, like a scarred and shaggy courtesan.

These English. Every clerk, every driver, every drayman and barrelmaker and ale-pourer has his hand out for coins, and doubtless every gaoler and prince, courtier and headsman, as well. They conceive of no superior system, indeed no alternative, anywhere in this world. And so I freely handed them my trash. Some were as grateful as children, while others betrayed no emotion at all, merely pocketing the payment as their due, a gift of nature like birdshit and rain.

I pulled from my pocket a thumb-sized paving stone. I dropped it into the gaoler's palm, where it reflected the sunlight in a dozen directions. His nostrils flared as he drew in a breath.

"God's mercy," he said.

The English routinely invoke their God when startled, or provoked, or overwhelmed by their own natures. They pray without cease, without thought, without result.

"The ninth hour," he told the stone, "at Traitors' Gate."

. . .

Traitors' Gate was a floating wooden barrier tapping mindlessly in the night tide across a submerged arch, set low in the fort's Thames-side wall. No two public clocks in England quite chime together, but somewhere during the ninth-hour cacophony, the gate swung open without visible human hand, and an empty punt slid from the shadows, tapping to a halt at my feet. I stepped down and in, half expecting the punt to slide from under me and make its return voyage without my assistance. Instead, after a respectful pause, I picked up the pole that lay in the bottom of the boat and did the work myself, nudge by nudge into the shadows, ducking as I glided beneath the arch. The soggy gate creaked shut behind.

Just inside the fortress, the stone marched upward in steep and narrow steps, at the top of which stood, all in red, my hulking friend the gaoler. He was alone. He silently waited as I climbed the slimy stairs to face him, or more precisely to face the teats that strained his tunic. He reached out both ham-sized hands and kneaded my arms, legs and torso. He found neither what he sought nor what he did not seek, and was quickly satisfied. He stooped, with a grunt, and picked up something from the cobbles.

"You're the ratcatcher, if anyone asks," he said. He handed me a long-handled fork and a pendulous sack. "And there's the rats to prove it," he added. "Wait here. When I cough twice, enter behind me, and keep to the right. Follow my taper, but not too close. If I meet anyone, keep back and flatten yourself against the wall like the damp. You might even kill a rat or two, if you've a mind."

I held the heavy fork loose at my side, where I could drop it on the instant if I needed to kill someone, and watched the gaoler lumber into the wall and vanish, through a previously invisible slot perhaps an inch wider than his shoulders. Finally I heard the double cough, fainter and from much farther away than I expected. I slipped into the door-shaped darkness.

We encountered no one, quickly left any trafficked levels of the vast and ancient keep. The dark corridors and archways we passed through and the stairs we climbed were broad and well-made and perhaps once were grand, but time's ravages were not being repaired. In spots we crunched through fallen mortar and stone. Even the rats were elsewhere. The walls were windowless, save for the occasional slitted cross that traded no light for no view.

Finally we passed through a series of large chambers, in the fourth of which the serpent-fire before me guttered as in a draft. My guide stood before an iron-banded oaken door, its single barred window the size of my head. He gestured me close, relieved me of the rat-sticker and sack, and whispered, as urgently as a lover.

"I'll be watching. You leave in a quarter-hour, and whether you walk or I drag you is no concern of mine. Keep your treasonous voices low. Take nothing he offers, leave no marks on his person, and for the love of God, give him no ink or paper; that's powder and shot to the likes of him." He inserted into the lock an iron key fully as long as the rat-sticker. The gears clanked and ground, and he hauled back the door. "Company for you, sir! Oh, Christ, not again. Whyn't he just pull his gentles, like the others do?"

The room was larger than I expected, and more finely appointed. The chairs, tables, washbasin and chamber-pot were old but finely made; the twin windows were grated but high, deep-set and arched; a river breeze stirred faded tapestries that covered the walls with the rose that was the sigil of the ruling house. In the far corner was a makeshift altar, a cross of two bound candlesticks upon an upended stool, and before it, in a pool of shadow, knelt a naked man with a bloody back, who slowly gave himself one, two, three fresh strokes across the shoulders with a knotted rope.

Judging from the fresh wounds amid the scarring, he had been at this for some time.

As I walked forward, the door thudded shut behind. "My good sir," I said.

The kneeling figure paused a few seconds before flogging himself again, and again, and a sixth time, each impact a dull wet smack. As I drew close enough to smell, I saw the shadow on the flagstones was in fact a broad spatter of blood.

The prisoner spoke without turning. "You've made me lose count. Well, no matter. I can start over from One, as must we all, each day." He flexed the rope, as if to resume.

"Good sir, please. My time is short."

His laugh, as he turned, was a joyless bark. "*Your* time?" The engravings I had studied were good likenesses. The Roman features were intact on his blunt, handsome face, but his jawline was hidden by a fresh grey curtain of beard that ill became him. "May I assume, sir, given your evident longing for conversation, that you are not here to murder me?"

"No, indeed."

"Ah," he said. He brought one foot beneath him and stood, slowly but with no evident need for support. "One can imagine worse fates, my good Sir Interruptus, than to be murdered in the act of prayer." Something passed over his eyes then, perhaps only the sting of the wounds as he donned, without flinching, the robe that hung on the bedpost. "Ay, *much* worse. The killers of Thomas Becket, even as they hacked away, did the work of God in making the saint's most heartfelt desire manifest. They delivered him sinless unto his Maker." He glanced at his blood on the floor as he cinched his belt. "I fear for his shrine at Canterbury, and for his relics. In these fell days, it is not only the living who suffer. A good even to you, Master Jenkins!"

After a long pause, the shadow beyond the window in the

door replied, "And a good even to you, sir."

"As for you," the prisoner said, smiling, "we reach an even footing. You impeded my task; I impeded yours. State your business, please, sir, and your name. I have not so many visitors that they grow interchangeable to me."

"I call myself Aliquo," I replied, "and I bring greetings to you, Thomas More, from your old friend Raphael Hythlodaye, and from my homeland of Utopia."

I bowed low before him.

"Please give my Utopian friends my best regards," More said, "and tell them my answer is no."

· · ·

The next afternoon, moments after I stepped from the inn where I had broken my fast, a man planted himself before me on the street, so that I would have to go around him, or stop. I chose to stop.

"You have seen me before, I believe," said the man.

I peered into his bearded face. "I have," I said. "You were outside the Tower yesterday. You were with ... the lady."

"I was," he said, "and I am, and I am here on her account only. I am to bring you to her."

"That is quite impossible," I said. "Who is this lady, who makes such demands of strangers?"

"You are a stranger to her, but not to her father, I believe. Her name is Margaret Roper, born Margaret More." He studied my face. "This changes your resolve, I believe."

"Yes," I said, though I had resolved to accompany him the moment I recognized him, in hopes I might see his mistress again—even if he led me straight to the chopping-block on Tower Hill.

Where he led me, instead, without further speech, was to the city's largest temple, dedicated to the name of a first-century persecutor of the enemies of Rome, who reversed himself to aid those enemies, but remained, throughout his life, in the service of a more perfect, more organized world. A thousand years later, his temple's interior was scarcely less crowded than the streets outside.

At home, upon entering a temple, all men would proceed to the right, all women to the left, and all would maintain their proper places until departing. Here, all was confusion.

"There," said the manservant, stepping aside. "Go to her, and if you speak falsely, then God help you."

Far ahead, across the echoing marble, a line of supplicants, in all modes of clothing, shuffled step by step into an airy chapel, and past a chest-high marble tomb minded by a droning guide. Toward the back of this line was she who had summoned me, she who already had claimed dominion over me with a single glance, though I had yet to realize it.

I went to her.

She watched me approach. She was nearly my height. Her eyes! ... I dare not describe them. She looked into mine, and then, without moving her head or glancing away, she refocused, and looked at me again. I knew in that moment she had seen me more clearly than her father had, than the gaoler had, than anyone had since home. I held my breath, sure she would turn away. Instead she gravely bowed her head, reached for my arm, and guided me into the line at her side. The stooped crone behind her hissed at my insertion, but a steely glance from Madame shushed her.

"Do you speak Latin?" Madame asked me, in that tongue.

"I do, Madame," I replied in kind.

"Do so, in this public place. Here, in this procession, we are pilgrims only, and will draw no attention. You know who I am."

"I do, Madame."

"Have you seen my father?"

"I have, Madame."

"You have an advantage over me, then. How is he? In mind, spirit and body?"

"In mind, keen. In spirit, resigned, but anxious for you. In body, intact, save for the injuries he inflicts himself."

"God inflicts them," she said. "So he told me, when I was a girl, and saw the bloody linens. A man who would keep secrets from his own household should do his own washing. Now tell me who *you* are."

"Only your servant, Madame," I said.

She blew air from the corner of her mouth. "Please. You are no one's servant, least of all mine. Who are you?"

We neared the tomb and the guide, his pockmarked face, his maimed hands. Many in line had some scar, or limp, or hump.

"Call me Aliquo," I said.

"Your position?"

"In this land, only emissary."

"From whom? What business had you with my father?"

Heeding her manservant's warning, I chose the truth.

"I offered to free him," I said, "and to convey him home in triumph."

Her eyes widened. "You are mad. How? Home to Chelsea? Home to me?"

"No, Madame. To my homeland across the sea."

"The impertinence! What name is given this homeland?"

"It is called Utopia. Your father wrote of it."

She laughed aloud, and a score of heads turned our way in shock as the echoes rained down from the arches above. Beside the tomb, without interrupting his recitation, the guide shook his head, placed the stump of a finger to his chin, and blew.

"He wrote of it, indeed!" she said, in a lower voice. "A fairy-story for his friend Erasmus, invented of whole cloth! A series of japes at the follies of the day."

"Is all this a jape?" I asked, with a gesture at the soaring chapel all around. "Is this statue atop the tomb a jape, because he has a silver head, as the king did not in life? Mere representation is not a jape, Madame. Your father represented us, but we are not his invention."

By now we had reached the tomb. It bore a plaque, in Latin:

Henry, the scourge of France, lies in this tomb.
Virtue subdues all things.
A.D. 1422.

"Above, you see good King Henry's funeral achievements," droned the guide, in nasal English, as he studied Madame for signs of outburst. "His battle helmet, sword, shield and saddle. Note the dents in the helmet, through which good King Henry's life was spared, glory be to God. ..."

As she passed, Madame addressed herself to the marble of the tomb. "I have met many scoundrels," she said, "but never one claiming to have stepped from the pages of my father's books. And whom do you claim sent you, on this mad errand? King Utopia the Nineteenth?"

"Our king, Madame ... is not like yours. He is more like the officers of this temple. He has unique responsibilities, yes; he has certain authorities, in certain settings. Yet I was not sent by him, Madame, but by a council of the people."

"An emissary from a headless land. Interesting. But this might explain why, a mere half-day after you stepped ashore at Woolwich, having left your private cabin on the *Lobo Soares*, out of Lisbon, before even buying a meal or engaging rooms, you proceeded not to York Place but to the Tower, and sought an audience not with the king, but with a condemned prisoner. A strange emissary, indeed."

"Madame is well informed."

"Madame is wholly *un*informed," she retorted, "on the one subject of any importance. They keep me from my father, and thus I must make do with the world."

"You call your father condemned," I said, "yet you grieve too soon, surely. He is not yet tried, much less convicted and sentenced."

"That is a truth so strictly and carefully laid as to be a lie," she said, "and one more lie to me, however small, will earn you an enemy beside which our present King Henry would seem a stick-puppet. Do you believe me?"

"I do, Madame. Tell me, the man in the tomb … he is the current king's grandsire?"

She winced. "No relation. After good King Henry died, his widow married a Tudor. And there Katherine lies, as if in life. So they say."

Only if in life she was drawn, shriveled and waxen of complexion, I thought, but said nothing. Where one might have expected an effigy lay instead the body, not even shielded but available to all. Katherine was blessedly clothed, arms folded across her sunken breasts. The one-eyed gentleman in line before me, his absurd rapier hilt stuttering along the pedestal as he walked past, half-burst into tears, bowed and kissed Katherine's face.

"I apologize for my countrymen," said Madame. "They prefer their women venerated and dead. Some attribute miracles to this poor corpse, and seek her elevation by Rome. Humph. 'Twould truly *take* a miracle, now—and our current king has rather discouraged miracles." She had looked almost merry, enjoying my discomfiture at the spectacle before me, but now her face grew taut like Katherine's. She shook her head, and the moment passed. "Tell me, friend Aliquo," she continued. "What becomes of Utopians when they die?"

"Burned to ashes, Madame."

"What, no burial?"

"No room, Madame. Ours is an island nation, at its widest scarcely 200 miles across. We must colonize the mainland as it is."

"And Utopian souls? What becomes of them?"

"They … remain. Invisible, but among us still, seeing and hearing all. They observe, are pleased to be addressed and honored, but they cannot participate."

"Interesting. And have your dead ones traveled with you, here to *our* island nation?"

"I hope not, Madame. This place would be most … distressing to them."

"I know how they feel. My father refused you, of course."

"Yes, Madame. Doubtless you'd have thought him mad, otherwise."

"No. But I know that even locked in that fortress, he is the king's servant and God's, and if it's the will of both that he—that he—" She faltered. "He would have refused you, had you come at the head of a legion. My father is the best man in the kingdom, and how I have prayed he were otherwise."

We had left the chapel and entered the cathedral's main chamber, where the line of supplicants broke apart and flowed into the larger crowd. We walked slowly together toward the west door, where her manservant stood, his gaze intent upon us, poised as if to spring.

"Madame, I have told you what you wanted, and I have only troubled you with my tidings. I am sorry for that. I pray you grant me leave."

"Stay a moment, friend Aliquo. I am told that earlier today, two cut-purses were found dead in a rain-barrel in Woolwich, a quarter-hour after you set foot on the dock. Their necks were broken. Does this news surprise you?"

"No, Madame. Many rough men meet such fates."

"Oh, indeed. Tell me, why did you *not* bring a legion? Why did your headless land send only you, alone?"

"My people have faith in me, Madame."

"I think it's because you didn't need a legion. I think you could have brought my father out of the Tower unscathed and singlehanded, had he but said the word."

"You think me a wizard, Madame."

"No. I think you're a killer, and I have a job for you. I want his head."

"The king's head? Now *you* are talking madness, Madame."

"Henry? Fie! What need would I have for that? Not Henry's head. My father's. More's. You have told me something of your land's customs, regarding the dead. Let me now tell you something of ours. When the headsman on Tower Hill separates my father's pate from his shoulders, his poor skull will be taken to London Bridge, impaled on a pike and mounted atop the Stone Gate, to feed the ravens and remind all Henry's subjects of the fate of traitors. I would spare my father that. I want his head. I want it brought home to his family. I want it brought home to me."

At that moment, I could have turned and walked out of the temple, the city, England, her gaze entire, perhaps even beyond the range of my memory of her. Instead I tarried, forever.

"Do not ask this of me," I said.

"My family is broken," she said. "My friends fear to be seen with me. My servants have multiple employers. My enemies watch me, and all others avert their eyes. I have no one else to ask."

I glanced at he who stood apart, glowering at me. "But your manservant?"

"That is William, my husband," she continued, looking only at me, "and he is a good man, but for this task, Aliquo my killer, my emissary from the land of dreams, I have no need of a good man. I have need of you."

. . .

"Ho, you knaves, you fishwives!" bellowed my leather-lunged boatman as he sculled straight across the paths of three score other vessels, missing each by the width of a coat of paint. Whenever the river ahead seemed passable, he changed course and sought congestion once more.

London may once have been a great city, but I was privileged to see it too late, in its twenty-sixth year of groan beneath the man Henry. And swirling among all was the reek of the Thames. That foul brown stream flows more thickly above its surface, and knows no channel, but floods all the nostrils of the town.

I had struggled on foot onto the city's single bridge, in hopes of achieving a perspective not granted to the scullers below—only to gain a fine view of the tradesmen's booths that line the thoroughfare on both sides. Each swaybacked roof sprouted a thicket of faded standards that snapped overhead like abandoned washing, their tattiness mocking the very memory of festivity.

Finally, midway along the span, I entered a public garde-robe—for which honor I waited a quarter-hour in line, as some men around me gave up and relieved themselves standing— and once inside, I peered through the privy-hole, to obtain a fine round view of the Thames, my only one since setting foot on the bridge. Amid cascades of filth from above, a grimy boy of perhaps ten summers sat, fishing, in a vessel the size of a largish hat.

"Ay, look out there, you swag-bellied antic!"

The boatman's roar returned me to my present sorry state. I was under no obligation to More's daughter, I still told myself; but there was no harm, surely, in seeing whether her task could be quickly discharged, before my departure for home. A Utopian may be forgiven the odd good deed. But I had seen enough already to complicate matters. I had hoped, once having achieved the battlement, to lift down the pike and use it to bridge the gap to the next building; or, failing that, simply to dive over the wall into the water. But the battlement was twice as high as the adjacent roofs—about twelve stories to their six—and as the Stone Gateway perched atop a bridge that was itself eighty feet above the river, any dive from the height would be two hundred feet, and fatal. A head dropped into the river would be lost on the instant, while throwing it onto the adjacent roof would be a desperate move; the twice-unlucky head would roll off, and land who-knew-where.

No, the only feasible way to bring down the head would be to carry it down the stairs and out the front door. And the only feasible way to gain the battlement in the first place was via the same stairs in the reverse direction, up. Neither up nor down looked likely, short of a safe-passage guarantee from Henry himself.

Would Madame recognize her own father's head? Or, more to the point, would she recognize a head *not* her father's? The thought of substituting a more easily recovered head gave me no pride, but that at least would be feasible, and would give the lady some measure of comfort. Yet I did not wish to see her so easily gulled.

I leaned an elbow on the saxboard, let the river lap my thoughts as the Stone Gateway bobbed before me. Assume, then, that the battlement was impregnable. From execution site to point of display, the head must travel more than a mile through the London streets—the teeming, crime-infested, unpredictable streets.

Why, anything could happen. And only fivescore cutpurses, fishwives, alemongers, soldiers and spies would have to be bribed to look the other way.

And once the display was over, well, the head would have to make its way downstairs again, to clear a space on the battlement for the next statesman.

"What do they do with the heads, after?" I asked the boatman.

His grin had gaps into which a mouse could wriggle. "Into Mother Thames they go, milord—and don't they make a pretty splash!"

So I could just wait beneath the bridge until the head was thrown to me. A tempting plan. A Simple plan. A foolish plan. I would gain only an unobstructed view of the thing sinking to the bottom of the river. And this was, of course, the thought with which my musings began; I had rounded the globe and met myself upon return.

"Oh, is that the state of it, y'say?" roared my boatman, in response to the ribald gestures of a passing fisherman. "Ye don't fray me, you cullion! I'll cuff you like Jack of Lent, I will!"

•   •   •

The trial, and the sentence, and the execution, went as Madame had foreseen. One always should trust the natives. By then, I had settled on bribery and substitution. Cross the smallest number of palms with a few paving-stones, replace the head to conceal its absence, and be done.

Utopia borders the land of the savage Zapolets, useful neighbors in that they always are willing, for pay, to perform errands that are too base for Utopians. There is no dishonor in hiring them, as Zapolets are debased already. London, too, has its Zapolets, and so, a week after More's severed head took its place atop the Gateway, I found myself directly beneath, alone in a boat, by midnight, having silently rowed myself into place, awaiting the descent of my package.

Above me, a low whistle—and again.

I crouched in the boat and looked up at the flickering darkness. Sound was magnified beneath the stone arch, and I heard as if in my right ear someone grunting and panting from exertion. In moments, something came into view, swaying in mid-air like a pendulum, ever closer. A heavy sack was being lowered to me.

Just as I reached up and took hold of it, someone on the bridge shrieked. Suddenly the full weight of the sack was in my hands, and I lurched off balance, nearly upset the boat as I sat heavily on the bench amidships. A hot, iron-smelling liquid pelted me from above, and then something plunked into the water beside me. In the torchlight I registered the staring, agape face of the poor Zapolet I had bribed, as his severed head rolled beneath the river's leathery surface. Just before it vanished, I snatched it by the hair, swung it streaming into the floorboards. The act was instinctive; it might come in handy. Then an arrow studded from above into the bench between my thighs. Thus encouraged, I set down the sack and rowed for the far riverbank.

Sounds carry on a river, but I heard none as I reached the stilts of some enterprise built over the water—a tannery, by the smell of it. No voices called after me. I ducked my head and rode the boat into darkness, till it bumped the barrels lashed to the quay. I tied my boat fast, risked a candle, and peeled back the sacking, to see the head for which I had paid a guard's life. I stared into the broad, lumpy face, its cheek triple-scarred long ago, as by a rake.

For my troubles, I now owned two severed heads, neither of them More's.

• • •

In mid-climb, my feet against the outer wall of the Gateway, I clutched the rope, straining to hear and see what was happening on the battlement above. Had my hook been noticed? Apparently not. I heard a murmuring conversation among guards, perhaps three men, but they were distant. I pulled myself up to the edge of the wall.

More than once, in my slow progress up the wall—one window level at a time—I had been tempted to let that damned not-More head that weighted my shoulder-sack, and became only heavier each minute, simply drop into the Thames. But no, a substitute head would be useful. With luck, no one would notice that More was missing.

I waited there, just beneath the battlement, for the guards to go below. Possibly they would not, in which case I would have to kill them all quickly and silently. I determined to give them a quarter-hour, and began to mark my heartbeats, as I looked out over the nightscape of the city. But sooner, all three voices moved into the stairwell, and I clambered up and over.

I counted my way to the More-pike, hoping the heads had not been rearranged since sunset, easily lifted the heavy pole out of its socket and stepped backward, laying it onto the flagstones as silently as I could. The head end necessarily was heavier, and hit first, bouncing once. I walked up the length of the pike. I reached beneath the iron band— grimacing as my fingers dented the head's tarred surface— and tugged.

The head did not budge.

I put both feet against the severed neck, braced myself, and pushed.

The flesh buckled.

I pushed again, and the head slowly began to stutter up the pike.

I was thus occupied when I heard voices ascending the

stairs.

Frantically, I managed to slide the head clear of the pike just as the first guarded crested the roof—facing southward and away from me, thank Mithras. The head fell only an inch or two to the roof. I let the pike down quietly and rolled sideways, putting a low wall between myself and the guards. I hoped they were not in the habit of counting the pikes.

I flung a pebble into the far corner of the rooftop, hoping it would make a noise loud enough to draw their attention. I suppose it landed. If so, it made not a sound.

One guard began walking the battlement toward me. His attention was directed outward, however. Sitting with my back to the inner wall, willing myself to disappear into the shadow, I watched him stroll into view. He stopped, still with his back to me, and stared downstream. A few steps, and he'd all but trip over the pike, and More's head.

I risked a glance behind me. One guard was picking his teeth, another leaning on his elbows, both looking across Southwark.

I stood and crossed silently to my guard, swinging the bag with the not-More head. It clouted the guard at the base of the skull. As he dropped, I kicked him between the shoulder blades, and he toppled over the wall. I dived for cover again. Only someone who was listening for it, as I was, would have noticed the splash, far below.

The two remaining guards continued their murmurous conversation, on the far side of the platform. I rolled into a crouch, looked over the crenellated wall that sheltered the stairs. My new friends were standing just barely within the torchlight of a taper on the far wall. They stood side by side facing the city, overlooking the rooftops that lined the bridge below. I wished them to separate, willed them to do so, but my will failed. There they would stand, barely a man's width between them, until they registered their companion had not rejoined them, whereupon they would seek and, not finding, sound an alarm. How to separate them sooner?

Water, moaned a voice at my feet.

You scarce will believe, ye who read this letter, that I did not spring backward, though my leg muscles spasmed in that desire; my overriding desire, to produce no noise whatsoever, saved me, I think. I only hopped, once, silently landing in place with my feet planted a bit farther apart, to either side of the lump of darkness I knew to be More's head. I did not cry out. I did not breathe. I only stared, stared down at the darkness between my feet, desperate to resolve a shape that, as I stared, began to move, to rock to and fro, like an inverted turtle, until it tipped and rolled to a stop against my left boot, its staring eyes reflecting the moon as its only movable limb, its long adderlike tongue, probed the air. Of course, I thought with insane clarity, that's how he could roll over. Face down, he pushed away the stone floor with his tongue.

Water, More repeated, more loudly this time.

The guards! They would hear!

With no more thought than this—nay, with no thought at all—still on the keen iron edge of terror, and preferring to be anywhere but against that More-head, I stood and strode forward, fast, noiseless, toward the two guards, who marvelously yet had heard nothing, still had their backs to me. In mid-stride, slacking neither my pace nor my direction, I returned the favor, turned my back to them, walked backward until their faces came into view and my shoulder blades thumped against the wall between them.

"Wha?" said the one on my right.

I smashed the heels of both hands into the guards' noses. As they fell backward I fell forward atop them, rode them down to the floor and crushed their faces with all my weight, my arms locked in place like bars. Out of respect, I did not watch. Instead I looked to the stars, found Ophiuchus beset, the writhing serpent-head and serpent-tail to either side, and the scorpion beneath his feet. The guards made scarcely any noise, only a grunt or two and one gurgle, as a gentlewoman's stomach might have done, and yet after they died, as I relaxed and flexed my cramping arms, the tower was quieter still. I saw the guttering taper, the flailing flags, but their sounds did not register. As I re-crossed the platform in search of More (his eyes! his tongue!), I moved in a silence like that of a dream, or of a daze from a clout on the head. I heard only the blood and snot and eyestuff pattering from my hands, which I held away from my body as if to distance myself from what I'd done.

I had killed before—had, indeed, likely killed the first guard, not five minutes earlier—and I have killed since, but my work atop Stone Gate that night, and as I left that accursed tower, was of another order. I blamed More, at the time. Whatever animated his head, I felt, was animating me. My body would ache for a fortnight.

I rounded the wall. More's head was gone. No—it was there, nose wedged into the join of wall and floor. But surely I had left it over there, beside the pike?

Water, said More's head.

Loath as I was to touch the damned thing (abomination! impossibility!), I wanted nothing from life, at that moment, but to heave More over the parapet, give him all the water he could drink, and to cast myself in after him. Perhaps I should have done those things, or one of them.

"Hush!" I said.

When would the next guards come on duty? When would the absence of tramping footfalls overhead be noticed? What signals, what duties, would be missed? I worked quickly. Ignoring More, I freed not-More from his sack, with some effort—I had to shake it, my assault on the first guard having got head and fabric somewhat intermingled—and it finally rolled onto the floor with a deep groan that made me yelp in horror. But 'twas only More again, complaining. I jammed the pike into not-More's neck, working it in deeper than necessary, wishing it were More. I hoisted the pike with effort, the head now even heavier at the weighted end of a pole, and set the hilt into place with the first sense of relief I had felt in an hour. I stepped back, snatched up the taper, and held it high, to check my handiwork. As he flickered into view, not-More sagged sideways, and I was sure for a moment that its savaged flesh would tear away and drop it into the Thames—but it held, and I foolishly continued to hold aloft the light, in a terrible elation, until a voice from below cried:

"Ho! What's the matter up there? Who's light?"

"No matter," I cried, even as I returned the taper to its sconce—too late. I heard behind me, from the outer wall, a scrape like nails against flint.

"What's this?" said the same voice—no longer loudly, but half to himself, in a sort of wonder, yet distinct for all that. I looked at my grappling hook as it twitched, flexed, skittered sideways, like a crab in lantern-light. He who had yanked it bellowed, "Intruder! Ho, the tower! Hoy!"

I snatched up More. He tried to bite me, the wretch, as I shoved him into my sack. To fling the hook over the wall was the work of a moment. With my snarling burden I strode away from my ruined lifeline, to the head of the wooden stairs, saw no one, and sprinted down, three planks at a time.

I found myself in a narrow stone chamber, barely wider than the flight of stairs. Beneath the stairs were casks and crates, but no guard, and no doors either. The only door faced me, a stone archway that framed a landing and a more substantial set of stone steps headed down. I had just reached the top when I heard a roaring and pounding from below, as if a cohort were charging, and torchlight flared and brightened 'gainst the stone wall visible at the curve.

I dropped my More sack—he squeaked as he hit the floor—and looked about, gauged my position. Above, in the open air, I would gain room to work, but so would they. Here was better. I stepped back three paces, positioned myself, and waited, as that fell force rose within me.

The leader of the party gained the stone landing but stopped at sight of me. I wonder what he saw. I stood unarmed, hands and sleeves besmirched with gore, a twitching sack at my feet. I know that I smiled. But what more did he see? Whatever it was, it stopped him like a barred gate, and the others clustered behind. Five total. One axe; three swords; the fifth, a torch in one hand and a rapier in the other. Fine.

"Which of you," I asked, "is the youngest?"

They said nothing, but two in the back glanced at the torchbearer, a beardless boy. They all looked wary, but he, terrified.

Their leader looked me up and down. "Who the fuck are you," he snarled, "to question us?"

I smiled even wider. "I'm the ratcatcher," I said, and sprang.

Afterward, I rose from my work on the floor and faced the one I'd left standing. The boy's quaking face was red with blood not his own. His shaking torch cast shadows that rocked the room. He choked back something, and dropped his weapon with a clang. He kept the torch, though. He was a dark-eyed, lovely boy. I have never been partial to boys.

"Your job," I said, "is to run below, and tell the others."

His jaw worked, his throat pulsed. He made no sound.

"That I am coming," I said.

Still he stood, trembling. The room filled with a smell harsher even than blood, and a puddle spread at the boy's boot.

Christ, cried More, muffled by sacking. *Christ!*

I took one step toward the boy, pursed my lips, and blew air into his face.

With a wail, he leapt into the stairwell, somehow kept his footing, and ran downstairs screaming, just ahead of me. Still he held on to the torch. O dutiful boy! Excellent boy! More clamped beneath one arm, my way lighted by the now much older once-boy, I ran in a downward stone spiral, around and down, around and down, past windows of increasing size, around and down, deeper into the swirling river-stench, until I reached a window just large enough, and vaulted through, knowing not whether I was over roofs or over water but hoping I was low enough. I was over water, and low enough. I plunged beneath the surface and sank, afire with sudden cold but glad of the respite from the smell. As I dropped ever deeper, my cheek was brushed by what may have been a kicking rat, my shoulder bumped by what may have been a spiraling turd, my chest gnawed by what was certainly the struggling head of my lady's father, biting at my heart as we descended into the dark peace below London. Ay, low enough!

• • •

I dared not return to my inn, in my bedraggled state, with my unpredictible charge. Instead I repaired to a haven I had noted earlier—a nearby plague-house, marked by a bundle of straw on a pole extending from an upper window, and a foot-high cross slapped on the door in red paint. Local gossip said the surviving family members had long decamped to the country-side, and the neighbors dared not set foot in the place. From the adjoining rooftop, I gained entrance to the house via its upper storey. I made fast the shutters, risked a single lighted candle, and gnawed the bread, cheese and onion I had stowed there before my assault on the Gateway.

Then, somehow, I slept.

I was awakened by More.

Where is the light?

Be silent, I said. The candle is beside you. Look.

I pulled the bedraggled thing from the sack, set it on the table. His neck looked to have been cut clean, but at an angle. The head listed to the right, as if cocked to hear a confidence. The skin puckered on that side, beneath More's weight.

Where is the light? Ay, am I damned? Am I such a sinner as that?

I cannot say, I told him. But you must be quiet, in any case.

God knows, I am no heretic, said More. *I sought out heretics. I had them killed. They put God's word in the English tongue, in the mouths of fishwives. They rejected the Apostle of Rome. They were protestants to God. I was Lord High Chancellor, but I served the Lord who was higher still. They were as bad as Luther, and Luther is the shit-pool of all shit.*

Were they beheaded, too? I asked.

No, burned, said the head. *Purified in the flames, and delivered shriven unto God. It was all I could do for them, poor misguided devils. I hope soon to clasp their hands, my prodigal brothers. And yet.*

Yes, I asked.

Where is the light?

I turned the head to face the candle, my fingers sinking into his temple as into a soft pear. This made the lace atop the table twist into a gyre; it was intimate with More's neck, now.

More moaned. *Where is the light? Ah, Christ my Savior, what is this place?*

I believe it's an apothecary's, I said. We are upstairs.

But where?

London, I said, mere rods from the Stone Gate. You've not gone far.

Ah, Christ, I smell it! The Thames!

You'll not smell it long. I'll deliver you to your daughter.

My daughter? Where is she? What business have you with my Meg?

She tasked me with an errand, I said. With the delivery of your head.

He emitted a wail, like a cat that is trod upon.

Ah, you wretch! you cullion! you ass-spreading ingle! You are a worse shit even than Luther. Meg wanted only my head, but you! Pestiferous, stew-dwelling, punk-eating maltworm! You have stolen my soul!

Hush, man. I have only your head. I know naught of your soul.

He wailed the louder, though his lips were closed. I seized his screaming skull two-handed, wrenched at the jaw until, with a tearing sound, it opened a space. I snatched up an onion, wedged it into the opening. The wailing continued. I seized the candlestick, toppling the candle, and smashed the head with the base. I saw only that I had opened a savage dent, as the flame toppled into my wine and went out, leaving me in the dark with this howling dead thing. In despair, I cried:

Shut up! For Meg's sake, shut up!

Meg, it said. *Meg.* And said no more.

*   *   *

At the time arranged, I stood 'midst the merrymakers on the Bank, on the lip of a bear-pit, a laden pouch slung over my shoulder. The bear below was a sleepy-looking fellow that lumbered in circles along the earthen wall and swatted at the refuse hurled down. Its bristly collar was all a-point with spikes. These did little to allay the general impression of boredom. The criers' voices were hoarse and listless, even as they insulted one another and their customers.

"Ale and elderberries!"

"Sweet-meats!"

"Flawn!"

"Here, this Florentine you just sold me—it's all fat in the middle!"

"Well, it suits you then! Out of my way. Florentines!"

Likely customers ogled an oyster-wench's ample bosom and, secondarily, the tray of shellfish her teats partially shaded. A gatherer outside a theatre collected admissions, one clank at a time, in a glazed money-box. At his waist swung the hammer that at day's end would smash open the profit—or the head of any coxcomb who tried to relieve him of it.

"Suckets, Milord?"

"No, no," I said, waving her past.

Suckets, said More.

She showed no sign of hearing it, but I stepped away, pressing the pouch closer 'neath my elbow. *Suckets,* More repeated. Through my sleeve and the fabric of the pouch, I felt something bite at my arm.

"Any ginger-bread?" asked another.

"Alas, no, but some lovely marchpane, me sister's known for it. Melts on your tongue, it does."

"Just like your sister!" Much laughter.

"It's yer fat stewed prune I wants in me mouth, love, if it's not been sucked off by now!" Even more laughter. The bear rumbled and farted, and the air above his pit fairly shimmered with the stink.

Damn you! I cannot eat! cried More. *And yet I starve!*

His was louder than any voice in the crowd, and yet no one reacted. So I did not react, either.

"Oh, you squirtings! Weasel-beak! Get on with your saucy selves. Ah, there's a love," said the hag, curseying to a gentlemen whose brocaded back was to me. "I thank you, sir."

"Away with you, then," he said, turning: William Roper, and alone in the crowd. He met my eye and cocked his head toward the street, then turned and walked away. I followed him across the thoroughfare, his feathered cap my guide through the throng. I followed him into an alley and around a stack of barrels. Madame stood there, her face streaked with tears. She twisted a bit of cloth in her fingers.

Meg, said More.

"It's you!" she said, and took a wild-eyed step toward me—but stopped herself, and so did not rush to me, lay hands upon me, embrace me. "So William was right after all," she said, more calmly. "I was sure you were seized, or dead."

Meg! Ah, Meg! Finish me!

To the horrid voice in my pouch, she reacted not at all.

I bowed low. "Alive, and free to serve Madame," I said.

"Free." She looked all about, at an overhang of verminous thatch above, at a puddle of piss below, at the leaden sky and the barrel-staves, at everything but me and my noisy pouch.

I glanced at her husband, who gave me only the smallest shake of his head in reply.

"Here, Madame," I said, and gestured at the pouch that swung heavily at my side, still wailing and moaning.

Drown me in the river, Meg! I am your father! Burn me in a pyre! Meg, you silly bitch, listen! Meg!

Madame made as if to reach for the flap, then snatched back her hand with such haste I heard it slap against the front of her dress.

Looking neither at him nor at me, she said, flatly, "William."

Roper, sparing me a cold glance, stepped forward and lifted a corner of the flap a few inches. The moment he lifted it, More's puling ceased.

"Why, 'tis not him," Roper said.

"You lie, sir," I said.

Roper's face twisted in anger. "Dare you speak so?"

Madame looked faint. "What wrong have I done thee to warrant such cruelty?"

Roper and I spoke at once.

"Madame, please."

"Silence, dog!"

"See for yourself."

"Meg, let's away."

"I will see," she said, silencing us. She lifted the flap, looked in, and breathed, "Oh."

As I watched her face, her features seemed to smooth. The lines of care and middle years filled in like canals. Her eyes shone.

"That such a small vessel," she murmured, "could contain such a great head."

"Meg! You are mistaken, surely."

"No. Look, William. Do you not see the mole upon his cheek, the cleft in his chin? As a girl I tried to hide flower-petals in there."

Her husband looked again.

"He is much diminished," Roper said. "And yet."

"Enough," Madame said, stepping away. "The task is concluded. Take him."

I thought this meant concealed guards, that the moment had come, and I was ready. But she only watched as Roper gently lifted the satchel off my shoulder.

"When they told me he was gone," she said, half to me and half to no one, "my own head went a-rolling. I had no mind, no purpose. I wanted only to be in the street, in the crowds. In my slippers I walked through the muck, seeing nothing, facing no one, until I was brought up short ... by whiteness. White on white, like a heap of saint-souls. I stood, marveling, before a shop-window full of Low Country linen. So, so beautiful. Mother used to say, ah, Meg, it's a shame to bring it home, it ne'er can be so pure again. I suddenly had a single thought: a winding-sheet. Father must be wrapped for burial. Of course. But I had no purse. I had left the house in such grief and such haste, I had come away with nothing. Yet I pointlessly, automatically patted the little sewing-pocket of my skirts, and pulled from that pocket three gold sovereigns, which were not there before. And so I came home no longer mad and pitiable, but sensible, and done with my errand, and this winding-sheet was worth two pounds at the most." She flapped at me the bit of cloth she'd been a-worrying. "Just look at it! Little better than dagswain. Such is the world without my father, friend Aliquo: petty miracles, and petty frauds." She shook her head, seemed to focus on me. "But my household will e'er remember your good offices. I pray you, seek your perfect homeland. I hope it exists—but you'll not find it here." Her eyes ceased to see me. "Ay, not here."

She and her man turned and walked away. "We'll pickle him, I think," I heard her say, "with some elderflower."

As that grim burden swung at Roper's hip, down the alley and into the street, her father's not-voice resumed its wailing.

God damn you. God damn you! God damn you ALL!

I stood at the alley's mouth and watched them grow smaller in the distance, the voice diminishing all the while, until they could not be seen, and More could not be heard.

. . .

Freed of my burden, freed of my hopes, I walked southward,

away from the city, toward the sea. I moved among women and men, but saw no one, heard nothing.

Two days later, I crouched on a quay on the wet lip of England, hidden behind shipping-barrels, and removed from my pouch the not-More head I had carried all that way.

"Farewell, friend Zapolet," I told it, and laid it onto the surface of the water, as gently as More must have laid his firstborn babe, wiggling and shiny, 'pon her coverlet. I watched the Zapolet's staring head roll 'neath the waves, as the babe sinks into the adult. Then it was gone forever.

I re-entered the crowd and found a line to stand in, waiting to book passage. Something tugged at my breeches. A grimy child, of indeterminate sex, holding a tray of sweetmeats.

"Suckets, Milord?"

Suckets, repeated More.

I bellowed and whirled, my feet crushing the scattered sweetmeats as the child fled. I stared into the incredulous faces of strangers jostling to get away from me. Gulls shrieked. The ocean heaved. Ships' colors whipped in the hot wind.

Thou fool, said More. *Whose head do you think I'm in?*

. . .

I write this letter in an English inn, a half-day's walk from London.

I said at the outset that I had failed, and so I believed at the time. Perhaps I will believe that again. In the meantime, with every northward step away from home, questions roil in my head—philosophical questions, such as those chewed after dinner, in the refectories of Aircastle. I will pose them to you.

Was I treated well, or ill, when my lover's husband discovered me in the arms of his wife, and assumed the entire fault was mine?

Was I treated well, or ill, when I, a mere girl, was charged with "forbidden embraces," with "defiling the marriage bed"? When my lover was persuaded to swear untruths against me, to save herself?

Was I treated well, or ill, when I was sentenced to slavery? When I was assured my bondage would be temporary if I was good, and if I denied my nature forevermore? When I was told, moreover, that I was fortunate, that voyagers stepped onto our docks daily in hopes of achieving slavery in Utopia, so preferable to freedom elsewhere?

Was I treated well, or ill, when my natural strength and agility placed me in endless daily training, in service to a citizenry that viewed combat and assassination as tasks fit only for mercenaries and slaves?

Was I treated well, or ill, when I was ordered to rescue a half-mythical figure in a faraway land where even my sex must be denied and disguised, if I am to function at all, and promised my freedom if I succeeded?

It is true, my former fellow citizens, my former masters and mistresses, I did not rescue More. He is dead. He reminds me daily of this fact, and of the impossibility of a better world to come, though in an ever fainter voice, one that I am growing used to. Mostly, now, he speaks a single name.

More is unsaved, and yet, I write you today as a free woman, to say farewell.

Our homeland is not perfect. No homeland is. But all lands can be made more perfect—even this England. And all lands have perfection within them: somewhere, sometime, someone.

Thus ends my story and my service, ye Prince and Tranibors of our good land, ye Syphogrants and families thereof.

May my example be instructive to you and to your assigns. Though I never return to Utopia, never walk again beside the Waterless Stream, I will feel my people with me always, all those stern and rational generations. I will always be your agent, but I serve another, now.

The Substance of My Lives,
The Accidents of Our Births

by José Pablo Iriarte

I seem to make an outcast of myself every time I'm a teenager. Which is fine, I guess. I'll take one good dog and one good friend over being a phony and fitting in.

Alicia points. "There he is, Jamie!"

A couple hundred feet away, our trailer park's newest resident grabs a box from the van parked in front of his single-wide. He's gray-haired and buff, like if The Rock were an old man.

Alicia and I are sprawled on top of a wooden picnic table in the park's rusted old playground.

She frowns, her eyebrows coming together to form a tiny crease above her nose. "I've never known anybody who killed someone before."

I shrug.

"I mean, maybe I have, I guess, but I've never *known* I've known them. Know what I mean?"

"No."

I don't really care about the new guy, even if he did murder someone once. I'm mostly just out here to not have to listen to old Mrs. Francis concern-trolling my mom. When I was a kid who sometimes acted like a boy and sometimes like a girl, it was "just a phase." Now that I'm sixteen, it's "worrying" and "not safe for the younger children" and something we should "talk to a therapist about."

What Mrs. Francis doesn't know is that I remember every life I've lived for nearly four hundred years—not in detail, but like a book I read once and have a few hazy recollections about. In over a dozen lifetimes I can recall, I've been male and female enough times for those words to mean little more to me than a particular shirt—not who I am.

My mom's too polite to tell a neighbor what she can do with her un-asked-for parenting advice. Trailer walls are thin, though, and if I have to hear it too . . . well, Sabal Palms Trailer Park might end up with two murderers living in it.

Next to me, my dog Meetu nudges my hand with her head, asking for more scritches. She's supposed to protect me from people who are as bothered by me as Mrs. Francis is, but would rather use their fists to try and fix me. People like Connor Haines, the biggest asshole in the eleventh grade. But the reality is that Meetu is basically a teddy bear trapped in a pit bull's body.

Alicia shifts on the table. "I can't believe my mom let him rent here." Her mother manages the park, so I guess she could have blocked him if she'd wanted to.

"Even ex-murderers gotta live somewhere."

She gives me her patented don't-be-obtuse combination eyeroll and headshake that I've never seen anybody else quite match. Even when it's directed at me, I can't help but grin.

"There's no such thing as an 'ex-murderer,'" she says. "Once you kill someone, you're a murderer."

I brush my hair out of my face. "He went to jail. He did his time, right? They let him out, so where else is he gonna live?" We've certainly had other people with checkered pasts here.

"They shouldn't have let him out. You take somebody's life, you ought to rot for the rest of yours."

Meetu shoves her giant head under my arm and rests it

on my lap. Guess I'm not going anywhere for a while.

"There's no heaven," Alicia declares. "The Jesus freaks are wrong about that. There's nothing but this. If people realized that, they'd take this life more seriously. You only get one."

She's wrong, but I can't explain to her how I know, so I don't bother trying.

A woman about my mom's age helps the man unpack, while a toddler stumbles around the grassy area in front of the trailer. He seems kind of old to have a little kid, but maybe he's making up for lost time.

"I can't understand what kind of woman would want to live with a killer, much less have a child with him." She peers at the table beneath her and runs a fingernail along a carved heart that's older than we are. "Not that I get wanting to be with *any* man."

The new neighbor comes out for another load. He glances our way, and even at this distance, our eyes lock, and a cold itch runs from the small of my back to the top of my scalp.

I know him. I know him *from before*.

I don't mean I know his soul. I know *him*.

Alicia gives me a little shove, and I realize she's been talking at me for a while.

"Are you okay?"

I blink. Even Meetu looks concerned, her muscular head cocked.

"I'm fine."

"Are you sure?"

I nod, but she doesn't stop staring and looking worried, so I add, "You're right. It's weird living next to a murderer."

Her face softens. "I didn't hurt your feelings, did I? When I said . . . that? I wasn't talking about *you*."

"Nah," I say. "I know you weren't."

The new guy goes back into his trailer.

"What did you say his name was?" I ask.

"Benjamin," she answers softly. After a few quiet seconds, she adds, "You did a really nice job on your nails."

I glance down at my newly red nails. She's painted them for me a couple times before, but this is the first time I've done them myself. I'm grateful that she doesn't qualify the compliment. Doesn't add, *for a guy*. But of course she wouldn't—that's why I—that's why she's my best friend.

• • •

I try to let it go. So I've got a neighbor that I knew in a past life. So he's a convict. The past is dead. Who cares.

Over the next couple days, though, my mind keeps returning to Benjamin. I feel like he was important for some reason. By the middle of the week I admit to myself that I'm not going to move on until I figure out what role he played in my life.

I'm not quite sure how to do that, though. I could ask Alicia for help. She's got a laptop and internet. I don't even have a smartphone. I don't want to open up the can of worms that is my past lives, though, so instead I decide to see what I can find out at the library.

I feed Meetu an early dinner while Mom's still at work, grab my backpack and bus pass, and head out.

Once I'm there, I have to face the fact that I don't have the first idea how to research anything about this guy. I don't even know his full name.

What's B's last name? I text Alicia.

Avery. Why?

What do I say that won't make her ask a thousand questions I don't want to answer? *Just wondering.*

UR totally gonna snoop arent you?

I consider possible deflections. Lying to Alicia feels scuzzy, though, and anyway, I can't think of any lies to tell. *maybe just a little*

I stare at my tiny screen, worried that she's going to offer to join me. After a minute her reply shows up, though, and it's just *haha well lmk what you dig up.*

I sigh, feeling both relieved and ashamed of my relief.

Even with his last name, I struggle. I don't know how to weed out other people named Benjamin, other people named Avery, other murderers. I don't even know when he went to jail—how long is a sentence for murder, anyway?

Finally I stumble across what I'm looking for—a news archive from the 1970s, with a grainy black and white photo of a man that looks a lot younger, but that's definitely him.

A Vietnam War veteran, possibly shell-shocked and deranged since coming back. A crime of passion—the victim, his best friend's wife. A body dug up by the shore of Peace Creek, not far away at all. Then I come across a photo of the formerly happy couple: Larry Dearborn and his wife Jamie.

Janie. Not Jamie. Janie. But the name doesn't matter.

It's me.

$\bullet \quad \bullet \quad \bullet$

It's raining when I stagger out of the library. On the bus ride home I lean my head against the window and watch the torrents sheeting down the glass.

Janie would be in her sixties, if she'd lived. I don't remember ever being old. I always seem to die young. I don't remember dying. End-of-life memories are hazy, same as beginning-of-life memories.

I glance away from the window and notice a little girl staring at me from the seat across the aisle. Her father sits next to her, but he's focused on his phone.

"Are you a boy or a girl?" she asks.

Before I can catch myself, my stock answer comes out. "No."

She tilts her head in confusion.

I imagine how I must look to her. Rain-soaked long hair, purple V-neck, red nails. Hell, she's just a kid. "I'm a little of both," I add.

Her eyes widen. "Oh!"

I turn back toward the window. Now that I've seen the photos and read the articles, bits and pieces of that life are coming back to me.

Benjamin looks like I imagine a murderer would—big and tough and unhappy. The newspaper says he killed me.

So why does that feel wrong?

• • • • •

The next day, school drags on more than usual. I can't focus on Henry James or rational functions when my alleged murderer just moved into the neighborhood.

My walk home is the vulnerable spot in my routine, because Meetu's not with me. So of course that's when Connor Haines ambushes me.

He's sitting on the concrete Sabal Palms sign outside the trailer park. His sycophant friend Eddie stands by his side.

A spike of fear travels through my body.

"What's up, Jimmy," he calls.

I don't bother correcting him. I was "Jimmy" when he met me—it was only four years ago that I decided "Jamie" fit better. More importantly, Connor doesn't care.

I consider my options. I could turn around. Go inside the Steak and Shake one block down and wait him out. Or I could run and try to reach my trailer ahead of him, and hide out there. But if I wanted to hide, my hair would be shorter and my nails wouldn't be red. It may cost me, but I won't start running or hiding now.

They fall in step with me as I pass the sign.

"Where's your dress, Jimmy?" Eddie asks.

Eddie is smaller than I am. I'm not a fighter, though, and he can be brave knowing he's got Connor backing his play.

"It was too ugly for me, so I gave it to Connor's mom."

I barely see Connor's fist before it hits my face. I stagger sideways, tasting blood.

"Why you gotta be such a freak, Jimmy?" Connor asks. "I don't care if you like guys, but why you gotta act like a girl?"

My clothes aren't particularly girlish today: blue jeans and a teal Polo. And I'm neither a gay boy nor a trans girl. Trying to explain is a losing game, though, so I just try to push past.

Eddie's fist lands in my stomach, driving the air out of me.

Connor grabs my arm. "Don't walk away when we're talking to you, Jimmy. It's rude. A real lady would know better."

"What's going on fellas?"

Benjamin's standing a dozen feet away. His arms are crossed, his sleeves barely making it halfway down his bulging biceps.

"We're just talking to our friend," Connor says.

"You've talked enough. Unless you want me to talk too."

Connor releases my arm and backs away. "See you at school tomorrow, Jimmy," he sneers.

"Yeah," Eddie adds. "Don't forget to wear your dress."

I watch them walk away. I understand what they're saying—sooner or later they'll find me when I have nobody to protect me.

"You're bleeding," Benjamin says. "Is your mom home?"

"She's at work."

I probably shouldn't say that to the convicted murderer.

"Why don't you let me help you."

My instinct is to mumble some excuse, but I don't believe he's a murderer. Anyway, I want to know how he fit into my old life and why everybody thought he killed me, so I follow him.

His trailer's one of the first ones, and I see his windows are open. Probably how he noticed Connor and Eddie harassing me.

I've seen dumpier trailers, but not often.

The previous tenant had been a hoarder. When she died in her trailer last year, Alicia and her mom had to clean the place out, and I helped. The place had been full of arts and crafts junk and half-eaten containers of food. We'd worn masks, and no amount of vacuuming and Lysol had made it tolerable inside.

Just goes to show there's always somebody desperate enough to settle for anything.

I don't smell the death smell anymore—what I smell is about a half dozen Plug-Ins, all churning away at once. I guess that's an improvement.

Benjamin and his family don't have much furniture. A worn futon backs up against one wall of the living room, and a rickety table leans awkwardly under the kitchen light. A makeshift bookshelf sags with paperbacks and magazines. I wonder if they're his wife's—girlfriend's?—and then my face heats up. I'm the last person who should be making assumptions.

His toddler lies in a playpen, her thumb in her mouth, snoring gently. I almost comment on him leaving her unsupervised—then I remember that he did it to save my judgmental ass from getting beaten even worse.

"I'll grab some cotton and peroxide. They split your lip."

I follow him to the table and sit on the edge of a vinyl chair. I will myself to keep still as he approaches, dripping cotton in hand. He's a heavy breather, and his thick fingers smell like peanut butter. Lucky I'm not allergic. This time.

My shoulder blades tingle as he sits across from me and begins dabbing at the blood on my face. His fingers are rough but his touch is gentle.

"Some people are just driven to destroy what they don't understand," he says. He gets up and runs a washcloth under the tap. "Hold this against your lip until the bleeding stops."

I feel silly having him take care of me; I can clean a cut for myself. It's not like I haven't been beat up before.

"Anyway," he adds, "I'm Benjamin."

"Yeah," I blurt out. Crap.

He glances up. "You know?"

"Sorry. My best friend's mom manages this place."

"What else do you know?"

I swallow, and it's all the confirmation he needs.

He sighs.

"I'm so sorry," I say. "Please don't tell? She wasn't supposed to say anything to me, but that's the kind of thing that's hard to keep to yourself."

Benjamin just grunts and sweeps up the bloody cotton balls.

"Anyway," I add, "I know you're not guilty."

He raises his eyebrows. "You *what* now?"

I study my fingers. "I can tell things about people."

He snorts.

I shrug. "Anyway, I'm Jamie."

"Short for James?"

"No. Short for Jamie."

"Well, I'm glad to meet you, Jamie."

I press the rag to my lip for a couple minutes, and then, to break the silence, I ask, "Who *did* do it?"

He frowns. "Not something I wanna go into, kid."

"Sorry."

"It's funny though. You remind me of her. You look like you could be her kid. I mean, if she'd ever had one." Another awkward moment passes, and he clears his throat. "So the landlady's kid . . ."

"Yeah?"

"I saw the two of you sitting together. The way you look at her. She your girlfriend?"

"We're just friends."

"Ah."

"We can be friends, you know. You can just be friends with people you're—you can be friends with people without dating them."

"Course you can."

I bite my lip, and flinch when I catch the split part. "Anyway, I don't think she sees me that way."

"Fair enough."

"Right."

"Right." He gets up from the table and begins washing some dishes while I continue putting pressure on my lip.

My mind wanders, trying to stitch together the bits of my last life that I remember. Being a little girl. Going to college. Dropping out to get married.

And I remember my husband turning mean. I remember going to our best man over and over again for advice—the only man Larry trusted me with. I remember deciding that I had to leave. I remember Larry—

Oh God. Larry did it. Larry was the killer.

Benjamin knocks a glass off the counter. He's not paying attention to the glass, though. He's staring at me, and he looks like he's glanced into hell itself.

Did I say that out loud?

"How do you know about him?"

Oops. Apparently I did. "Uh, lucky guess?"

"Right." He takes the rag from my hand, ignoring the still-running water. "Well the bleeding's pretty much stopped now. It was good to meet you. You'd probably best be getting on home now."

He doesn't seem to breathe at all as he talks, and before I fully realize what happens I am escorted out the door.

"You take care, now," he says, once I'm safely outside.

"Thanks, Benjamin," I say, but the door closes before the last syllable leaves my mouth.

Making my way home, I feel like I can hear all my past selves in my head, and they're all furious. That bastard Larry killed me, and he got away with it.

I want to punch something. I want to scream. I want to take my notebook out of my backpack and rip out every sheet of paper and crumple each one up. I want to break some pencils. I want to scream.

I want to cry.

What does it say about me if I was murdered any nobody cared enough to find out who really did it? They just found the handiest fall guy to pin it on and went on with their lives, and Larry Dearborn lived happily ever after.

I run through imaginary confrontations with Larry as I walk up to my trailer. I've never been violent—not in any of the lives I can recall—but right now I wish I had the talent for it.

Meetu wants to play when I open up the door—Meetu always wants to play. "Not now," I say, snapping the leash onto her collar. She understands lots of things, but "Not now" isn't one of them. Still, she's happy enough to go out for her walk.

I daydream about running into Connor and Eddie again while I'm out with Meetu. See how *they* like being threatened. Then I play out the rest of that scenario in my head—Meetu's fifty-eight pounds of love, but all anybody sees when they look at her is a scary, vicious killer dog. I imagine how people would react to *another* story about a pit bull attack. I imagine them calling for her to be destroyed.

No, if I do see those guys I'll keep a tight grip on Meetu's leash, even if they're messing with me, because I don't want to lose her.

That's what pisses me off—me and Janie and the other voices in my head. The Connors and the Larrys of the world always get away with the things they do.

There must be some way to make Larry pay. He doesn't know I exist. Has no idea that I know what he did. That I keep remembering more and more with each step I take.

He'll never see me coming.

"Watch your back, Larry," I murmur. "I'm coming for you."

Meetu thumps my knees with her tail. She doesn't know what I'm talking about, but she's game. She's always game.

● ● ●

"I'm telling you, he didn't do it!"

Alicia snorts. "You know this how? Because he told you?"

We're sitting on her bed. I avoid her eyes by focusing on her posters. Harley Quinn. Black Widow. Imperator Furiosa.

Alicia is into kick-ass women. I'm into her—something I'm better off keeping to myself.

"Listen," I say, "I'm pretty good at reading people. I believe him. He's already done his time, so he has no real reason to lie."

"His reason is to get people like you to trust him. Jesus, you went *into his trailer*?"

"I was bleeding."

"So?"

I pull my legs under me and face her. "Listen, enough people think I'm a flake. That both of us are. I've always had your back. Will you just go with me on this?"

She chews her lip. After a moment she sighs and says, "I'm not sure what you want me to do."

"You've got a computer. Do a search for this Dearborn guy. See what you can find out about him."

"What for?"

I smooth a wrinkle on her bedspread. Any answer would be impossible to explain. "I don't know yet."

She rolls her eyes, but she pulls her laptop off the nightstand and begins clicking around. For several minutes she makes random frustrated sounds as she repeats the same research I already did at the library. I don't want to admit to how much I've already obsessed about this, so I let her retrace my steps.

Finally she chuckles ruefully. "Good luck."

"What?"

"Larry Dearborn is *the* Dearborn in Dearborn Automotive. He owns that huge car lot out on Auburndale Highway. The football stadium at Lakeside High is named after him. He's loaded."

I frown. So he's rich too. Must be nice to literally get away with murder.

"Let's go see him," I say.

She scowls. "And do what?"

"We can pretend one of us is buying a car."

"Look, if you're right, then Dearborn's the dangerous one."

"He was dangerous forty years ago."

She shakes her head.

I try a different tack. "You're always saying you're bored here, surrounded by people who aren't going anywhere. You always say you want to do something adventurous, like join the Air Force. Well fine: let's have an adventure. I'm not saying to confront him or anything. I just want to see my—I just want to see Janie Dearborn's killer with my own eyes. He won't know that we know, so there's no reason to be afraid of him."

She narrows her eyes. Before she can raise an objection, I spit out, "What would Furiosa do?"

She makes a face. "I'm not twelve, Jamie."

"Sorry." I get up from her bed.

"Where are you going?"

"I'll go on my own," I say. "I'll take the bus."

"Don't," she says. "I think you're nuts, but I'll drive."

We tell her mom we're going to the library and breeze out before she can question us. Once on the road, we roll down the windows and turn north on state road seventeen. Alicia's mom's car is a beat up Saturn station wagon that's almost old enough to go to bars. It's sticky and hot and I almost think I should've gone by bus, except then I would have been alone.

The car salesmen close in like hyenas when we park, and immediately lose interest when we step out. I guess without an adult with us, they figure we're not car shopping.

I lead the way into an over-cooled lobby and cast about until I find a receptionist's desk.

"Hi," I say to the lady on the other side. "Is Mr. Dearborn here by any chance?"

She inclines her head. "And you are?"

"We are, uh . . ."

"We go to Lakeside High School," Alicia blurts out. "And, uh, we're on the yearbook staff. And since Mr. Dearborn's been so generous to our school in the past, we were wondering if he maybe wanted to take out a page in this year's edition."

I fight the urge to stare at Alicia. We actually *are* in yearbook, but at Pickens High, not at Lakeside. They've been leaning on us to sell advertising, and the last thing I've wanted to do is cold call on a bunch of local businesses so they can all treat me like some kind of freak. So here we are instead doing it for an entirely different high school.

I have to give her credit, though—that was some quick thinking.

The receptionist's expression softens. "Ah, yes. Well he doesn't really come in to the showroom anymore, but you're right, he might want to sponsor a page." She takes a random salesperson's card from a holder on the counter, turns it over, and writes something on the back. "You can visit him here. I'm sure he'd be thrilled to have visitors from Lakeside."

Something about the way she said that feels off to me, but I can't quite figure it out until twenty minutes later, when Alicia pulls up in front of the address on the card: Landmark Hospice.

"What's a hospice?" Alicia asks. "Isn't that like a cheap hotel for backpackers?"

"No, it's a place where people go to die."

"Oh."

We park for several minutes under the shade of an oak tree, until Alicia asks, "Can we go home now?"

I nod dully, staring out the window.

It's all so unfair. Larry Dearborn killed his wife—killed *me*—and he'll never face judgment for it. Never spend a day in prison. He made a ton of money, lived out his life, and got to the end without any consequences. Even if I found some way to prove he did it, nobody would prosecute him. Why bother?

. . .

The riverbed where the news said my body was discovered is just over a mile away. I take Meetu out after school a couple days later and wander around. Meetu runs back and forth between the creek and me, getting all muddy and messy.

I guess I have this idea that Meetu might dig up some bit of evidence, or I'll remember something about how I died that would lead me to discover something. Meetu's not that kind of dog, though, and anyway the police already went over this area when they found the body. What could I hope to uncover all these decades later?

And what would I do with it if I found it?

I don't actually have any memories of this place. I was probably dead or unconscious before Larry ever brought me here. I do remember more and more about our relationship. How his dark moods got darker and more frequent and how even getting promotions at work only made him happy for a day before he'd brood again. I remember the only place I felt safe being with his buddy Benjamin, and I remember Benjamin convincing me I needed to leave, and helping me pack. I remember taking my suitcases to his house one night, and trying to figure out where to go next.

I remember Larry showing up at Benjamin's place, enraged, and that's about all I remember. He must have killed me there, leaving plenty of evidence pointing at Benjamin.

Benjamin.

In all of my fury at Larry killing me and getting to live out his life without ever paying for his crime, I've hardly given thought to the man who *did* pay for it. I've been so focused on the unfairness of my death that I haven't thought about the unfairness of his life. I can't do anything about Larry, but can I do something for Benjamin?

I call Meetu to me and we start to walk back home. About halfway there Alicia's Saturn shows up and pulls off the road on the grassy shoulder.

"I had a feeling you might have gone out this way. You're obsessed, Jamie. I'm worried about you."

She helps me get Meetu into the back of the station wagon. There's one thing to be said about having a piece of crap car—you don't much care if it gets dirty anymore.

"I think I have an idea for how to clear Benjamin's record," I say.

She doesn't take her eyes off the road. "Oh?"
"Yeah. Can I borrow a dress?"

.   .   .

Alicia doesn't wear dresses much, and her fashion style is not quite what I'm looking for. She is close to my size, though, and she's willing to help, which counts for a lot.

She opens up her laptop and brings up a picture of Janie Dearborn—of her and Larry in better times. She's wearing a long denim skirt and a turtleneck and throwing her head back and laughing. I think I can remember that day.

"Freaky," Alicia murmurs. "She could be your older sister."
"Do you have anything like what she's wearing here?"
"Janie seems like the wholesome type. That's not me."
"Do you have anything that might be kind of close?"
She frowns, then straightens. "Actually, I might."
She heads not for her closet, but for the chest at the foot of her bed. She digs inside and tugs out a balled up wad of cloth.

"It's from my Aunt Hilda," she says, as if that explains everything.

She unrolls the bundle on her bed. It turns out to be a brown dress, with little pink flowers and ivory accents. It's nothing like the outfit in the news photo, but I understand why Alicia picked it. It's equal parts Brady Bunch and Sunday brunch.

"My aunt doesn't really get me," she says.
"No kidding."
"Mom made me wear it last time Aunt Hilda visited and then I dumped it here and haven't thought about it again." She holds the dress up to my shoulders and cocks her head appraisingly.

I quirk my lip. "It's . . . really ugly."

Alicia giggles. "You asked for a dress. You didn't say it had to look *good*."

I go to her bathroom to try it on. I stare at the mirror, trying to form my own opinion before I ask Alicia for hers. I worried that the dress was going to bulge and gap in the wrong places, but it's a modest cut, so it pretty much works.

I remember looking like this before. It looks like *me* in the mirror. Just a different me.

I try to imagine how Connor Haines would react if he ran into me like this. He and Eddie would probably go berserk.

Well fuck them. They don't get a vote.

I pull the door open and cross the hall back into Alicia's room. She paces all the way around me, nodding slowly.

"Now let's add some makeup," she says.

When I've worn makeup before I've always gone for subtle. Some foundation, a touch of eyeliner. Not trying to *look* like I have makeup on. After some false starts, Alicia and I manage to get a more blatantly feminine style that I'm satisfied with.

"Stand up," she says. "Let me see."

I stand by her dresser, suddenly self-conscious.

She raises her eyebrows. "I still hate that dress, but damn, you—" She bites her lip. "You're really pretty."

My neck and face heat at that. I know she doesn't mean . . . I know she's just trying to build me up. It's nice to imagine that she's serious, though.

The moment is interrupted by her mom coming home. When I see her car pulling into the gravel driveway outside, I want to grab my own clothes and hide in her bathroom until the danger passes. But I steel myself and stay right where I am. I've always figured that once you start hiding, it's hard to stop.

Alicia makes eye contact as the front door clicks unlocked, and I wonder if what I'm thinking is plastered all over my face.

"I'm home," her mom calls out, as if that weren't obvious.

A moment later she passes by the open door. "Oh, hey, I didn't realize you had somebody—" She blinks a couple times. "Oh. Hi Jamie. Alicia, can I talk to you?"

Alicia follows her to the master bedroom and closes the door. I pad out to the hallway in my bare feet. Sound carries pretty clearly through the thin walls of a trailer, and I don't have to put my ear up to the door or anything to listen to their conversation, even though her mom is obviously trying to keep it down.

"Honey, I know you like girls and not boys, and I know Jamie's confused about his gender anyway, but I'm not comfortable with a boy playing dress-up in your bedroom."

"Jamie's not confused about a thing," Alicia replies. "And anyway, they changed in the bathroom."

I step back into her room and close the door behind me, because I really don't want to hear the rest. I don't want to hear Alicia reassure her mom that she doesn't think of me "that way." I don't want to hear Alicia's mom—who has always been cool to me—say something I won't be able to forgive.

Some people have a hard time adjusting to me—I get that. I don't care what their process of working things out looks like if in the end they treat me like a person. But I don't want to test that resolution by knowing too much.

Alicia doesn't ask me to leave when she returns; she doesn't talk about the conversation at all. I don't either. I figure everything's fine until somebody tells me otherwise.

"We ought to buy you some shoes to go with that, instead of those flip-flops. I could drive you to the mall in Sebring. It would be fun."

I meet her eyes, wondering where she's coming from. Alicia's not usually into shopping.

"It would," I agree. "But I don't think anybody's going to

be looking at my shoes where I'm going. Some other time?"

She smiles. "Definitely." She raises both her eyebrows. "You gonna tell me what your plan is?"

If I did, I'd have to explain all sorts of things I'm not ready to. I shake my head. "You might try to talk me out of it."

She chews her lip; I can't tell if she's suspicious or hurt.

"I really appreciate your help," I say. When she doesn't reply, I add, "I better get on with this."

She finally meets my eye, and pulls me into a hug. "Be careful, whatever you're planning."

"I will," I say, and then I head out the door.

I should have asked for a ride—it would make things easier than taking public transportation dressed like this. But riding the bus will give me time to get used to the way I'm presenting.

All the way to Larry's street, I keep waiting for somebody to say or do something either because they've clocked me or because they think I *am* a girl. I wish I'd brought my ear buds, so I could block out the sounds of traffic and random conversation going on around me. That's stupid, though— what it would actually do is make me less likely to hear trouble coming.

Somehow I manage both legs of the ride and the transfer between. Everybody's too wrapped up in their own phones and music and worries to bother me.

At the hospice, I use the same story at the front desk that we used at the dealership. They give me directions to his room, and I walk past a courtyard garden, a nurse's station, and about a dozen doors with patient names written next to them in dry-erase ink.

I almost pass the door with Larry's name. I turn abruptly when I spot it, trying to project confidence, like I've been here before. I quietly close the door as I enter, and then blink as my eyes adjust to the darkness inside.

The curtains are drawn to block the low-hanging sun. Apart from the dim light slipping around the edges, the only illumination comes from a flatscreen television on the wall, bathing the room in a blueish glow. Flowers on a dresser cast sinister shadows that move with every flicker of the screen. In the center of the room, an oversized hospital bed dominates the space, undercutting the semblance of ordinary life somebody went through a lot of effort to create with the decor.

Larry lies on the bed, his head lolling to the side. I take in my first sight of him this lifetime. In my memories he is a giant, angry and frightening, out of control. He appears so weak and emaciated here that I can almost pity him—until I think about the lives he's destroyed. Mine. Benjamin's. Who else? Somebody like Larry probably didn't stop at one victim.

I walk up to the edge of the bed. I could take my revenge right now; nobody could stop me. I don't think it would make me feel better, though, and it wouldn't do anything for Benjamin.

And I didn't come here for revenge.

A television remote and call device is tethered to his bedsheet with an alligator clip. I loosen it, turn the sound down, and place it on the floor.

"Larry," I call out.

He makes a gross snot-clearing sound, but doesn't wake up.

"Larry!"

He blinks awake and looks at me, wild-eyed.

"Who the hell are you?" he croaks, scratchy and barely intelligible. More memories come flooding back—Larry suspicious, Larry dismissive, Larry belligerent. I feel this weird contrast, like a double-exposed photograph. Part of me remembers that I'm supposed to be scared when Larry's voice takes this dangerous tone, but he's not scaring anyone anymore.

"You don't remember me Larry? I'm hurt. I remember you."

"I've never met you in my life," he says, and starts patting around where his controller used to be.

"I remember that night at Peace Creek. You, me, and Benjamin. I bet he remembers it too."

He pauses in his search and stares at me again. Shaking his head, he gasps. "You can't be."

I stand over the bed. "Look at me."

"Janie," he whispers. His gaze flicks between me and the edge of his bed. Probably still looking for his call button. Then he reaches for something on the other side of him, which I hadn't noticed before. For a moment I think it's some kind of back up call device and my heart seizes, but it doesn't have a speaker or anything that appears to be a microphone.

I pluck the object out of his reach; it looks like some kind of self-dosing painkiller.

"Nuh uh, Larry. I'm talking to you. It wouldn't be very polite of you to check out."

"You're dead," he croaks.

"That's right. Soon you will be too, and I'll be waiting for you."

He stiffens, and I have this momentary worry that I will inadvertently cause a fatal heart attack or something right here.

I lean in a little closer. "I promise you it won't be pleasant. You let an innocent man pay the price for my death, but there'll be nobody to pay for you in the afterlife."

This seems to spark some fight back into him. "Benjamin wasn't innocent! He betrayed me! He had an affair with you!"

"Benjamin and I never had an affair," I say. I'm pretty sure that's true. "He tried to convince me to go back to you on the day you killed me." That part's definitely not true.

He clutches the bed railing. "What are you talking about?"

"I hitched a ride to the Greyhound station in Winter Haven, because I was afraid of you, Larry. Then I had second thoughts, so I called Benjamin from a payphone. He told me you were a good man, that you were just going through a hard time. He told me I should give you another chance, and he drove all the way out there to bring me back."

Larry sinks back in the bed and his face seems to cloud over.

"Listen to me!" I command. Then I remember that there are all sorts of nurses and other patients around, and lower my voice. "He wasn't taking me away from you. He was bringing me back."

Larry moans, his expression stricken.

"He was your friend right up until the end, and you took his life for it, as surely as you took mine. He deserved better Larry. So did I."

He grips my wrist; his skin is soft as tissue paper, but his grip is hard and a little painful. "You look so beautiful, Janie. Please don't leave me again!"

"I can't stay. My time is past, and you can't give me back what you took from me." I glare, and he tries to edge back from me. "But you can give Benjamin back some of what you took from him. You can talk to the police and recant. Tell them Benjamin didn't kill me. Tell them, Larry, or you'll see me every night in hell. I'll make you sorry. Believe me."

He raises a hand in front of his face. "Stop! I'll tell them! Please Janie!"

I take the phone from the bedside table and dial. As soon as I navigate my way to a human being, I pass the handset over.

"Don't let me down," I say, "I'm watching you."

He's sobbing as I give it to him, but he's coherent enough once he starts talking. When he does, I make my way from the room before anybody can show up and start asking me awkward questions.

• • •

I'm walking Meetu a week later when I pass Benjamin out in front of his trailer with his little girl, planting flowers, of all things. He waves, and I wave back before realizing he's actually calling me over.

"Damnedest thing happened," he says, getting up and brushing his hands on his jeans. "I got a call from my parole officer today. Larry Dearborn recanted. One of those death-bed confession things. They say that's how a lot of false convictions are overturned."

I do my best to feign surprise. "That's terrific!"

Meetu's tail thumps like Benjamin's a long lost friend.

"Yeah," he says. He pets Meetu, but his eyes stay on me. Looking *hard,* like he's trying to peer *into* me.

I'm not sure what to do, so I just shrug and say, "I'm glad you're finally getting some justice." The words feel stupid as they leave my mouth. He already served the sentence for this crime, and nothing can give that back to him.

As if he's read my mind, Benjamin says, "It'll make it easier to find work. Lot of people wouldn't look beyond that one line on a job application, before. Once people get a word for you—like *convict*—they think that word is all there is to know."

I nod.

His little girl makes mud pies in the dirt, and I think about how clearing her father's name will affect her future.

"I could watch her for you," I blurt out. "While you look for work." My face heats up. He may treat me like a person, but that doesn't mean he wants me watching his kid.

"That would be great."

I scratch Meetu, trying to act like it's no big deal.

"So." He nods toward Alicia's trailer. "You gonna ask that girl out? Don't tell me you're not interested."

"I'm . . . not *un*interested." I take a slow breath. "I guess I'm afraid."

"Afraid she sees you different from how you see yourself."

I sag. "Yes."

"I hear you," he says. "But if you don't take a chance on somebody disappointing you, you never give them a chance to surprise you either."

When I don't respond, he adds, "Will you stop being her friend if she says no?"

I shake my head.

"Then there's no sense wanting something and not at least trying."

I glance at the trailer. At the rainbow blinds that mark her bedroom window. "Maybe I will."

He claps a hand on my shoulder. "Good luck."

It feels more like a command than anything else, and I take a couple automatic steps toward her trailer. By the time my brain figures out what my feet have done, it seems more awkward to stop than to keep going.

Anyway, Benjamin's right. He sees right through me, the same way I know the real him.

The same way Alicia has always seen the real me, I realize. My pace picks up a bit, and Meetu responds by bounding forward, dragging me along, like everybody's figured out my destination before me.

She comes to the door as soon as I knock. "Hey," she says.

"You doing anything?"

She shrugs. "Watching TV."

"Wanna come for a walk?"

"Sure," she says, stepping out onto the deck. "Did something happen? Is something wrong?"

"Nope," I say, leading her down the steps. "Nothing's

wrong at all."

We head down the street, quiet, like we don't need to babble to fill the space between us. To anybody watching us, we probably look like we're already a couple. Maybe by the time we come back, we will be. Maybe we won't.

Either way, we'll be okay.

The Rule of Three

by Lawrence M. Schoen

Popular culture failed to prepare me for first contact. Countless starships bristling with canon and rail gun turrets did not fill the skies. The aliens didn't flood our television and radio bands with messages of conquest or world peace or miracle cures. They didn't present themselves to the United Nations or to any government leaders. None of that. I was sitting in my condo in a suburb of Washington, D.C. when my mother phoned me from California. It was a Sunday after-noon. I'd just ordered a pizza and I'd planned to watch the big game on my new television. But my mother was on the phone. She'd just had a call from her own mother in her tiny mountain village back in China.

An alien had landed.

I charged the plane ticket to my credit card and was on a plane to Beijing two hours later. I didn't watch the big game and I never got to eat my pizza.

*   *   *

My father is an American who, fresh out of university, traveled to China, specifically Guizhou Province, to teach English. My mother was one of his students, a member of an ethnic minority known as the Miao people, who had left her tiny rural village on a scholarship as part of a poverty abatement program. They fell in love, moved back to the United States, and I was born. My maternal grandmother still lives in China, much as her ancestors did. She manages just fine without indoor plumbing or electricity. She's never owned a computer or a cell phone or a television. She raised her daughter, my mother, in a house that clung to the side of a steep mountainside half a kilometer from the same river where, according to a third-hand report from her much younger albeit blind neighbor who did own a phone and had actually placed the call to my mother, a "funny-looking fellow fell from the sky in a giant pearl and was teaching the village's children odd things."

I grew up a child of two worlds, which led me to work for the US state department. Which is probably why my mother called me.

The US government didn't know about any alien. Nor, as best as I could tell with a few oblique inquiries of my counterparts in Beijing, did the Chinese government. The only ones who knew that an alien was visiting Earth were my maternal grandmother, her blind neighbor, and no more than a dozen or so villagers and their barefoot children.

My mother had called me at noon. She passed along surprisingly good video shot by a local child on the blind neighbor's cell phone. I could hear the kid's laughing commentary as he panned back and forth capturing some trees along the riverbank before moving on to show the water and what looked like an enormous pearl floating there. The trees provided perspective. The pearl had to be at least two stories tall. It looked like nothing on Earth, and certainly nothing that had any business being in my grandmother's backward village. Except that's where it was. Not the place where an alien visitor, or an alien invader, would set down. There was nothing significant there, nothing of value, just a handful of people who—a lone cell phone notwithstanding—

had never joined the modern world. Nothing but my grand-mother.

In hindsight, maybe I should have passed the video on to my boss, turned the whole matter over to the state department. Probably. Except that thought didn't occur to me until *after* my plane had taken off and I was on my way. Instead, some dumb ass heroic notion had sent me racing off to save my grandmother from some science fiction nightmare.

.   .   .

Eighteen hours later, I arrived in Beijing feeling like I was dying. I'd used an American carrier that had opted to serve prepackaged Chinese food including at least one packet that had sat on the tarmac too long and spoiled. An hour into the flight and I was ill, very ill. I've never been sicker. I spent most of my flying time locked in an airplane lavatory as the world's worst case of food poisoning purged everything out of my body. I only managed to get back to my seat in time for landing. I wanted to die, but I had to get to my grandmother. With the help of the airline's customer service and endless apologies for the food poisoning, I transferred to a domestic flight leaving for Guizhou four hours later. I'd been upgraded to first class with the all the amenities, but couldn't bear the thought of eating or drinking anything. Three hours later, just after 1 a.m. local time, I stopped to pick up my rental car. There was a message from Mrs. Liu, my grandmother's blind neighbor, letting me know my mother had called ahead. My grandmother was expecting me and would have dinner waiting, no matter how late I arrived. The thought would have made me ill, but I had nothing left in my stomach. I hadn't even touched the stash of chocolate chip granola bars I'd brought for energy along the walk and I knew I wouldn't. I drove for three more hours to get as close as I could to the remote village where my grandmother lived. I hadn't slept on either plane; I'd crossed twelve time zones and been awake for about thirty hours, and still had several hours of hiking along a starlit goat trail.

Near the end, the sun was just starting to climb above the mountains, chasing the darkness from the narrow valley. The long walk in the dark had made me feel better. Not healthy, mind you, but not like I wanted to die. As I walked up the path to my grandmother's house I caught the scent of her sour fish soup and I thought it the most welcome aroma in the world. No sooner had my dear sweet grandmother seen me approaching her door then she ushered me in and set a bowl in front of me. I ate two servings, and with every taste of pickled chili, cabbage, tomato, and local fish I felt myself restored a bit more. I'd come home.

When I pushed back from the table, sated and feeling like a human being again, my grandmother said, "You look terrible. All that big city living is bad for you. You should eat real food."

"Yes, grandmother," I said. "Thank you for the soup. It was wonderful."

That made her smile. She squeezed my hand. "Do not try to charm me, boy. You didn't come so far just because you missed my cooking. You came because of the funny man, didn't you?"

Before I could ask her about the "funny man," she stood up and stepped through a hanging curtain that divided the space. Dutifully, I followed. Her entire house was one small room, smaller than my bedroom back home. One side was kitchen and workspace with a long table and a massive storage chest, the other her modest living area with her bed, a shelf, and a small lamp. There was no bathroom; all of that business took place outside. In one corner of the living area, she'd set up a cot for me, piled high with cloth blankets decorated with intricate designs of white and deepest blue.

"Sleep now. Travel makes us wise in time, but first it makes us stupid. Sleep off the stupid. We'll talk when you're rested."

I was born in China, but I grew up in the west. I graduated from Stanford University in California with a bachelor's in experimental psychology and earned a law degree at Harvard. I've studied under brilliant professors and met some of the smartest people in the world. None of them was ever wiser than my grandmother. I went to sleep.

. . .

Blame the food poisoning. Blame the jet lag. Blame both, if you like, but I slept about twenty hours. That's only an estimate because my phone had run out its battery while I slept and my grandmother had no need of clocks. It was still dark, but a faint light came from the other side of the wall hanging. I pulled it aside and found my grandmother tending to a large pot of fermenting leaves. She was making indigo. It didn't matter that more than ninety percent of the world had switched over to synthetic, mass-produced indigo decades earlier. This was the way she'd learned to do it seventy years ago, as her family had always done it going back for centuries since they'd first come to this valley. And to hear her tell it, they'd done it that same way even before then.

Saying nothing, I moved to the kitchen and peered into her cupboards until I found what I needed to brew us both tea. I filled two cups and crossed the few steps to her workspace. She paused to accept her cup, sip, and savor the tea for a moment, then returned to making indigo. I drank my tea and waited. Back home, I'd have been impatient. I'd have seen waiting for this old woman to be overindulgent and a waste of my time. But that was half a world away, a different culture, and arguably a different time. This was my grand-mother's world. Simply being there somehow allowed all of the rush in me to drain away. I didn't worry or fidget. I spent the time studying her face as she worked, the myriad lines and wrinkles in her skin as the years shrunk in upon her, the bright light that still burned in her eyes, the barest tip of her tongue peeking out between her lips as she concentrated on her task.

In time she set aside the pot of leaves, smacked her lips, and picked up her tea. "You have questions," she said. "You are the most inquisitive boy I have ever known. Ask them."

"Why do you call him the funny man?"

She snorted, almost spilling her cup. "Because he is funny. Don't ask stupid questions."

"People can be funny in many different ways. I wasn't there to see, so how was he funny?"

"Well, for one thing, he was naked."

"That's odd," I said, "But I wouldn't have called that funny."

"That's not the funny part. But if he'd worn clothes I wouldn't have seen it."

"Seen what?"

"He didn't have a penis," she said.

I must have blushed because she added, "I thought living in America made you more worldly. Anyway, maybe 'man' isn't the best way to describe him, but he didn't have the curves of a woman. So, yes, I thought that was funny."

"Mrs. Liu told Mother that you said the man fell from the sky in a pearl."

"That's right."

My grandmother had always been very literal. "How could a man, even a funny man, fit inside a pearl?"

"Oh, well, it was a very large pearl, larger than this house. I know you must have seen the pictures Mrs. Liu sent."

"And you're sure it wasn't an airplane or a helicopter?"

"I told you, it was a pearl, glossy and slightly off-white. It couldn't have been a plane or a helicopter. It didn't make any noise. Not a sound."

"How did you happen to see it?"

"I was on my way down to the river to carry water back. It crossed the sky and then fell silently into the river. I saw it. I kept on to the water's edge and by then the funny man had waded to the bank and was teaching the children."

"What children?"

"Some of the village children help me carry water back up here. They wait for me down there with their own buckets. But they'd abandoned their buckets and instead gathered around the funny man in the tall grass. He was talking to them, linking his fingers in theirs. He did this with several of them in turn, just for a few moments. Then they'd both laugh and the child would start plucking up blades of grass, causing them to light up and float up and away."

"What do you mean 'light up and float away'?"

She scowled. "It was just what I said. I didn't say it made sense."

"Then what happened?"

"I called to the children to stop goofing off and come help me with the water. They did, and the funny man just looked at me. But I had to get back to my dye work and turned to come back up the mountain. But I thought it was important, so later in the day when I went to visit Mrs. Liu I told her about it—"

"And she phoned Mother, who phoned me," I said.

She scowled again. "You interrupted me. You don't come into my house and interrupt me. Ever."

"I'm sorry, Grandmother," I said. And I was.

• • •

I retraced my steps partway down the dirt path I'd taken earlier, turning right at a branch point I'd missed on the way up. The left-hand route would eventually lead back to where I'd parked my rental car; the path I now walked took me around to the river. The water came into view while I was still high above it. There, sitting a third submerged in the current, just as my grandmother had described it, floated an immense two-story pearl. It gleamed rather than glistened. Looking closer I realized that the water did not go around it but rather appeared to flow through it, as if the massive pearl wasn't there at all, just a bizarre holograph in this place that saw so little technology.

The path turned, pulling the river from my view. I continued my descent and heard peals of laughter, high-pitched and innocent. Soon, the path curved again and I arrived at a small sward that continued on a short distance and ended at the shore. I could see the pearl again, closer and even larger than before, but I ignored it. Sitting in the tall grass, giggling and carrying on were seven children ranging from three to eight years of age. Seated in their midst was my grandmother's funny man. He appeared naked and pale, almost the same shade as the giant pearl in the water behind him but without the luster. An alien.

The children ignored me. The three oldest seemed to be plying the alien with pieces of fruit and what looked like an earthen jar of warm beer. The rest were engaged in some game that involved plucking blades of grass, breathing upon them, and tossing them into the air where the wind carried them up and away. The blades of grass seemed to catch the light as they rose, sparkling. Except, there was no wind, and this portion of the valley was still in shadow. The alien rose, tousled the heads of several of the children, took a swig from the clay jar before, and stepped toward me. Now that it was standing, I could confirm that other detail my grandmother had shared. Its overall body shape was masculine, long and lean like a swimmer. The junction where its legs joined its torso was smooth and sexless. No bellybutton either, as it happens.

"Part of you is dark with unlife," it said. "I can barely see you."

It took me a moment to process the words. I don't know, maybe I was expecting English or Mandarin. Instead, it had spoken in the same language of the Miao people that my grandmother had grown up speaking. The language of this valley, of the children who had stopped laughing and were watching us intently. The language I had learned from my mother as a child and studied as an adult from a university professor who, with western arrogance, had called it Hmong. I understood all the words, but they didn't fit together meaningfully.

I turned my gaze to the children, paying attention this time, focusing on the impossibility my mind had rejected at first glance. The blades of grass they plucked and cast away, they actually glowed. They actually floated.

"What are the children doing?" I asked.

The alien smiled. "They are altering the grass. A simple trick I taught them in exchange for teaching me their language."

"How did you do this? And what exactly are they doing to the grass?"

It frowned. "I am sorry. These are worthy questions, but I lack the concepts to form them properly in your words. They are only children. I had hoped they might in time bring me to one of their parents, or bring an adult to me. Someone who could teach me more of your language."

This was the opening. If not actually first contact, then first significant contact. "I'm an adult. Can I teach you?"

The alien sighed. "Not yet. Perhaps never. As I said, part

of you is dark with unlife."

"What is unlife?" I asked. Then added, "Which part?"

Instead of answering, the alien knelt alongside the oldest child, a boy, offering its hand, palm outward and fingers spread wide. The boy met it with his own and they interlaced their fingers. Both closed their eyes and leaned into the other until their foreheads touched. Only a moment passed. Both smiled, released the other's fingers, and the alien stood and faced me again.

"Your clothing. Your shoes. And . . . something else, in your . . . pocket? Yes, in your pocket."

I reached into my pants and pulled out my useless smartphone.

"That, yes. Dark with unlife."

"Of course it's not alive. It's a phone."

"You misunderstand. Not not alive. Unlife."

"And my clothes?" I asked.

"More of the same. You are dim, difficult to perceive, and the clothes make it harder still. These children are bright."

I looked down at my clothes. I'd worn top-of-the line cross-trainers because I knew the dirt paths on my grandmother's mountain would have ruined my normal dress shoes. My slacks were khakis, polyester with a permanent crease. My shirt was a cotton/polyester blend, pale blue, long-sleeved, buttoned down the front, brass stays keeping the collar flat. I was the poster boy for the US State Department's diversity program. In contrast, the children were dressed in simple, homespun shorts tied off with handmade rope. They wore shirts or open vests of the same material. Most of them were barefoot but a couple had sandals, crafted from the same hemp as the belts.

"I'm sorry," I told it. "I don't understand. They're just clothes."

"It is the Rule of Three," it replied.

I shook my head.

"Your shirt. Did you make it?"

"Make it?"

"Did you weave it yourself?"

"No. I . . ."

"Did the individual who wove it also harvest the plants from which it was made?"

"I'm fairly certain they did not."

"And was that person the same as the one who planted and tended those plants?"

"What's your point?" I asked. "Probably dozens, even hundreds, of different people were involved in the manufacture of my shirt. The textile industry is broad and far-reaching. Especially when you factor in distribution and sales."

The alien frowned. "I do not know many of those words. But consider the children's clothing. Describe their origins. Did they make them?"

"Their parents probably did. Or they bartered with a neighbor for them, either finished goods or the materials to make them."

It nodded at me and smiled. "If I make a thing, I am one and the thing is full of the life that I gave it. If I pass that thing to you, you are two, and the thing still feels its connection to me and so retains that life. If you give the thing to another, that person is three. The thing still holds the link to me, my life still resonates within it. The distance does not matter, but the number does. Three is the limit. Pass the thing I made on to a fourth person and it can no longer detect me. The connection is broken. Unlife rushes in to fill the void. As a result it cannot be easily perceived. It is dark, inert."

I swallowed. "You're describing virtually all manufactured goods. Everywhere."

"Not everywhere, but yes, much of your world is dark, roiling with unlife. I'd feared finding any people at all. My time on your world is very brief, but I needed to speak with someone I could perceive. This valley has only a few specks of the dark. I came here and found these children. They brim with life. But not you, you appear dark to me."

Inspiration struck and I began unbuttoning my shirt. The children giggled when I pulled it off and cast it aside. "Better?"

The alien smiled. "Much. You remain dim, but the dark does not cover you as it did before."

I unlaced my shoes, removed them and my socks. I didn't much care for children, certainly I had no desire to produce any of my own. But these were here and I'd learned to work with the tools at hand. I beckoned to one of the older children and bartered three promised granola bars for his vest which I wrapped into a crude kilt. Next I took off my pants and underwear, removed my fancy watch and my college ring. I left them all in a pile and stepped closer to the alien.

"And now?"

"Now I see you more clearly. You are still dim, your body darkened by unlife it has absorbed, but with each moment you improve."

"Absorbed?" I thought of the last meal I'd had before leaving D.C., a burger grabbed at the airport moments before boarding my flight. Prepackaged beef patty, shipped frozen from some warehouse, stamped out on an assembly line probably hundreds of miles away. The same for the bun, the slice of processed cheese, the fries guaranteed grown from Idaho potatoes halfway across the country. How many hands had touched them, from cow and farm to the moment I ate them? Almost everything I'd eaten as an adult failed the alien's Rule of Three. The same would be largely true of anyone living in any city in the world. The food that sustained them, that became their muscle and bone, that gave them life, all of that was unlife to the alien. Was that what it meant when it said it feared finding any people? Were the vast billions of the world dark to it? And if so, how was I only dim?

My head spun, and only part of it was the strange explanation of the alien. Only part was meeting an alien. I was also light-headed from jet lag and a need for more sleep and a mostly empty belly despite the glory of my grandmother's soup and . . . the soup. Was that why the alien found me growing less dim? Had the food poisoning purge from my plane flight also rid my body of some of the effects of food that didn't pass the Rule of Three? Did that apply to everything I put in or on my body? Not just food but all of my vitamins and supplements, any medicine I'd ever taken, aftershave and cologne. The particulars didn't matter. Only the Rule of Three. "Right," I said. "Absorbed. Got it."

*   *   *

By some unspoken agreement all of the children got up to go. Each held a bit of light green fabric they'd somehow woven out of grass. They passed these to two of the older boys who caused the individual pieces to come together in seconds. The one who had loaned me his vest stepped up to me and presented a pair of faintly glowing shorts. I turned my back as I slid them up my legs and removed my makeshift loincloth. Then, waving goodbye and shyly saying farewell they ran off, whether to continue their play elsewhere or head to their respective homes I couldn't say.

My shorts gleamed, a soft pulsating of light that beat in time to its own rhythm, faster than my heart's. They felt . . . light.

"You will not fly away," said the alien. "I did not teach them that."

"But you could have?"

"Perhaps. I do not know the limitations of what they, or you, can learn. But it is likely."

"What did you teach them?"

"Only external workings. To speak to the grass. To persuade it to change its nature."

It was one thing to be standing around chatting with an alien, but something quite different to abandon all scientific rigor. Still . . . , "Grass can talk?"

It smiled. "No, not as we do. But all living things contain information. They know themselves and communicate that knowledge internally. May I show you?"

It closed the distance between us and offered me one of its hands, fingers spread. I hadn't noticed before, but its little finger was actually a second thumb. I raised my own hand, lacing my fingers through with its five digits. There was a tingling sensation. Time stopped. There was a feeling I can only describe as what a cup must feel when it is full of tea, drunk from, then filled again. Then my hand was free and the alien took a step back. In that moment it stopped being just an alien. It had a name. My mind held the idea of speech sounds that I couldn't pronounce, sounds that didn't exist in English or Chinese or any language on Earth. A single syllable that came close to sounding like Foom, a Miao name that meant "bless."

"Ah, so much better," it said. "Not surprising, you have vocabulary and concepts the children lacked. To resume, no, grass does not speak. That is but a metaphor. Rather, I taught the children how to coax the grass to alter the substance of its own genetic code to achieve several specific effects."

"Like glowing?"

"Utilizing some of its stored energy to self-illuminate, yes."

"And the floating?"

"Mmm, harder to explain. You do not have the science for this, your approach to technology is all dark."

"What do you know of our tech?"

"Only what I gleaned in our brief melding. The core of it, what you call hypothesis testing, we share that, but your focus is all external, and most everything you learn you apply to endeavors that violate the Rule of Three."

"Which makes them dark? And, part of unlife?"

Foom nodded again. "Yes, you understand perfectly."

. . .

My mind reeled as the implications dropped into place, one by one. From the moment of my mother's phone call, through a day's worth of air travel, amidst the puking and shitting of food poisoning, driving and hiking to reach a tiny village of people who live as their ancestors did a thousand years ago, through all of that I hadn't dared ask myself why I had come. I wasn't representing the US State Department; maybe they'd have sent me as part of a team because of my connections and language ability, but maybe not. I certainly wasn't here at the behest of the Chinese government. I hadn't come so I could be the first westerner to meet an alien—that was crazy, dangerous, and meaningless. Looking back, I'd like to think that at some unconscious level, a glimpse of Mrs. Liu's video was all I needed to know that Foom represented the future, that it had arrived essentially at my grandmother's doorstep, firmly rooted in the past. I'd come to be a bridge, and in that moment, having the alien confirm my understanding, I knew the world was screwed.

There was no falling back on the classic trope of taking Foom to meet with world leaders. It wouldn't be able to perceive them. Whether it was foie gras or prime rib, a fast-food cheeseburger or a cup of insta-noodles, antibiotics or cholesterol-lowering meds, there wasn't a president or king or diplomat on the planet that wouldn't appear dark to the alien. And even if they deliberately purged themselves as I had unwittingly done, if they ate my grandmother's soup or dined on fish caught and cooked by their own hand, still the things they placed the most value on, computers and air conditioning and cars and smartphones and hospitals and organ transplants and electrical grids and highway infrastructure and missile defense systems, all the things we'd accomplished as we moved from the agrarian world through the Industrial Age, past the Atomic Age and into the current Information Age, all of it was dark. Unlife.

While these thoughts poured through my brain, Foom stood still as a statue. It didn't breathe. Had it been breathing before?

"Your vocabulary improved after we . . . touched," I said.

"We shared," it replied. "I acquired more of your language, more sophisticated concepts, the patterns of your cognitive processes and decision making heuristics. I have a much fuller comprehension of humanity as a result. Thank you."

"You said 'share.' What did I gain in return?"

"Insight." It smiled, lips parting wide enough to show me that it didn't have teeth. "Your previous world view was built upon numerous philosophies you believe to be universally true. I have shown you that while such beliefs may hold true at the local level, at a truly universal level there is only the Rule of Three. You're working through the ramifications of this even now."

Popular culture was wrong. Foom wasn't here to end war or share cures for all known diseases. It said it wouldn't be here long. Anything that was going to be gleaned from it while it was on Earth would happen in a very short window of time. There would never be any US ambassadors or diplomats here. Nor any Chinese officials. There was only my grandmother, blind Mrs. Liu, some children who'd learn how to make floating, illuminated grass, parents who had no idea their kids had made alien contact, and me. More realistically, I was on my own.

.   .   .

"I have been exploring your solar system for most of a century," Foom said.

"Why?"

"Cataloging." Foom led me down to the riverbank. A giant pearl sat in the water not ten meters away. "You would call me a completist. Visiting each and every one of Jupiter's moons alone took more than a decade. Some were truly majestic. Which is not to say your own moon is not interesting, but I am still processing what I learned there. It was my penultimate destination in this system. I saved your world for last."

We stepped into the river and were quickly engulfed above our waists. The water was cold but the current not especially swift.

"Did you find life anywhere else in our solar system?"

"Life, yes, but nothing alive that was also self-aware and sapient as you are. And I found death, too. But only on your world is there unlife. Your pardon, can you swim?"

"Excuse me?"

"I would have you step inside my home but the river bottom drops away deeper before we will quite reach it."

"Yes, I can swim."

"Very good. Let us do so now."

And so we swam. As we drew closer I could see the pearl did not rest upon the bottom of the river, but floated partially submerged. Before we reached it, Foom dove down a meter or so and swam straight into the curve of the pearl. It passed within without a ripple. Closing my eyes, I followed.

I didn't hit anything and a few moments after I should have struck the side I opened my eyes and swam up for air. I broke the water's surface and found myself somehow inside the giant pearl. The nacre of the inner walls glowed, revealing a curving ramp that wound up the middle, opening onto ledges and alcoves above. Foom had already reached the ramp and climbed out of the water, waiting for me on a low bench extruded from the inner wall.

Foom was an alien. It had come to Earth from the stars, which meant that I was inside its spaceship.

"Explain something to me, please," I said.

"Of course."

"This is your home?"

"It is."

"But it's also a vessel, right? It's how you traveled to my world."

"Yes, your understanding is true."

I shook my head and followed him from the water. "I don't think it is. How can a vessel that travels between stars not violate the Rule of Three?"

"Because I made it myself."

"How is that possible? Sure, you say you've been in this system a century so you're longer lived than my kind, but how could one person make something as complex as a spaceship by themselves?"

"It's my home. Who else would make my home?"

"But how?"

It waved me to the bench, the twin thumbs of its hand wiggling in an odd gesture. "Yours is not the first dark world I have visited. Everything you know of technology exists in the dark. Your people have breached your atmosphere, even stood upon your moon, by means of this technology, and spread unlife along the way. I cannot perceive such vehicles directly, or the people I assume traveled within them, only the darkness they define. You force your technology to shackle the universe to do your bidding, rather than work with those same forces to express themselves in ways of mutual benefit."

I waved at the gleaming surface all around us. "I don't understand."

"Do you understand beer?" Foom asked.

"Beer?"

"A beverage. The children brought me some. It is . . . refreshing."

"I know what beer is."

"Do you know how to make it?"

"What?"

"The ingredients. The process."

I flashed back on my sophomore year at university and the roommate who turned his half of our dorm room into a brewing den. "Um, grain, barley I think . . . and hops . . ."

"So you simply bring together barley and hops and you have beer?"

"What? No, you have to ferment it."

"How?"

"Uhh, you heat and crack the grain, then you mash it, which means soaking the grains in hot water so the sugars come out."

"Why do the sugars do that?"

"I don't know. Enzymes? My chemistry isn't very good."

"Then what?"

"You pour off the hot water with all the sugars, then you add the hops and you boil everything. You cool it and filter it, and then you add yeast which turns the sugar into alcohol. That also releases carbon dioxide, which is why it has bubbles. And you get beer."

"Do you enjoy beer?" Foom asked.

I couldn't help but grin. "I do, sure. Most people do."

"If you had never seen beer, never tasted or smelled it, had no knowledge of it, do you believe you could look at the components, the barley and hops and yeast and water, and see the thing they could become?"

What kind of a question was that? Beer was . . . beer. It was omnipresent, had always existed, hadn't it? But thousands of years ago, maybe not. Someone must have discovered fermentation, airborne yeast landing in a rain barrel that had some rotten fruit in it or some such. Maybe something like that had happened many, many times before someone took a swig that led to the first hangover.

"No, I guess not."

"It is a natural process. To brew beer you work with the substances of nature, following their own paths. In the case of beer those parts are external, but even so the Rule of Three is present at every step. I created my home in much the same way, though perhaps more directed. An internal pathway."

It held out its hand before me, pressing the tips of its thumbs together. A tiny whitish drop formed where they touched. It grew into a small bead.

"You asked before about the thing I taught the children that made the grass float. This is like that, but more so. Whereas they taught the grass to change its nature, I have taught myself to change mine. Like barley and hops giving way to something unimaginable until it occurs, so too did I create my home."

The bead had grown to the size of a fat pearl, grayish and iridescent. Foom parted its thumbs and the newly created pearl hung in the air. At a flick of its fingers it floated up then down then twice around its head before coming to rest upon my hand.

"How . . . ?"

"It is like your beer. A miracle until you know the way. To be fair, this is a small thing. It would take you at least a year of practice to make one as large as my home."

"You're kidding, right? You're saying I could do this?"

Foom reached out for my hand again, pressing the new-formed pearl against my palm. "Surely there are things your people do that are not all dark, things of wonder like your language and beer. These are precious and I hope to experience more of them, but in truth what interests me more is art."

"Art?"

"Every sapient people manifest their culture, producing records of who they are. Such art transcends mere language, often outliving the organisms that produced it. I hope to encounter some in this narrow slice of your world untouched by unlife. This is why I have come."

. . .

I returned to my grandmother's home late in the afternoon trading my western clothes for a simple shirt and trousers that had belonged to my grandfather, lying untouched for longer than I'd been alive. Both were short on me. Decades earlier my grandmother had acquired the cloth from another neighbor and then sewn them herself, making me the third in the chain of possession and thus acceptable under the Rule of Three. I ate a dinner prepared by her hand from food she had grown herself. I slept better that night than I had in years, probably the result of my exertions hauling water up for my grandmother and applying myself to chores that at her age went undone until some neighboring teen was sent over to help. I dreamed that the dark was leaving me, replaced by nutrients that met the alien's rule, or sweated out of my body in service to exertion that served that same rule. And I dreamed of beer, appreciating it as I never had before.

Foom had been unacquainted with beer before meeting the children. It had immediately grasped the process of water and sugar being transformed to alcohol and carbon dioxide, but fermentation itself was new, a miracle. And clearly, it wanted more miracles. So much of the world's food had converted over to manufactured production. Even naturally grown products were transformed. Something as simple as corn was not left alone but converted into high fructose corn syrup, an additive that by alien standards darkened everything it touched. But surely other natural processes remained. Bees still made honey and wax. Milk and rennet produced cheese. Foom would regard any of these as miracles, and what knowledge might it offer in trade?

I returned to the river in the morning. No children awaited me, though whether they'd taken the day off or Foom had sent them away I couldn't say. The alien swam from its pearl home and clambered onto the shore, naked as the day before.

"There is less of the dark about you," it said. "Do you feel it?"

"I suppose I do. I've been thinking about that, and about our conversation in your home yesterday. I have a proposition for you."

"What specifically? We spoke of many things."

"Trade. I could show you things, like the making of beer. What kinds of things could you show me in turn?"

Foom's face broke out in a wide toothless smile. "I would teach you new ways to view your world, and skills with which to experience it."

"What would that mean, pragmatically? Are you talking about ending disease? A stop to aging? Space travel?"

"Yes, all these things are possible, but I will expect a fair accounting, an introduction to processes untouched by the dark, such as the creation of beer. Or better still, some example of art, if it is to be found here."

"I think I can make that happen. What do you know of batik?"

. . .

With no small portion of apprehension, I persuaded Foom to return with me to my grandmother's home. She'd finished her work with the indigo yesterday and was carving designs into cloth in preparation for dyeing. She met us at the door with more of my late grandfather's clothing.

"You are a funny man," she said. "And I am an old woman. But you are no child wearing your innocence instead of clothing. If you wish to come into my house you will put something on. Or you can go away. I don't care which."

I flinched. I hadn't expected any of this, and my imagination flared with the horror that generations of diplomats would have experienced at my grandmother's handling of the first alien to visit the Earth.

Foom didn't so much as blink—could it blink?

"Of course, Grandmother. Your generosity honors me." It turned its back to her, much as it had seen me do when the children had presented me with shorts to wear yesterday, and donned the ancient trousers and shirt. The faded colors accentuated its pale skin but my grandmother was satisfied. She welcomed us into her home, taking a seat at her worktable and gesturing for us to watch her as she picked up a small knife and dipped it into a tiny pot of boiling wax. I'd seen her do this a hundred times. My mother had learned to do it as a child and practiced the technique well into her teens until a social program had sent her to school, ultimately leading her to meet my father.

"What is she doing," asked Foom.

By this point my grandmother appeared to be attacking a large white cloth stretched before her, the blade of her knife imparting a delicate pattern of wax where it touched.

"This is batik," I said. "The style dates back more than a thousand years, back when nothing on this planet was dark."

Foom nodded with approval. "Unlife has never touched it. But what is it?"

"Art. She is creating a pattern on the cloth with the wax."

"And the art is the interplay of the wax and the cloth? It tells a story?"

"Not exactly. The wax is temporary. It gets melted off."

"So this is ephemeral art? The art is the memory of the pattern of where the wax previously had been?"

"No, something else entirely. When she has completed the pattern in wax, the cloth will be boiled in an indigo dye." I directed his attention to the pot of leaves that would soon produce the dye.

"The white cloth will become blue," Foom said. "But you said it will be boiled? Surely the wax cannot endure. The intricate patterns lost."

"The wax is lost, yes, and deliberately so. But before that happens, it will have blocked the dye from staining that portion of the cloth. Where it had been, the cloth will still be white—"

"And the pattern preserved!" Foom practically shouted. "Do you have examples of this? Please, I must see."

This was my mother's family's calling. Generations had spent their entire lives weaving cloth, making indigo dye, and designing the most astonishing batik patterns. Some of the greatest art of the Miao people had been created in homes like this, saved up week upon week and carted over the mountains from tiny villages into the towns and cities where time and progress existed, where commerce replaced barter, where unlife had developed and spread.

My grandmother was an artist—though she would have scolded me to be called such—with decade upon decade of experience and expertise. A buyer in distant Shanghai sent an agent twice a year, buying up everything she'd created for a fraction of its true worth. But there was little my grandmother needed or wanted. A few chickens, seed for her garden, a whetstone to sharpen her knives once in a great while. Some money too, but she never touched it, letting it accrue in an account to pay for my mother to fly in once a year for a visit or to be spent on scholarships for the village children who opted to leave this life behind and attend school in the distant city.

While my grandmother sat engrossed in her work, I led Foom to the trunk at the back of the room. I hadn't been here in years, but there was nowhere else for her to keep her finished work. I lifted the lid and revealed what I can only describe as vast tapestries of her art.

Silently asking permission, the alien took them out of the trunk one by one, unfolding them and holding them at arms' length. The designs were flawless, intricate, breathtaking. Some were fanciful, birds and fish and scenes of nature. Others were purely abstract, complex patterns that predated Mandelbrot's awareness of fractals but spoke to the same geometric subdivisions going smaller and smaller. Each was a piece of perfection.

"This," said Foom, "this is what I hoped to find. This is all from one."

"From one?"

"One source, one origin. The cloth, the dye, the vision. All from her."

"Right," I said. "Your Rule of Three. So, she could give one of these to someone else and it wouldn't go dark?"

"No, it could pass to yet another's hands and still not be dark."

"Would you like one? Something to decorate your home?"

"Such a treasure?" Foom's voice dropped to a whisper, not that my grandmother had given any indication of hearing him before. "She would gift me with such a thing?"

"If I asked politely," I said. "Especially if I explain that you have come from so very far for just such a thing as she's made and already forgotten about in this trunk."

"That would be wondrous," it said. "But, might I ask some more? Is it possible she might share her knowledge, teach me to do this batik myself?"

I smiled, thinking back on all the times she forced me to sit at that same table with a knife and a square of practice cloth during one of my mother's visits, when all I wanted to be doing was playing outside with the local children.

"I think that would make her very happy."

. . .

Grandmother agreed to teach Foom, but would have none of his finger-melding knowledge transfer. She taught him as she'd been taught, as she'd taught my mother and tried to teach me, sitting at the same table with her, a knife in one hand, a small pot of liquid wax within easy reach, and a blank cloth on which to practice the most simple of designs. Foom was an apt pupil and I'm not sure who was more pleased.

The next day the alien arrived at my grandmother's house at first light, joined us for a simple breakfast, and then set to work which usually involved a brief lesson and hours of practicing what he'd learned. Maybe it was the extra thumbs, maybe the fact that its remarks hinted that it was several hundred years old with several times the experience any human being could amass. Maybe the alien was just a batik prodigy waiting to happen. Whatever the reason, after five days of learning basic techniques and simultaneously observing my Grandmother's work, it seemed to be patterning its cloth with the confidence and speed of its teacher. The proof of it came at the end of that fifth day when its cloth was stained with dye and the wax boiled away leaving unmarked cloth where it had been.

The result was breathtaking, a miniature tapestry of blinding white and brilliant blue, a set of panels that showed the solar system and Foom's pearl home spiraling ever closer to the Earth.

"This is good," said my grandmother. "You possess a gift limited only by your dreams."

"My people do not dream," said Foom.

"Funny man, perhaps you just don't remember them when you awaken?"

It smiled. "That might be. Certainly I have thought about what it might be like to dream."

"That is a good start. Next time, draw your thoughts upon the cloth."

"The cloth?" I said. I'd been sitting at the same table with them, scribbling notes in a handmade notebook I'd bartered from one of the neighbors.

"The patterns we make speak more clearly than words," she replied. "If you were a better student you would understand that. The funny man does."

Foom bowed its head. I pushed back from the table to make tea for all, as that was about the extent of my contributions to the batik these past several days. After I'd poured their cups and sat back with my own, the alien looked up and placed his hand over my grandmother's, not in the laced fingers way it had used with me and the children, but a simple and direct touch to add significance to the words that followed.

"What knowledge may I offer you in turn, Grandmother?"

"Knowledge? Pfah! I am an old woman. I live as my mother lived and her mother before her. The world has changed. As my daughter and grandson insist, but not so much here. There is no knowledge I need that I have not had since his mother was a little girl."

"But this is a great gift you have shared, which I will share with many others when I return home. Surely there is something I know how to do that you would like."

"I am content that you have learned so well so fast. My grandson hungers for new things. If you want to teach something, teach it to him."

The alien turned to me. It still hadn't tasted its tea and I set my own cup down under the weight of its regard.

"I have only learned this batik because you suggested it. It seems a reasonable solution to share knowledge with you, and when you visited my home you expressed an interest in how I had made it. Shall I teach you?"

"Too much talk," said my grandmother. "If you insist on yammering, do so beyond my hearing. Go. Away with you."

We left our tea and slipped out of her house, taking the path back toward the river.

* * *

"Everything I can do stems from a simple precept," said Foom. "The mind shapes the body."

"I'm not sure I understand. That's pretty broad."

"Do you still have the bead I gave you? You saw me create that. I could not always do so."

"Wait," I said. "I thought that was just something your people can do. A biological ability."

"It is, but not innate to us. The mind shapes the body. We have learned new processes, taught ourselves to create what we need rather than suborn the environment to meet our needs. Thus we preserve the Rule of Three."

"You make . . . everything? But how?"

"Think of beer, the miraculous chemical processes that transform water and grain and hops. You are aware that your body performs many processes of similar astonishment, from transforming the nutrients you ingest into the energy necessary to move you about, to encoding your sensations into memories that can be stored in complex networks and accessed in a myriad varieties."

"I . . . suppose. But those are all just biological processes. It's all internal."

"Not always. Your females produce milk to nurture their young. It begins as an internal process but the result exists outside the body."

In that moment I thought my brain might explode. Was Foom suggesting that a lactating mother's breast milk was on a par with its space craft? I thought again of bees making honey and wax. I thought of beer, from the perspective of the yeast converting the sugar. "I suppose that makes sense."

"So. What if you could teach your body a new process? To produce something you desired, within yourself rather than having to rely on your environment?"

I laughed. "What, you're saying I could train my body to brew beer?"

"Why not? It already knows how to break down much more complex matter than grain. But that's not what you want, you want to be able to create your own home like mine. Perhaps one day to travel beyond your world as I do."

"And that's possible?"

Foom laced its fingers with mine. "The universe is nothing but possibilities. But what you desire requires much practice. Let us hope you will be a better student of this than you were your grandmother's batik."

. . .

The next several days blurred together. This wasn't like when Foom had shown the children how to manipulate blades of grass, how to change their nature. That had been rote memorization, revealing a simple truth, a fact. What it was teaching me was the underlying structures that would allow me to alter my own biology to achieve my desires, and to do so without conscious thought. The goal, in the end, was to make it as effortless as taking an evening stroll. That's all well and good for an adult who's been walking his entire life, but not so easy for an infant whose world has only been crawling. And yet, in time, all of us learn to walk and scarcely think about the how of it for the rest of our lives. Those first days were like taking my first stumbling baby steps again, certain that at any moment I would land on my face. Except this time I was mucking about blindly with my own biochemistry.

On the third day, I had learned to sweat at will. By the fourth, I could control the process so that only my palms perspired. On the fifth day, I could alter my sweat glands to produce other substances and that's when the real change happened. It wasn't just what I was doing, it's how it made me feel. Bliss. That's the only word that can describe it. Using the Rule of Three internally, to create from my own body the thing I desired was . . . numinous. Like everything in the universe was right where it was supposed to be, and that my small actions were a contributing part. The sensation overwhelmed me at first, but quickly receded into the background, leaving me free to continue.

I focused on the bead Foom had given me, probing it, trying to understand it in ways that I can no more describe than I can tell me how to play piano or ride a bicycle. I just did it. And on the sixth day, after an hour's effort I could cup my hands together and produce a hollow bead of shining nacre that defied gravity and responded to my will. I'd like to say that on the seventh day I rested, but it was more like a coma. I passed out on the grass by the river and Foom must have carried me back to my grandmother's house. I awoke on the morning of the eighth day and saw her expression go from worry to a scowl. I knew I was fine.

"This is difficult for you," said Foom later that day, as we sat once more by the river. "There is no more complex substance on your world. It will take a year or more of practice before you can produce a vessel like mine, but the same principle applies to convincing your body to produce anything you like."

"You're saying I could sweat beer?"

It smiled that toothless grin. "Easily. And unlike the beer you've described from your homeland, the kind brewed in factories and transported vast distances to be sold in warehouses and then moved to stores and only then to the individuals who will drink it, your beer obeys the Rule of Three. It isn't dark. Nor will its consumption contribute to the darkening of others."

"But I can only learn to make it if I have actual beer to work from, to teach my body the template."

"That is true of anything you produce. It must adhere to the Rule of Three or you will be unable to master it."

"And you're the same way? With the things you make?"

"I am." It pressed the fingers on its left hand together, and as it pulled them apart drops of indigo dribbled free. "I have learned to make your grandmother's dye. Prior to meeting her and being exposed to it I could not do this. But now that I know it, I can teach others. This is what my people do, why we travel the galaxy."

That was key. This ability I'd gained, it wasn't just limited to me. Everything Foom had shown me, and everything I did with it going forward, I could share. "So, while it may take me a year to create a ship like yours, I could be showing others the same thing and with enough of us working on it, we'd have a fleet of ships. Enough vessels for humanity to join your people out among the stars!"

"Oh. No, that's never going to happen."

"What? Why not? You said I could do it. That it would just take time."

"And that is true, but you need to understand, most of your planet, most of your population, is dark. The most 'advanced' human beings are also those who are most distant from the Rule of Three. You are a blight and you are killing your world. That's part of what drew me here—your efforts to leave your own gravity well, to travel to your moon and one day to the other worlds of your solar system. If you had been content to remain here, I probably would not have come to such a dark place, not even to complete my cataloging of this system. But you were not, and the risk of you using your technology, dark and unliving as it is, to spread into space, that is too great."

"I don't understand," I said. "What are you going to do about it?"

"What needs to be done. Better for your species to die out, even if that includes some members of humanity who do live by the Rule of Three. When you are all gone, when the only inhabitants remaining live by the Rule of Three, your world will heal itself of the dark. It will become a paradise again. In time a new sapient species will rise, and Earth will have another chance."

"But . . . human beings will have been eradicated?"

"You understand me perfectly. That is my task while I'm here."

"I can't let you do that!"

Foom tilted its head, first right and then left. "You've already been a great help to me. Just as you've been learning from me, I've been learning about human bodies from you."

. . .

With a sudden burst of energy it leapt to its feet and jumped into the river, waving for me to follow and calling out, only his head above the water. "Come with me. The thing I've been waiting to show you is ready. And I cannot advance things to their next stage until you see it." Without waiting for me to follow it dove beneath the water, surfacing several meters away as it swam toward its home.

"This isn't happening," I said to myself, maybe to the river. "I misheard or didn't understand. It can't seriously have a plan for exterminating the human race."

I hit the water and swam after Foom. I came up at the bottom of the giant pearl as I had before, and ascended the ramp in a slow spiral. Halfway up I found Foom waiting for me on a bench in one of the alcoves opening off the central ramp. A naked man sat with him, slumped as if asleep. I stared at them both and Foom grinned back at me. Moments passed before I found my voice. "That's . . . me!"

"Yes," said Foom. "I made a clone. It was simple, really; your cells already contained their blueprint. I just nudged them forward to aid me in the next stage of my work. But first I require your assistance to quicken this body."

"Quicken it?" I averted my gaze from the clone. It was like seeing my own corpse.

"The body lives, but isn't alive. I'm sorry, the language I have from you lacks the nuance I need to explain."

"Try," I said. I didn't know where to look. "Try real hard."

"I accelerated its growth to bring it on a par with your own age, but it is not otherwise a reflection of you. To continue my work, I need you to connect with it, bring it in accord with yourself."

"And how am I supposed to do that?"

"Everything in it is primed to recognize you. We need only give it a push to connect. Give me your hand."

It spread its fingers for me as it had before, all while lacing the fingers of its other hand with those of a hand of the sleeping clone. There was no tingling this time, rather a sense of falling. Not a flailing or tumbling kind of fall, more like a plummet, the personification of my lifelong relationship with gravity. I plunged into myself, nonsensical as that sounds, as if I had just dove into a pool of me, a lake, an ocean. I didn't surface, I just kept falling ever deeper.

When I came back to myself it was to discover I had laced my free hand with the clone's. Foom had released both of us. I was staring at the clone, but also staring at myself from its eyes. And it was like looking upon the face of creation, like being fully aware at the moment of one's own birth. The earlier sensation of bliss I'd experienced working the Rule of Three paled by comparison. I was suffused with a rapture beyond my own comprehension.

I let my hand drop away from my doppelganger's.

"This is impossible," I said, and heard two voices. The clone's rasped a bit, speaking its first words. My words. My clone.

The alien gave me one of its toothless grins. "I would suggest you forget that word. It will only hold you back."

In other circumstances that would probably have been encouraging. But even overflowing with the exponential joy coursing through me, I still wanted Foom's creation of my clone to be impossible, because more than anything I needed its plan for extermination to be impossible. And if I admitted the reality of the one, what would hold back the other?

"So . . . are you saying all things are possible with your Rule of Three?"

"Ask yourself rather, how can you realize the concept of free will if you accept limits upon yourself?"

I wanted limits. I desperately wanted to limit Foom's ability to wipe out humanity. "And you're going to teach me that? To transcend all limits?"

"Nothing would please me more. I believe you have the potential, with sufficient practice. And the clone should be an aid in this. Meanwhile, I can continue my own research, with the help of you and your double."

I shook my head. "What research? Is that why you made a clone of me?"

"Your duplicate will be the proving ground for my work, but before I can begin that piece of it I must first obtain a detailed understanding of the workings of the human male reproductive system. And I can't do that without your help."

It was a day of casual threats of extinction, of feeling my consciousness centered in two separate bodies, of drowning in euphoria, but even still the non sequitur of Foom's reply stopped me cold. Was I being propositioned by an alien?

"I don't know how to respond to that."

From between the thumbs of one hand Foom conjured up a palm-sized nacre cup. "As soon as you provide the sample we can return to the riverside. Then you can resume your practice and soon realize there is no such thing as impossible."

"Sample?"

"Yes, please. A sample of your ejaculate. I will analyze it and perfect my understanding. I cannot use your double's; because of the accelerated growth I utilized, it would be unreliable."

It handed me the cup.

. . .

The less said about providing a sperm sample for a sexless alien, the better. Suffice it to say that I did what was necessary, with my clone miming my every movement, and then the three of us wound our way down the ramp and swam out of the pearl and back to the riverbank.

Controlling the movement of two bodies at once is crazy difficult if you try to do both at once. I started swimming and then switched my attention, seeing the world through my clone's eyes and started it swimming, too. Back and forth was odd but easy, and we made it to shore without incident.

Foom busied itself with its analysis for the rest of the day, encouraging me to use the time to practice my new knowledge of generating floating nacre beads as a template for shedding my concept of impossibility. Somehow having two bodies at once was oddly synergistic, as if I was both watching another person doing it and adding my clone's efforts to my own. More, the feeling of bliss that filled me while I worked helped to distract me from Foom's ultimate goal. The result was that my clone and I both produced hollow beads twice as large as I'd managed only an hour before. My control over the beads also grew. I sent the pair of them—mine and my clone's—soaring high into the sky, feeling a connection to them long after they were lost to sight. I must have remarked on this out loud because Foom looked up from its own wool gathering to say "Automaticity" and then went back to work.

That first pair of larger beads had to have taken more than an hour—I'm not certain, I'd left my watch with all of my other dark items, back at my grandmother's home. The next pair took less than half that time and were a third larger. The third set was fully four times the size of the first one I'd made, and accomplished in less than ten minutes. Automaticity, yeah.

I was getting . . . well, not *tired*, exactly, but I needed a break from sweating balls of flying, alien nacre. Now that I had the knack of it, Foom had said that I could make anything I was familiar with. I gave a pass to its idea of producing beer, but thought instead of my grandmother's soup. I closed my eyes and the memory of it was still vivid in my mind, the range of tastes from the pickled chili to the succulent fish pulled from the nearby river. It was so vivid I swear I could smell it. My clone made a throat clearing noise and I looked over to see it sitting there with both hands cupped together. He held soup. I shook my head at him and we both focused. Nacre formed in his hands, encapsulating the soup. A similar ball appeared in mine and when it was complete I caused it to fill with more soup, then set both to floating a few feet above our heads. I smiled from both bodies, the absurd idea popping into my head that if I ever got back to the USA, I was going to make a killing in soup delivery. I tried producing other foods and failed. My memories were vivid, full of taste and temperature and mouthfeel, but when I tried to actually exude them I fell short. They were all foods from back home, tainted by too many hands and time and distance and thus far removed from Foom's Rule of Three. I didn't understand how that should matter but it did. The technique came easier with each creation and I was getting used to the feeling of universal joy that using it brought. I felt certain I could make anything now, provided I'd experienced it personally and that the past event subscribed to the Rule of Three. I saw a lot of locally sourced restaurants in my future.

It was a silly and charming thought, and almost enough to distract me from Foom sitting across from me working on a method of ending the human race to keep us from spreading our madness throughout the rest of the galaxy. Almost.

. . .

Late in the day Foom laced its fingers with my clone's and I felt my consciousness pushed aside. Not entirely out, but no longer in control of my doppelganger. There wasn't the exchange of knowledge and insight that had accompanied this gesture in the past. I followed the alien's focus, using everything I'd learned in the last few days. I could see what it was doing, but not understand it. "Can you explain what's happening?" I asked.

"I am crafting what you would call a retrovirus from your double's cells. Actually, many variations of this retrovirus. If I am successful, one of them will rewrite your gonads and ultimately alter the viability of any spermatozoa they produce. He'll still produce semen in the normal fashion, but it will be inert for reproductive purposes. No 'Jing'."

Foom grinned as it said that last word, lapsing from the Miao tongue into Chinese for an old word from Chinese medicine for 'sexual energy' that I must have picked up years ago and long since forgotten. Apparently, it had pulled more than just the one language from me.

"Shooting blanks, as the Americans would say," I added.

"Thus ensuring the extinction of your species without causing any physical harm to the living."

"Maybe not physical, but what about emotional? Most people want children, long for them. Millions, maybe billions, will be devastated when the world comes to understand what you're setting in motion."

The alien pulled its fingers back and my full awareness snapped back into place, leaving me regarding it from two perspectives. But something had changed. I hadn't returned to being one mind in two identical bodies. Something was wrong with my clone, which meant something was wrong with me, just not the first me. I pressed my hand to my double's forehead. He was burning up. I turned to Foom for an explanation, but it was oblivious and still caught up in our conversation.

"It is not that I lack empathy," it said. "But nor can I predict how the members of another sapient race will react, most especially not a race that has no knowledge of the Rule of Three and is so dark and wrapped in unlife. They exist beyond my awareness. Perhaps an effective analogy would be to liken them to the ants that live beneath your feet. When you walk upon the grass here, do you consider what impact your passage has upon them, their tunnels, their dwelling places?"

"So, we're ants to you? So far beneath your notice?" I suddenly felt chilled, or rather, my clone did. It made no sense. I could feel the warm sunlight on my skin.

Foom frowned. "You focus on a portion of the analogy I did not intend. I was not expressing superiority but rather ignorance. I can no more plan for human emotional suffering than you can take into account the daily acts and aspirations of ants. The virus I have crafted will ensure there is no pain. That much I can do. It is why I made your clone."

My clone began coughing and couldn't stop. He took a drink of water from one of the clay jugs we replenished from the river. It didn't help. "What, it's okay for my clone to suffer?"

"You are not dark. You have purged the unlife from yourself. I did not wish to risk harming you in the event that my first attempts at producing the virus damaged you in any way."

"What about emotional damage? Don't you think I'm upset by your plans for humanity?"

"Not directly, no. You have no children. No plans for any. Your major empathic ties are to older relatives, your parents and your grandmother. They will, in all probability, expire well before you do. They will feel no impact from the sterility imposed on your species. You are of an age such that your friends who are likely to wish offspring have already conceived and birthed them. Again, no impact. The same for associates of these friends. The Rule of Three applies. Any further and your upset is abstract and irrelevant."

It was becoming more and more difficult to argue with Foom as the clone's physical distress grew. By now he was lying on his side, still coughing. He was shivering uncontrollably. I felt aches in his arms and legs, his neck. His head pounded and his throat felt raw. All of it was vivid and real but also removed, confined to that other body.

"What's happening? Why do I feel so sick?"

For the first time, Foom looked genuinely concerned. "You are unwell?"

"Not me, him!"

The alien spared a glance at the duplicate it had made and nodded. "Ah, my apologies. It is temporary, I assure you. Your double is serving his purpose as a proving ground."

"Why is he sick?"

"His body is responding to the assault of two hundred thirteen variations of the virus I have developed. I am confident that one of them will be successful. Once I determine which, these trials will conclude. I will only inflict a single virus on humanity, with no more additional impact than a mild instance of influenza."

"So, that's it? You'll be done and all of humanity is screwed? No appeal?"

Foom rose and laced its fingers with the clone again and again I felt my awareness of the body shunted aside. The sudden relief from his symptoms stunned me with just how sick he was. "A moment . . . yes, the testing is complete. I have isolated the successful virus." It freed its fingers from the clone's hand and the chill and fever and ache and nausea all rushed back to me. Foom resumed speaking but I couldn't fully focus on its words.

"There is nothing to appeal. If your people could embrace the Rule of Three then they would be able to effortlessly counter any virus. Doing so would be proof that they will not succumb to the unlife that covers this planet."

"How long do we have?"

"Do you mean your double, or are you asking me about your species?"

"Wait, what? The clone is dying?"

"Of a certainty. His body's attempts to fend off so many distinct viral attacks have triggered a cascade failure. He is burning himself up. I can terminate your connection with the body if you like."

"Yes. Wait, no. Just no. What about the rest of humanity. How long does it have?"

Foom raised both hands, palms up, directing one at me and one at my clone. "That depends. Will you continue to aid me?"

"Of course not. I'm not going to help you to wipe out my species."

It nodded. "I understand. Then it will take longer, several hours at least." Nacre spheres the size of softballs grew upon each outstretched palm. Something sloshed within them. "These vessels will contain the virus in a sustaining aqueous medium. I will need to produce thousands of them, pausing to replenish myself several times before I complete the process. When I am done I will scatter them throughout your stratosphere, blanketing the planet. Without a mind to guide them, the ozone there will begin to dissolve the shells, releasing the virus to rain down upon your people. Within days, every male of every age will have been exposed and rendered infertile." It tossed one of the spheres to me. I slapped it aside and it landed in the grass.

"And I suppose you're just going to sit back and watch?"

It frowned again. "No, I will have left before that. I intend to take my leave of you once I have launched the virus into your sky. I had hoped you would understand, I take no pleasure in denying you the stars. You yourself may one day manage to use what you've learned to leave here."

Lost in some fever dream just a few feet away, my clone moaned. I'd just been offered the stars and I felt myself dying.

• • •

There was nothing more to say. Foom excused itself and went off to its ship, to rest or replenish or whatever it needed to do before beginning the seeding process that would destroy humanity.

"What am I supposed to do?" My clone turned back to me with a look of complete helplessness that I knew showed on my own face. I pondered the question and then answered myself, letting the words fall from my double's lips as he slipped in and out of consciousness. "Our grandmother would chide me for tackling such a difficult question on an empty stomach." At a thought, a pair of my soup spheres fell into our respective hands and irised open, delivering a welcome ripple of bliss. "Our grandmother is wise," I said, and ate the soup.

• • •

It's a difficult thing to hold your dying self in your arms. To feel your own life trickle away and yet continue to live. To sip comfort food from an otherworldly bowl and know there is no comfort to be had. My mind slipped free of him, returning my previous singularity. I sat there, rocking him silently, until his body grew cold. It took a long time. When I could at last let him go, I eased his lifeless body down and left him lying supine on the grass. I looked up to find Foom sitting near, hundreds of virus-filled nacre spheres already floating above its head.

"He's dead," I said.

"Of a certainty."

"Why? You said that knowledge of the Rule of Three could save him."

"Yes, easily. You would only need to focus on the attacking virus while it remained in the host body, engineering a counter virus from it to reverse and restore what had been changed."

"Then why didn't you? He didn't have to die!"

Foom paused, two new spheres finished. "Why does this upset you? He wasn't truly alive, just an outgrowth of yourself, and you are fine. He served the purpose I created him for."

"To kill all of humanity!"

"No, to spare you. I told you, I needed your biology to produce the virus. But I consider you an ally. You have shared your grandmother's art with me, taught me your language, introduced me to marvels here on your world. I could not repay that with your death."

"So you just had me experience it from a slight remove? Is that your idea of kindness?"

"I offered to sever your connection earlier. You chose to decline. I'm sorry if the outcome is other than you expected. I thought you understood how things would end from the beginning. Now, please, I need to focus and continue my work."

"Finish your death spheres," I said.

"The virus will *not* result in anyone's death. Your double succumbed to the sheer weight of hundreds of viral attacks, not a single one."

"Fine, sterility spheres."

"An apt name."

• • •

Foom continued producing the nacre spheres that would destroy humanity. It's not like I could have stopped it. Instead I positioned my clone so that he looked like he was asleep instead of dead. I plucked handfuls of grass, and using the external version of the technique Foom had shown me caused them to weave into a shroud. More trickles of bliss. I wrapped my double once, twice, then bound the grass closed around him. I've never been especially religious, but I'd attended plenty of funerals. I spoke prayers for the dead in three languages, wondering if there was an afterlife for cloned bodies that had never had a soul of their own, wondering if, when my own passing came, my spirit would be divided.

When I was out of words and empty of emotion, I did a variation of the tricks Foom had taught the children. The grassy shroud around my clone flared with light and began to rise into the sky. It would precede Foom's virus spheres. Indeed, I intended it to go far higher, carrying my double beyond the Earth's grip. At least he would get to space.

• • •

"I am done," said Foom.

"Done?"

"With the sterility spheres. All I have left to do is send them on their way, and then depart myself."

Like a magician performing some big reveal it crossed its arms over its torso and then spread them wide. Thousands of spheres that had been hanging motionless just above its head took off, flying straight up. In the last instant before they were lost to the eye, they spread out in all directions and kept climbing. Then they were gone.

"That's it, then. End of humanity."

"Do not be despondent," said Foom. "The last generations of your people will still endure for many years. And the rest of the galaxy will be spared the inevitable dark that your continuation would have brought. Nor will you be forgotten. I will share your grandmother's batik with my people. I cannot properly describe how much you have enriched us."

"Right. And you've killed us by way of thanks."

The alien ignored me. "I will always treasure the gift you asked her to give me. As you have seen, I keep few personal mementos of my travels, but this will inspire me for centuries to come. As will the memory of the time I shared with you. Thank you."

I glared at it, but Foom just stood staring back at me, waiting for some response.

"Right. Got it. 'So long and thanks for the fish.' Will you just go?"

The alien nodded. It walked to the river, dove in, and swam toward its home floating in the water. Moments later that magnificent pearl rose up from the river and drifted lazily away, rising above the valley, over the mountain tops, higher and higher to visit other worlds, study their wonders, maybe take home a few treasures, maybe leave behind a promise of extinction for its next hosts.

. . .

I think I sat there in the grass for hours, staring up into the empty sky. But the sky wasn't empty. It contained thousands of nacre spheres waiting to decay and infect every man on the planet. How long before nations began realizing that the birth rate had ground to a halt? The limited reserves at sperm banks would only delay the inevitable. In less than a hundred years, humanity would be wiped from the Earth.

I didn't know what to do. I could flee, rush home armed with the knowledge that the future had been stripped from us. I could try to warn the government, here in China, or back in the US. They wouldn't believe me at first, but a quick demonstration of creating my own nacre spheres would silence some of the doubts, and the utter lack of new births would do the rest. Not that it would do any good.

And yet . . .

I went looking for that first sphere full of the virus that Foom had lobbed at me, and found it right where it had fallen. The alien hadn't sent it off with the others. Was that an oversight or had it left the sphere behind deliberately, intending for me to find it? I unsealed it, ignoring the trickle of joy that using the technique brought, pressed my face to the opening and inhaled a dose thousands of times greater than would reach anyone over the next several days. I switched my focus inward, awash in bliss as I tracked the infection spreading through me. Time fell away and I dove deeper, seeing the mechanism that performed a tweak that would work on any adult male. I should have been impressed by the masterstroke of genetic engineering, but it all looked so easy when you knew what to look for. I touched a portion of the virus, held it tight, changed it, and set it free. It quickly attacked the original virus, rewriting it to undo the sabotage, leaving me whole again. Or whole until other bits of unaltered virus still in my system rendered me sterile again. Another touch and I'd suborned more of Foom's work and repaired myself again, then purged any remaining trace of the alien's original virus from my body.

I focused on what I'd changed, concentrated on creating a new sphere in my hands, and filled it with the antivirus I'd envisioned. I had a cure. I just didn't have enough of it.

* * * *

Foom had said the thing was possible, that an antivirus could be used to reverse its virus while it lingered in its victims. I'd made the cure and seen it work. But how much time did I have to produce and distribute it to the entire world? How long would the original virus linger after it had done its work?

I was running before I even knew where I was going. Down the dirt paths where days before I had seen the children scatter. It was nearly dusk, but that didn't matter. I ran until I came across the first house and pounded on the door, calling for any children inside to come out and play, babbling about glowing grass. An adult opened the door and began shooing me away. Behind him a child peered out, one of the ones who'd first taught Foom to speak a human language. I ignored the adult and called for her to find her friends, all of them, and meet back where Foom had shared his magic. I conjured a quick nacre bead and sent it flying over to her. She snatched it from the air, darted around her father, and vanished further down the dirt path. I spun around, ignored the angry man behind me, and headed back to the clearing where, with luck, the children would find me.

• • •

Soon five of the original seven had arrived. It would have to be enough. I didn't think I could spare the time to wait for the missing two. One by one I laced my fingers with theirs and shared knowledge the way Foom had with me. I showed them the nacre bead that I had managed on that first day. It was one thing, one substance, a tiny hollow sphere. A pearly, empty marble. I made up a song on the spot for them to sing, about dancing beads floating above their heads, making a game out of how many they could manage. And as they filled the air with their creations I gathered them to me, one by one, and poured my retrovirus cure into them and sent them flying away to rendezvous with Foom's spheres. Night had fallen but I didn't care. The kids kept making their hollow beads, getting better and faster at doing so, and I kept filling them up and casting them into the sky. First hundreds, then thousands. We worked through the night, the older children taking a moment now and then to set some of the grass aglow.

By dawn I'd long since lost count, but surely we'd launched more than five thousand tiny packets, each instructed to seek out Foom's larger spheres, punch through them, and rewrite its virus. Three of the children had fallen asleep and the other two had slowed down. I was exhausted as well, drained. I felt like I hadn't eaten in weeks, drunk in days. But we'd done it. Or I thought we had. Maybe not all of them, but nearly. Most. I hoped so, anyway.

• • •

The next morning found a gathering of children clamoring for me outside my grandmother's door. The five who had helped the day before had been joined by the missing two from that first day in the clearing, and another six besides. They'd brought water from the river to free me up from that chore and plaintively asked if I was free to come play. Several of them held out hands full of nacre beads for my inspection. The new children looked at me with yearning and hopeful eyes.

I led them back down the path to the spot where Foom had held court. I began by lacing fingers with all of them, bringing the new recruits up to speed on the game of illuminating blades of grass and making them float. I shared the concept of exuding the nacre and the first hints of how to make the resultant beads fly. In turn, I asked them for the stories of their lives and their families. I asked them for their hopes and dreams. And I asked myself how the Rule of Three might best be tailored to serve them.

It became apparent that they couldn't do the work internally. They could learn to copy anything put in front of them, as they had that first day with the nacre beads that I'd then filled with the retrovirus. But they could not imagine a thing they had experienced and produce it fresh as an act of will. I didn't know if this was a talent that came with adulthood or something I could do because Foom itself had taught me and I lacked some necessary piece for imparting it to another. Time would tell. Meanwhile, there was plenty to do with the things in front of and all around us.

Several days later, after starting our morning session, I left the children and paid a visit to Mrs. Liu, my grandmother's blind neighbor. She very generously allowed me the use of her phone, which I discovered she kept charged using a single solar panel on top of her tiny house. I phoned home. Specifically, I called my boss in the state department. After a few minutes of her yelling at me that I'd worried her by vanishing, yelling about my failing to show up for work, and yelling with relief that I wasn't dead from the mystery strain of influenza, I learned the important details. All over the world people had come down with what looked to be the flu. Men and women both, though men fared worse. Most people recovered after a day. Even so, a tiny percentage had died, much as happened with every flu, but the sheer number of people affected meant the deaths reached into the tens of thousands. Then, just as quickly as it had begun, the pandemic had passed. She asked where I was and I told her I was visiting family. She asked when I'd be back and I told her I'd always liked her laugh. Then I ended the call. I returned the phone and asked Mrs. Liu if she needed anything. I helped her with a few minor chores for less than an hour and then returned to the children.

They'd come a long way in just a few days. I had, too. Together we were altering some of the local trees, teaching their limbs and leaves to absorb light throughout the day and return it as radiant heat from their trunks after the sun set. We were changing grass to grow longer and weave its blades into rounded walls and floors and roofs, creating living houses more durable than anything the Miao people in this valley currently enjoyed. And we all learned to copy the food that each child brought so that they returned home with enough to feed their entire families.

As the days turned into weeks, weeks into months, I shared and taught other things I knew. Every day was something different but topics included Mandarin and English. Arithmetic and basic algebra. What I remembered of philosophy and economics and astronomy and the scientific method from my college classes that seemed so very distant now. We talked of outer space and had sober discussions of what it meant to have met an alien. And every day, at one point or another, we'd all grow quiet and gaze upward and speak of visiting the stars. I was getting better at creating my own nacre spheres now, producing orbs the size of beach balls that I could wrap around some of the smaller children, giving them giggling rides high above the trees.

Foom had promised to share my grandmother's batik with people throughout space. I intended to bring her soup to them as well.

Messenger

by R.R. Virdi & Yudhanjaya Wijeratne

We looked to our neighbors in times of war to be our enemies. It was the wrong place to look. We should have turned our gaze upward, to the sky—to space. In our preoccupation with ourselves, we missed them—the others.

Picture this, if you will. One moment, I was checking out of three years of reserve duty in the Indian Army, putting down my rifle and walking up the old beaten path to the house. My little one shrieked and bounded towards me. The wife, eight months pregnant, looked on fondly.

The path was overgrown: it was my job to trim it, to keep the weeds from spilling over into the driveway. It needed cutting. The little one needed new shoes. The car had rusted a bit. It was mundane as far as a life goes, but I was happy have these chores to return to. A simple life—a good one.

The next thing I remember, my wife was gone, my child was gone, my house a smoldering ruin. And I was wading through fistfuls of ocean, screaming in rage and pain as I poured missile after missile into the Enemy.

. . .

It started, as far as we know, with an asteroid. Or what we thought was an asteroid.

NASA did their jobs, running their instruments and coming back shaking. Ordinary asteroids are fused lumps of rock and ice that look like potatoes tumbling through space. This one looked like a sleek cigar of mostly metal.

The press went wild. They called it Oumuamua, Messenger, a Hawaiian name that meant little to us.

People who knew what it might be—or suspected—called it Rama and waited with bated breath. Messenger zipped through our solar system and left. And those who remembered their Arthur C. Clarke heaved a sigh of relief. Sometimes you don't want it to be aliens, even if they might give you the grand tour of the universe.

A year later, another Oumuamua—smaller, sleeker— slammed into the Moon. That first Messenger must have figured out what our instruments were like. By the time we knew it was coming, it was already too late. It hit the dark side of the Moon with the force of thirty-three nuclear bombs. A star blossomed on the dead lunar surface. The sun must have thought the Moon was winking at it.

There were those in the space industry who wanted to go look at this thing. Launch a probe, maybe a lander, figure out what the hell happened.

It's the damned Moon, we thought. Who cares what happens up there? Besides, who had the money for a space industry, anyway? The economy was tanking, populations were on the rise, the world was going to shit, and the only thing I paid attention to those days was my horoscope: Goals you are trying to reach slip out of your grasp. Work harder this week.

We should have paid attention. We didn't.

Within weeks, the first of Them landed. It streaked through the atmosphere, burning, screaming, and hit the south-west of India like the wrath of God. The explosion rocked the entire state of Karnataka. Downtown Bangalore became a smoking hole twenty feet deep with towers toppling around it like so many toy bricks. Glass shattered for miles around. Cars melted in the heat.

And something stood there in the carnage. Or tried to. Something burned, like wreckage, cracked and shattered with the heat of re-entry. Something with a great head and parts that spun and moved and steamed. Something with a mouth hung open, drooling fire and slavering.

Parts of my house cracked and steamed. From the ruins of my house came the awful smell of hair burning and flesh roasting.

It tottered. It screamed.

I tottered. I screamed.

It keeled over and died.

I keeled over.

I wish I'd died.

* * *

The orders came the next day as I lay empty-eyed at my friend Bhanu's place, thinking of her. Thinking of my Divya and my Anisha. And the unborn child. In the background, the TV blared. An overly made-up news anchor blabbed on and on and on about lights in the sky.

Bhanu came shaking his phone at me. "Arjun-ji! Arjun-ji! There's more coming! They're calling us up! They're fighting!"

My fists clenched. My knuckles cracked.

"Let's go," I growled. "Let's show them what all seven hells look like."

As I left, I saw the evening moon, climbing high in the sky: except where I had once shown my daughter the hare on the Moon, there was now a trickle of darkness, like a great black spider creeping around the edge.

* * *

And that was how I became one of the first Shikari.

This is me now. They call me Vishnu's Vengeance. A hundred-meter machine of gleaming alloy punched out by Tata-Leykham Industries. My fingers are steel. My fists can crush buildings.

Once I dealt out death, one man at a time, with my INSAS assault rifle, my fingers sweating in my gloves and my heart thumping at a thousand beats per minute. Now I cradle a gun ripped straight out of a Russian battle tank—a smoothbore that I call Padma, Vishnu's lotus. It is an apt name for this gun. It has laser sights and an autoloader that would make an artilleryman green with envy.

My fingers do not sweat, and my heart is a nuclear battery that will burn for five hundred years. I am a god of death.

And I wait in the darkness for my enemy.

It was not easy, becoming what I am. They only took those of us with nothing to lose. Not all of us who went in made it out. Those who didn't die went crazy. But I held on. My anger grew with time. I screamed their names in the darkness—Divya and Anisha, Divya, Anisha—until the words turned into a mantra and became my will. And by the time the neuro-doctors strapped me in for processing and gave me the final contest forms, my hands shook so badly with anger that I snapped the pen and stabbed the paper. Maybe I was already insane.

Maybe I still am.

For when you take a man's reason for life away from him, what more does he have to fear?

My enemy is wading now. Unlike the first mistake, this one gleams silver. Long, sleek metal legs slam into the ocean floor. Blue circuit traces cover the turtle-like shell in the middle.

"Babaji, the Enemy is a Spider-class," says Bhanu in my ear. I can vaguely hear the roar of helicopter blades underneath the crackling audio. "Five legs, low center of gravity. I think we see a tail."

Babaji. My crew call me Father. I am their Head, their Commander...their god.

"Telemetry confirms the Enemy is bearing three degrees to the left, speed thirteen knots, over," crackles another voice. That is Sanjaya. In the Mahabharata, the great Sankrit epic, Sanjaya is an advisor to the king: his is the gift of seeing things happening a great distance away. How fitting that a Sanjaya fulfils the same role for me today. He is a good kid, young, a little awkward, but as sharp as a fine razor when he sits at that screen. "Babaji, I recommend you adjust main gun by 13-by-3. This should be a nice clean one, over."

I raise my gun and sight carefully. I stand still. It must be a strange sight: an iron giant standing in the ocean before a city.

I fire.

The 125mm projectile leaves the reconfigured tank gun with a thunderclap. The strike is instantaneous: the armor-piercing spike of tungsten slams into the Enemy at a thousand meters per second. It rips a shoulder clean off the grotesque creature. It screams from some hidden mouth—a sound that will give children in this city nightmares for decades to come. Instead of blood, it leaks lightning.

I fire again, and again, and again, walking forward as I do. My aim is true. Padma never fails me. Rounds slam into the monster, ripping chunks out of the carapace. Gleaming layers of soft white and silver dance in the moonlight. And now for my grand finale. I switch to a special round—a 145 monstrosity tipped with uranium—and fire right into the hole at its heart. The round arcs slow and hits with a dazzling light that blinds us all for a second. I can hear Bhanu and Sanjaya cursing.

The Enemy screams one last time and falls. Mission accomplished.

I make my way to the smoldering corpse and stare down at it with an almost human-like fascination. I've seen these before. Nothing's new...except the smell. I don't take it in with the clinical—analytical—dispassion I'm supposed to.

A pixelated curtain of static white, tinged with hints of obsidian threads, washes over my vision. The hulking monstrosity is gone, and something makes it way to tickle my senses. Something I should have forgotten.

It's an acrid odor, clinging to the inside of my skull with hooks, refusing to let go. It's the smell of the past—of burning buildings, searing ozone, sizzling flesh—of a life gone by. Something I'd been made to forget, something human.

Shikari don't smell. We process. We analyze threats. We neutralize them.

The jarring white carpet fades and my vision returns to normal. I brush it from my mind and bend to grab hold of one of the construct's legs. A quick tug tells me the limb will hold under the weight and the tug of the ocean. I wrench on the creature and move toward the shore, keeping my mind on the task of retrieval.

We shouldn't be studying these things, hauling them back to shore. We should be burying them. A few more rounds would turn each corpse into slag fit to sink to the ocean floor to join centuries of refuse.

I wade through the water, giving no mind to the waves crashing harmlessly against my body. Every impact does nothing but jar a memory out of me. I remember the days when, in what little free time I had, I paddled against the water and fought to not drown under high crests of seafoam.

Now I tower above it all. The waves do not touch me the way they used to. I near the shore, monster in tow, when another bout of discordancy lances through me, body and mind. My limbs grow distant and weary. Vishnu's Vengeance is nothing but a hollow dream. I'm no longer of steel strength and resolve, of lightning computer thoughts and processes. I'm of something hot and heavy—something weary. A spot in my chest, something I'd left behind, burns and beats out of sync. Something wracks lungs I don't have, feeling like they're being wrung by iron cables till every bit of air is squeezed out of me.

I remember tottering. I'm screaming.

And it passes again.

My fist tightens around the leg I'm holding. The shore nears, and a crowd gathers along it. Strobing lights cascade off the tops of vehicles to spread out of the sands ahead, bathing the grains in faint blue. I twist and heave to pull the monster's carcass through the final bit of water, sending up a new row of waves to crash before the onlookers. An alarm cuts through the din, wailing, and giant radiation holograms light up the air, almost as tall as I am. Ants—men—in white hazmat suits form a wary perimeter around the corpse. I need to remember they're people. People: soft, organic, thinking—always thinking, worried, letting emotions drive them.

Curiosity. That's what's in their minds. That itch. The yearn to know. They had to understand what I'd killed. But what's there to understand?

I was supposed to kill it. That's all you could do to one of those. And I did my job. It should burn, much like a home—people, a little girl and her mother.

Everything flashes, and I become myself again. Vengeance. The thoughts leave me, and I am free to watch the little dots of white run toward the monster. They slow the closer they get. They inch, much like insects, concerned the immobile mass would somehow find a second life and wreak havoc again. It wouldn't. Vishnu—I—had made sure of that. I'd made it burn. And it wasn't enough.

More ants scurry around the fallen enemy, making their way close enough to touch its legs. They likely whisper among themselves over the marvel of creation the thing is.

I don't see it. All I see is a burning house, a fading pregnant woman, the ashes of a little girl.

The coldness flickers again. Then, all feeling, like the visions, fade.

Scientists motion at neighboring crews to bring their tools over. They cut through its body with methodical precision, loading the bits onto heavy machinery so they can haul it off to wherever.

Curiosity. One word. Five syllables. The promise of understanding. It'll make the fight easier. That's their thinking. It's what drives the little insects before me into their joyous circle around the harbinger of our doom.

Shikari are not to be curious. We're decisive. We burn what needs to be burned.

My vision refocuses on the enemy and I raise my cannon. The small forms, clad in white, do not register as anything important. They're nothing more than concentrated pillars of carbon, hydrogen, nitrogen, calcium, and phosphorus. Base elements. The enemy still lay before me. It wasn't gone, not completely.

But I could fix that.

I feel the charge rush through me as the cannon arm primes. I know what comes next.

The house on fire, smoldering ruins and bodies, and smoke blanketing the air above.

My arm grows distant and hollow, unresponsive. I stop, aware of what I was trying to do. The cannon lowers, and I turn my back to the people on the shore, fixing my gaze on the horizon.

Am I a man dreaming that I am a machine, or a machine dreaming of being a man?

● ● ●

Back in the hangar, anxious tech-priests scuttle around me, tapping, tinkering. Little two-legged ants crawling everywhere. Phantom itches on my skin.

"It's not the radiation, Babaji," says Sanjaya, a worried voice in my ear. "Your outer skin registers a few rads, but the inner skin is completely untouched. Electronics, neural conduits, all in perfect working order. Your gun arm might need a re-servicing, but that's it."

I KNOW WHAT I SAW. I KNOW WHAT I FELT.

"I know, Babaji, but I can't explain it," he says, a desperate note entering his voice. "It's not hardware."

"Maybe you need some rest," says Bhanu.

Unasked, the question on all their minds, the problem none of them will say out loud: Babaji, maybe you're desyncing.

LEAVE ME, I growl.

They bow and back away. My children fear me. I sigh, the hangar reverberating with the emptiness I feel inside. But before they can leave, an alarm screams, and the voice of Command and Controls drills into my skull.

VISHNU TO BAY SIX. VISHNU TO BAY SIX. WE HAVE A SITUATION.

Bay six. My main reactor re-ignites. I break into a run, ripping cables out of my plugports. This is not good.

● ● ●

Bay Six is fifty kilometers away, a vast fortress that dwarfs my own waterside dwelling. My bay is low, sleek, and modern—designed to be broken apart, towed down to wherever I'm needed, and re-assembled. Bay Six, on the other hand, is an immense thing built out of ten-ton blocks of stone. It is more than a launch pad, it is a temple. A shrine.

To the greatest and most fearsome of all of us.

A shrine to Kali, Goddess of Destruction.

My target is along the coastline, which lights up on my heads-up display. My steel feet claw small valleys in the soil. The lights of Chennai strobe in and out in the background, throwing small shadows of me onto the floodlit waters. For a moment I am a man again, with outsized legs, chasing a metal giant in the darkness.

Bay Six, all towers and spires, sits on a high artificial hill. The whole thing is lit up in a ghastly red. Alarms blare from inside. I can't jump, but one push from me and the gate crumbles, and my steel bulk is in the main courtyard.

It's a large place, almost ten square kilometers of stone and buildings. There should be people here, a veritable army, but nothing. There are vehicles, but they lie scattered and abandoned. The army flags are burning. The stone is slick and coated with a thick black.

SANJAYA?

Oil, I think. I follow the oil trail inside. Bay Six has three courtyards, one inside the other. I pass through the second courtyard, and here the metal of the military gives way to something older and more sinister. Giant stone frescoes adorn these walls, depicting the Mother Goddess in all her aspects: Kali creating, Kali destroying, Kali dancing on the body of her consort, clutching the severed heads of her enemies in her four arms, her tongue lolling with madness.

Except here, instead of the black-skinned goddess I grew up knowing, Kali is a metal giant. As I draw closer, the shapes resolve themselves: Kali, four-armed, wearing a skirt of human heads. Kali, holding her own severed head in her hands, the head drinking oil out of the stump of her metal neck, trampling a couple in the throes of passion.

The oil that I've been following is everywhere. It coats the walls. It drips from the severed heads of the statues and the frescoes.

SANJAYA?

A hiss, a whine of static. "Babaji...signal...block...reports...Kali...full desync," comes the familiar voice. A hiss, a crackle. "Power...authorized..."

The voice fades away. I have a bad feeling about this.

The Kali technicians have always been more than just technicians. They worship her. My children call me father, but Bay Six... We've all heard the stories. It's no small thing to see your gods come alive. And servicing the Mother Goddess has always been more than just an oil change.

I prime my lesser cannon and break through into the third and final courtyard. And I stop, and I shudder, even though I cannot feel horror in this frame.

Ants lie everywhere, lit by the flames that adorn the walls. In the flickering, I can see white hazmat suits. Cultist robes woven with technician insignias. Army uniforms. Great piles reach up to my knees, staked through and pinned with great metal rods. Arms wave and mouths scream in agony. From them ekes a slow, unceasing river of what I had mistaken for oil.

And above them, kneeling, is the four-armed Shikari herself. The firelight flickers across her red metal skin. The gaping maw is open in a terrible silent parody of laughter, the arms wrapped around her body, shaking. A necklace of severed heads bleeds onto the carapace.

KALI, DESTROYER OF ALL THINGS.

The gaping mouth closes, the great metal face droops to one side, the eyes shine a terrible and brilliant red.

VISHNU, PRESERVER, PROTECTOR, she greets me. HAVE THEY SENT YOU TO TAKE MY TOYS AWAY FROM ME?

I raise my main gun in response. She shakes her head, and out of the throat comes something like a chuckle.

YOU THINK YOU COULD TAKE ME? She roars, spreading her four arms wide. Flames sprout from her mouth, charring the closest of the piles. ME, THE FIRST, THE MOST TERRIBLE?

I CAN TRY, I say, BUT I'M NOT HERE TO FIGHT. POWER DOWN, KALI.

She screams at me, a sound that will carry clear to the cities nearby and make grown men tremble, and leaps. It's a noise that could make my unflexing steel buckle and warp. But I'm ready. I leap back and fire, aiming for the knees. My trusty Padma spits hellfire. Kali's left knee explodes. The great arms miss me by mere feet.

She makes no attempt to defend herself, but claws at me, as if to rip me apart with just her hands. I swing out of the reach of the crushing arms. My autocannon rake her sides as I roll. She staggers, crushing corpses, swearing. Her curses are a stream of napalm. I kneel in the slick ooze and fire again. She slumps, red eyes confused.

WHY? HAVE I DONE SOMETHING WRONG?

THIS IS TERRIBLE. THIS IS EVIL.

The great head lolls about. Something is happening inside. WE ARE TERRIBLE! WE ARE GODS! THEY WORSHIP US AS GODS! WORSHIP DEMANDS SACRIFICE!

I look down at the screaming heaps of dying men and women. WE WERE SUPPOSED TO PROTECT THEM.

She wavers, as if confused. And then some part of her—the part that once knew love and duty, the part that signed on a dotted line—regains control, and she realizes what she has done. She screams, a long, wailing shriek that will haunt my nightmares forever.

. . .

"That's the fourth," says Sanjaya softly. "Kali-Shikari is too unstable. I think they'll retire the whole line."

"It's the arms," says Bhanu, who has studied these things. "Too many arms, too much weaponry. Too different from the human body-map. I'm going through her technicians' logs, and it turns out she's had the symptoms for months. Memory loss, confusion, the shakes. Nobody reported it. They were too busy worshiping her."

They speak to me from the comfort of a helicopter gunship, safe in the distance, as I accompany the long train towing the bodies of men and women out of that terrible place. Long lines of the living, men and women, are converging on the site, the charnel stink keeping them away from me, but still close enough that I can hear their wailing. The families of the dead, probably. There are picket lines and a politician holding court. I pause to look at them, and they shake and back away.

"Six hundred staff," says Sanjaya. "She butchered six hundred."

IT'S NOT JUST THE ARMS, I want to tell them. SHE BE-CAME WHAT THEY THOUGHT SHE WAS. SHE BECAME A GOD.

But I don't. Instead, once the train is done and the officials have made the appropriate noises, I wade into the ocean. The waves wash over me. The moon is bright tonight, like an iridescent pearl, and the water rocks me gently as my feet sink into the ocean floor.

"Babaji?" tries Sanjaya, ever faithful.

LET ME BE, I tell them, weary beyond all measure in a body that can never feel tired. Kali's scream still rings in my head. LET ME REST.

It is hard to see a Shikari gone bad. It starts with little things—anger, memory loss, small tics and tremors. The human mind is a fragile thing. We were meant for a fleshy prisons, not these bodies of steel and alloy that they put us in. Touch. Taste. Adrenaline. Dopamine. Oxytocin. Emotions. These things matter. The software that they wrap around us tries to simulate this stuff, but nothing's perfect. Eventually, the sheer wrongness of it gets to you. Once the neural feedback loops kick in, you're done for. Anxiety, terror, depression—they told us this in boot camp. It starts with the shakes. Then the blackouts. Time lost, unaccounted for. Then the hallucinations. Psychosis. The fragmentation. And not always in that order.

The Kali line has always been a bit on the manic side. There are others that have just stopped moving, lost all will, until the techs ripped them apart and dug into the brains and found nothing, just dumb software running routine checks, the ghost of a pilot somewhere inside occasionally lighting up something in a poor imitation of life.

The techs call it desyncing. We—those of us who fight— call it death. All we had to do, they said, was hold on long enough until they'd figured out how to make AI that could do the job.

All we had to do was kill and kill and kill until we die, screaming, inside the metal tombs our own bodies.

A new voice penetrates my skull. "Vishnu, this is Command. Report for debriefing ASAP, over."

The waves wash against me in silence.

"Vishnu, I repeat, this is Command. If you can hear me, report for debrief immediately, over."

I HEAR YOU, COMMAND, I say at last. I'LL BE THERE SOON.

And in the darkness, my hands shake.

• • •

Command is an old man in battle fatigues, tall but bent with age, surrounded by a rolling office of technicians and soldiers who all seem to have the same face. The only one in nonregulation uniform is the psychiatrist, a woman dressed in short, strangely utilitarian green. They make me go over what happened.

I play back all my logs, explain my interpretation of the incident. The technicians make notes and parse the data, making incomprehensible noises to each other. The psychologist walks dangerously close to me, heels—who wears heels in a military base?—clack-clack-clacking against the steel, peering up at me. The old general is frowning. I have the strange feeling that I've seen him before, but for some reason—maybe because this place is shielded—my facial ID system isn't working properly.

"And you're one hundred percent positive you saw no signs of desyncing before this? One hundred percent?"

MY LAST DEPLOYMENT WITH HER WAS IN SEPTEMBER.

"Dammit," he says. "We're losing them faster than ever."

"Perhaps it's the upgrades, sir," one particularly noisy technician volunteers. "The neural load on Kali must be very high already, and those six arms... It's not like we're built to operate six arms—"

The general quells him with a look. She mumbles and falls silent. The psychiatrist, meanwhile, has come to a stop in front of my arm.

"Vishnu-ji," she says. "Why is your hand twitching?"

BATTLE DAMAGE, I say automatically. NEURAL FEED-BACK FROM REPETITIVE GUNFIRE. IT HAPPENS.

I don't know why I said that. It's not true.

The psychologist doesn't believe me. But I am a god, dammit. You will believe me. My twitching hand curls into a fist.

"Leave us," the general says to the psychologist.

She hesitates. "Sir, I am mandated by the High Court—"

"This is a military facility, Doctor Chaudury, and when I

say leave, you can either walk out or be thrown out."

He waits until her clack-clack-clacking has died down, then turns back to me.

"Lieutenant," he says. "I'm talking to the man I once signed up and trained for this job. The man inside this tin hulk. You there, Officer?"

I AM VISHNU.

"Lieutenant Arjun Shetty," says the general coolly, looking straight into my eyes. Eyes the size of his head. "They can put you in a glorified metal uniform, but you're still the boy I took and trained into this."

I AM VISHNU, SIR.

But suddenly I know him. And suddenly I can see the faces of the people standing around him. They're not the same faces at all. The only thing they have in common is that they all look terrified.

"I know you're dying in there," he says, not breaking his gaze. "I know you've fought for your country and you've done us proud. But there aren't enough of you. Not enough Shikari, not enough soldiers like you willing to put their hearts on the line for our country. So I'm going to give you an order: if you're going to crack, you'll tell us. You won't hurt anyone. You were built to protect. Vishnu. Shetty. You are protectors. You don't fall apart on us the way that bitch did, you understand?"

My fists clench and unclench. One of them is shaking, and I can't control it, but I can still salute.

SIR.

They haul me into a metal coffin and take me home. On the way back, Sanjay keeps trying to tell me something.

"The DRDO research guys made a huge breakthrough, Babaji," he keeps saying, over and over. "It looks like those creatures are silicon-based through and through. Silicon-based! It's not armor but skin! Just like you, Babaji. They say it looks like every inch of that body can suck up silicon, basalt, carbon, all sorts of material, and use it to heal and grow. Their neurons look like transistors! They say the skin samples even look like they can replicate! Sand, Babaji, sand!"

THAT'S GOOD, I say, not really listening. I'm trying to keep my hands from shivering. Open. Close. Open. Close. There is a darkness closing in that is more than just the darkness of the transport vehicle.

"Explains why they hit the Moon, yah? All that material just lying around. They hit the Moon, replicate, replicate, leap down the gravity well to the Earth, and we have so much more silicon lying around, our crust is like twenty-five percent silicon . . ."

SANJAY. I DON'T WANT TO KNOW WHAT THEY'RE DO-ING ON THE DAMNED MOON. JUST TELL ME IF THIS MEANS WE CAN KILL THEM FASTER.

Sanjay, for once, ignores me, too caught up in his own excitement. He starts yapping on and on about logic gates and electromagnetic fields and disruption flows. All I hear is "EMP" and "bomb."

"That's why that Japanese Shikari was doing so well, Babaji! The Matari, remember? Susanoo or some strange name like that. Electrical discharge weapons? Their Lightning Whip technology?"

THAT'S GOOD, SANJAY, I say slowly, letting the darkness take me. Open. Close. Open. Close. THAT'S VERY, VERY GOOD.

.   .   .   .

I dream. I dream of darkness and moonlight on the ocean, of thunder and lightning, of a man screaming in pain as his wife and children die.

And in my dreams, the darkness rises and crashes into me, bowling me over.

. . .

I wake.

The ocean swells. My quivering hands: waves roll, I shake. Roll. Shiver. Roll. Shudder. Roll. Shake. There's a voice in my ear and a terrible buzzing in my head.

The moonlit ocean touches my skin, and I taste the ghost of salt water in a mouth that no longer has anything to taste with.

Not far from me lies a dark and terrible shape, bleeding a thick ichor that turns the dark ocean silvery.

It wasn't a dream. I've blacked out. The ruins of my delivery vehicle lie twisted and mangled on the shore. There's a crater of some kind there that I can't process. The road is twisted, tangled.

Am I desyncing? Is this fear that makes me shake? Fear is for ants. I am Vishnu. I get to my feet. Warnings, error messages. My servomotors are screaming. L3 and L4 command relay nodes are down; the backup routing system has taken over my entire left side. My secondary batteries have almost been ripped out of my ribcage. My cannon is almost out of bullets.

"Baba-ji—" Crackle, hiss.

The Enemy lies just a stone's throw from me, bleeding but conscious. It reminds me of a time where I perused the Internet, looking at the bizarre crosses of creatures artists came up with. This one falls somewhere between a lobster and a scorpion. Four crustacean-like pillars support its bulbous body, all layered in glistening chitin. Segments of folded shell stretched out far behind its body. I can see where my bullets have blasted it to bits, gouging out silvery chunks of flesh the size of men. A pair of pincers, broken and shattered now, sit at the ends of knobby limbs protruding from below its flat skull.

A great eye turns in its face and rolls to greet me out of that nightmarish bulk. Curved, sickle-like mandibles erupt in a terrible grin from what might be its face. Something thrashes behind it, stirring up new waves that bow out to the sides before falling flat. Another of the appendages breaches the surface of the water, flailing alongside the first.

Even in death, it challenges me. I fire once, twice at that hideous eye. At this range, the bullets explode with so much ferocity they reduce the entire head into silvery rice and curry.

And suddenly there is a great thunderclap as a meteorite hits the ocean not far from where I stand, sending up a wave that smashes into me like the fist of God himself. I'm picked up and flung head over heels. For once, my thoughts are cold, analytical. A new Enemy, I decide immediately as I scramble to my feet in the mud.

There's no ceremony in its arrival. The creature shakes itself, sending beads of water back into the ocean. Its carapace is the color of burning rock. Ripples of red light dance over its shell, winking out of existence as it turns to face me.

The fear drains away. Vishnu doesn't do fear.

Something like fangs click together like a helicopter's blades against stone. Something like arms bare. Something like a mouth screams.

It's a challenge. One I intend to meet. It rushes me, moving through the water with an ease that shouldn't be possible for something with its body.

I swing Padma around, operating with the efficiency only programming and nerves of fiber optics can bring about. I fire. Twin reports ring out, deafening my auditory systems to all other noises hanging below the explosions.

The Enemy reels as plumes of fire blossom over its plate-like chest. Tails whip across the surface of the ocean in a frenzy. Silver collides with water, foaming on contact and sending up pillars of steam that vanish almost as quickly. The monster's body cracks like it's being pelted by a storm of river stones. But it doesn't stop.

I take it for what it's worth: A minor problem. Solution: Destroy the Enemy without reservation. Maximum effort and energy expenditure.

I re-prime my cannon, loading up all secondary barrels. I'm down to my last two uranium slugs. It's too precious to fire. But I have my flechettes, tucked away somewhere in the terrible ingenuity of Padma. The gun spits once, twice, thrice, peppering the Indian Ocean with razor-sharp slugs of steel that rip through the air like a metal storm.

The feedback is terrible. A lance of cold electricity rakes the inside of my left arm as I track the creature's movements. It surges forward, tails beating across the ocean to the sounds of wet thunder. Calculations flood my mind to answer a problem I hadn't even considered: How fast is it closing in versus the speed of my cannon and the resulting explosion radius?

Answer: Too fast.

A part of me pauses at the results. I see the numbers and know the exact measures I need to take, but the math doesn't add up. My vision flares. The math always adds up. Not now. The numbers make sense, but not to a man who remembers a burning building, smoldering bodies, and that he's tottering in place.

Vishnu screams at me, clearing my vision, commanding me to fire. But I am Vishnu. And I'm torn. Something visceral manifests in my gut, knotting and writhing like a bundle of spastic eels.

I lower the cannon.

And the Enemy slams into me.

I teeter, but something keeps me from falling over. My body pivots and I feel it grow farther away. One of my fists balls and crashes into the side of the Enemy. Another thundercrack as its shell splits from the impact.

Vishnu screams at me. The cannon. The cannon. My hand shakes, and the cannon feels like a dream. I can't make sense of it. It's formless—an idea that a man who's lost everything clings to. A tool for revenge that can't come. My other hand forms a stiff shovel, plunging itself into broken shell as it tries to stitch itself back together.

A terrible warmth spreads over my fingers as I root through its insides. Its silvery mass clings to my digits, registering a series of numbers related to bodily temperature, volume, and the chemical makeup of the Enemy.

I push the data aside—push Vishnu aside. A primal scream builds in my chest, rattling its way through my throat. It's the noise of a man who has lost everything. A man who's nursing the fire of a burning building deep within him. The kind of fire that sets your marrow alight.

I use it to drive my hand deeper into the Enemy, rooting around inside its body. A mass, like a bundle of roots, brushes back against me. I close my fingers around them and rip. The mass resists me, sending the crustacean-like monster into a twitching frenzy.

It thrashes, trying to shake me free. One of its pincers clubs my side as it brays in warbling tones.

The impact shakes through me, registering on two levels: Vishnu takes it in with a calculation reserved for machinery. Sensors, feedback, line failures, energy pathways recalculated, recalibrated.

I feel like I've been hammered by clubs.

The creature yowls, mandibles clicking in staccato beat.

I ignore it as the heat inside me builds.

"Vishnu—Babaji, come in. Your readings...all over the place. We think you're desyncing, Babaji. Repeat—desyncing. Acknowledge? Return to base. Babaji!"

Desyncing, me? My minds turn to Kali. Vishnu remembers her, a goddess. A destroyer. I remember what she'd been pushed to. What she'd done. And how she went out.

I CAN'T LEAVE NOW, I try to tell the crackling line, but nothing meets me but the hiss of static.

One of the Enemy's tails lances overtop its body, coming down to drive the bony spear-end into my shoulder.

Instinct, not programming, drives me to reach overhead and grab hold of the monster's tail. I dig fingers of steel, driven by man's iron resolve, into the armor-skin. I hold tight, remembering my other arm—remembering Vishnu. I prime my cannon, load my last uranium slug, and fire point blank.

The explosion knocks me back like a ragdoll. Sensors in my arm scream. Brilliant light, too many shades for me to make out, wash over my sight. The heat prompts a series of numbers to scrawl over my vision. I tune it out, feeling the inferno instead. I'm reminded of the first time I touch my hand to a gas burner, despite my mother's warning. The heat is of a temperature where all I feel is just the first flash. The rest is a numbing weight I can't process. My skin is heavy. Too heavy. The Enemy is screaming. It is reeling.

I stagger back, planting my feet as Vishnu's thoughts echo in the background.

"Babaji—" Static crackles behind his words. "—desyncing. Return—"

The words fall away, carrying no meaning to me.

Water plumes in the distance. A second pillar erupts next to the first formation. Two more creatures, mirroring the one in front of me, emerging, skins glowing red and steaming from the heat and the water.

Vishnu runs a calculation on the odds of survival.

I ignore it, fixing my gaze on the thing that staggers and screams. My chest aches. Vishnu tells me, us, that our plating is scorched. Bits of my torso are slagged to near unrepairable status. My cannon tires to prime itself, failing. The weapon's mouth is the sort of orange you find in volcanos and metal shops. The metal warps in front of me, losing the hot and violent color as bits of globular steel fall into the ocean to send up gouts of steam.

I twist, jamming the burning and ruined weapon into the dying Enemy's face, pressing those terrible snapping mandibles into the ocean, holding it down until the tail stops whipping and the arms stop ripping at my skin.

"Babaji, disengage. Babaji, come home! Desyncing—You're—"

Maybe I am. But I have a duty. Then they made me Vishnu, The Protector. I/we won't fail. Can't fail.

"Babaji, your mind...the signals. Come back!"

I/we force my/our wrecked cannon deeper into the shattered shell, twisting the arm back and forth until it buries well within the Enemy. The weapon still pulses in accordance with our will. The knots in our stomach, the molten anger, the cold crackle of Vishnu's resolve... We channel it all.

Electricity arcs through us, making its way into the weapon, where it all goes wrong. Everything within our arm expands. The power falters for a wink, flashing out before coming back to scream. Fire builds within the cannon and finds its way out. Metal warps and gives way under the explosion. Carmine light, tinged with smears of vermillion, blossom across our vision and deep within the Enemy's body.

I stagger back from the force. Hydraulic fluid, along with an assortment of other viscous liquids, stream from the remnants of my arm. The Enemy before me is a ruined and smoking shell. Noxious white bubbles out from what's left of its shell, spilling onto the ocean.

I ignore it all to focus on the two creatures closing in. Vishnu is screaming that his systems are shutting down. His systems? My systems. We're supposed to be one. I'm not sure what changed.

"Babaji…"

Vishnu's screams are distant now, growing further away. The darkness swirls on the moonlit sea. My limbs are like grains of sand, loose and crumbling before me. I stagger forward a step, sinking deeper into the ocean.

"Babaji, disengage. Come back. Come back!"

Flicker. I can see them. I can see my wife and daughter. There they are, standing on the water. She's running to me, leaving her mother behind. Something's wrong with the way she runs.

Flicker. My daughter closes on me, mandibles clacking a discordant and percussive beat. Except she's not my daughter anymore. She's the Enemy.

Enraged, we right myself, twisting to launch an uppercut with my remaining fist. I fall short. Pincers slam into my shoulders. The pain drives Vishnu back into me, or me back into him, like two lightning bolts striking each other. The world becomes a pixelated haze that takes its time to clear. I/we can feel it, the steel skin tearing, the servomotors dying, the energy delivery subsystems winking out in showers of terrible sparks.

Our ruined forearm hisses spitefully, still steaming. It punches through the air-water almost of its own accord. The metal catches the moon's light in full for a passing second, looking like it's made from pearls, not steel, and then it buries itself in a mouth full of shredding teeth and is ripped from me.

Metal screams. We scream.

"Babaji, other Shikari incoming. Come home. Babaji!"

The Enemy in front of me opens a pincer and slams it into our torso, braying in a challenge.

We answer it in kind, releasing a warbling cry of whining metal and the cavernous booms of combustion engines.

We shove the creature back.

"Babaji, stop. You're desyncing. Stop."

Wrong. We're not desyncing. His words make no sense to a machine. We're merging. Becoming something more. Vishnu is more than a machine now, more than a man.

The second Enemy arrives, slams into me. A knee joint explodes.

We scream again, clawing, gripping, pushing both creatures in front of us with our one good arm and the tottering bulk of our chest. We dig deep, clawing at what I can of our operating system core. There are things here we can use. The chemical makeup of the fluids pouring out of me. The conduit lines that spark in their death throes. And, here, here—our nuclear heart, the great engine-furnace that powers our every move.

Kali died deluded: a goddess of death, meant to bring that to our enemies. She brought it out on our subjects, on the ants, on our families.

Vishnu would die concluded. Resolved. A protector. Sparing the ants. Keeping them from screaming, burning, teetering and tottering like a man had so long ago.

We scream louder, pushing the Enemy back, hanging onto it like grim death. We need to get them out. We need to get them away. Our heart responds to old subsystems buried deep within me, throwing up a myriad of fail-safes in my way. Are you authorized to do this? OP-4 level clearance required. Are you sure? Runtime diagnostics required. Confirm damage threshold?

A blazing pincer cuts through the night, burying itself in

our side. It digs in. Metal mandibles sink into our shoulder. We are being pulled apart.

"Babaji!"

That's what they call us. We're their god. Their protector. My wife. My daughter. My crew. All of them.

"Babaji!"

Vishnu. That's who that title belongs to. Not the man inside him. Am I still one?

Are you sure you want to do this, asks our heart. This will result in critical damage.

We don't want to destroy our heart. But yes, yes, yes, a thousand times yes.

The ocean threatens to swallow us now. It creeps over my waist as the light before my eyes dims. It drags us away, machine and monsters locked in terrible combat, towards its dark depths.

Are you sure you want to do this?

Damn right we do. We are a god, and you will listen.

Command accepted. Nuclear core critical. System will destruct in 3...2...1.

And then the world explodes. Wiping out the monsters, wiping out the machine, wiping out the man. A new sun is born on the Indian Ocean.

And finally, there is peace.

Excerpt from The Tea Master and the Detective

by Aliette de Bodard

The new client sat in the chair reserved for customers, levelly gazing at *The Shadow's Child*—hands apart, legs crossed under the jade-green fabric of her tunic. The tunic itself had been high-quality once, displaying elegant, coordinated patterns, but it was patched, and the patterns were five years old at least, the stuff that got laughed at even in a provincial backwater such as the Scattered Pearls belt. Her skin was dark, her nose aquiline. When she spoke, her accent was flawlessly Inner Habitats. "My name is Long Chau. You have a good reputation as a brewer of serenity. I want to use your services."

The Shadow's Child stifled a bitter laugh. Whatever her reputation was, it hadn't translated into customers fighting to see her. "Go ahead."

That gaze again from Long Chau. *The Shadow's Child* was used to respect or fear; to downcast eyes; to awkwardness, even, with people who weren't used to dealing with a shipmind, especially one that wasn't involved in passenger service.

The Shadow's Child's body—the metal hull that encased her heartroom and her core—was far away from the office compartment they were both in. The avatar she projected into the habitat wasn't much different from it: a large, sweeping mass of metal and optics that took up most of the office, shifting between different angles on the hull and ports, giving people a glimpse of what she was really like— vast enough to transport merchant crews and supplies, the whole of her hanging in the cool vacuum of space outside the orbitals of the Scattered Pearls belt, with bots crowding her hulls and sensors constantly bombarded by particles. She could have made herself small and unthreatening. She could have hovered over people's shoulders like a pet or a children's toy, as was the fashion amongst the older shipminds. But she'd lived through a war, an uprising and a famine, and she was done with diminishing herself to spare the feelings of others.

Long Chau said, "I'm going into deep spaces to recover something. I need you to make a blend that keeps me functional."

Now that was surprising. "Most of my customers prefer oblivion when they travel between the stars," *The Shadow's Child* said.

A snort from Long Chau. "I'm not a drugged fool."

Or a fool at all. The name she'd given, Long Chau, was an improbable confection of syllables, a style name, except as style names went it was utterly unsubtle. *Dragon Pearl*. "But you're drugged, aren't you?" *The Shadow's Child* asked. She kept her voice gentle, at that tricky balance point where customers had trust, but no fear.

An expansive shrug from Long Chau. "Of course I'm drugged." She didn't offer further explanation, but *The Shadow's Child* saw the way she held herself. She was languid and cool, seemingly in utter control, but that particular stillness was that of a spring wound so tight it'd snap.

"May I?" *The Shadow's Child* asked, drifting closer and calling up the bots. She wasn't physically there, but physical presence was mostly overrated: the bots moved as easily as the ones onboard her real body.

Long Chau didn't even flinch as they climbed up her face. Two of them settled at the corner of her eyes, two at the edge of her lips, and a host clung to the thick mane of her hair. Most people, for all their familiarity with bots, would have recoiled.

A human heartbeat, two: data flowed back to *The Shadow's Child*, thick and fast. She sorted it out easily, plotting graphs and discarding the errant measurements in less than the time it took the bots to drop down from Long Chau's head.

She gazed, for a moment, at the thick knot of electrical impulses in Long Chau's brain, a frenzied and complex dance of neuron activation. For all her computational power, she couldn't hope to hold it all in her thoughts, or even analyse it all, but she'd seen enough patterns to be able to recognise its base parameters.

Long Chau was drugged to the gills, and more: her triggers were all out of balance, too slow at low stimuli and completely wild past a certain threshold. *The Shadow's Child* accessed Long Chau's public records, again. She finally asked a question she usually avoided. "The drugs—did your doctor prescribe these to you?"

Long Chau smiled. "Of course not. You don't need a doctor, these days."

"For some things, maybe you should," *The Shadow's Child* said, more sharply than she intended to.

"You're not one."

"No," *The Shadow's Child* said. "And perhaps not the person who can help you."

"Who said I wanted to be helped?" Long Chau shifted, smiling widely—distantly, serenely amused. "I'm happy with what I've achieved."

"Except that you came to see me."

"Ah. Yes." She shook her head with that same odd languidness. "I do have... an annoying side effect. I'm more focused and faster, but only in a narrow range. Deep spaces are well outside that range."

The Shadow's Child had never dealt very well with dancing around the truth. "What are you talking about? Anxiety? Traumatic reaction?"

"Fuzziness," Long Chau said. "I can't *think* in deep spaces."

It wasn't unusual. Time and space got weird, especially deeper in. It took effort to remain functional. Some people could, some people couldn't. *The Shadow's Child* had had one lieutenant who spent every dive into deep spaces curled up on the bed, whimpering—it had been a hundred years ago, before the brews got developed, before brewers of serenity started doing brisk business on space stations and orbitals, selling teas and brews that made it easier for humans to bear the unknowable space shipminds used to travel faster than light.

"You could stop taking the drugs. It would probably help," *The Shadow's Child* said.

"I could." Long Chau's tone made it clear that she wouldn't even consider it. *The Shadow's Child* thought for a while, reviewing evidence as she did. Long Chau was entirely right. She was no doctor; merely a small-rank brewer of serenity struggling to make ends meet. And she just couldn't afford to ignore a customer.

"I could make a blend that would suit you," *The Shadow's Child* said.

Long Chau smiled. "Good. Go on."

Deep spaces. She hadn't returned to them since the Ten Thousand Flags uprising—since her entire crew died and left her stranded. *The Shadow's Child* hesitated again—a moment only—and said, "I don't want to be responsible for accidents. With all that you have in your body, I'd want to monitor you quite closely after you drink the blend."

"I'll have your bots."

"Bots won't be able to react fast enough, with the time differentials. I want to be with you in deep spaces. And it won't come cheap."

Long Chau was silent for a while, staring at her. At length, she stretched, like a sated cat. "I see." She smiled. "I hadn't thought you'd want to return to deep spaces, even for a price. Not after what happened to you there."

It was like a gut punch. For a brief, startling moment *The Shadow's Child* was hanging, not in a comforting void, but somewhere else, where the stars kept shifting and contorting. The dead bodies of her crew littered her corridors, and the temperature was all wrong, everything pressing and grinding against her hull, a sound like a keening lament, metal pushed past endurance and sensors going dark one after the other, a scream in her ears that was hers, that had always been hers...

"How—" *The Shadow's Child* shifted, showing her full size, a desperate attempt to make Long Chau back away. But Long Chau sat in the chair with a mocking, distant smile, and didn't move. "It's not public, or even easily accessible. You can't possibly have found—"

Long Chau shook her head. Her lips, parted, were as thin as a knife. "It is my business to work out things that other people don't pick up on. As I said—I'm more focused. You hesitated before saying yes."

"Because you're a difficult customer."

"It could have been that. But you kept hesitating afterwards. If you'd simply decided to accommodate a difficult customer, the moment of decision would have been the only time you slowed down. There was something else about this bothering you."

"It was a fraction of one of your heartbeats. Humans don't pick up on this."

"They don't." Nothing ventured, again; no hint that she found the silence awkward or unpleasant.

The Shadow's Child hesitated—again for a bare moment, because what her customers did with her blends was none of her business. But she'd just committed to being in deep spaces again, and that was beyond her short limit of unpleasant surprises for the day. "You haven't told me what you need to find in deep spaces."

Again, that lazy, unsettling smile. "A corpse."

Then again, perhaps she was wrong about the unpleasant surprises.

• • •

The Shadow's Child was putting the finishing touches to a test batch of Long Chau's blend. The sweet, intoxicating smell of honeydreamer saturated the room. Two bots clung to the inside of the teapot, taking samples and comparing them to the simulations' results—almost done...

Someone knocked at the door.

"Go away," *The Shadow's Child* started, and then she saw it was Bao, the woman who collected the rent for the compartment that served as her office and laboratory. Her heart sank. "I'm sorry. I didn't mean to be rude." The rent. It had to be the rent. *The Shadow's Child* had scrapped together everything she could in the last days of the year and barely met the deadline, but there were few rules where the Inner Habitat families were concerned.

"May I?" Bao asked.

The Shadow's Child hesitated, but of course Bao would simply be back, if she said no. Bao was polite and pleasant, but unrelenting—which was why the Western Pavilion Le family, who owned *The Shadow's Child's* compartment, employed her.

"Come in," *The Shadow's Child* said. She and Bao had this uneasy relationship, not quite friendship but almost. Bao had been one of the only people willing to risk renting space to a mindship—someone who needed a compartment to receive visitors in-habitat, but who didn't really live there, physically speaking, whom you couldn't easily intimidate or frighten with a couple of toughs if the rent wasn't paid.

The Shadow's Child had the bots prepare tea, but Bao waved a hand. "I won't be long." She pulled up the same chair Long Chau had settled in, and sat, gazing back at *The Shadow's Child*, cool and collected. Unlike Long Chau, her tunic was the latest fashion. The calligraphied verses, bold and forceful, came from Ngu Hoa Giang, the current darling of the Imperial Court. Bao's face was impeccable, with the peculiar smoothness of successive rejuv treatments—and her bots, instead of riding in her sleeves, hung in a jewelled cascade from both her shoulders, an effect that was all the more striking because Bao wore her hair short, in defiance of all conventions. "This is a business visit, in case you had doubts."

"The rent," *The Shadow's Child* said. "I can pay—"

Bao shook her head. The bots moved, slowly. "You did pay." Her voice was low-pitched, and confident. She picked up the tea from the bots, breathed it in; but didn't drink. She never did, when on business. She always said she'd feel personally implicated if she shared food or drink, though she enjoyed the smell of it.

"Then I don't know why you're here." She didn't mean to be this impolite, but it was out of her before she could think.

Bao sighed. "The Western Pavilion Le own the compartment. There's not much that escapes them. Your revenue—"

"It's good enough," *The Shadow's Child* said. She forced

herself to be nonchalant.

"Is it?" Bao's gaze was piercing. "I said business, but perhaps it'd be more accurate to say I'm here as a friend. Or a concerned relative. You may not need much space, or that much money to pay for it—"

If only. She should have had money for her repairs, but everything had gone into making sure she wouldn't find herself homeless. Shipminds such as her were meant to be the centre of families: grown by alchemists in laboratories, borne by human mothers and implanted into the ship-bodies designed for them, they were much longer lived than humans—the repositories of memories and knowledge, the eldest aunts and grandmothers on whom everyone relied. They were certainly not meant to be penniless and poor, and *The Shadow's Child* would die before she'd beg from her younger relatives—who were, in any case, even worse off than her. Their salaries as minor scholars in the ministries paid them a pittance, and they could barely afford their own food.

She could have remained as she was, in orbit around the habitats. But without office space, how could she practise her trade? No one would take a shuttle to come onboard a distant shipmind, not when there were closer and better brewers of serenity available. "I get your point," she said. "And I'm grateful, but—" But she didn't need more stress. She didn't need her niggling worst fears to be proved right.

Bao pulled back the chair, and rose. "But I'm not good news? I seldom am." She shrugged. "I know you won't consider passenger service—"

"No," *The Shadow's Child* said. It was reflex, as if someone had pushed, hard, on an open wound and she'd screamed.

"The money is far better. Especially you—you're a troop transport. You could take on a lot of passengers and cargo each run." Bao's voice was soft.

"I know."

Bao was smart enough to drop the subject. She looked at the bookshelves: not physical books, because *The Shadow's Child* would have needed to read them through her bots, but a selection of the ones in her electronic library, displayed in matching editions in a riot of colours. "I see you have the latest Lao Quy. It's well worth it, if you need a distraction. She's really got to be a master of the form."

Bao and *The Shadow's Child* shared a fondness for epic romances and martial heroes books, the kind of novels scholars looked down on as trash but which sold thousands of copies across the belt. "I haven't started it yet," *The Shadow's Child* said. "But I liked the previous one. Strong chemistry between characters. And to have set it in a small mining operation was a smart change of setting. I loved the mindship and their habitat's Mind lover, trying to find each other after decades had passed."

"Of course you would. She's good," Bao said, fondly. "This one is different. I'd argue better. We can talk about it later, if you want, but I wouldn't want to spoil the experience." She looked at the blend on the stove, and shook her head. "I'm not going to keep you from your customer."

A customer *The Shadow's Child* didn't *like*, but she'd pay handsomely, and—as Bao had all too clearly reminded her—*The Shadow's Child* couldn't afford to be picky.

.   .   .

The Shadow's Child had to take Long Chau onboard, of course. When Long Chau's footsteps echoed in the corridors of her body, it was an odd and unsettling feeling. She'd taken on a few passengers for the army after Vinh and Hanh and her crew died, but everyone had been so careful with her, as if she were made of glass. And after she'd been discharged she'd refused to take on further passengers.

She had no need of sensors or bots to follow Long Chau's progress through her. The footsteps, slow and steady—each of them a jolt in the vastness of her body—went through room after room, unerringly going towards the cabin she'd set aside for Long Chau. From time to time, a longer pause, feet resting lightly on the floor of rooms, a faint heat spreading outward on her tiles: once, near the seventh bay, staring at the scrolling display of fairytales Mother had brought back from the First Planet; another time at the start of the living quarters, reading the Thu Huong quote on houses being a family's heart—new paint and a new calligraphy, replaced after the ambush. *The Shadow's Child* had had network decoration, once: a wealth of intricate interlocked layers only visible with the proper permissions. But she'd lost everything, and she hadn't seen the point of putting more than basic work into this after she was discharged.

When Long Chau reached the cabin, she found a table and a chair, and a cup of steaming tea set there. She raised her eyes, as if she could see *The Shadow's Child* hovering somewhere above her. It was pointless: everything around her was the ship. All *The Shadow's Child* really needed to do was focus her upper layers of attention on this room, while in the background the bots and everything else continued to run without any input, and the solar wind buffeted her hull as her orbit swung her around the habitats—all familiar sensations that barely impinged.

Long Chau pulled up the chair, settling down into it without any apparent nervousness. Her movements were slow and deliberate. *The Shadow's Child* felt it all. The scraping of the chair, all four feet digging into her floors; Long Chau's weight shifting, lightly pressing down on top of the chair. "You're quite lovely," Long Chau said.

It'd have been a compliment from anyone else. From her,

though, said with an utterly impassive face? *The Shadow's Child* couldn't be sure. Not that she should have cared, except that it would affect her relation with a customer. "Your blend is on the table."

A raised eyebrow. "So I've seen." Long Chau considered the cup for a while. *The Shadow's Child*'s bots climbed up onto her face and head again. She let them, without even so much as a reaction. The dense, urgent pattern of her brain activity was now available to *The Shadow's Child*. She'd had enough time now to build a model of what Long Chau considered normal, and nothing there was surprising.

"It's not poisoned." The smell of honeydreamer saturated the room, bringing back, for a brief moment, memories of *The Shadow's Child*'s first disastrous attempt at cooking it, when the bots had failed to remove the carapaces and they had popped in the heat, sending shards flying all over her compartment.

"Of course it's not," Long Chau said, with a hint of annoyance. She raised it to the light, lips slightly parted; stared for a while longer. "It's fascinating, isn't it, that a few herbs and chemicals can have this effect?"

Hours of poring over Long Chau's metabolism and brain patterns, reconstructing the drugs in her system—trying to find out which compounds would keep her functional, guessing at what she might call "slow thoughts", wondering if the mixture would flat-out short-circuit her neurons, make her suicidal or, more likely, even more reckless and over-confident, with the risk she'd endanger her own life on a whim ... "Are you mocking my work?"

"On the contrary," Long Chau said. Her face was set in a peculiar expression, one *The Shadow's Child* couldn't read. "Merely appreciating the value of localised miracles." She sounded... utterly earnest, in a way that disarmed the angry reply *The Shadow's Child* would have given her.

Silence stretched, long, uncomfortable. *The Shadow's Child* became aware again of her core in the heartroom, of the steady beat that sustained her—pulsing muscles and optics and brain matter, holding her connectors in an unbreakable embrace. One two, one two...

In the cabin, Long Chau appeared utterly unfazed. She merely raised the cup to her lips after a long while, and drank from its thin rim in one long, slow go—didn't even seem to breathe while doing so—and set it down on the table. "Shall we go?"

The Shadow's Child didn't need to move to dive into deep spaces. She'd already asked for permission from Traffic Harmony, and within deep spaces it wouldn't matter if they overlapped another ship. She watched Long Chau, because it was her job.

A centiday since she'd taken the blend—fifteen outsider minutes—and no visible effect yet. The tea *The Shadow's Child* had given Long Chau was a mix of a downy white Dragon Quills with a stronger, more full-bodied Prosperity Crescent, with fried starvine root and crushed honeydreamer, scattered among the downy leaves. She watched Long Chau's vitals, saw the minute changes to breath and heartbeat. The hands moved a fraction faster as Long Chau got up and stared at the walls—*through* the walls.

"I'm not there," *The Shadow's Child* said.

"You're in the heartroom. I know." Long Chau's voice was mildly irritated. "I'm familiar with shipminds, though I've seldom had the occasion to go into deep spaces."

While she was speaking, *The Shadow's Child* plunged into deep spaces—not far in, just enough on the edge that she could see Long Chau's reactions. "Tell me about the corpse," she said. Around her, the corridors shifted and changed. A faint, trembling sheen like spilled oil spread across the walls, always in the corner of one's eyes. Outside, the same sheen stole across the habitats, the sun and the distant stars—a distorted rainbow of colour that slowly wiped them out. Her hull was awash with faint cold, the brisk flow of stellar wind around her replaced by a faint, continuous pressure. It should have felt like coming home—like a fish diving into a river at the end of a long, breathless interval onshore—but all she could feel within her was tautness, and the rapid beat from her heartroom, everything pulsing and contracting in ways she couldn't control.

It would be fine. She wasn't where it had happened. She wasn't deep in—just at the very edges, just enough to keep Long Chau satisfied. It would be fine.

"You said any corpse would do," she said.

"Of course." Long Chau appeared utterly unfazed by deep spaces. *The Shadow's Child* would have liked that to be a front, but Long Chau's heartbeat, even and slow, said otherwise. "I'm writing a treatise on decomposition. How the human body changes in deep spaces is a shamefully undervalued area of study."

"I can see why you'd be a success at local poetry clubs," *The Shadow's Child* said, wryly.

It didn't seem to faze Long Chau. "I would be, if I had anything to do with them." She looked around her. The walls had caved in now, receding in what seemed a long and profound distance; the table was folding back on itself, showing the metal it had been made from, the bots that had hammered it into shape—the broken scraps of what it'd be, when it finally broke down, every moment existing tightly folded on top of one another. "How deep are we?"

Two centidays since she'd taken the blend. She seemed fine. Unfair. Heartbeat normal, veins slightly dilated but not past the expected top of the range, pupil constriction slowly easing up—the activity map almost a match for when she'd sat in *The Shadow's Child*'s office. *The Shadow's Child* tried to calm herself down. She stretched her core in the heartroom, slowly and deliberately, away from Long Chau's prying eyes. A good thing she hadn't boosted up the arrogance: it was an easy way to keep people functional in deep spaces if they had enough self-confidence to start with, but she didn't think she could have borne the result for long.

"Not very deep," *The Shadow's Child* said. "I'd rather keep you in safe areas." It was untrue.

"And yourself from unpleasant memories," Long Chau said. "It makes sense." And then, with an odd expression in her voice, "You're not recovered. Even being here makes you nauseous."

"Shipminds don't get nausea," *The Shadow's Child* said. It was a lie—especially now, with no distance between her body and herself, she felt rocked by alternating waves of warmth and cold, her core coming apart in ten thousand pieces in the heartroom. She forced herself to be calm. "And you have no idea what you're talking about. You're guessing."

"I don't guess." Long Chau's voice was curt. "You were in an accident during the uprising. A mission gone bad because of lack of information. Something that badly crippled you, and left you in deep spaces for some time."

She—she'd hung around in places where nothing made sense anymore, with no one alive onboard anymore. The crew was gone, and Captain Vinh was lying curled just outside the heartroom, her hands slowly uncurling as death took hold. Nothing but the sound of her panicked heartbeat, rising and rising through empty corridors and cabin rooms until it seemed to be her whole and only world—she was small and insignificant and she would be forever there, broken and unable to move and forever forgotten, her systems always keeping death at bay...

Long Chau was still speaking, in that same dispassionate tone. As if nothing were wrong, as if she could not feel the chills that ran up and down the corridors, the pressure that was going to squeeze *The Shadow's Child* into bloody shards. "There is no information about you during the uprising, and you're in surprisingly good shape considering your age, and the fact that you're barely scraping by earning your living. That means either a wealthy family—but you don't have the accents of wealth—or that the military shouldered your maintenance until a few years ago." Every word hurt—the currents of deep spaces pressing against her hull, again and again, drawing the will to live out of her—but she couldn't commit suicide because everything was offline or broken.

"But you haven't been with the military for the last five years or so. That ugly gash on your hull, just below the painting of the Azure Dragon gardens, is around that age and no one fixed it. Which means you were discharged shortly after the uprising. You're completely traumatised, but showing no other sign of damage. Meaning whatever happened was under the military's watch, and they repaired it for you. So a mission gone wrong."

"I. Am. Not. Traumatised." It felt like swallowing shards of glass. She'd still be there, body non-functional, coms dead, if another mindship hadn't happened to go by and notice a light blinking on her hull—near that painting Long Chau was so casual about.

It had only been a bi-hour or so, in outside time—eight centidays, nothing more—not even the time it took for a banquet, such a pitiful duration to someone like her. Except that, in deep spaces, it had felt so much longer.

"You tiptoe around deep spaces like a mouse around a tiger's claw." A gentle snort from Long Chau. "See. I don't guess."

"You—" *The Shadow's Child* tried to breathe, to say something, anything that wouldn't be a scream. Outside, the currents of deep spaces bathed her—clinging, lightly, to her hull—like hands, awaiting the right moment to curl into claws. "You have no right."

Long Chau looked puzzled, for a moment. "Why not? You asked me to prove it."

"I didn't."

A long, awkward silence. "Oh. My apologies. I thought you'd want to see how I'd come to those deductions."

The Shadow's Child was still shaking. "No. I don't."

"I see." A long, careful look. "I'm sorry. I didn't mean to hurt, but it doesn't change that it did happen." A further silence. Then, "Tell me about the wreck."

A customer. Long Chau was just a customer. And *The Shadow's Child* needed those, no matter how eccentric they might be. She had to remember that—but all she wanted was to drop Long Chau off on the habitat and forget any of this had ever happened. "There is no shortage of wrecks here. *The Three in the Peach Gardens* isn't very far in, and he was carrying passengers when he died."

"How long ago was that?"

"Not during the uprising. Five years ago," *The Shadow's Child* said. She'd picked a ship she hadn't known, not even as a distant acquaintance. She supposed it'd be different, to see a wreck washed by the tides of deep spaces rather than a recent corpse, but she wasn't sure enough of how she would react.

She'd stared at ships' corpses, back then, after the ambush—at twisted, inert metal, at dead optics, at broken hulls, the damaged wrecks all around her, the lucky ones who'd died—knowing that her own damage wasn't severe enough and that she would merely remain trapped, for moments that would stretch to an eternity.

Long Chau laid a hand on the wall. Her touch was a jolt, a small pinpoint of warmth in the vastness of *The Shadow's Child*'s body. "I see. Fresh is better, from my point of view.

The older corpses just become unrecognisable." She shook her head. "Not much to work on." And then, looking up once more, "You're not disgusted, are you."

"By what you want?" *The Shadow's Child* forced herself to be casual. "I've seen corpses during the uprising. They don't frighten me."

Excerpt from Fire Ant

by Jonathan P. Brazee

Chapter 1

No bonus on this run, Beth told herself as she read the analysis.

Pilot Two Floribeth Salinas O'Shea Dalisay, Hamdani Exploration Corps, ran through her Hummingbird's diagnostics one more time, hoping that she'd missed something, but no. Another dry well.

Beth had been on a long run of dry wells since her last hit: sixteen missions, sixteen times without a bonus. With her expenses, all conveniently taken out of her pay by Hamdani Brothers, that left scant little to send home to her family. She *needed* a bonus.

There was no use wasting time hanging in the barren system. The data she'd collected had been uploaded to corps headquarters, so her work here was done.

She shifted her body in her harness. In zero-G, she didn't have bedsores per se, but she did have contact spots, irritation from where her harness and even her flight suit rubbed her. Her piss tube, which was hypo-allergenic and guaranteed not to irritate, felt like sandpaper. Her finger hovered over her console for a moment as she considered returning to the station. She'd been out for over 62 Standard days—1,494 hours, in fact—and that was a long time to be stuck in her Hummingbird, relying on drugs, nanos, and the devil the Hummingbird pilots called the "stretcher" to keep her muscles from atrophying. Her body cried to get out of her suit, to feel gravity, to walk, to stand naked in a shower as water jets scrubbed off the stink and itch of deep space. She needed the taste of a cold Coke to wash out the days of the food paste the pilots called "slime."

Can't make anything going back, she told herself. *Maybe the next one's it.*

With a heavy heart, she pressed the "Next Mission" button, waiting for HQ's response. Anagolay would be running her calculations, determining what system among the vast reaches of the galaxy would offer the best probability of providing the raw materials that HB needed to fuel its factories. Even better than that, which system provided the best chance at an Alpha world, a planet that could host human life. This was the proverbial golden ring for the pilots of the Exploration Corps. Finding one would set up Beth for life. She could return to New Cebu and open up her own store. With her family's future secure, she could think about finding a husband and starting her own family, raising kids who would never have to leave New Cebu in order to make a living.

Light years away, Ana's circuits did their thing, and the AI sent out a response: SG-4021. The designation meant nothing to her. It was simply one more star system among the 100 billion in the galaxy. All the low-hanging fruit had long been plucked, systems where scans had indicated planets that could support life with minor or no terraforming required. Systems with easily harvested heavy metals had already been explored. Now, 400-plus years since the Grand Expansion, corporations, from the big zaibatsus such as Hamdani Brothers to small indies, searched the black for other jewels to be exploited. Only a tiny fraction of the galaxy's systems had been explored, so no one knew what treasures were out there, waiting to be found.

By accepting the orders, Beth had just locked herself in the *Lily* for another 12 days at a minimum. The thought almost overwhelmed her, and she could swear her piss tube shifted, rubbing her raw.

She could have refused. The OPW Union, which was relatively powerless in most ways, had still managed to get some regulations enacted for deep-space pilots. Commercial pilots, those working for corporations, could only be required to conduct two missions before returning to their bases. Two missions, however, would barely pay for expenses for most of them. Beth wasn't a pilot for charity—her family needed the support. So, this would be Beth's fifth mission on this run.

The trip to SG-4021 would take place in two steps. First, she had to accelerate to a minimum of .54 of the speed of light before entering the gate. The transport back to Nexus Prime would take no sidereal time at all, and only a few moments to reach the next gate to take her to her destination. Then it would be the long deceleration process into the system proper where her scanners could analyze it.

The math was too complicated for a human brain to grasp, and Beth didn't even try. She trusted Ana's vast computing power and her little Hummingbird's ability to make the transit. Fly-by-night indies often got lost between systems, never to be heard from again, but not HB pilots. All of the pilots resented the zaibatsu's roughshod manner, but it was still one of the most competent. The HB Explorer Corps hadn't lost a Hummingbird in over nine years, which was one of the reasons Beth had accepted the contract with them. She had to endure the long, lonely trips in deep space, but she was not particularly brave. As a child and teen, she'd never been bit by the wanderlust bug. She was supporting her extended family, like most Off-Planet Workers, and that required her to survive the work.

New Cebu was a relatively poor world, with the wealth highly concentrated among the planet's Golden Tribe. The masses were dirt poor, but they were the planet's most valuable resource. They became the beasts of burden for all the jobs that the GT's wouldn't sully their precious skin with.

Beth stretched her legs as the *Lily*'s navigation system inputted the instructions. They didn't stretch far. Beth stood 4'6" in her bare feet (137 cm in Universal Standard) and weighed 72 pounds soaking wet (32.6 kgs). She'd always been the smallest girl in her class, but her size had plucked her out of housekeeping at the Montclair Resort on Bally's World to become a pilot in the HB Explorer Corps. She'd received bonuses on three of her first seven missions, earning more than she could have made throughout her 15-year housekeeping contract.

The money might be her primary motivation, but over time, Beth realized she liked being a pilot. Despite the long hours in her cramped cockpit, despite the lack of real food, of tubes to take care of her bodily waste, despite the loneliness, she felt at home in space. She liked flying her Hummingbird, of being the first human to enter new solar systems. She might long to get out of her little ship at the moment, and she was frustrated by her string of dry wells, but she was glad she wasn't cleaning toilets for rich folks anymore. Beth might still be an OPW, but she'd lucked into one of the best jobs someone from her background could have.

Her console command light turned green. She could still refuse the mission without penalty. Every pilot thought that canceling a mission after accepting it would have dire consequences. The pilots might have named Ana after the old Filipino goddess of lost travelers, but the AI belonged to HB, and she was programmed to improve the bottom line. It would not be beyond HB to punish those who canceled missions with systems that had a lower probability of earning the pilot a bonus.

She didn't hesitate. She pushed the command, then flipped down her entertainment screen. Bobo had sent her the link to a two-hundred-year-old feline opera series, and she'd been saving it so she could binge watch it.

She had the time for that now.

.   .   .

Beth ran through the checklist. If something were off, lights would be flashing red, but company policy was company policy, and HB *loved* checklists. She quickly scanned as she watched the timer count down until the *Lily* would enter the gate she'd left three days before. This might be the last time it was ever used. There hadn't been enough in the FR-30072 system to warrant another mission, but the law was the law, and not even the most powerful corporations would fight this. Once set, a gate remained in place, its coordinates logged. Anyone could use it, and unless HB registered a claim, anyone could make do with the system as they would.

There was a vibrant gleaning industry in space exploration. Smaller companies, some being one-man tramps, constantly scanned the data bases, looking for something missed by the larger corporations, or more likely, systems that were not cost-effective for the big boys, but in which a small, low-cost operation could salvage a few BCs.

There was nothing in the last system that would even pique the interest in the gleaners, though. Beth was pretty sure that she was the first and last person to ever travel there.

The green status light started to flash amber, and Beth tensed. She couldn't help it. She'd been through 87 gates in her short 22 years, yet she still had to fight the nervousness that welled up each time before the jump. The gates themselves were essentially foolproof—it was the calculations to enter the gate where a mistake—a fatal mistake—could occur. A vessel could theoretically come apart if it hit the gate off-line, but a more likely accident would be to be sent off to who-knows-where.

Beth would just as soon not experience either one.

The readout reached ten seconds, and time seemed to crawl for her as the remaining seconds ticked off. At three, she raised the silver crucifix that hung around her neck and kissed it while staring ahead at the outside display. Some of her fellow pilots closed their eyes, but Beth wanted to see what was coming—which was a little foolish, because unlike just about every holovid made, there was nothing to see. No stars pulling into lines, no flashing colors. One moment she was in one part of the galaxy, the next she was somewhere else.

The *Lily* passed through the gate and was immediately picked up by Ana on the other side. Within heartbeats, Ana reprogrammed her navigator, took control, and shunted her towards an outbound gate. Still travelling at slightly over the minimum required .54C, it only took her a few seconds to reach her new gate and make the crossing to SG-4021.

Beth would always swear that she could feel a tiny tug as she passed through a gate. Most science-types would scoff at her. It was true that in a very real sense, her body was stretched across the galaxy, her nose lightyears from her butt, but as the saying went, it happened too quickly for her body to realize it was dead and cease functioning.

She took a deep breath, happy to have survived yet again, one of the millions of crossings that would happen today, all without incident. She gave a quick look at her displays. The ship's AI had taken readings the instant the *Lily* had entered the outer system, categorizing stars to confirm her position.

This was high-level math, taking into account the ship's supposed position and how long the light from distant stars would take to reach the target system, then comparing that with known star signatures. It was a matter of bracketing, taking a reading, adjusting, and bracketing again until a confirmation was achieved. Despite the computing power of the ship's AI, it took five seconds to confirm that she had reached SG-4021.

The first order of business was, as always, to launch the return gate. Without it, she'd be stuck in the system forever. Even at maximum speed, she didn't have enough food or O2 to make it back to civilization. The *Lily* might eventually make it, centuries or millenniums from now, but she would be a desiccated mummy, far beyond caring.

The AI immediately shifted its scanners to start analyzing the system. A Hummingbird was designed to explore the galaxy, but its scanners were limited. More powerful scanners could easily be put onboard, but the corporate bean-counters stressed weight over anything else. It took more powerful—read *expensive*—engines to get heavier craft up to gate speeds, so every ounce possible was stripped from the exploration scouts. That was why each pilot was in the smallest 2% of humanity. That was why Beth had no real food on the voyage, subsisting on the densely caloric "slime," paste designed to keep a person alive and not much else. That was why the only physical item Beth had been allowed to carry with her was her small silver cross.

The big ships, be they military or corporate, were powered by the terribly expensive FC engines, but those were limited by economies of scale. Smaller craft, such as Beth's Hummingbird, had to make do with the older tech Bradstone engines, and their ability to push craft to gate speeds was a geometric function.

What's that?

The *Lily's* scanners weren't that effective this far out, but they weren't useless. They were picking up something, something very interesting. The fourth planet from the primary was well within the Goldilocks zone. Her heart jumped.

Don't get excited, Floribeth Salinas, she told herself.

There were thousands of planets discovered that fell within the temperature range that supported Earth-type life. Of those, a grand total of 132 had been discovered that either could support human life as is or with minimal terraforming.

Still, the prospect was exciting. There was more to analyze as she shot towards the system's center. An asteroid belt showed promise of valuable metals, and a small inner-planet probably had fissionables, but her attention remained locked on Planet 4 as the *Lily* slowed down. She'd pass by the asteroid belt close enough to confirm the amount and ease of extraction of the metals, but she'd set a course to enter an orbit about the planet so her scanners could make a detailed analysis.

Beth had already sent a confirmation of arrival to HQ, but she hesitated to send anything more yet. Call her superstitious, but she didn't want to jinx herself. Once she knew something for sure, she'd report.

Beth had never been overly superstitious growing up, but five years as a pilot had changed that. The bulk of HB's pilot corps was Filipino, but there were Brazukas, Ukies, Canucks, EnBee's, Canos, Thais, and others, all OPWs, who plied the black for the GTs, and no matter which planet they were from, pilots became superstitious. Her cousin Bobo said it was because deep space was just too vast for the human mind to comprehend, and superstition was merely a way to try and control the uncontrollable.

Beth raised her cross and kissed it.

. . .

Over the next 26 hours, as the *Lily* passed the outermost planet's orbit and entered the system proper, Beth was focused on her displays. Even this far out, she could tell that the mineral potential in the asteroid belt was significant, more than bonus-worthy. Her dry streak was over, and she'd have a tidy sum to send home. She wanted more, though, and she hoped the beautiful planet four out from the primary would provide that. She already knew it was in the Goldilocks zone, she already knew it had an atmosphere that contained at least some O2. She already knew that the gravity was 1.12 Earth Standard. Those were all well and good, but she had to get the *Lily* in orbit for a more detailed analysis. There were too many possibilities that could render the planet a bust.

Still, Beth spent much of the time daydreaming how she would spend her bonus. She considered, then rejected half-a-dozen ventures. If she was smart about this, she could not only live comfortably for the rest of her life, but live *well*.

She catnapped a few times, drifting off to sleep, but the excitement was too much of a stimulant. There was nothing she could do to affect the outcome, but she was afraid of falling asleep, then waking up to find out she'd been dreaming. She had to speed things up, or she was going to go crazy.

On her current trajectory, the *Lily* would reach SG-4021-4 and slip into orbit in another 32 hours, 13 minutes. The ship was a fairly simple craft, all things considering. Beth had to bleed off her speed, or she'd simply shoot right past the planet, hence the somewhat circuitous route into the system. There was another way, though, that could be taken when the conditions were right. Beth could use the gravity of one of the system's gas giants to slow the ship down—if they were in the correct position relative to each other. As luck would have it, that might be the case.

Beth queried her AI, and the numbers looked good. She could nudge the *Lily* in front of SG-4021-8, gaining a little velocity, but bleeding off more by turning the ship away, letting the planet's gravity act as a drag. This would take some tricky maneuvering—she didn't want to use the planet for the more common gravity assist trajectory, the slingshot which would increase her speed. She'd have to rely on "icing" the *Lily*, swinging its aft end around at full power to push the ship into the right trajectory. She ran the preliminary calculations, and she had a 23-minute window remaining to initiate the change of course.

"How much time will the maneuver save me?"

"Four hours, five minutes, and thirty-two seconds, depending on time of initiation," her AI passed into the implant behind her ear.

That's all? That's not much.

She knew she'd probably be better off taking the standard trajectory in. Deviating from the tried-and-true always introduced a degree of risk. On the other hand, four hours was four hours, and the risk was tiny.

Screw it.

"Initiate new approach," she said.

Immediately, the view on her display shifted as the *Lily* turned to its new course. She zoomed in to SG-4021-8, a large, yellow orb, grimacing for a moment as the image of her little *Lily* getting caught up in the planet's gravity well took over her mind. The chances of that happening were miniscule—something would have to seriously go wrong, but Beth had a tendency of worrying about a worst-case scenario. She adjusted her display, zooming in on SG-4021-4 again. It wasn't the lovely blue of Earth, Society, or any of the water worlds. From this distance, it was a dusky tan, but that was not necessarily a bad sign.

Floribeth, she named the planet, soaking in the sight.

Not that she had naming rights. Some of the early ex-plorers had planets named for them, but in today's universe, the corporations that discovered most of the usable planets decided on the name.

Her route was on her display, and the numbers calculated out. The *Lily* was functioning at peak performance—she might bitch about HB, but they kept the Hummingbirds in top condition. The bottom line was that everything was progressing as planned, and for the first time since her initial readings, Beth began to relax.

The gods of the universe were a fickle bunch, however, and just as Beth's eyes began to flutter closed, her alarm jerked her back to full-alert. She immediately checked life support. A Hummingbird was not very robust, and it was possible that a tiny bit of space flotsam had pierced her repeller field, all the protection her scout ship had. To her relief, the life-support system showed green.

"What's going on?" she queried her AI, checking the output of the engines.

They were operating smoothly. With life support and engines green, pretty much anything else could be handled.

"Foreign object alert."

Beth's heart, which was still racing, slowed down slightly. The AI had the authority to take emergency evasive action to protect the *Lily*, so the mere fact that it hadn't meant whatever it was that had triggered the alert was not an immediate problem. It was probably a swarm of debris in her path. Space was big, and her ship was small, but with enough space rubble along her route, the AI had most likely calculated that the risk of colliding with something her fields couldn't handle had risen from highly unlikely to just unlikely.

She punched up the alert message, figuring that the worse-case scenario would be that she'd have to change course, even reverting back to her original approach. Disappointing, but not really a big deal.

Only, the alert was not for something along her current path. To her surprise, the foreign object alert was for something in the vicinity of SG-4021-4. She scrunched her brows as she considered that.

Planets often had objects around them, from moons to rubble that had been captured over the eons. They tended to be in stable orbits and easy to avoid. Beth wasn't sure why the AI had triggered the alert and was about to query it when she realized that the object's track was not a regular orbit. Whatever was out there was leaving the planet on a separate course.

"What is it?"

"Undetermined."

The *Lily's* scanners were designed to analyze planets, but over broad spectrums. They were not designed to analyze small objects, particularly at this distance.

There was only one thing it could be, she knew: a claim-jumper.

HB had the license for the system, she was certain. Their legal team would never make the mistake of letting something like that slip through the cracks. Some tramp explorers poked around the galaxy, trying to find a lode, but they didn't get in the way of the big boys once they'd registered a claim.

"Ping that ship," she told her AI. "And get ready to send back a report."

Beth felt a surge of anger. If Floribeth was, in fact, a Class A planet, she was bound and determined to protect the claim. A simple warning and capture of the claimjumper's engine signature, and whoever was out there would run like a barrio cockroach when the lights came on.

She waited for the response, which she expected would be an apology, then a break for a gate. That confused her for a moment, though. The *Lily* should have picked up the presence of another gate the moment she entered the system.

Were they waiting to drop the return gate?

That was stupid. Regulations were sometimes there for a good reason, and even the foolhardiest tramp explorer would drop a gate the moment he or she arrived.

Come to think of it, how did they get here? Through what gate?

For the last 40+ years, all gate coordinates were registered. Sure, a little bribery could open a gate belonging to a planetary government or a smaller corp, and anyone could use a gate—after paying the appropriate fee—once it had been registered, but there was no way HB would let someone through one of their gates before the destination was examined for potential value.

The investigators are going to have a field day with this.

"Ping them again."

"There is no response."

"If they think that staying quiet is going to do them any good . . ." she muttered to herself.

"What kind of ship is it?"

The *Lily's* relatively weak scanners would be more than capable of identifying the ship. All ship engines had a transmitted signature that could be traced. It would be a simple matter of matching the signature with the Directorate database.

"It is not a ship," the AI told her.

"What? Of course, it is. Look at the track."

"I repeat, there is no signature, and scans do not match anything in the database."

"That's impossible. It has to . . ." she started to say before a thought crossed her mind.

Not all century ships, the vast behemoths that first took

mankind to the stars, had been accounted for. They'd all been tracked, of course. Anything moving through space collided with tiny particles that then emitted tiny pulses of power, faint, but still there. But the galaxy was huge, and some of the traces of the big ships, which travelled much slower than modern vessels and didn't have the luxury of gates, had simply gotten lost in the noise.

"Could this be a lost colony?" she asked aloud, but more to herself.

If it were, then her bonus would have to be huge. No "lost" colony had been found for a couple of centuries.

"Negative. No century ship could have traveled this far from Earth by this time."

Beth's excitement faded. She really had no idea as to where she was in the galaxy. The *Lily* could flash from one side to the other if the math was correct, but the century ships, without gates, had to traverse the black in the old-fashioned way. Even today, with gate technology, most of the inhabited worlds were in Earth's neighborhood.

So, what the heck is that? she wondered as she watched the track of the object. It was as if it had been flung out of the planet and was now forging its own path.

"Is there volcanic activity on the planet?" she asked.

"Negative."

It had been a long shot, but Beth was wracking her brain for possible answers.

Oh, well, I guess I'll find out soon enough. It looks like our paths are converging.

As soon as the thought had formed, Beth felt a cold chill sweep over her. Space was too big, even within a system, for coincidences like that. If their paths were converging, then there was a reason for that.

That was not a ship . . . at least a ship known to man. It was not a natural phenomenon. As the ancient saying went,

"Eliminate the impossible, and what ever remains, no matter how improbable has to be the truth."

"But that's impossible, too," she said aloud.

Unconsciously, her hand reached forward to the mission abort. Push it, and the *Lily* would head back to the gate and the nexus. Her mission would be over. If that really was a Class A world, she'd be giving up her bonus, to be awarded to whoever followed her.

She brought her hand back down. She didn't know what that thing was, so she didn't know if she was in danger. She didn't know if she was safe, either, but the planet was just sitting there, waiting for her, and she wanted it.

"I want full scans on that object," she ordered the AI. "Maintain present course."

She tore her attention away from the object for a moment to check her track. She was already speeding up as the eighth planet pulled at the oblique on her little scout. She'd be icing soon, and the full force of the gas giant's gravity would begin to slow her down. Something about that nagged at her, tickling the back of her mind, but she couldn't grasp it, and in frustration, cleared her mind, dropping an old episode of "The Syntax Gambit" on the display, blocking out the readings, tracks, and everything else. Her AI would let her know if anything changed, and she could lose herself in the opera. She'd seen it ten times if she'd seen it once, and the hopeless love of Jeremy always tugged at her heart.

She tried to lose herself in the story, but for once, she wasn't as deeply invested as she normally was. Her mind kept drifting to Floribeth and the unknown object. She stopped the opera once to go over her SOP, but there weren't any instructions. It was obvious that she should shoot back a message to Ana at HQ, but she didn't know what to tell them that wouldn't make her sound crazy, get recalled, and then lose the bonus to someone else.

She turned back to the show, and just when Meng died, leaving the distraught Jeremy considering suicide, it hit her.

The *Lily* and the object were on a meeting course, but she hadn't performed the icing turn yet. Whatever—whoever—was out there, understood what she was doing, understood that she was coming in and from what direction.

It was impossible, but it was the only explanation. Whatever was out there was coming for her. In her heart, she was sure whoever it was was not meeting her for a civil hello.

If that was a human ship, then by not having an engine signature, by not answering, those in the ship wanted to eliminate her. Beth hoped that was the case. Because if that was not a human ship . . .

It was beyond comprehension. Everyone knew they were alone in the galaxy, at least in so far as a space-going race. It was possible that there was sentient life hidden among the millions of planets, but humans would have detected the signs of movement at speeds, like the swish of bioluminescence that marked the passing of a shark in the oceans of Mother Earth.

If that thing out there was a primitive craft of some sort, native to the planet, then there would be a plethora of signs of the civilization that created it. No, that ship—and Beth knew in her heart that it was a ship—came from outside of the system. It wasn't human.

Shit!

Beth grabbed the manual controls and whipped the *Lily* around, pointing her past the other side of the gas giant looming large in her display. She pushed the power to the max as alarms blared.

"Give me a gravity assist course at max speed to the gate!" she shouted.

Within seconds, a path appeared on her display. She gave the ship a minor correction, and she was hugging the inside of the route. She knew she should turn over the ship to the AI, but she just couldn't release control.

"What's the other ship doing?"

"The unidentified object is adjusting course."

"To where, damn it!"

"Towards SG-4021-8."

Beth felt a surge of hope. The alien ship was still half a system away, and while the *Lily* was only slowly picking up speed, that was a lot of space to make up. With the gas giant's help, her ship was going to make use of a significant burst of speed. She hoped that would keep her far enough in front of the ship to make it to the gate.

She pulled up the alien ship's track. It was accelerating as well, and at a slightly faster rate than the *Lily*.

Beth had a love-hate relationship with her Hummingbird. It was small, barely a floating coffin, and she hated being cooped up in it. But it was also reliable and had returned her from 48 missions so far.

"Make it one more, baby."

The problem with a Hummingbird—or any corporate exploration scout—was that it was made with economy in mind. The costs for a quicker, more maneuverable craft like a Directorate Wasp, were exponentially higher. The corporations didn't care if their OPW pilots spent several days accelerating and then decelerating through gates. And when kilograms mattered, there was nothing to waste in the way of defenses. Corporate scouts were rarely pirated, and it was far cheaper to replace a lost scout and give a nominal payout to the pilot's family than build more robust ships.

Her ship had never let her down, but she'd never been in a race before, and this was one she knew she couldn't afford to lose.

With the first surge of panic subsiding, she turned the *Lily* over to the AI, trusting it to take the quickest, safest pass.

Scouts were not made to withstand the pull of something like a gas giant, but the AI would know how close it could take the ship without risk.

For the next 22 minutes, Beth stared at the blip on the screen, only looking away to check her speed. She'd already bled off the bulk of her velocity by the time she'd punched it. A Hummingbird's little engines weren't the most reactive, but the gas giant's gravity had already accelerated the scout far beyond what its engines could do. In a little more than 53 minutes, the *Lily* would start whipping around the planet, gaining even more speed.

The alien ship was gaining, but not fast enough, she thought. Along with the slingshot, and with the *Lily*'s engines screaming, she thought she could reach the gate within 19 hours. She'd know for sure once she broke free from the gas giant's grip.

As she watched the blip on her display, something happened. The blip split in two, one speeding up—quickly.

"What's that?" she asked, her voice breaking.

"Two objects have detached from the primary object. They are accelerating at a high rate of speed."

"Uh . . . how high a rate?" she asked, not really wanting to know the answer.

"Unable to determine using fold scanning."

"Fold" scanners were an important piece of any interstellar craft, from scout to battleship. The *Lily* had an array of inexpensive, but accurate scanners that relied on the visual spectrum. For Floribeth, that meant the scanners were "seeing" the planet almost 50 minutes after the fact due to the speed of light and the distance. The fold scanner, which worked through physics that Beth didn't even try to understand, could "see" things in what was close enough to real time that the lag didn't really matter. Fold scanners didn't show much detail, but the little scout's scanner had been enough to pick up the alien ship—and whatever had detached from the ship and were heading towards her.

"What is their current velocity?"

"Inadequate data input."

"*Guess*, damn it!"

"Approaching .58C."

That shocked Beth. It normally took the *Lily* three days to reach the .54C necessary to pass through a gate, and even at those slow speeds, they would be enough to smush Beth into a red paste without the g-compensators. Whatever was coming her way had to be accelerating at tremendous levels. Nothing alive could survive that.

Could it?

"When will they reach us?"

"Inadequate data input."

Beth started to yell out, but she stopped, took five slow, deliberate breaths, then said, "Make the best possible estimate."

"Fifty-one minutes, thirty seconds, with approximately a one-minute margin of error."

"And when will we pass behind the SG-4021-8?"

"Fifty-five minutes, twenty-two seconds."

Beth's vision started to close in. Whatever was coming her way was going to catch her before she could get the planet between them. She had to goose more speed out of the *Lily*.

She checked her readouts, but the little engine was at maximum output. There was no magic gyvering that could suddenly turn the scout into a fighter.

What about you, big boy? she wondered.

The gas giant loomed large, but her trajectory already had her skirting the very edge of the safe zone. She checked the blips chasing her again—they had already closed the gap significantly.

For all she knew, the blips were a floral delivery service, sent to welcome her to the system. Beth doubted that, though. All she had were two sets of blips, and she thought the two objects that made up the lead blip had malevolent intent. If there was one thing she was sure of, it was that she didn't want to let whatever was represented by those blips catch her.

"Bring the course to here," she said, swiping her finger on the display to indicate a new course.

"Negative. That course is not within accepted safety parameters."

"Neither is getting an interstellar missile up our butts. Do it."

"Negative. I am not authorized to allow you to put Hamdani Brothers property in jeopardy."

Beth wanted to scream in frustration. The *Lily's* AI, like everything else on the ship, was a basic model, adequate to do the job, but not much else. It was nothing like higher capability AIs that had simulated personalities and could function more like humans.

Beth was not going to sit there and argue with a bunch of silicate cells when their very survival was at risk. She didn't even hesitate. Flipping up the cover near her right hand, she hit the switch.

Immediately, the ship's AI went dead. The ship still functioned as a basic numbers cruncher, and it would keep the ship operating, but it no longer had the independent capacity that made it an AI. That part of its silicate circuits had just been fried. Beth took control of the *Lily* and swung it on a closer line to the planet.

She almost expected to feel a surge as the gravity pull got stronger, but that was ridiculous. The *Lily* was going through heavy acceleration even without the change in course, and her g-compensators, well, compensated.

Beth didn't think the change in course would speed her up significantly, but what it did was shorten her distance to travel until she was behind the big planet. She hoped that would be enough.

The planet grew larger and larger, and twice, Beth had to zoom out on her display. All the time, the leading blip, which had now split into two separate blips, closed the distance. She kept running the calculations, and as the alien torpedoes, as she was now calling them, came closer, the calculations became more accurate. It soon became apparent that her change of course was not enough. She was going to get caught a minute too soon.

"They can probably follow me around the planet, anyway," she muttered.

She nudged the course over, closer to the planet, so that she would pass right alongside the exosphere. Alarms blared, but mercifully, the AI didn't say a word.

"This is it," she told herself as she reached the planet.

Outside, immense forces were pulling at the *Lily*, something it was not designed to take. It even shuddered, something Beth had never felt before. Beth almost panicked, knowing she'd hit the limits of the exosphere, and she was afraid she'd bounce off, exposing the ship to the torpedoes that were on her ass. With a firm hand, she steadied the scout, wishing now that she could turn it back over to the slagged AI.

The first torpedo materialized on the visuals. An egg-like spheroid, it didn't look like a torpedo. Beth was tempted to close her eyes, but if she was going to die, she wanted to see it coming.

But it didn't come. It started to slow down. The *Lily* shuddered more violently, and something broke free to lodge beneath her right foot, but on the display, the first torpedo began to yaw. Suddenly, it swerved and dove into the planet, as the *Lily* began to whip around the gas giant.

Where's the second one? Where is it?

The gas giant was big—huge, in fact. But the *Lily* was moving very fast. Within moments, the ship slingshotted around and broke free of the planet's grip, heading back out into space. Beth kept it on course to reach the gate, but she ran every scanner she had back toward the planet, looking for the second torpedo. It never appeared.

Somehow, by some miracle, she had shaken the alien craft, and the *Lily* was still intact. She pulled up her cross and kissed it.

Beth switched the fold scanner to the remaining blip, the one still far behind. It was still accelerating, but with the gas giant's assist, Beth had opened up the distance. It had shifted course as well, moving to an intercept that steered clear of SG-4021-8.

Beth ran several scenarios. She wished she could turn the AI back on, but disabling it was a safety option, in case an AI went rogue (which was an extremely rare occurrence). As such, it would take a tech to install a new AI. Still, even without the AI making the calculations, it became obvious that unless the ship chasing her had something else up its sleeve, the *Lily* should enter the gate with around 40 minutes to spare. She was still nervous about another set of torpe-does, but after an hour without any more being fired, she began to relax. She even fell asleep for two hours.

Eighteen hours, twelve minutes, and fifteen seconds after slingshotting around the gas giant, Pilot Two Floribeth Salinas O'Shea Dalisay, Hamdani Exploration Corps passed through the gate. As per regulations in existence since the formation of the Directorate, but never followed, as far as she knew, she triggered the self-destruct, and the gates to and from SG-4021 were reduced to their component atoms.

Excerpt from
The Black God's Drums

by P. Djèlí Clark

The night in New Orleans always got something going on, ma maman used to say—like this city don't know how to sleep. You want a good look, take the cable-elevator to the top of one of Les Grand Murs, where airships dock on the hour. Them giant iron walls ring the whole Big Miss on either side. Up here you can see New Algiers on the West Bank, its building yards all choked in factory smoke and workmen scurrying round the bones of new-built vessels like ants. Turn around and there's the downtown wards lit up with gas lamps like glittering stars. You can make out the other wall in the east over at Lake Borgne, and a fourth one like a crescent moon up north round Swamp Pontchartrain—what most folk call La Ville Morte, the Dead City.

Les Grand Murs were built by Dutchmen to protect against the storms that come every year. Not the regular hurricanes neither, but them tempêtes noires that turn the skies into night for a whole week. I was born in one of the big ones some thirteen years back in 1871. The walls held in the Big Miss but the rain and winds almost drowned the city anyway, filling it up like a bowl. Ma maman pushed me out her belly in that storm, clinging to a big sweet gum tree in the middle of thunder and lightning. She said I was Oya's child— the goddess of storms, life, death, and rebirth, who came over with her great-grandmaman from Lafrik, and who runs strong in our blood. Ma maman said that's why I take to high places so, looking to ride Oya's wind.

Les Grand Murs is where I call home these days. It's not the finest accommodations: drafty on winter nights and so hot in the summer all you do is lay about in your own sweat. But lots of street kids set up for themselves up here. Better than getting swept into workhouse orphanages or being conscripted to steal for a Thieving Boss.

Me, I marked out a prime spot: an alcove just some ways off from one of the main airship mooring masts. That's where the gangplanks are laid down for disembarking passengers heading into the city. Concealed in my alcove, I can see them all: in every colour and shade, in every sort of dress, talking in more languages than I can count, their voices competing with the rattle of dirigible engines and the hum of ship propellers. It always gets me to thinking on how there's a whole world out there, full of all kinds of people. One day, I dream, I'm going to get on one of those airships. I'll sail away from this city into the clouds and visit all the places there are to visit, and see all the people there are to see. Of course, watching from my alcove is also good for marking out folk too careless with their purses, luggage, and anything else for the taking. Because in New Orleans, you can't survive on just dreams.

My eyes latch onto a little dandy-looking man in a rusty plaid suit, with slicked-back shiny brown hair and a curly moustache. He got a tight grip on his bags, but there's a golden pocket watch dangling on a chain at his side. A clear invitation if I ever seen one. Somebody's bound to snatch it sooner or later—might as well be me.

I'm about to set out to follow him when the world suddenly slows. The air, sounds, everything. It's like somebody grabbed hold of time and stretched her out at both ends. I turn, slow-like, to look out from the wall as a monstrous moon begins to rise into the sky. No, not a moon, I realize in fright—a skull! A great big bone white skull that fills up the night. It pushes itself up past the horizon to cast a shadow over the city underneath, where the gaslights snuff out one by one. I gape at that horrible face, stripped clean of skin or flesh, that stares back with deep empty black sockets and a grin of bared teeth. It's all I can do not to fall to my knees.

"Not real!" I whisper, shutting my eyes to make the apparition go away. I count to ten in my head, whispering all the while: "Not real! Not real! Not real!"

When I open my eyes again, the skull moon is gone. Time has caught up to normal too—the sounds of the night returning in a rush. And the city is there, spread out again: breathing, shining and alive. I release a breath. This was all Oya's doing, I know. The goddess has strange ways of talking. Not the first time I've been sent one of her visions—though never anything so strong. Never anything that felt so real. They're what folk call premonitions: warnings of things about to happen or things soon to come. Most times I can figure them out quick. But a giant skull moon? I got no damn idea what that's supposed to mean.

"You could just talk to me plain," I mutter in irritation. But Oya doesn't answer. She's already humming a song that whistles in my ears. It's about her mother Yemoja leading some lost fishermen to shore. The moon is Yemoja's domain, after all. Giving up, I turn back, hoping to find my mark again—but instead, I'm startled by the sound of footsteps.

My whole body goes still. Not just footsteps but boots, by the way they fall heavy. More than one pair too. I curse at my bad luck, ducking back down into my alcove. I chose this spot special, because it's some ways off from the usual paths people take—just near enough for me to see them, but far enough to keep out of their way. No one ever comes this far out, to this part of the wall. But those steps are getting closer, heading right for me! Cursing my luck twice again, I scramble back to huddle into a far corner of the alcove, where the shadows fall deep. I'm small enough to curl into a ball if I draw my knees up under me. And if I go real still, I might escape without being seen. I might.

I'm expecting constables. Rare to see any of them up here, but could be the city's decided to do a sweep for one reason or the other. Maddi grá coming up, and they like to make everything look respectable to visitors—respectable for New Orleans, anyway. Maybe someone's complained about all the street kids up here picking pockets. Or worse yet, could be the city's workhouses and factories need more small hands to run their machines—machines that seem to delight in stealing fingers. I grit my teeth and ball up my fists as if trying to protect my own fingers, not daring to breathe. Damn sure ain't going to end up in one of those places.

But the figures that enter my alcove aren't constables. They're men, though, about five of them. I can't make them out in the dark, but by their height and the way they walk they have to be men. They're not wearing the telltale blue uniforms of constables though, with the upside-down gold crescent and five-pointed star stitched on their shoulders. These men are wearing dull faded gray uniforms that almost blend into the dark. Their jackets got patches on the front that I recognize right off: white stars in a blue cross like an X over a bed of red, the letters *CSA* stitched underneath. The brisk twangs that roll off their tongues are Southern, but like those uniforms, certainly nothing made in New Orleans.

"Alright then," one of them says. "You can get us what we want?"

"Deal already set up, Capitaine," another voice answers, real casual-like. This one's a Cajun. I'd recognize that bayou accent anywhere. I lift my chin off my knees to risk a peek from under the lid of my cap. The one talking that Cajun talk ain't got on a uniform. He's wearing some old brown pants and a red shirt with suspenders. I still can't make out any faces, but can see a mop of white hair on his head almost down to his shoulders. "Dat scientist be here next day, on a morning airship from Haiti. Gonna see to meeting him myself."

My ears perk up at that. A Haitian scientist? Meeting with these men?

"How long we have to wait?" a third voice asks. This one's impatient, almost whining. "Captain, we don't need all this fuss. I say we just snatch him when he gets here. Put him on our ship and fly off. Have him in Charleston in no time."

The Cajun makes a tsking sound. "Ma Lay! Do dat, brudda, and you get de constables involved. Dey gonna cost you mo dan I do. Not how we do tings down here, no."

"Seems all you folk *do* in this city is drink and gamble and eat," the third voice sneers.

The Cajun chuckles. "We like to pass a good time. Make music and babies too."

The first voice, the one both men called Captain, steps in then. Sounds like he's trying to keep things from boiling over. I glance to those black-booted feet, realizing I hadn't pulled my sleeping blanket into the corner with me. That was careless. But nothing I can do about it now. My heart beats faster, hoping none of them steps on it or bothers to look down.

"So after this scientist gets here," the captain is saying, "then what?"

"When he get settled, I set up de meeting between the two of you," the Cajun answers. There's a pause. "You got what he coming all dis way to get? You don't deliver, he might run."

"We got his jewel, alright," the third voice says in his usual sneer.

The Cajun claps, and I imagine him smiling. "Den it should work out fine." He extends a hand and the captain offers over a thick wad of something. The unmistakable beautiful sound of crisp bills being counted fills up my alcove.

"You'll get the rest when we see this scientist—and his invention," the captain states.

"Wi, Capitaine," the Cajun replies. "You give him his jewel and he gonna hand over dat ting you want." He stops his counting and leans in close. "De Black God's Drums. Maybe you boys able to win dis war yet, yeah."

The captain dips his head in a nod before answering. "Maybe."

There's some more talk. Nothing important from what I can tell. Just the questions and assurances of men who don't trust each other and who up to no good. But I'm only half-listening by now. My mind is on the words the Cajun said: the Black God's Drums. With a Haitian scientist involved, that can only mean one thing. And if I'm right, that's big. Bigger than any marks I was going to pinch tonight. This is information that's gonna be valuable to somebody. I just need to figure out who'll pay the highest price. Long after the men leave my alcove, I sit there thinking hard in the dark as Oya hums in my head.

   . . .

Two nights later, it's all hustle and bustle the Sunday before the Maddi grá. Most times like now I'd be mixed up in all that tumult, getting ready to strut and sashay with the best of them. But not tonight. Tonight, I got a meeting. And some information to sell—or trade.

I cut through the Quarter, to get a glimpse of some of the action—and mostly to do some light pocket-picking along the way. I'm small enough not to get noticed. Just a bit of Oya's wind is more than ample to send wallets or bills flying. The goddess disapproves of my using her gift this way, and tells me as much, tickling the way she do in my head. But she also understands I got to keep my belly full, and lets me do as I need. Makes her grumble some, but I don't pay her no mind.

I change my route when I catch sight of some Bakers though. Their faces are powdered with flour to match their white jackets and pants; only bit of colour on them are the blood red kerchiefs around their necks and the rouge on their cheeks. They swagger about, thumbing the handles of flat wooden paddles fitted into belts at their waists: whole lot of them just itching for a fight. The Guildes of New Orleans are out strong tonight—Bakers, Boilermakers, Mechanics, you name it—and touchy about their territory. Then again, when ain't they? There'll be some blood flowing before the dawn come, you just watch. And that kind of trouble I can do without.

It's as I'm trying to duck away from them that I end up running into someone. Usually Oya's gift lets me move light on my feet, so that I slip around and about other people like a passing breeze. But this time it don't work for some reason. I hit the other person head-on, so hard it sends me bouncing off him to fall right on my backside.

Blinking, I look up to find a tall skinny man in a tight black suit, like what the morticians who run the city's best funeral parlors wear. When I see his face, I almost try to scramble back and away. It's a skull, bone white and grinning like the one in my vision! Only this isn't no phantom. You don't bounce off phantoms, I tell myself, trying to be sensible. Looking closer, I realize his face is really a mask—white bones painted on black cloth.

I breathe easier, feeling kind of foolish. It's a little early for masking, true. But no accounting for when some folk decide to start their Maddi grá. The man tilts his head to the side to peer down at me, with blue eyes like chipped bits of ice.

"Best watch where you going, cher," he scolds playfully, stressing that last word as he takes in my clothing. He extends a suntanned hand towards me, with long spidery fingers and red tattoos painted on the knuckles. I'm about to accept his help when Oya hisses loud in my head. Dammit! It hurts! It sounds like a rising wind in a fierce storm moving through trees, or blasting down a corridor between buildings. I snatch my hand back, just to make it stop. Something in those icy eyes turns hot for a moment, but the man just drops his hand to his side and laughs—a cackle coming from behind that grinning skull that raises up bumps on my skin.

"Suit yourself den, cher." He shrugs. Moving around me where I still sit, he makes his way down the street. He don't walk, though. Instead, he does a funny little soft shuffling dance with his feet while mouthing the words to some tune I never heard before:

> *"Remember New Orleans I say,*
> *Where Jackson show'd them Yankee play,*
> *And beat them off and gain'd the day,*
> *And then we heard the people say*
> *Huzza! for Gen'ral Jackson!"*

I shake my head. An unusual fellow, no doubting it. Probably why Oya took a disliking to him. She can be particular like that. But being strange ain't no crime. Not in New Orleans. Could be he got something to do with the vision she sent me two days back. Or she think he do. Only, he ain't the first or last skeleton I'm gonna see at Maddi grá. Can't go off chasing after every one just to figure out what's got her so prickly. My hands full as it is. Picking myself up, I spare one last glance for the odd man then turn and set out again on my business.

By the time I reach Madamesville I can hear the bells at Saint Louis tolling the hour. I stop once to let a mudbug scuttle down Robertson. Its six iron legs clang heavy on the cobblestones while curving pipes on its back belch out black smoke, looking like some big old crawfish what crawled out the bayou. The constable driving the thing squints my way through a pair of bronze goggles. He looks me over once, then turns back in his cushioned seat to continue his rounds without stopping. No time for a street rat like me when there'll be all kinds of mayhem out tonight. I cross behind him and arrive at my destination.

Shá Rouj isn't the best bordello in Madamesville, certainly nothing like the big mansions up on Basin Street. But it ain't one of the tucked away 50-cent joints either, that some say got more rats than ladies. Madame Diouf keeps it nice, with bright cherry red paint and white shutters, all behind fancy iron railings that twist and curve into ivies. A great big cat's head, painted black in a red top hat and a gold monocle, grins down at me from the roof and winks a lazy mechanical eye. I tip my cap and wink back for luck before stepping through the front door.

The stink of cigars and too-sweet perfume hits me right off and I wrinkle my nose at the mix. The house is full tonight, more than usual. There's men sitting on rose-coloured sofas and chairs or standing about—drinking whiskey and rum, keeping up a loud chatter that rolls and echoes about the room. The women on their laps don't wear much beyond stockings, frills, and lace corsets, but their painted faces are always smiling. I see one tug her ear and a server man in a white wig, bright gold breeches, and a long fancy red coat—with tails even—rushes to keep everybody's cups full.

Shá Rouj was built to look like free New Orleans. It lets in men of any colour and offers women just the same—big Dutch gals, scarlet-haired Irish, dark senoritas, midnight-black Senegalese. And like New Orleans, Shá Rouj is neutral territory. Where else can you find Frenchie corsairs making all nice with British Jack Tars? There's Prussians, New Mexicans, Gran Columbians—even some Kalifornians, in their peculiar Russian dress. I count about a dozen black men, all showy and boisterous. Haitians by the looks of it, all gussied up in blue and red uniforms.

I pick through the crowd, searching for one face in particular. My eyes fix instead on some men sitting in a corner and drinking quietly—all in familiar dull faded gray uniforms with the Southern Cross battle flag on their sleeves, the words *CSA* inscribed beneath in red stitching. Confederate States soldiers. Air Force, by the badges on their shoulders. My heart thumps as I wonder if they're the same ones from the other night in my alcove. Pretty certain no one saw me. But still, I walk the other way, keeping a good bit of distance between us. Funny to find Confederates in here anyway, what with all this open miscegenation. They keep to themselves, their eyes wandering every now and again to a knot of loud-talking officers in unmistakable dark Union blue—New York Bowery Boys by those rough accents and their sheer bawdiness. Any other day these allies and enemies might be at each other's throats. But tonight they share the same space and mind their manners. Because this is New Orleans—one of the few nonaligned territories in the now broken United States.

New Orleans been free now going on more than two decades—ever since the slave uprising in that first year of the war. Caught the Confederates by surprise. They got so scared, they let the Free Coloured militias join up to help put it down. Only the militias switched over to the slaves and both of them took the city. After that, Union ships and troops came in and got into one big batay with the Confederates. Was them two that burned Old Algiers. New Orleans hunkered down and waited it out. Finally, the Haitians and Brits and Frenchies sent their airships to stop the fighting. Truce was signed making New Orleans a neutral and open port.

Free Coloured men tried to cheat the slaves soon after, hoping to put them back on the plantations. But when it looked like another uprising was brewing, they passed emancipation real quick. A council runs New Orleans today, made up of ex-slaves, mulattoes and white business folk. Brits, Frenchies, and Haitians patrol our harbors and skies to keep the peace. Confederates and the Union ain't had a big tussle in fifteen years—not since the Armistice of Third Antietam. But if that war ever starts back up, New Orleans gonna find herself right in the middle of it again. Folk say that's why we live every day chasing the good times. Because you never know when the bad might come.

"Goad a'michty!" I look up to find a round splotchyfaced Scotsman in a milk-white suit pointing a thick forefinger at me. Two plump octoroons hang off his arms, with piled-up hair and red crescent moons on their cheeks, wearing nothing but frilly pink corsets and black striped stockings. "Lad's too young to be here, d'ye think?" he protests to no one in particular.

"Not a lad," I mutter, pulling off my cap to reveal a thick halo of black hair and a nut-brown face.

The Scotsman's eyes widen then narrow hungrily. Rum and wine got his face as ruddy as his side whiskers. "Hou much for the wee one?" he asks aloud. I think he's joking. Maybe. Oya don't. There's a rumbling thunder in my ear. She's protective like that.

"Too young for you, sir," another voice puts in sternly. "And not for sale."

I turn to find a woman striding down a set of stairs towards us, her hand lightly trailing the wooden bannister. She'd be tall even without the evening heels, with black skin and hair turned a dark smoky gray. Her face is striking, as beautiful as a painting I once seen of the Queen of Sheba. She moves like she's walking on water, the roomy skirts of her ruffled blue dress swishing about her legs in waves. In my head Oya's anger settles, and she starts up another song about Yemoja—who tricked her from her throne under the sea.

"Guid eenin Madame Diouf," the Scotsman greets her, stumbling into a bow that almost topples him. "I meant no offense."

The proprietor of Shá Rouj blinks once before smiling. I'm always envious when I look into those black eyes, like what I imagine the deepest part of the sea must look like. Mine are murky as swamp water, a plain muddy brown.

"No offense taken, sir," she croons in her Afrikin accent. "Have you tried the special whiskey I've had shipped in? From a distillery in your native country. A place called Orkney? Compliments of the house for you, sir." The Scotsman's face lights up and he begins to babble on excitedly about having family from this Orkney, forgetting I'm even there. Madame Diouf listens politely, then at her nod the Scotsman is pulled away by his escorts, their hips swaying with loose flesh that seems to push him along between them. She promptly turns her attention to me, showing an appraising eye. "Little creeping vine. What brings you here tonight?"

"It's just Creeper, Madame Diouf," I respond.

The older woman grimaces. "Mondjé! I prefer the name your mother gave you, *Jacqueline.*" She runs her fingers through my unkempt hair and tugs at the too-big brown coat on my small frame. Oya scowls as deep as I do. We don't like being fidgeted with. "This hair could use braiding! And what is all this? Where did you get those ridiculous trousers? Do you want to be mistaken for a boy?"

I pull away, putting my cap back on and tucking my hair beneath. "On the streets, better people make that mistake."

Madame Diouf puts on a severe frown. Damn Afrikin. Even that's beautiful. "You aren't out there running with those Guildes, are you?" she asks. "Gangs of thieves and worse!"

"I don't have nothing to do with any Guildes," I retort, somewhat offended. As if I'd take on dressing up like one of those clowns.

Madame Diouf looks me over skeptically. Then that beautiful face softens. She leans down, smelling sweet like honey and jasmine. I get dizzy in the haze of her. "You have no need to stay on the street, Jacqueline," she reminds. "Your mother was like my own daughter. Enough schools in the city to take you in."

"Tried that already," I shoot back. "Those girls hold their noses around a 'pitènn's daughter.'"

Madame Diouf stands up and lets out a string of curses in her mix of Creole and Afrikin talk. It's impressive enough to raise my eyebrows. "What nerve!" she huffs. "Mothers just two steps out of chains and they're putting on airs!" She pats my head again, then runs the back of her long fingers across my cheek. "Well, I'll have one of the girls set up a bath for you. Have them braid your hair up at least, yes? Get some proper clothes on you too. And stay and take some food. To maig' comme coucou! Put some fat on those bones!"

By the time I'm led to a kitchen table in the back of the house, I been freshly soaped, scrubbed and washed, and had my hair tied down in thick braids. Kept my own clothes, though. No matter what Madame Diouf think, dresses don't do me no good on the street. I settle down into a chair and busy myself licking grease off my fingers as I pull meat from a bit of fried pork. Oya's disappointed there's no hen. I stay away from the roast mutton, though, which the goddess abhors. Eat that and she'll have me bringing it back up half the night.

From where I sit I can see everything in the main room. I watch all the cavorting and carrying on as the women of Shá Rouj smile, wink, laugh, and wiggle every bit of money from their customers—who willingly hand it over. Whole lot of these men gonna have lighter pockets by the end of the night, if not plain empty. They may not know it, but as soon as they walked in here, they never had a chance. The group I'm expecting has to be coming here. Got it on good information they would. Just need to bide my time. My doubts are still nagging me when they finally push through the door. I sit up, squinting to make sure. No doubt about it. That's them.

The first one in is a trim dark-skinned man with long hair like a Choctaw. But he's a Hindoo, I can tell, those other Indians from the Far East. More than a few of the women glance at his pretty face, and he flashes back a smile that makes even me blush. Didn't even know men could have eyelashes that long. At his side is a tall broad black man with a shadowy beard peppered over with white and a serious-set face. The old-time blue military jacket with gold epaulets marks him as a Haitian; his countrymen in the room raise their drinks in salute and he answers with a deep nod, his stone face unchanging. Behind the men are two more figures: one is the biggest Chinaman I ever put eyes on, wearing a tall wide-brimmed tan cowboy hat, of all things, and a long matching frock coat; the other—she turns out to be exactly who I came all this way to see.

The captain of the airship Midnight Robber is as tall as I

remember—not so much as most men, but a good height. She wears snug-fitting tan britches on long lean legs, and the red and green jacket of a Free Isles flyer. Her coils of black hair are pulled back by metal clasps above a dark brown face with the kind of big eyes men like talking about. She scans around the place, one hand dropping to rest on a pistol at her waist. At a call from the Hindoo, she moves to join her group, walking with a slight limp. The other men in the room look her over, some curious, others admiring. Seems they uncertain if she's up for sale too. But she ignores them, instead shouting for a drink and settling into a sofa. Some of Shá Rouj's finest wares soon arrive, one of them squealing as she falls into the captain's lap. A stab of jealousy from Oya startles me. I push it away, trying to focus.

Now what? The information I got is something I'm certain this group will be keen on. And I have it in my mind to make a trade. But not like this. Too many eyes here. I glance to the Confederates. Seems they noticed the captain too. And they're doing a bad job at not staring. Definitely too many eyes. No, I'll have to wait to get her alone. I settle back, finishing my meal and trying to be patient.

I blink awake. Images of me in a burgundy dress dancing with a machete in the middle of a thunderstorm melt away with my dream. I'm thankful at least it's not about giant skulls in the sky. I curse beneath my breath, though, blaming Madame Diouf a little, and myself more, for dozing off. A hot bath and a full stomach? What was I thinking! Thankfully, I look around to find the crew of the *Midnight Robber* just where I'd left them. The Hindoo is standing on a table, drunk off his ass and reciting something like he's a theatre actor. The women around him clap while the Jack Tars roar in approval. But damn my luck, the captain's gone! I search the room. Could she have returned to her airship? No, not by herself. Remembering the woman in her lap, my gaze moves to an upper floor. Of course.

I push away from the table and walk through the kitchen to the back door. Heading outside, I make a half-circle around Shá Rouj 'til I find a good spot on the railing to pull myself up. My nickname on the streets is Creeper, and for good reason. Just like ma maman in the sweet gum tree, I'm a damn good climber. Got people to saying I remind them of one of those creeping vines that make their way up the side of buildings. Tonight, my nickname does me well. Didn't want to take the stairs right there in the open. No one's watching out here, though.

Reaching the second floor I hoist myself onto a balcony and peek inside a window. Some bodies moving in the shadows make Oya titter. Not the right ones, though. Takes about three more bits of peeping 'til I find my captain. She's lying facedown on a bed, her back rising slightly with her snores. Movement makes me pull away quick. A second woman is getting up from the bed. She walks to bend over a white porcelain basin on a dresser and spends some time washing before slipping her meager clothing back on. After deftly lacing up a frilly corset in a mirror, she stops to lay a kiss on the captain's bare shoulder before leaving.

Now's my chance. Pulling open the shutters I lift the window and ease myself into the dark room, taking care not to get my coat caught on anything. When my shoes touch the floorboards there's a creak that makes me wince, but I gingerly begin to make my way over. My mind races, trying to think of the best way to wake the sleeping woman I've gone through all this trouble to see. She solves my dilemma for me.

"Don't take another blasted step," a singsong Free Isles accent warns. The captain rises up from the bed and I find myself staring down the skinny barrel of a gold-plated pistol. I can't help admiring the gilded handiwork—Free Isles issue.

She reaches up to turn a handle on the wall, pumping gas into a pair of hanging lamps. We both squint at the brilliance.

"What the ass?" she asks in surprise. "I thinking you is a bandit or a jumbie, but you just a boy?"

"Girl," I correct, tilting my head to let the light take in my face: baby cheeks, small mouth, round lips and all.

"Girl, then," the captain repeats, unfazed. She doesn't even stop to button up her corset. Her large eyes look me up and down, passing judgment. And she hasn't put the gun away. "Somebody hire you to come here and steal from me nah? Put a knife in me neck?"

I shake my head. That odd bit of jealousy comes again from Oya. But there's a strange familiarity too. "Here to see you," I tell her. "I got information. Information to trade."

She frowns like she don't believe. "What you have to trade with me?"

I hesitate. I'd seen this discussion going different, certainly not under gunpoint. Figure now ain't the time to play coy. "The Black God's Drums," I blurt out.

That gets her interest, for sure. Slowly, the captain lowers her pistol, her face flat and unreadable. Refastening the buttons on her corset, she grabs a white shirt from the brass bedpost and begins slipping it on. "Talk," she orders. "Now." Her voice is alert, with a tone that says she's not having any nonsense. So, I talk.

"I like to sleep up on one of Les Grand Murs," I begin. "There are alcoves there no one checks, where I can see airships come in everyday. I like watching the people—"

"Good place for a thief to mark she victims," the captain cuts in wryly.

Well yes, I think, but that's beside the point. And rather rude to point out. "Saw you and your crew get off this morning," I continue. "Two nights back though, saw something else—a Confederate airship."

The captain shrugs. "New Orleans open to them jackass like everybody else."

"It's who's waiting for them," I explain. "A Cajun with white hair. He brings the Confederates down to my alcove. If I hadn't been tucked into my corner they'd have seen me. But they don't. And I listen to them talk. Confederates say they're here to get the Black God's Drums. Cajun says there's a Haitian scientist willing to exchange it for something."

The captain's brow furrows. "Exchange for what? Money?"

I shake my head. "Not money. They were talking about a jewel."

The captain goes quiet for a while. Her eyes are set on me but I can tell her mind is elsewhere. When she finally speaks, it's a question. "You know what that is—the Black God's Drums?"

I nod. I'd put it together plenty quick as soon as I heard it.

"Shango's Thunder," I answer. In my head, Oya dances at hearing her husband's name.

I used to ask ma maman to tell me the story over and over again, about how Haiti had gotten free. She would talk about the mulatto inventor Duconge, who was raised up in France but returned to the island where his mother was born as a slave and offered his inventions to the black generals of the uprising. When Napoleon's armada came to take back the island they saw dozens of cannons on the highest hills, all shooting into the air. The Frenchies laughed, thinking the blacks couldn't aim. They stopped laughing though when the sky turned dark as night, and a storm came that wiped them from the sea. *Like the hand of an angry god,* ma maman would say.

"In Haiti, the weapon is named for other gods of storms—like Hevioso from Dahomey and Nsasi of Kongo," the captain relates. "But in Trinidad we name it for Shango, the Yoruba orisha of thunder. Name seem to catch on."

Oya grumbles with indignation across my thoughts: something about haughty Dahomey and upstart Kongo gods. Wasn't just them or Shango. She was there too, dancing in the whirlwind, dashing those Frenchie ships to bits and sending thousands of men to lay with Yemoja beneath the sea. Them Frenchies still down there with her mother now, she says, their bones and spirits held close.

"Only a few know its secret code name," the captain goes on. "'The Black God's Drums.'"

"Well, that scientist is going to give your secret weapon to some Rebs," I say.

Her face goes grim. "That's no good," she murmurs. "That's no good for nobody."

That last part I already know. Anything that helps those Rebs is bad trouble. I was born after the Armistice of Third Antietam, when the Union and Confederates, all battered up and starving from eight years of war, had called a truce. Might have been good for the white folk, but it doomed those blacks what hadn't made it to the Union. I've seen the tintype photographs from inside the Confederacy. Shadowy pictures of fields and factories filled with laboring dark bodies, their faces almost all covered up in big black gas masks, breathing in that drapeto vapor. It make it so the slaves don't want to fight no more, don't want to do much of nothing. Just work. Thinking about their faces, so blank and empty, makes me go cold inside.

"So what you want trade with me for this, lickle gal?" the captain asks.

I frown. Who's she calling lickle? No longer under the gun, I move to sit in a chair and lean back—trying to look casual and at ease. "I want to go with you when you leave," I say.

That makes her eyebrows rise. "Go with me? Go where?"

"On your airship, the *Midnight Robber*. I want to be crew."

She screws up her face, looking at me as if I've jumped out my skin and done a bloody jig around the room—then laughs. The sound makes me bristle. "What I want with a lickle gal on me ship?" She gives a brief, sharp suck of her teeth. "You think I want pickney to mind?"

"I don't need minding," I snap, my temper getting the better of me. Oya disagrees, whispering a lullaby. I push it away.

The captain leans forward, pinning me with her gaze. Those large eyes are as dark as Madame Diouf's. "You ever been on an airship?" she asks gruffly. "Know one end of it from the other?"

That wasn't fair. "I learn fast!" I counter.

The captain shakes her head, pursing her lips and this time sucking her teeth for a long while—the way old Creole women and Madame Diouf do. "What schupidness is this? Girl like you should be in school, learning your maths and letters, not gallivanting about on some airship! What your mother and father would say?"

"Nothing," I retort, biting each of my words so they're forced out. "They're dead." This sends her quiet. "Papa died in one of the tempêtes noires." *You took him, Oya,* I accuse. The goddess don't deny it. Just keeps humming. "I never knew him. The yellow fever took ma maman three years back."

The captain searches my face for truth and decides she's found it. "I sorry for that," she says at last. "Still—"

"You knew her," I break in. I take off my cap and step further into the light. "Ma maman. She used to work here, for Madame Diouf. And the two of you..." No need to say the rest.

The captain looks puzzled for a moment. But when she sees my face fully those already large eyes go even bigger.

"Rose," she whispers, speaking my mother's name. She

stares, as if only now truly seeing me for the first time. "That same little nose and small eyes! Oh gosh, you Rose's daughter!" Then, more subdued, "I didn't know she had a child."

"Ma maman kept me away from her customers." This makes the captain flinch, but I just shrug. "It was work. She didn't have no shame in it. And I don't have no shame for her. I used to see you, though, coming here as crew with other Free Islanders, before you had your own airship. You couldn't have been much older than me."

"And how old is you now?" she probes.

"Sixteen," I declare, trying to sit up a little taller. She frowns dubiously. "Fine, fifteen," I amend. She frowns further. "Fourteen," I mutter. I refuse to admit thirteen.

The captain barks a laugh. "I was well past nineteen before I jumped on any airship! My grandmother would have put licks on my backside if I was even thinking it so young. At your age, all you should be studying on is your schooling and how some boy might like you so and dreaming about when you marry."

I make a face. Next thing she'll have me in frilly dresses and ribbons. "You don't seem to like boys," I remark.

This actually makes her smile. Her teeth are straight and white as pearls. "Don't think because you playing sneak-foot behind me that you does know my mind," she reprimands in a firm tone. "I like boys—men. Sometimes. And I get my schooling!"

"So, you plan to get married?" I say mockingly, folding my arms.

She snorts loudly. I almost smirk at that. Hard not to admire a woman who's not afraid to let out a good snort. "Not if I can help it. Eh! Stop with all these blasted questions! I a grown woman, and I don't need answer to you!" I watch as she swings her legs over the edge of the bed. And it's then I notice one of them isn't whole. Her right leg is only a thigh of smooth brown skin fitted snug into a metal casing; the rest is made of twisting copper rods that flex like muscle and bone. There's a steel ball joint where a knee should be and the calf is covered by a leather brown boot. So that explains the limp. She didn't have that when she visited before. I open my mouth to ask about it then clamp it back shut. None of my business.

She looks up to me, noticing my staring—and suddenly there's light. Gold like the sun, so much it hurts my eyes. She's bathed in it, all through her twisted coils of hair and covering her skin. I blink and the light's gone, leaving twinkling stars in her eyes. In my head Oya thunders, pushing words from my lips I don't mean to speak aloud.

"Bright Lady!" I blurt out before I can stop myself. The rest blares through my thoughts. *Oshun! The Bright Lady! Mistress of Rivers! Oya's sister-wife! Shango's favorite!* How hadn't I noticed it before? So that explained Oya's odd emotions, the jealousy and familiarity. More than one goddess shared this room.

The captain goes stiff as a beam at my words and her eyes narrow. So she knows about the goddess hovering about her, then. I can see it in her face, in the way her lips are pressed together all tight. But she hasn't accepted it. Well, that's none of my business either. I turn my head and say no more.

The magic of those old Afrikin gods is part of this city, ma maman used to say, buried in its bones and roots with the slaves that built it, making the ground and air and waterways sacred land. Only we forgot the names that went with that power we brought over here. Since Haiti got free, though, those gods were coming back, she'd said, across the waters, all the way from Lafrik. Now here's two of them in a bordello in New Orleans. Who knows what that means.

In the awkward quiet, the captain stands to slip back on her britches, then her remaining boot. "I'm going to find my crew," she tells me finally. "See if they think you talking true or just trying to sell me one big nancy-story. Wait here. I'll be back."

She buttons her Free Isles jacket and walks to the door. "What's your name?" I call out quickly.

The captain turns back to me, hesitant before deciding. "Ann-Marie," she answers. "Ann-Marie St. Augustine."

"I'm Creeper," I reply. She pauses at that. Everyone does. But she nods.

I wait until she's gone. Then I disappear through the window into the night.

Excerpt from
Alice Payne Arrives

by Kate Heartfield

CHAPTER ONE
Concerning a Robbery and What Comes After

1788

The highwayman known as the Holy Ghost lurks behind the ruined church wall. Lurking has a different quality to waiting, she reflects, having time for reflection. Waiting is what she did for the first five years after Father returned from the war in America, much changed.

That's how everyone put it, that first year.—*How is Colonel Payne?—Oh, people say he is much changed.* Now, people use the same tone to say the opposite.—*How is Colonel Payne?— Oh, he's much the same.—No change? His poor daughter.*

Alice grew tired of waiting for change. Colonel Payne's poor daughter does not fade into the background; she hides in it. She's quivering in the saddle: rider, hat and gun, all cocked, after a fashion.

Ah! There it is. A carriage comes rattling around the corner, the horses' gait slowing as the slope rises toward Gibbet Hill.

Alice lurks halfway up. Behind her, on the summit, there are no trees but those of the Tyburn sort, swinging with cages and corpses, as a warning to highwaymen. It seems to have worked. She has this section of Dray Road, fenced in with trees and ruins, all to herself. The road here is a hollow way, a track worn into the ground over the centuries, its banks curving up like the bottom half of a tunnel on either side. A trap for her victims.

What a gaudy contraption the Earl of Ludderworth uses to get around the country in, half-painted in gold as if he were Marie Antoinette, its four lamps lit although the sun is still bloodying the forest. Four horses, plumed. That dark bulk on the seat is the coachman and footman, both liveried like dancing monkeys, no doubt. Inside, it's big enough for four, but there will only be two. The odious earl will be travelling with his manservant. That makes four men, two of them armed with swords and probably pistols too. Loaded? Maybe, but not cocked.

Her left calf nuzzles her horse's belly. Havoc's withers twitch and he steps quietly to the right, making no sound until she taps fast with both legs and they are out in the open. By the time Havoc stops in the middle of the road, where he has stopped so many times before, she has both pistols in her hands.

"Stand and deliver!" she growls.

The first time she did this, she felt exposed, despite the hat low over her forehead, the black mask and green kerchief, the long grey cloak, the breeches and boots and gloves. She and Jane had meant it half as a lark; Jane was not convinced Alice would go through with it until she had. It was revenge, the first time, against a teacher of the pianoforte who preyed on any girl who was not sufficiently warned by her friends. Revenge, and a little much-needed money.

Now it is a regular affair, this robbery on the road. There are plenty of villains making their way through Hampshire, ready to be relieved of a purse, a blow struck in secret for womankind. Despite the fact that all the victims are men of suspect character when it comes to women, no one has made that connection, or suspected that the Holy Ghost is a woman, much less that it is Alice. All her skin is covered, lest the colour of it call to any local's mind Colonel Payne's poor daughter.

Today, after a dozen robberies, she does not feel exposed. She doesn't feel like Alice Payne, sitting on a horse in the middle of the road, in a disguise. She is the Holy Ghost, and she is about her vengeful business.

The coachman moves—reaching toward the seat beside him? A pistol there?

This would make a convenient moment for a partner to ride out of the woods, up to the side of the coach, a second pistol in hand. But the Holy Ghost doesn't have a partner on the road, not a human one, at least.

So she pulls the trigger in her left-hand gun and the lamp nearest her breaks and goes dark. Bullet meeting glass makes a satisfying smash that never fails to frighten cowards.

The coachman flinches, freezes.

"Hands in the air!"

His hands go high.

This is the dangerous moment. She keeps her distance, watching the windows of the coach. She's not too worried about Lord Ludderworth himself; he seems unlikely to start a fight with someone who can fight back. He presses his advances on the vulnerable: young girls, girls in service. In any event, he's a horrible shot. At more than one tedious shooting party, she's watched him fail to hit pheasants that were practically presented to him on plates. But his manservant Grigson may be another matter.

"Your money or your life! I'd rather the money, if it's all the same to you, but I'll not hesitate if it's the other."

And now, the pièce de résistance.

Six feet down the road, right beside the stopped carriage, the automaton slides out of the gorse bushes.

There are a dozen good spots for it, all along the roads of this county. Three of them happen to be near churches, and one near an abbey, which has given rise to the Holy Ghost nickname. A reputation is good for a highwayman. When people know what to expect, they aren't so afraid as to do foolish things. A well-known robber who puts on a predictable show is an institution, and the good people of England will hand over their tolls with due resignation and respect.

In the twilight, the sight of Alice's automaton sends shivers down her own skin. The carved wooden head, painted white with blue eyes and red lips, as still as a Madonna's. The grey cloak, the same colour as her own, the hood brought over the head. The outstretched hand.

The coachman crosses himself.

The coach window clicks open a crack, wide enough to admit a gun—she breathes, keeps her seat still and remains calm—but instead, out sneaks a purse in pudgy, ringed fingers—the hand of Lord Ludderworth himself. The hand that lifted her skirt when she was fourteen, that has squeezed every housemaid's breast between London and Bristol.

The little purse lands in the wooden hand and the automaton stands motionless for a moment, then flips its hand to let the purse drop into the box. The box clacks on the cart rails, a few yards up the hill along the side of the road to where Alice sits on Havoc.

The automaton lets Alice keep her distance, and it gives the villains a show for their money. A story to tell.

It is noisy, but it is not meant to fool anyone. Everyone knows it is a machine and that only inspires all the more awe. Ghosts and fairies litter history, but machines that can move like humans are the stuff of dreams.

Jane's work never ceases to amaze her. Her darling Jane, working on her gears and springs in her study, believing that one day, her toys and curiosities will bring Utopia. For now, this one brings Alice a living and brings a little justice to the world, and that is good enough for Alice.

Alice never lets the pistol in her right hand droop, keeps her wide gaze on the coachman, the footman, the open window. At the edge of her vision, she pokes the hook she's attached to the end of her riding crop into the handle of the box, lifts it by the handle, drops it into her lap. She unties the purse, still watching the coach, lifts a coin to her mouth and bites.

The automaton nods its head, as it always does after three minutes.

There is a long silence.

She shifts in the saddle. Almost done. Almost safe.

Havoc's head snaps up, but he's a steady horse, steadier than his mistress. He stands and waits.

"That'll do," she says, trying not to let the relief into her voice. "Ride on. The toll's paid."

An easy night's work. The manservant Grigson never made his appearance. She watches the coach rattle up Gibbet Hill for a moment.

Then she ties the purse to her belt. She jumps Havoc up onto the bank and rides him more or less the same way. She'll have to ride fast if she's to beat the frightened coachman to Fleance Hall with enough time to change her clothes and fix her hair.

And then, after the world is asleep, she'll return for the automaton. It has slid back into its hiding spot in the bushes.

She grins as she rides through the paths that she and Havoc know well. The new purse bangs against her hip. That will buy Father a month's freedom from his creditors, at least.

At the sound of hoof beats, she snaps her head around, as beneath her Havoc's muscles run taut as rope.

Behind her, and not very far, a man on a grey horse. He's hatless, and she recognizes his face at once. Grigson.

The manservant was never in the coach. He was riding behind, waiting before the bend in the road, waiting to pursue the thief rumoured to haunt Dray Road.

Damn Lord Ludderworth. So stingy he'd rather risk his right-hand man than lose a bit of gold.

The bank is easily five feet higher than the road here and she can see the carriage rattling along up the hill, bearing the earl to safety while his servant tries to capture the most notorious highwayman this side of London. Well, he won't get his chance. Havoc is a fast horse and she knows these woods like no one else does. There's a deer path up ahead that will take her to a winding, deep creek ford where she can double back without being seen, if she times it well.

As she steers Havoc's nose that way, she glances behind her.

Damn! Two more men, on her right; Grigson approaching behind.

The one way they won't expect her to veer is left.

She pulls Havoc to the left and spurs him to a gallop. The carriage is rattling up the hill, and here on the higher ground the banks flatten out, so that the road is no longer a hollow way. Havoc does not even break his stride as his hoofs hit the dirt of the road, just behind the carriage. She'll cross behind it and—

A horse whinnies in fear, up in the team, and the carriage careens off the road, rocks as the wheels hit the grassy banks.

Alice keeps Havoc at full speed. Her leg grazes an old milestone stuck in the grassy bank. She turns parallel to the road again, heading up the hill, to put the carriage between herself and the three pursuers. Typical of Lord Ludderworth, to wait until he was out of danger before loosing his ambush!

There are few trees here to hide her. She glances back: the three horsemen were surprised by her sudden turn back to the road and she's put a little distance between them. Once she crests the hill, and is out of their sight for a moment, she'll double back to the right and find the creek bed.

She glances once more at the road and squints, frowning. The carriage is out of sight; it must have been travelling faster than she realized and crested the hill already, despite going off track for a moment. That must be a fine coachman to get the horses in hand so quickly after they took fright at Havoc's approach. Perhaps they bolted.

The air seems to shimmer the road like a soap bubble, just there by the old milestone. It's mere fancy—everything looks strange at twilight—and she can't afford a second look.

Over the hill, hidden from view for a moment, Havoc veers back over the road toward the creek. She races along the most winding paths to Fleance Hall, where Alice Payne is expected.

CHAPTER TWO
In Which the Wrong Mistress Is Persuaded

1889

Prudence opens the hackney door before it stops and jumps onto the snow. Her motherfucking Victorian boot heels stick with every step, but after she gets out of the drift and up onto the frozen ground, she can run, holding her skirts.

The Mayerling hunting lodge sprawls red-roofed against the bare Austrian hills. It's just past dawn, with a murmur of cowbells and lowing not too distant. Here, though, everything is quiet.

She had better be wrong. Oh, she had better be wrong. Mary Vetsera is only seventeen, and Crown Prince Rudolf has only been screwing her for a few months. Besides, Mary's a baroness, hardly the one he'd choose for a suicide pact. He's always used Mitzi for playing to his Byronic self-image: his Viennese demimonde "dancer," so nicely shocking to the Austrian court.

It has taken Prudence seventy-one attempts at 1889 to convince Mitzi to refuse to die with Rudolf, to report his suggestion of suicide to the police.

Seventy failures and now, at last, success. Two nights ago, Rudolf came to Mitzi and she refused to die with him. They cried. Prudence was there, the maid in the next room, listening, ready to comfort Mitzi the moment her lover left. Rudolf even promised to get off the morphine. If he doesn't kill himself, he'll live with his syphilis for decades. Everything will be fine.

Mitzi has told the police twice that Rudolf is suicidal. They never do a damn thing about it. But at last, Prudence thought she had saved them from their suicide pact. Mitzi was upset, but resolute. Strong. Any moment now, she should hear from General Almo, saying: You've done it. Mission complete. Come home.

Home being the year 2145, for lack of anything better.

And then yesterday afternoon, the letter arrived, from Rudolf, saying good-bye. It might seem a lover's farewell, nothing more—but Prudence has misgivings. No word from Almo, no word from the future that the past has been changed. She asked her most useful gossip where Rudolf had gone that day, and she heard: Mayerling. With Mary Vetsera.

She runs to the gatehouse and peers inside. One guard, but not at his post: he's in the courtyard with another man, hitching two horses to a calèche. It's six thirty in the morning, early for Rudolf to have asked for a carriage, but then this is a hunting lodge.

She can tell the other man by his whiskers: Loschek. Rudolf's valet. The man who always sleeps in the room next to Rudolf and whatever woman Rudolf has in his bed on any given night.

Rudolf has sent the man in the bedroom next to his own outside, away from him. To hitch the horses? Or to get him away?

She darts inside the gate and around the corner to the window Mitzi snuck out of a few months before, to get away from Rudolf in one of his moods. As Mitzi's maid, Prudence knows well enough which room Rudolf uses as his bedroom when he has a lover here.

He had better be sleeping. Oh, she had better be wrong.

Goddamn those Misguideds. The damage they cause! The more they encourage Rudolf's liberal tendencies, with their agent-tutors and agent-friends, the angrier Rudolf becomes with his tyrannical father. The worse Rudolf's melancholy, the more entrenched Rudolf's conviction that there is no point to his own life beyond sex and drink. The man who could save the world from the First World War, squandered to syphilis and depression.

The Misguideds are now trying to fix the suicide problem, just as Prudence is, but they're working with Rudolf. The Farmers can't get close to him, so Prudence was assigned to Mitzi. Ten years ago. For ten years she's been reliving 1889, getting it wrong, getting it wrong.

She puts her boot on the drainpipe and thrusts her knife between the window and the sill. No matter where she goes in human history, she always carries a knife.

The window budges, at last, and she pulls it open and heaves herself through.

This time, there's no chair in the hallway on the other side, so she falls to her stomach, knocking the wind out of herself. She waits, prepares herself to pose as yet another new mistress if anyone but Rudolf comes, but there's no one. Silence.

A shadow moves, far down at the other end of the hall. A guard.

She'd like to unbutton the awful boots but there's no time so she tiptoes as softly as she can, opens one door and then another.

She knows, as soon she opens the right room, that she was not wrong. She's seen Rudolf's dead face many times. The image of her failure.

She steps inside and closes and locks the door behind her. She can't be discovered here. There might still be time; he might be alive.

He's slumped on the floor, blood trickling from his mouth.

Gore on the wall behind him.

There's an empty glass; there's a gun; there's Mary, on the bed, not sleeping.

Prudence kneels by his side, this asshole of a prince whom she's never met but whose life she has been trying to save for ten years. Another failure. Under her fingertips, no pulse.

"Major Zuniga."

She stands quickly and turns, dizzy for a moment. On a chair: a red felt hat, with black feathers.

General Almo stands in his fatigues, a time portal behind him. Why the hell did he shimmer here himself? He's never done that, not in any of her past failures.

Any moment now, the valet will return. Almo turns and locks the door, as if he's had the same thought. The key was in the keyhole. There is a hairbrush on the dresser, and by the bed a pair of dove-coloured women's shoes . . .

"It's earlier this time," she says, and her voice is full as if she wants to weep, although she has no more reason to weep than she's had the last seventy times. But this time, she thought she had it. She saved Mitzi's life. She thought she'd saved Rudolf's too.

"And he's chosen a different partner, I see."

She nods. "Mary Vetsera. She's just a girl. But now we know that's a possibility. It won't happen again, sir."

"There won't be an again. I'm reassigning you."

She has to lean against something but there's nothing to lean on, nothing that isn't covered with Rudolf's blood. She steps closer to the general, rooting herself in the movement.

"Sir, I can do this."

"No. You can't."

He's a big man, and seems even bigger here, in this room. There is too much history here for these four walls to contain.

"If it's . . . I know there are limits to what a woman of colour can do in this setting, but I can work with Vetsera just as I worked with Mitzi. I've got a prep package to be an American artist, like Edmonia Lewis. Vetsera could be convinced to take art lessons."

"It's not that. We're shutting down this mission. Putting our resources elsewhere, in 2016. Let's try 2016 again."

"But 2016 is *completely fucked*," she says, trying to keep her voice even. "You know that. Sir. We have to go back earlier."

He shakes his head. "Obsession happens to all of us but we have to see it for what it is. It's my fault. I wanted this too. I let you stay here far too long. But no single moment of history is everything. It's a long war, Major Zuniga. If we fight one battle forever, it will never end."

She nods, because she doesn't trust herself to speak. He's right. The war of attrition for human history will never end, not if the Farmers keep fighting the Misguideds battle to battle, moment to moment.

General Almo is right. It is pointless to keep trying to push history one way while the Misguideds are trying to push it in another. But he doesn't have the courage to do what needs to be done. The only way to end this war, to end all wars, is to stop anyone from changing history ever again.

CHAPTER THREE
Companions; or, How Alice Is Transformed

1788

Alice loses her pursuers at the creek bed. Havoc picks his way back up the bank and into the woods, where he knows the paths to home.

She urges Havoc to go faster, although it's nearly too dark to see. She does not dare light the mica lantern in her saddlebag. She needs to return unseen. By now, Lord Ludderworth's carriage will have arrived at Fleance Hall. Alice is meant to be at the door with Father to greet their guest, to distract his attention from the fewness of servants with bluster and goodwill.

There's a lantern at the second servants' entrance, around the back of the house, where Jane waits, holding a candlestick.

She takes Havoc by the bridle and says, "I'll tie him here and stable him later before the groom does his rounds."

The fact that the groom is also kept busy being the coachman, the footman and man-of-all-work makes taking horses out of the stable very convenient. Before Father went away to war, Fleance Hall had nine servants. Now it has four: a cook, a housemaid, the groom and the indefinable Satterthwaite, her father's butler/valet/man-of-business.

"Your gown is just inside." Jane points. "What kept you, Alice? Your father has been asking—he thinks I've gone up to your room to help you with some womanly requirement."

"Time for that later," Alice says, and kisses her, snaking one arm around her waist.

"Go on," Jane hisses, pushing Alice, but she's smiling. "Your father's guest will be here any moment."

Alice slips through the propped-open door into the little anteroom, where her clothes are laid out on the bench. Her best yellow gown, of course. Jane's lit two candles on the wall sconces, but it's still gloomy. She kicks off the high riding boots and wriggles out of the breeches. She's shivering in her shift when Jane slides in and closes the door behind her.

Ten years they've lived together now at Fleance Hall. It was Father's idea to bring his cousin's ward here to be Alice's companion, when he went away to America to fight. Alice was only twenty-two then, and Father held great hopes that she'd marry. Truth be told, she's never done much to encourage proposals, and actively discouraged them whenever any of her lovers got too close. In those early years, while Father was away, Jane was a friend. Over the last year, she's given Alice a reason to discourage proposals forevermore.

She plops the purse full of coins and rings into Jane's white hand.

"Ah, you and Laverna got your man."

"We did." Laverna is the name that Jane gave the automaton, early on: the patron goddess of thieves.

Alice wriggles into her slim modesty petticoat, then pushes the clothes over enough on the bench to give herself room to sit, and points her toe. Each white stocking rolls up under Jane's white fingertips, which brush the tops of Alice's bare knees, under the modesty petticoat.

"You know," Jane says, "I was never jealous of any of your lovers, but sometimes I feel a little jealous of Laverna."

"She is your creation, darling."

"All the more reason. I don't trust anything I build. Do you remember the walking doll I made for Freddy Combles last Christmas? I swear it used to migrate through the house in the night. I was glad to be rid of it."

She glances up and Alice offers a weary smile.

"What is it, Alice? What did keep you, on the road?"

"Ludderworth's servants chased me. Don't worry, Jane, they didn't get close. But they did delay me. I can't believe Lord Ludderworth isn't here already. He must have stopped to wait for his servants. Lucky for me he did."

Alice puts her hand on the petticoat, keeping Jane's hand there, and Jane slides her fingers up the inside of her thigh. Under the shift, under the petticoat, there is nothing between them. Jane's thumb and finger find their places with absolute confidence as Jane leans into her and says against Alice's lips: "Later."

Alice groans theatrically and stands up so Jane can wrap the stays around her body and lace them down the front, over the stomacher, shaping Alice into the role of Miss Payne. Jane knows every inch of her body, where it will give and where it will swell. Jane slides the wooden busk between shift and stays, and together they tie the yellow petticoat around her waist. A gauze fichu over the shoulders, then she slips into the gown like a jacket and Jane closes it in front, working fast, thrusting the pins into the stays.

"Damn it," Jane swears around the pin in her mouth. "It's crooked here."

"Never mind that," Alice says. She steps into the yellow silk shoes and picks up the white-ribboned cap, the only thing left on the bench, and pins it quickly over the back of her hair. It was braided under the hat, and the frizzes that have come free around her forehead will look just fine with the cap.

It's only Lord Ludderworth, anyway. If her gown is pinned crookedly and her hair a little wild, what does it matter? It's been years since she could afford to keep a lady's maid. She is thirty-two years old, keeping herself and her family under this roof by dint of adventure, and she does not give a damn if her bodice is straight.

She tugs the sides of the fichu a little more closely together over her cleavage, and runs down the hallway, leaving Jane to gather the cast-off highwayman's clothes and hide them in her study. The housemaid never ventures in there; she's afraid of all the machines and instruments, and especially of the frogs in jars.

Alice runs, one hand holding her skirt, the other skimming the walls that she loves, although the paper is peeling. Through the parlour, empty, lit only by embers. Voices in the hall just inside the main door. She runs past Satterthwaite at the door and comes skidding to a halt on the chequerboard floor, the only part of the big house that is scrubbed to a polish and brightly lit.

The four men in the room turn to look at her.

Father says, "Alice! At last!"

Standing beside Father is not Lord Ludderworth, or even Lord Ludderworth's coachman or footman, but the manservant who chased her on his horse. He's wet with sweat and too alarmed to do anything but bow his head.

"You remember John Grigson. Lord Ludderworth's manservant. These two men with him are servants of the earl's household as well."

"Of course," Alice says, bowing her head. "Mr. Grigson."

"Miss Payne," says Grigson, glancing from Alice to her father and back. She's seen people do this her whole life, contrasting her father's pale skin with her own. She takes after her Caribbean mother, whom she does not remember. Grigson is black himself, though, and usually it is white people who have more difficulty with the existence of Alice. It dawns that his hesitation, his glancing from face to face, has little to do with her. He's had a shock. God, could he have some idea that she is the highwayman?

"Lord Ludderworth went on ahead of us," he says. "How can it be that he has not arrived?"

"What do you mean?" Father barks. "You mean to say that your master is somewhere out there on the road, still?"

Grigson shakes his head. "That he is not, Colonel. I'd stake my life."

"Then where, man?"

CHAPTER FOUR
On the Nuclear Option, with Cocktails

2070

Prudence pauses outside the yellow-brick house and pulls out her EEG scanner. Just to be safe. Two people inside, both of them neutrals. She chose Helmut and Rati with care: radical conservatives, young enough with nothing to lose and smart enough to have dangerous confidence in their own decisions. To the scanner, that's neither Farmer nor Misguided, but neutral. A person with extreme tendencies on either end of a spectrum sometimes registers the same as a moderate.

The retina lock on the door is disguised as an old-fashioned peephole, because the only houses that would have such security in this part of suburban Toronto would be drug houses. Prudence would rather not attract any official attention. No records.

The lock clicks and she turns the doorknob.

"I'm home," she says, stepping into the dim hall.

She means it as a joke, but it feels true. Even before she set up her rogue project in this ugly little house, Prudence Zuniga always had a place to stay in 2070. Most of her friends—well, colleagues—are here, and this time around, her sister.

This year is the destination of choice for discerning time travellers.

2070: Later than the biggest waves of History War refugees and the backlash to them.

2070: Twenty-one years earlier than the beginning of the History War itself, although the first rumblings of that war are now only a year away. Teleosophy begins as an intelligence wing of the U.S. military in 2071. Twenty years later, it will explode into a global war between the Farmers and the so-called Guides.

The technology of 2070 is advanced enough to make life comfortable. Time travel is new but available for those who can pay; upstream in earlier centuries, the only travellers are military like Prudence. The war won't get bad enough to visibly affect contemporary life until after the Anarchy hits in 2139. That leaves plenty of time for a human to live out a life. Sure, the climate's a mess already by 2070, but it's a catastrophe, not yet an apocalypse.

Visit 2070: It's Not an Apocalypse. Yet. This Time.

She hasn't written marketing copy in . . . what? How many years of her life? Too many to do the math. The voice of it in her head twists itself ever more cynically but never goes silent. Of course, propaganda isn't all that different. She spent several years behind a desk doing propaganda for the Mao and Peron projects, and various European Union campaigns, before Almo recruited her out of the communications branch.

Farmer agents never lie unless it's absolutely necessary.

She's learned how to make the truth do what she wants it to do.

If Project Shipwreck works, though, there will be a lot less demand for her unique set of skills.

Helmut and Rati emerge at the top of the basement stairs.

"Anything I should know about?" she asks.

Helmut shakes his head. "We're still running reliability checks. Getting better. Point-two percent."

Prudence sighs. Not nearly good enough. But she won't wait any longer.

"You look exhausted," Rati says. "Is 1889 not going well?"

They are both looking at her with concern. They're too goddamn young, too new, to know that it's perfectly normal to be exhausted.

"Not going at all, anymore. General Almo's closed it down."

"Closed it down?" Rati asks. She's the sharper of the two. "You mean he . . . gave up?"

Prudence walks the room, checks their work. They've been busy. They're dedicated, these two. They're ready. "He wanted to reassign me to goddamn 2016, which if you ask me is too late to do any good for the timeline, and too early to do any good for the History War. I convinced him to send me here to do Berlin Convention sabotage instead."

If he suspects anything, he'll suspect that Prudence wants to spend time with her sister. It's one more reason she chose to make this time and place the headquarters for Project Shipwreck. She has a plausible reason to want to come here.

"The leaders won't lead," she sloganeers. "So we have to."

Rati frowns. "Now? But you said . . ."

When they began, three years ago in Prudence's lifeline, it

was an experiment to see how much EEG-scanner coverage they could achieve, worldwide. They were going to turn the network over to Teleosophic Core Command, or said they were.

Prudence, Rati and Helmut have mainly kept up that fiction even among themselves, but the network has been basically complete for months and they haven't discussed handing it over to the TCC. Even if they could convince the TCC to send a generation of Misguideds downstream, they could never convince the TCC to end time travel altogether. Project Shipwreck won't be nearly as effective if they allow the enemy to develop counterstrike ability. Mutually assured destruction is exactly what Prudence and her protégés are trying to avert.

So the three of them have drifted, from rogues to traitors.

"Almo doesn't have the stomach to win," says Helmut. "He just gave up on preventing the First World War."

"Exactly," says Prudence. "The Command has just shown it is not interested in putting an end to this war. Too many generals behind desks and not enough of them out in the field to see what the enemy is doing. I've seen, over the last ten years, just how fanatical the Misguideds can be. There is no winning against a cult in a war of attrition. The only way is to burn it all down. Almo can't see that. So it's up to us."

They're quiet.

"And what about the 1788 component?" Rati asks.

"I've chosen the naïf and I'll go today. Jane Hodgson. You two know that name?"

Helmut shakes his head, but Rati says, "The inventor of the helidrone?"

Prudence smiles. "Just the kind of person we want, don't you think? She dies in poverty, so I think the reward, and the lure of a scientific machine she's never seen, will do the trick."

Helmut shakes his head. "It's a weak spot, but I don't know what to do about it. I'd go myself, happily, but we just can't be sure that the causality won't glitch. I was hoping to figure it out, but—"

Prudence raises her hand. "Hodgson will work out. And if she doesn't, there are plenty of other people in 1788 who will take the job."

Helmut nods. "All right. Once that's in place, we're ready."

"Ready? You just said point-two percent!"

He blushes. "Point-two percent may be as low as I'll ever be able to get it. EEG scanning has inherent limits, and there will always be some false positives."

"OK. Let's think about the consequences of that. The global population of Misguideds, as of July 1, 2070, will be roughly two-point-two-six billion. Right? Which gives us a false-positive of . . . let's see . . . oh, four and a half million people. Four and a half million people who are actually neutrals, or maybe even Farmers. People like us."

Helmut frowns, and his face goes pink.

"Yes," says Rati, glancing at him, and back at Prudence. "But it's not as if we're killing them."

"No, we're not killing them," she says. Her voice still sounds like a rusty hinge. "Probably. But it's the goddamn nuclear option, isn't it?"

Their eyes go wide. Shit. She has to tread more carefully here. She's taking them for granted.

These two kids are working with second-rate equipment, putting all of Rati's ill-gotten funds toward the power cells. They've disguised their workshop to fit the period, as much as possible, and to fit their cover story, should any of their fellow Farmers find them. These two young people have chosen not only to blow up their own chances at making a better world, but to blow up everyone else's chances too. She's already asking too much of them, but goddammit, she's going to ask for a little fucking humanity too.

"Look," she says. "Our energy supply is going to be extremely touch-and-go as it is. Nobody has ever done anything like this before. Ever. We're moving two billion people five centuries downstream. I would like to have a little wiggle room in my calculations. OK?"

Helmut nods, although he's still a faint salmon colour. White people: always showing their emotions in their skin. Date the Walking Biogenuine Mood Avatar. Never Be in Doubt of How He Feels Again.

They both nod, dutifully, devotedly. They are exhausted, poor tadpoles. And she needs to do a better job of morale.

"Let's get a drink," she says. "I think Orbital Decays are still popular in Toronto in 2070. You like cocktails, Helmut? Of course you do. Everybody likes cocktails."

They close down the displays, power down the cooling fans and the Faraday decoy rig.

She hangs back, trudging behind them like a chaperone while Helmut and Rati chatter their way down the sidewalk, into the streets of Toronto. It takes twenty minutes to get to the gentrified part of the neighbourhood. They order their cocktails and sit in a dark booth in the back, watching the life of an ordinary bar. Rati has her scanner on the table. It blinks orange, green, blue, as people pass by their table.

"You're worried," Prudence says, grimacing a bit at the sourness of her Orbital Decay. The mix of shrub syrup and gin always takes a few sips to taste anything but awful.

"Not worried," Rati says, stirring her own Decay so the tapioca pearls dance and swirl in the martini glass. "Just . . . wondering. Thinking about the timing. You keep a diary, right? You've been at this longer than I have. Can you really know that this is the best of all plausible worlds?"

"I'm sure it isn't," Prudence says. "But I know it isn't the worst."

CHAPTER FIVE
In Which Mr. Grigson Gives His Account

1788

"But do you mean to say," says Father, "that you and His Lordship did not travel together, or that you did? Elucidate."

Father is florid already, well past the heady certainty that no one can tell he's had two mugs of cider if he pronounces his diphthongs with austerity, and venturing into gleeful indifference.

Grigson glances at her again. "I do not wish to frighten Miss Payne, but—"

"Miss Payne does not frighten easily," says Father, loudly, regretfully.

It is irritating, the way Father becomes all the more imperious after each of his absent episodes. Mr. Brown the groom found him wandering on the hills again, just last week, and Alice held Father's hand while he stared into the posset of cream and strong sack that Cook made for him, while all the servants tried not to show their concern. And then the next morning, he was back to being this other new version of himself, disagreeable and unkind, as if in compensation for his vulnerability the night before.

Grigson looks back at her. She smiles sweetly.

"We were expecting trouble," Grigson says. "There have been so many tales of the Holy Ghost in this county lately. So my lord asked me to ride a little behind, so that if he were robbed, I could give chase. It all happened just as he thought it would. Just as the stories say: the man appeared, and then the apparition. A creature of wood and gears, if you ask me, although I could only see the shape of it from where I was. As soon as the coachman had driven my lord up Gibbet Hill, I spurred my horse and my companions did the same. He veered back across the road, around the carriage and out of view over the hill. The carriage horses spooked and ran up onto the road bank, but we three followed the highwayman. I lost him in a creek bed. I had half a mind then to return and find the automaton and smash it to bits—"

Alice's intake of breath is loud; the man pauses; she covers it up by fluttering her hand to her mouth, hoping she looks overwhelmed at his manly energy. He is handsome. Good arms, nice legs.

She has always dismantled Laverna during the night, after her prey has passed. If they find it, there is no clue that could betray her, and she does not think anyone would trace it back to Jane—people tend to leave her to putter about in her study, the harmless companion, bookish, fancies herself a scholar . . . Still. Laverna is theirs, their private secret, and she does not want their secrets smashed or studied.

"Go on, man," says Father, "and never mind what you had half a mind to do. Where was his lordship then?"

"Upon the road, or so I thought. A fear struck me that perhaps we had driven the highwayman to take some desperate action. Perhaps he thought we'd recognized him. So we returned to the road, back to the spot where we left it, and then rode as hard as our horses would go, straight to Fleance Hall."

He pauses, and takes a deep, shuddering breath.

"I did not pass the carriage. And it was not here when I arrived."

"What do you mean?" Alice asks sharply. "It could not have vanished. There are no side roads, no paths big enough to take a carriage, not between here and Gibbet Hill."

That's the very reason she chose that spot to waylay Lord Ludderworth, once she heard that Father had invited him to Fleance Hall. He was a fish in a pond. So where is he now?

"You mean to say the whole carriage has vanished?"

Father asks.

"And the three men in it."

"Three? What three? Who was with the earl? Your tale is all tangled."

"I mean, Colonel, that the earl was driven by his coachman, and that there was a footman too, riding on the seat."

"It must be just on the hill somewhere," says Alice. "Perhaps the coachman couldn't get the horses back onto the road, and decided to wait for help."

"Begging your pardon," says Grigson, "but there are few trees on the hill. Not much to hide a carriage behind."

"You could have passed very near to it without seeing, in the dark," she says. "Or they turned around to drive back to London, although why they would, when they were three miles from Fleance Hall, I can't imagine."

It must have been fancy, that shimmer in the air beside the road near the last place she saw the carriage. But perhaps her fancy had some cause. Perhaps her eye caught sight of something her mind did not have time to understand.

"Satterthwaite," says Father, his brows knit. "Have the groom ride to the New House and fetch Captain Auden."

Is he getting up a search party? They'll find the automaton. She has to get out before them and dismantle it. Damn that earl! Where can he have gone?

"What do you want with Wray Auden, father?" Alice asks. "Do you think the carriage passed our lane in the night and went on to New House? It's possible, I suppose, although we have the lantern lit."

"That is possible, yes," says Father, adopting a pompous set to his jowls to camouflage his suppressing of a belch, "but I want Captain Auden because he's the parish constable. There's been at least one crime done tonight, and maybe more than one. It's time this highwayman was caught."

Excerpt from Gods, Monsters, and the Lucky Peach

by Kelly Robson

The past is another country; we want to colonize it.

-1-

The monster looked like an old grandmother from the waist up, but it had six long octopus legs. It crawled out of its broken egg and cowered in the muddy drainage ditch. When it noticed Shulgi, its jaw fell open, exposing teeth too perfect to be human.

It recoiled and hissed: *Oh – shit – shit – shit – shit – shit – shit.*

Shulgi hefted his flail in one hand and his scythe in the other. He knew his duty better than anyone other than the gods. Kings were made for killing monsters.

.   .   .

On one of Calgary's wide, south-facing orchard terraces, Minh pruned peach trees while paying vague attention to ESSA's weekly business meeting. Minh and her partners were all plague babies. They'd worked together for nearly sixty years, so unless a problem cropped up—an over-budget project or a scope-creeping client—their fakes could handle the meeting nearly unmonitored.

No problems this week. Nobody playing diva, simply letting their fakes walk through the agenda. Everyone except for Kiki, the firm's ridiculously frenetic young admin. She was playing with an antique paper clip simulation, stringing them into ropes. The clips clicked against the table.

Kiki, stop it, Minh whispered. The sound is driving me nuts.

I didn't know you were lurking, Kiki replied. I thought I was all alone here.

The meetings are important. Sit still and listen.

Easy for you to say. You don't spend every Monday morning with a bunch of fakes. I bet you're halfway up a tree right now, aren't you?

Minh didn't reply. She was in a tree—four legs wrapped around the trunk of Calgary's oldest peach. She'd just started the late-winter pruning. Below her, bots gathered the dropped limbs and piled them on a cargo float. A cold downwash funneled through the orchard, the wind caught and guided by the hab's towering south wall. Minh pinged the microclimate sensors. A few more weeks of winter chill and the trees could start moving into bud break.

Since I've got your attention, Kiki continued, you might want to look over the RFP coming up next. It's a big river remediation project funded by a private bank. You've never seen anything like it. You're going to disintegrate.

Kiki shot her the request for proposal package with a flick of her fingernail.

Minh dropped out of the tree and spread the data over the orchard's carefully manicured ground cover. She hadn't seen a new project in ten years. The banks weren't interested. Calgary and all the other surface habitats struggled to keep their ongoing projects alive. Some of the habs—Edmonton, notoriously—had managed the funding crisis so badly, they'd starved themselves out.

Before she'd even finished scanning the introductory

material, Minh's blood pressure was spiraling.

A time travel project. Aren't you excited? Kiki whispered. I nearly blew apart when I saw it.

Half the RFP made sense. Past state assessment, flow modeling, ecological remediation—her life's work, familiar as her own skin. The rest didn't make sense at all. Mesopotamia, Tigris, Euphrates—words out of history. And time travel—those two words raised the hairs on the back of her neck. Her biom flashed with blood pressure alerts.

It's intriguing, whispered Minh. Why didn't you send it to me earlier?

Kiki jangled the paper clips. It's been in your queue for two days. I've been bugging your fake about it. You never look at your RFPs before the meeting. None of you do.

Yeah, well, we're busy people, Minh replied absently.

When the plague babies had moved to the surface six decades earlier, in 2205, they'd been determined to prove humanity could escape the hives and hells and live above ground again, in humanity's ancestral habitat. First, they'd erected bare-bones habs high in the mountains, scraping together skeleton funding for proof-of-concept pilot projects. For the first few ecological remediation projects, the plague babies donated their billable hours, hoping to lure investment and spark population growth.

It worked. Not quite as quickly as they'd hoped, but over the decades, the habs proved viable. Iceland and Cusco were booming. Calgary wasn't quite as successful but momentum was building. Then TERN developed time travel, and every aboveground initiative had stalled.

Why would TERN get involved in river remediation now? Hadn't they ruined her life enough already?

Minh's biom slid an alert into the middle of her eye. Blood pressure wildly fluctuating, as if Minh couldn't tell. She'd been light-headed ever since opening the RFP package. Her field of vision was narrowing. Her fingers itched to dial a little relief into her biom, but no. Minh had promised her medtech she wouldn't meddle with her hormonal balance, so instead of hitting herself with a jolt of adrenaline, she circled the peach tree's central leader with two legs and hung upside down, rough bark against her back, and let the blood cascade to her brain.

Back in the meeting, the fakes finished walking through the project progress reports. Nothing over budget. No problems. The fakes approved them all.

"Okay," Kiki told the fakes. "On to new opportunities."

Watch this, she whispered to Minh. I can turn these fakes into scientists.

Kiki fired the time travel RFP onto the table.

"The first one is for Minh. River remediation, and it's big. Thousands of billable hours."

All round the table, the fakes dropped away as Minh's partners engaged with the text.

Kiki grinned at Minh. *See? It's like magic.*

Mesopotamian Development Bank

Request for Proposal (RFP 2267-16)

Past State Assessment of the Mesopotamian Trench

Due March 21, 2267 at 14:00 GMT

The Mesopotamian Development Bank is embarking on a multiphase initiative to remediate the Mesopotamian trench. This project will restore 100,000 square kilometers of habitat, including the natural channels of the Euphrates and Tigris rivers, their tributaries, coastal wetlands, and terrestrial and aquatic species. The restoration project will support a network of arcologies across the habitat.

The Bank is seeking a multidisciplinary project team

to execute a past state assessment supported by the Temporal Economic Research Node (TERN), a division of the Centers for Excellence in Economic Research and Development (CEERD). The successful proponent team will assess and quantify the environmental state of Mesopotamia in 2024 BCE. The project will include complete geomorphological and ecological baselines, responses to stressors, and processes of change and adaptation. The data gathered will guide and inform future restoration projects in an effort to impose a regular climatic regime across the Mesopotamian drainage basin.

"This project is too good to pass up," said Minh. "I want it."

"You can't be serious, Minh," David said. He was out of breath, puffing hard. "Nobody hates CEERD and TERN more than you."

Minh pinged his location. David was cycling the Icefields Guideway, climbing Sunwapta Pass without boost assist.

"It's a great job," said Minh. "I've already started working on the proposal."

Kiki rolled her eyes. Minh ignored her.

"This isn't a job, it's a joke," said Sarah. "You can't do an ecological assessment on a hundred thousand square kilometers in three weeks. Three years wouldn't be enough."

Zhang shook his head. "Maybe if we knew this bank, but we've never even heard of them."

Kiki fired a documentary onto the table. "The Mesopotamian Development Bank specializes in West Asian projects. They're designing a string of habs for the Zagros Mountains. Look at this design. You're going to collapse."

The table exploded into a full-blown architectural simulation, the angles and planes of a huge ziggurat echoing the peaks and crags of the surrounding ranges. In comparison, Calgary was a pimple on the prairie.

"Put the doc away, Kiki," said Sarah. "It's just pretty pictures to attract investment."

Kiki slapped the doc down. Minh threw some numbers into an opportunity-assessment matrix and fired it onto the table.

"If we win, the follow-on work could be massive," she said. "Make the client happy and they'll keep us fed for decades."

Minh's partners reviewed the figures in the follow-on column.

"I like the numbers," said Clint. "But the job's got to be wired."

Kiki leaned over the table, braids swinging. "If they already know who they want to hire, why bother with a public procurement process? Private banks don't need procurement transparency."

Easy, Minh whispered. I'm handling this.

"I want this job," said Minh. "I've already started putting together my team."

David said, "If you win, your team can't pull out. The Bank of Calgary would peel the skin off us."

"It won't be a problem," said Minh. "Who wouldn't jump at the chance to time travel?"

-2-

When the new stars appeared, Shulgi was in the arms of his new wife, a soft, fragrant widow who spoke with an endearing lisp. Still young, she'd already brought two healthy children into the world with ease. She was a proud and capable mother, and when she'd promised him more children than any of his other wives, Shulgi laughed.

It was his last moment of joy.

. . .

The next day, Kiki showed up at Minh's door.

She was huge. More than half a meter taller than Minh, Kiki outweighed her by at least sixty kilos. Like all fat babies, she was flawless. Perfectly proportioned and so healthy, her flesh seemed to burst with the pent-up energy of youth.

She wore an all-weather coverall and lugged a backpack. Her brown face was pearled with sweat, and her pedal clips scraped over the catwalk grid as she shifted the heavy pack from one shoulder to the other.

"Hi," Kiki said. "Sorry to surprise you. I told your fake I was coming, but I guess you haven't checked your queue yet."

Kiki belonged to one of the half-assed hybrid habs the fat babies were building up north. Minh couldn't remember which one. She pinged Kiki's ID. Jasper, right.

Minh blinked up at her. "Did you bike all the way here in one day?"

She'd never given Kiki much thought, aside from the occasional administrative tangle. But here she was, large as life. One of Minh's neighbors, a sanitation engineer with cat's-paw prostheses, tried to edge by on the atrium catwalk. Kiki's backpack was in the way. She shrugged it off and hugged the wall to let them pass.

"I left at dawn," said Kiki. "I wanted to take the scenic route, but Jasper doesn't have rights to use the Icefields Guideway. I had to go through Edmonton. Haven't been back there in five years—not since I got out of the crèche. It's falling to pieces. A ghost town."

It was rude to keep Kiki standing outside, but showing up

at her studio uninvited was rude too. Minh crossed her arms and leaned against the doorjamb.

"What are you doing in Calgary?" she asked.

Kiki grinned. Even her teeth were big.

"David's giving me full-time hours to help you with the time travel proposal. If we're going to work together on a big job, I need to able to talk to you. Your fake hates me."

Minh drew herself up a bit taller. No use. If she wanted to talk to Kiki eye-to-eye instead of staring at her sternum, she'd have to climb the doorframe.

"I don't need help. You shouldn't have come all this way."

"Your fake said the same thing. You haven't changed your mind, have you? You seemed excited in the meeting. Excited for you, I mean. You don't exactly emote."

Minh had been ignoring her project deadlines to do preliminary research on West Asia. A literature search on the Tigris and Euphrates left her with a shortlist of several thousand papers, all three hundred years old, but no problem. She knew how to decipher old academic English. The time travel aspect was another matter entirely. No information available at all. If anyone had ever done an ecological assessment using time travel, they weren't talking about it. TERN's nondisclosure agreement had fangs. Big ones.

Minh tried to keep her expression as bland as a fake.

"No, I haven't changed my mind. I'm working on the proposal."

"Then you need help. I checked your utilization projections. You have three report deadlines over the next two weeks. You're in the middle of pruning the orchard on Crowchild Terrace. Plus, you must get pulled into lots of maintenance work. Calgary is an old hab. Falling apart."

"You don't know what you're talking about." Minh hooked a leg on the wall and drew herself taller. "Calgary is doing just fine."

Kiki's face fell. "Sorry."

"I don't have to work in the peach orchard. I do it because I like it. I planted the first trees myself."

Kiki winced. "Come on, Minh. I dropped all my other jobs to work on this. If David throws me back to quarter time, Jasper will be in deep trouble. We traded my extra hours for an advanced civil engineering seminar from U-Bang. Half the hab has already started the course. Maybe you don't need me, but it can't hurt. Give me a chance."

Minh bit back a retort. If the fat babies had stayed in Calgary instead of running off to start their own habs, they'd be fine. Or if they had to leave, at the very least, they could build aboveground using Calgary's hab tech, which was time-tested and proven. Racking up a trade deficit with the Bank of Calgary was better than taking handouts from Bangladesh Hell.

But the young had to go their own way. Minh had to admit she'd been the same, back in the dim and distant past.

Remembering her youth didn't make dealing with fat babies any easier. Minh found young people exhausting. Five years' teaching at the University of Tuktoyaktuk hadn't helped. When Tuk-U shut down, giving up face-to-face teaching was almost a relief.

Minh had been heartbroken, though. Tuktoyaktuk was a jewel box of a hab. The crowning glory of the Arctic, on the wide, fertile Mackenzie River delta, the hab represented the dreams she'd worked toward all her life. But Tuktoyaktuk had failed. Calgary couldn't support it. The bankers hadn't been clever enough. After the university shut down, Minh had tried to block the Bank of Calgary from leasing the hab to CEERD, but she'd lost that fight too.

Losing Tuktoyaktuk still hurt. For Minh, the time travel project was an opportunity to poke CEERD in the eye—not only for Tuktoyaktuk but also for creating TERN and inventing time travel in the first place. If they hadn't, life on the surface of the planet would be different. The banks would still be interested in the investment opportunities the habs offered, and the populations of the hells would be looking to the future instead of the past.

If only she could figure out a way to win the project. Minh couldn't deny her proposal would have to be unusually clever. Winning depended on finding the right strategy, which would take a lot of research. Minh couldn't work twenty-hour days, not anymore. A lifetime of abuse had nearly ruined her health. She needed to find a thin edge and wedge it hard. Kiki might be that edge.

"Fine. You can help. But you can't stay here. I don't have room."

Kiki peered over Minh's head into the studio. Her eyes went wide.

"Wow. Your space is tiny. I bet you can sit on your sofa and reach everything with your tentacles."

"They're called legs."

"Sorry. Legs. You're a firm partner, a senior consultant. You helped build Calgary. But your home is barely bigger than a sleep stack." Kiki's voice rose, incredulous.

"Ecologists don't impress the bankers. You should know that by now."

"So, are we working, or what?"

Minh stood aside and let Kiki into the studio. She loved her home, especially the ten square meters of window looking west at the front ranges of the Rockies, but with Kiki inside, it suddenly felt small.

I'm getting old, Minh thought. *Set in my ways*. Kiki was just an average young human, energetic and disgustingly healthy. A few weeks working together wouldn't do Minh any harm. And a little youthful enthusiasm wouldn't hurt the proposal at all.

-3-

Lounging in the comfort and luxury of the palace's inner courtyards, enjoying the company of his wives and children, Shulgi might have been the last to notice the new stars if one of his falconers hadn't sent word.

New stars were powerful portents, but their interpretation depended on the skill of the seer and the clarity of their conversations with the gods. Anyone could pretend to read an augury; anyone could say the gods talked to them. But gods rarely spoke plainly. For Shulgi, the gods' voices were usually only echoes of his own desires.

Shulgi only truly trusted one priest: Susa, who spoke for the moon.

.   .   .

Minh put Kiki to work researching time travel, tasking her with prying up details about TERN and their technology. It wouldn't be easy. CEERD moved mountains to keep their think tanks' intellectual property classified as trade secrets. Even when the World Economic Commission ruled entire sectors of their work public domain, they shared as little as possible. Those lawsuits ate millions of billable hours.

Minh thought Kiki wouldn't last long working out of her little studio, but it was fine. Kiki left whenever she got restless, and Minh was in and out too. But on the second evening, Minh came home late from a friend's centenary to find Kiki on her sofa. She hadn't bothered to slide it into sleep config. When Minh nudged her elbow with a toe, Kiki didn't even move.

Minh borrowed a hammock from her neighbor and slung it in front of her window. Kiki slept through the whole noisy operation.

The next morning, Minh woke with her nose grazing the glass, drinking in a two-hundred-degree panorama of bright late-winter morning, brown hills in the distance and blue sky above framing the high front ranges of the Rockies, the half-frozen Bow River snaking toward Calgary. A familiar view, but its beauty could still put a crack in her heart.

Minh stayed in the hammock all morning, throwing the West Asian climate data into a key-value database, then painting the mountains with data, using the view for a playground as she ingested enough data to fake an expertise in the ecology and geology of West Asia.

Kiki's feet bumped the wall as she stretched out on the sofa.

"Sorry." Kiki gathered up her clothes and began stuffing them into her backpack. "I couldn't get a sleep stack. Tonight, I'll find a lolly and double up."

Kiki kept her head down, braids veiling her expression.

Why would Kiki insist on staying in Calgary? Jasper must be full of friends, lovers, crèche-mates. Once the proposal was submitted, Kiki would drop back to quarter time. It could take months to replace the billable hours she'd dropped to work with Minh.

But if she wanted to be in Calgary, it must be important. The reasons were none of Minh's business.

"It's okay," Minh said. "You can have the sofa."

"Really?" Kiki's grin shone brighter than the sun coming through the windows. She trotted into the bathroom. Her voice echoed off the tiles. "Thanks, Minh. I don't like to fuck strangers, actually. Or anyone, really. I don't get much out of it."

Minh's eyebrows rose. Maybe that was why Kiki was in Calgary. Taking a break from the hormonal atmosphere at home.

"That must be hard in Jasper. You'd be odd person out."

"Yeah, Jasper's pretty sticky."

"So, what do you do? Dial up the oxytocin and join the crowd, or hibernate and avoid it?"

Kiki stuck her head out of the bathroom. The beads on her braids clicked against the doorjamb.

"Don't you know? Jasper doesn't offer full biom control. We can't float the license fees."

Minh gritted her teeth. "Oh, right. I forgot."

Personal autonomy was a central tenet of the above-ground movement. When the plague babies ascended from the hells, they'd spent years in clinics and hospitals, poked and prodded by surgeons and physical therapists. Escaping that life was one of the reasons they'd moved to the surface in the first place. The habs offered their people complete power over their own bodies. Minh had managed her own health since she was twenty.

Trust the fat babies to throw that freedom away.

"I tried joining in the sex games a couple of times, but I don't see the point. I'd rather spend my time doing useful work, you know?"

Minh nodded. "Doing important work is all that matters."

Kiki grinned. "No wonder you and I get along so well." She disappeared into the bathroom again.

"Do we?" Minh muttered, scowling.

Maybe they did. Kiki approached time travel research with energy and determination, quickly accumulating a pile of annotated bookmarks for a solid and substantial literature search report. Minh was making progress too, soaking up old West Asian ecological research papers.

She was itching to dive into a work plan draft, but her project deadlines loomed. Mesopotamia would have to wait. Minh put the research aside and tried to drum up enthusiasm for yet another Icelandic adaptive management review. But that evening, Calgary's water recirculation system blew. All available residents were pulled into the refit. Minh spent an eighteen-hour shift crawling up and down pipe shafts, troubleshooting the repair bots.

When Minh dragged herself home from her first shift, Kiki was waiting.

"I'm still researching time travel," Kiki said. "If you want, I can pull work plans from old proposals so you don't have to face a blank page when the refit is done. Just point me in the right direction."

Minh peeled off her wet coverall. "Dig out the proposal for the Colorado River current-state assessment. The target area is about the same size."

"Which bank is remediating the Colorado River?"

Minh shut herself in the bathroom and threw her clothes in the sink.

None of them, she whispered. They yanked the funding ten years ago. Make a list of all the data-gathering tech we used in Colorado. Satellites, cameras, sampling, and so on. We'll have to take all the infrastructure back in time with us.

You'll be launching satellites?

Of course. I'm not going to measure river flow with a handheld doppler.

No water in the shower, not until the refit was done. Minh slathered herself with cleanser and toweled herself dry. Then she gripped the shower walls with her three right legs and hung upside down. She loosened her left legs and slid open the shield protecting the teratoma on her lower hip. After cleaning it thoroughly, she slathered the prosthesis socket with lubricant gel. Then she repeated the process on her right side. When she was done, she hung from the wall and let her arms hang, stretching the kinks out of her back and shoulders.

Careful curation of her glucose and blood oxygen levels had kept her alert through the whole long shift, but now she needed rest. Her body thrummed with exhaustion.

If she couldn't fall asleep naturally, she'd ping her medtech. In the past, she would have tweaked herself asleep. No more, though. She'd done enough damage. Standard hormonal protocols only from now on.

Which gave Minh the glimmer of an idea.

She wrapped herself in a soft jumper and opened the bathroom door.

"TERN must have a standard project protocol. They take tourists to the past. No way they do it without power and tech."

Kiki nodded. "The only official information is from the marketing for TERN's package tours. They claim ambient power is fully available in the past. I've tried to get more specifics, but I get canned replies saying TERN's intellectual property rights are ratified by the World Economic Commission."

Minh snorted. "CEERD and all its rotten think tanks believe if they game the system enough, the World Economic Commission will turn them all into private banks and then they can roll around in their credit."

Kiki laughed. "You really hate them."

"They're greedy. But maybe we can make it work for us." Minh hooked a leg on the hammock and hauled herself up. "What have you found out about the client?"

Kiki sat cross-legged on the sofa, in a nest of quilts.

"The Mesopotamian Development Bank was created last year. Their identity isn't public yet, so all I have are rumors. They might be a mechanical engineer from one of the Siberian hives who developed a way to tunnel through burning peat, or a neurosurgical engineer from Bangladesh who found a new way to splice neurons."

"The World Economic Commission loves engineers."

Minh dimmed the lights and closed her eyes. Maintenance bots danced in patterns behind her eyelids. She'd never get to sleep.

"The client only just became a private bank, but they're already investigating a massive project. That's quick," Minh said.

"I guess they like Mesopotamia a lot."

"So it's a passion project."

Minh squirmed, trying to get comfortable. She slipped one leg out of the hammock and pushed against the window, rocking herself back and forth. Maybe it would help her get to sleep. She hated bothering her tech.

"A passion project," Minh repeated. "Which means . . ." Her biom nagged her, flashing unusually strident cortisol alerts and demanding rest. "I'm too tired to figure it out. Remind me about it tomorrow."

"Okay. And what about the project team?"

Minh hadn't even thought about team members yet.

"I'm working on it," she said.

–4–

Shulgi trusted Susa because she never told him what he wanted to hear. She didn't care for his good opinion and never made any effort to gain his favor. In fact, she hated him. The moment she got within ten steps of him, her nose would wrinkle up as though he smelled foul. It made no difference whether he were stewing in training-pit sweat or fresh and oiled from a bath. Shulgi never smelled sweet to her.

When Shulgi had become king, Susa ascended the dais of the moon. Her duty was to oppose him. As woman opposes man, as humans strain against the gods, as children defy their parents, Susa's right and duty was to say yes when he said no and argue against his every decision.

But she didn't have to take such pleasure in it.

* * *

By the time Calgary's refit was done, the Bank of Calgary was nagging Minh for a draft budget. The submission deadline was only a few days away, and Minh still hadn't done anything about her project team.

Ten years back, when news of the first time travel project hit, she'd been wrapping up the Colorado River current-state assessment. Her entire thirty-person multidisciplinary team camped on the edge of the Grand Canyon, accompanied by a professional media crew and a dozen cameras, exploiting the canyon's spectacular visuals as they trapped the documentary data for the final report. It was a waste of billable hours, but banks liked grand gestures and mediagenic visuals. The funding had been available back then.

The Colorado River was envisioned as the largest riverine restoration project ever undertaken, extending from La Poudre Pass to the gulf, supporting a string of habs—eight glistening green pearls along the great river from mountains to sea, providing habitat for a hundred million people within four centuries.

Minh had been skeptical. But there was no reason they couldn't remediate the first few reaches, support a few new habs. Even one would benefit the funding consortium eventually. She had planned to plant the first glacier seed herself. Maybe she would have even seen a little streamflow before she died.

Then the time travel news hit and all work stopped.

At first, the whole Colorado team was transfixed by the news docs. When they began arguing over the implications of time travel, some predicted disaster—temporal disturbances and out-of-control paradoxes. Most were enchanted by the possibility of restoring extinct species—rewilding on a scale they'd never dreamed of. Personally, Minh was excited by the idea of time-traveling adaptive management projects. She could initiate a restoration initiative, visit the future to see the results, then come back to the present day and fine-tune the approach. But her excitement was short-lived; time travel could only be used to visit the past.

Not even Minh foresaw what actually happened: the banks lost interest in everything aboveground, and especially in long-term ecological restoration projects.

People—especially bankers—had trouble thinking long-term, and nothing was more long-term than ecological restoration. Results took decades, even with soil printers, glacier seeds, climatic baffles, wind chutes—all the tech they'd developed. Even when harnessing the wind-sculpting and rain-generating power of the great mountain ranges of the globe, restoring natural habitats took vision, determination, and, most importantly, glacial patience.

Banks were not patient. When they saw a shortcut, they lunged for it. No matter if the shortcut was an illusion. No matter that time travel couldn't be used to change anything.

The funding pool dried up. Ambitious new restoration projects died in the planning phase, never to be resurrected. The habs formed desperate consortiums to keep their projects afloat, fees plunged in all related disciplines, and the few surviving projects operated on shallow budgets with skeleton teams.

After a long, dry decade, interest in ecological restoration was starting to trickle back, but the damage was done. The Colorado River would stay dry. Probably forever.

Kiki passed a mug of tea up to Minh as she lay in her hammock. She'd slept ten hours straight. Probably snoring openmouthed the whole time, judging by her throbbing headache.

"I'm looking through TERN's earliest docs," said Kiki. "Why were they so concerned with proving time travel can't affect anything? Wasn't it obvious? Time travel happened. Nothing changed."

Minh swished the tea around her parched mouth and swallowed.

"No, it wasn't obvious at all. You were still in the crèche, right? How old?"

"Thirteen."

"Easy to take things on faith at that age. I was seventy-three. TERN wouldn't share their research. No open peer review process, no repeatable results. Plus, their public relations department was releasing disinformation to keep critics confused. Everyone I knew was suspicious. How could we trust them not to mess with history?"

"TERN says that when they time travel, a separate timeline is spun off from ours, and when the time travelers leave, the timeline collapses."

Minh shrugged. "TERN can say anything they want. They have a monopoly. Nobody can prove them wrong, because nobody outside TERN knows how it works."

"Have you seen this?"

Kiki shot a doc into the middle of the room. The Pyramid of the Sun at Teotihuacan bloomed across the floor and stretched up to the ceiling.

Minh winced. Her headache pounded. She shot the doc out the window. The pyramid grew to full size over the river valley.

Sunlight bounced off the back of Minh's skull. She lifted a leg to her forehead and squeezed her temples. Her biom blinked a low-priority dehydration alert.

A hundred puffs of dust pocked the surface of the pyramid. The stones shuddered and slipped, then the whole huge structure disappeared behind a cloud of dust. When it cleared, the pyramid lay like a corpse, a pile of cold rubble across the Avenue of the Dead.

The doc overlaid the rubble with a dozen time-stamped satellite images of the pyramid in real time, here and now, whole and undamaged. Kiki killed the doc.

"Yeah, I've seen it." Minh clambered out of the hammock and grabbed a bottle of water. "When TERN finally proved time travel was effectively useless, I figured everything would go back to normal and the banks would get interested in us again. I was wrong."

"That's why you hate CEERD and TERN."

"One of the reasons." Minh drained the water bottle and wiped her lips with the back of her hand. "What have you found out about the project's restrictive parameters?"

"Payload," Kiki said. "That's the big one."

Kiki took her through a stack of bookmarks. She'd analyzed hundreds of time travel docs, estimating the mass and volume of the cast, crew, and equipment. Her analysis was confirmed by a stack of other calculations, including the capacity of time travel tourist groups, and details of all known artifacts retrieved from the past.

Kiki sat cross-legged on the sofa, pulled her braids back, and knotted them at the nape of her neck.

"TERN's maximum payload seems to be restricted by volume, not mass. The single heaviest item brought from the past is the Golden Buddha from ancient Thailand. It weighs over five thousand kilograms."

Minh flipped through the bookmarks and scanned the attached notes. Kiki's analysis was solid, her conclusions well supported. Impressive.

"You should publish these results," she said.

Kiki grinned. "I can't. It's TERN's intellectual property."

Then she whispered, I bet I'm not the first person to figure this out. Every time someone tries to publish results like this, using open and available information, TERN shuts them down. I've been whispering with a plague baby in Sudbury Hell who hates TERN even more than you do.

Okay, I get it. No more bad-mouthing TERN if we want to win this work.

Minh plucked at her temples with her suckers. The headache was easing off. Time to get to work.

Minh used Kiki's numbers to mock up the payload dimensions. The volume amounted to a little more than half her studio.

"This can't be right. There's no room for equipment."

"There is, actually. Almost everything can be fabbed." Kiki shot an array of color-coded rectangles into the mock-up, stacking them like crèche blocks. A large yellow cube flashed. "That's the fab, and the layer on the bottom is superdense feedstock. You can even bring a skip along for transportation. All you need are the skip drives, sensory array, and safety-foam canisters." A dozen shoe-sized pink boxes stacked on top of the yellow cube. "If you want to bring lots of satellites, it's easy. They're small. You can take plenty."

Minh paced the edges of the mock-up, thinking.

"People take up a lot of space. They can't be compressed."

Minh added blocks to represent monitoring and sampling equipment. She threw in a few placeholders for the team's personal effects, water treatment system, and a nutritional extruder. A third of the payload was still empty.

Minh's aches and pains faded into the background, overwhelmed by the electric thrill jolting from fingers to the tips of her legs.

"I got it," Minh shouted. Kiki jumped, startled.

Minh lowered her voice to a reasonable level. "This is how I'll win the project."

"You're sure?" Kiki asked. "You sound pretty sure."

Minh laughed. "No, but it's not impossible."

Kiki beamed. "How?"

"The client is asking for a multidisciplinary team. That's old lingo, from the big-budget days. Our competitors will stack their proposals with consultants—everything from fisheries biologists to fluvial engineers to statisticians. Big teams, lots of billable hours, like the old days."

"And our team—your team, I mean?"

"My team will be small." Minh grinned. "The smallest."

–5–

When Susa sent for Shulgi, he gathered his household and processed through the streets, accompanied by everyone who belonged to him, from his eldest wife to the child who swept the stairs. Susa and her people met them at the apex of the ziggurat. She looked agitated, tired, unwell, her skin sallow under the layer of cosmetic.

She tried to rush through their greeting ritual, as if she didn't have time to honor the gods, but Shulgi wouldn't allow himself to be hurried. With new stars watching, he told her, they mustn't scatter the grain of duty for others to glean.

The delay made Susa furious. When the ritual was complete, she spoke plainly.

The stars were the clearest augury she'd ever seen and could only be interpreted one way. The stars called for Shulgi's death.

• • •

Hamid's fake was dressed in cowboy gear. It looked like a refugee from a crèche costume party.

"I'm busy, Minh," it said. "Tell me what you want."

Minh ground her teeth in frustration. "I need to talk to Hamid."

Thousands of billable hours, Kiki whispered. Those are the magic words.

Hamid doesn't care. His lover is a private bank.

"What's it about? I'll pass the message on," the fake drawled.

"It's a new project. A unique opportunity. Can you boost me up his queue? Top priority."

The fake nodded and faded out.

"Wait," Minh said. The fake faded back in. She shot it the RFP package. "Tell him to look at this and think about the horses."

"The budget is due in ten minutes," Kiki said. "We need to submit now. No room to wiggle."

Their draft budget had two big blanks. Minh was still the only team member.

"Put Hamid in."

"Without his permission?"

"He's an old friend. And this is a just a draft."

"Okay. I'm putting myself in the other blank."

"Kiki—"

"Do you have a better idea? The bank will like it. Call me a placeholder. You can kick me off the team anytime you like."

"Okay, it's better than a blank."

"*Better than a blank*. That's my new motto."

Kiki sealed the budget and shot it upstairs.

When the Bank of Calgary called two hours later, they were both deep into editing—Kiki finessing a custom version of ESSA's history and past projects into an inspiring three minutes, Minh pulling the guts out of the old Colorado work plan and trying to reshape it into a credible approach to a past-state assessment.

Minh should have known the bank would jump fast. Calgary was deep into trade deficit. This RFP was a big ripe peach hanging on the branch. Of course the bank was itching to grab it.

Even so, Minh knew exactly what the bankers would say. It was what they always said.

The banker intercepted Minh and Kiki the moment they walked out of the elevator onto Calgary's bustling apex floor.

"These rates are too low," he said, ushering them into a glass-walled conference room.

He was young—a tall fat baby with bony wrists protruding from the sleeves of his banker suit. She'd seen him before, in the entourage of Calgary's senior account manager. Now he had his own entourage—three more fat babies, big-eyed and downy-faced. Looked like they were right out of the crèche.

"Where's Rosa?" Minh looked around for the banker she usually dealt with, an elegant white-haired plague baby who wheeled around in an antique chair.

"Palliative care. But she still has team oversight."

Minh winced. Rosa was only a few years older than her.

"About these rates—"

Minh cut the banker off. "I don't want to lose this job on price."

"There's no point in proposing a tiny team with cut rates. Your fees will be a minor line item compared to what TERN will be charging the Mesopotamian Development Bank."

"You think the client won't care what we cost? In my experience, private banks are cheap. They only value their own expertise. Everyone else is just a warm body."

"Not this private bank. Their pockets are deep."

"Oh, good." Minh plastered on a phony smile. "You've got intel. Tell me everything."

His eyes glazed over, descending into the data stream.

Minh exchanged a glance with Kiki. He's whispering with

Rosa, I bet. He's not as good as you are at running multiple streams.

Why are you poking him?

I want him scared of me. He needs to learn I can't be pushed around.

The banker looked up from his stream. "The Mesopotamian Development Bank is private."

"Obviously," said Minh. "Tell me who they are. What do they want?"

"Unknown."

Minh grimaced. All this would be so much easier with Rosa.

"You don't know anything about the client. You have no intel or insight, but you want to tell me how to budget this project."

The banker spread his hands in an awkward version of the conciliatory gesture bankers always made when they were out of their depth. He was trying to seem friendly and understanding, but his expression was wary.

"Our models show ESSA should be contributing more to Calgary's economy. Your firm has been treading water for years. You're a top consultant in two fields, fluvial geomorphology and restoration ecology. Clients should expect to pay well for your time."

Minh gave the banker an icy smile.

Watch this, Kiki. This is how I handle a bully banker.

Minh drew several of her legs up onto the table, held tight, and leaned in. "Let me tell you something." She smacked the glass with her toe and dropped her voice into its lowest register. "I've been running projects for forty years. Out there." She pointed out the window at the mountains. "In the real world, not hiding up here in the top levels of a hab someone else built, juggling numbers and pretending to be important."

He sat back in his chair. A shade of alarm contorted his young face, but then he relaxed.

Rosa's telling him how to handle me.

Minh lifted another leg and pointed at the underside of the glass spire overhead. "When I was your age, I helped build this hab. My team put the capstone into place. I know how to win a job and deliver results."

She gripped the edges of the table with two legs and thrust herself forward, right in the banker's face. "All you do is push deficits around and procrastinate until the hab collapses."

The banker looked ruffled, but Rosa was keeping him under control. "We'll take your budget recommendations into consideration. But one more thing—"

Here it comes. He's going to try to hobble me.

"Calgary doesn't want you to put yourself at risk on a dangerous project. Your maintenance contributions are valuable, especially snowpack management. Certainly, you should be on the team as project advisor, working from Calgary, but not project lead."

Minh pretended to consider it for a moment.

"There's a studio available," the banker continued. "High level, over a hundred square meters."

I bet that's Rosa's space, Minh whispered. Banker level.

"Which way does it face?" Minh asked.

"I don't—" The banker glazed over for a half-second. "East. It faces the old city."

Minh tapped a leg against the underside of the glass table, still pretending to consider the offer.

I've never seen you in diva mode before, Minh. You're pretty good at it.

This is nothing. Wait until you meet Hamid.

After letting the banker fidget for a minute, she said, "No, thanks. If you don't want us to bid on this project, we can flush our proposal, right, Kiki?"

"Sure. Iceland wants another adaptive management review. They requested a quote this morning."

The banker huffed and puffed for another ten minutes before winding up the meeting. As they walked to the elevator, he fell into step beside Kiki.

"Glad to see ESSA's finally doing succession planning," he said.

Kiki grinned at Minh, triumphant. See? I told you the bank would like having me on the team.

Excerpt from Artificial Condition:
The Murderbot Diaries

by Martha Wells

Chapter One

SecUnits don't care about the news. Even after I hacked my governor module and got access to the feeds, I never paid much attention to it. Partly because downloading the entertainment media was less likely to trigger any alarms that might be set up on satellite and station networks; political and economic news was carried on different levels, closer to the protected data exchanges. But mostly because the news was boring and I didn't care what humans were doing to each other as long as I didn't have to a) stop it or b) clean up after it.

But as I crossed the transit ring's mall, a recent newsburst from Station was in the air, bouncing from one public feed to another. I skimmed it but most of my attention was on getting through the crowd while pretending to be an ordinary augmented human, and not a terrifying murderbot. This involved not panicking when anybody accidentally made eye contact with me.

Fortunately, the humans and augmented humans were too busy trying to get wherever they were going or searching the feed for directions and transport schedules. Three passenger transports had come through wormholes along with the bot-driven cargo transport I had hitched a ride on, and the big mall between the different embarkation zones was crowded. Besides the humans, there were bots of all different shapes and sizes, drones buzzing along above the crowd, and cargo moving on the overhead walkways. The security drones wouldn't be scanning for SecUnits unless they were specifically instructed, and nothing had tried to ping me so far, which was a relief.

I was of the company's inventory, but this was still the Corporation Rim, and I was still property.

Though I was feeling pretty great about how well I was doing so far, considering this was only the second transit ring I had been through. SecUnits were shipped to our contracts as cargo, and we never went through the parts of stations or transit rings that were meant for people. I'd had to leave my armor behind in the deployment center on Station, but in the crowd I was almost as anonymous as if I was still wearing it. (Yes, that is something I had to keep repeating to myself.) I was wearing gray and black work clothes, the long sleeves of the T-shirt and jacket, the pants and boots covering all my inorganic parts, and I was carrying a knapsack. Among the varied and colorful clothes, hair, skin, and interfaces of the crowd, I didn't stand out. The dataport in the back of my neck was visible but the design was too close to the interfaces augmented humans often had implanted to draw any suspicion. Also, nobody thinks a murderbot is going to be walking along the transit mall like a person.

Then in my skim of the news broadcast I hit an image. It was me.

I didn't stop in my tracks because I have a lot of practice in not physically reacting to things no matter how much they shock or horrify me. I may have lost control of my expression for a second; I was used to always wearing a helmet and keeping it opaqued whenever possible.

I passed a big archway that led to several different food service counters and stopped near the opening to a small business district. Anyone who saw me would assume I was scanning their sites in the feed, looking for information.

The image in the newsburst was of me standing in the lobby of the station hotel with Pin-Lee and Ratthi. The focus was on Pin-Lee, on her determined expression, the annoyed tilt of her eyebrows, and her sharp business clothes. Ratthi and I, in gray PreservationAux survey uniforms, were faded into the background. I was listed as "and bodyguard" in the image tags, which was a relief, but I was braced for the worst as I replayed the story.

Huh, the station I had thought of as The Station, the location of the company offices and the deployment center where I was usually stored, was actually called Port FreeCommerce. I didn't know that. (When I was there, I was mostly in a repair cubicle, a transport box, or in standby waiting for a contract.) The news narrator mentioned in passing how Dr. Mensah had bought the SecUnit who saved her. (That was clearly the heartwarming note to relieve the otherwise grim story with the high body count.) But the journalists weren't used to seeing SecUnits except in armor, or in a bloody pile of leftover pieces when things went wrong. They hadn't connected the idea of a purchased SecUnit with what they assumed was the generic augmented human person going into the hotel with Pin-Lee and Ratthi. That was good.

The weird part was that some of our security recordings had been released. My vantage point, as I searched the DeltFall habitat and found the bodies. Views from Gurathin's and Pin-Lee's helmet cameras, when they found Mensah and what was left of me after the explosion. I scanned through it quickly, making sure there weren't any good views of my human face.

The rest of the story was about how the company and DeltFall, plus Preservation and three other non-corporate political entities who had had citizens in DeltFall's habitat, were ganging up on GrayCris. There was also a multicornered solicitor-fight going on in which some of the entities who were allies in the investigation were fighting each other over financial responsibility, jurisdiction, and bond guarantees. I didn't know how humans could keep it all straight. There weren't many details about what had actually happened after PreservationAux had managed to signal the company rescue transport, but it was enough to hope that anybody looking for the SecUnit in question would assume I was with Mensah and the others. Mensah and the others, of course, knew different.

Then I checked the timestamp and saw the newsburst was old, published the cycle after I had left the station. It must have come through a wormhole with one of the faster passenger transports. That meant the official news channels might have more recent info by now.

Right. I told myself there was no way anybody on this transit ring would be looking for a rogue SecUnit. From the info available in the public feed, there were no deployment centers here for any bond or security companies. My contracts had always been on isolated installations or uninhabited survey planets, and I thought that was pretty much the norm. Even the shows and serials on the entertainment feeds never showed SecUnits contracted to guard offices or cargo warehouses or shipwrights, or any of the other businesses common to transit rings. And all the SecUnits in the media were always in armor, faceless and terrifying to humans.

I merged with the crowd and started down the mall again. I had to be careful going anywhere I might be scanned for weapons, which was all the facilities for purchasing transport, including the little trams that circled the ring. I can hack a weapons scanner, but security protocols suggested that at the passenger facilities there would be a lot of them to deal with the crowds and I could only do so many at once. Plus, I would have to hack the payment system, and that sounded like way more trouble than it was worth at the moment. It was a long walk to the part of the ring for the outgoing bot-driven transports, but it gave me time to tap the entertainment feed and download new media.

On the way to this transit ring, alone on my empty cargo transport, I had had a chance to do a lot of thinking about why I had left Mensah, and what I wanted. I know, it was a surprise to me, too. But even I knew I couldn't spend the rest of my lifespan alone riding cargo transports and consuming media, as attractive as it sounded.

I had a plan now. Or I would have a plan, once I got the answer to an important question.

To get that answer I needed to go somewhere, and there were two bot-driven transports leaving here in the next cycle that would take me there. The first was a cargo transport not unlike the one I had used to get here. It was leaving later, and was a better option, as I would have more time to get to it and talk it into letting me board. I could hack a transport if I tried, but I really preferred not to. Spending that much time with something that didn't want you there, or that you had hacked to make it think it wanted you there, just seemed creepy.

Maps and schedules were available in the feed, tied to all the main navigation points along the ring, so I was able to find my way down to the cargo loading area, wait for the shift change, and cut through to the embarkation zone. I had to hack an ID-screening system and some weapon-scanning drones on the level above the zone, and then got pinged by a bot guarding the entrance to the commercial area. I didn't hurt it, just broke through its wall in the feed and deleted out of its memory any record of the encounter with me.

(I was designed to interface with company SecSystems, to be basically an interactive component of one. The safeguards on this station weren't the company's proprietary tech, but it was close enough. Also, nobody is as paranoid as the company about protecting the data it collects and/or steals, so I was used to security systems that were a lot more robust than this.)

Once down on the access floor, I had to be extremely careful, as there was no reason for someone not working to be here, and while most of the work was being done by hauler bots, there were uniformed humans and augmented humans here, too. More than I had counted on.

A lot of humans congregated near the lock for my prospective transport. I checked the feed for alerts and found there had been an accident involving a hauler. Various parties were sorting out the damage and who was to blame. I could have waited until they cleared out, but I wanted to get of this ring and get moving. And honestly, my image in the newsburst had rattled me and I wanted to just sink into my media downloads for a while and pretend I didn't exist. To do that I had to be secure on a locked automated transport ready to leave the ring.

I checked the maps again for my second possibility. It was attached to a different dock, one marked for private, non-commercial traffic. If I moved fast, I could get there before it left.

The schedule had it designated as a long-range research vessel. That sounded like something that would have a crew and probably passengers, but the attached info said it was bot-driven and currently tasked with a cargo run that would stop at the destination I wanted. I had done a historical search in the feed for its movements and found it was owned by a university based on a planet in this system, which rented it out for cargo trips in between assignments to help pay for its upkeep. The trip to my destination would take twenty-one cycles, and I was really looking forward to the isolation.

Getting into the private docks from the commercial docks was easy. I got control of the security system long enough to tell it not to notice that I didn't have authorization, and walked through behind a group of passengers and crew members.

I found the research transport's dock, and pinged it through the comm port. It pinged back almost immediately. All the info I had managed to pull of the feed said it was prepared for an automated run, but just to be sure I sent a hail for attention from human crew. The answer came back a null, no one home.

I pinged the transport again and gave it the same ofer I had given the first transport: hundreds of hours of media, serials, books, music, including some new shows I had just picked up on the way through the transit mall, in exchange for a ride. I told it I was a free bot, trying to get back to its human guardian. (The "free bot" thing is deceptive. Bots are considered citizens in some noncorporate political entities like Preservation, but they still have appointed human guardians. Constructs sometimes fall under the same category as bots, sometimes under the same category as deadly weapons. (FYI, that is not a good category to be in.)) This is why I had been a free agent among humans for less than seven cycles, including time spent alone on a cargo transport, and I already needed a vacation.

There was a pause, then the research transport sent an acceptance and opened the lock for me.

Chapter Two

I waited to make sure the lock cycled closed, and that there were no alarms from the ringside, then went down the access corridor. From the schematic available in the shipboard feed, the compartments the transport was using for cargo were normally modular lab space. With the labs sealed and removed to the university's dock storage, there was plenty of room for cargo. I pushed my condensed packet of media into the transport's feed for it to take whenever it wanted.

The rest of the space was the usual engineering, supply storage, cabins, medical, mess hall, with the addition of a larger recreation area and some teaching suites. There was blue and white padding on the furniture and it had all been cleaned recently, though it still had a trace of that dirty sock smell that seems to hang around all human habitations. It was quiet, except for the faint noise of the air system, and my boots weren't making any sound on the deck covering.

I didn't need supplies. My system is self-regulating; I don't need food, water, or to eliminate fluids or solids, and I don't need much air. I could have lasted on the minimal life support that was all that was provided when no people were aboard, but the transport had upped it a little. I thought that was nice of it.

I wandered around, visually checking things out to see that it matched the schematic, and just making sure everything was okay. I did it, even knowing that patrolling was a habit I was going to have to get over. There were a lot of things I was going to have to get over.

When constructs were first developed, they were original-ly supposed to have a pre-sentient level of intelligence, like the dumber variety of bot. But you can't put something as dumb as a hauler bot in charge of security for anything without spending even more money for expensive company-employed human supervisors. So they made us smarter. The anxiety and depression were side effects.

In the deployment center, when I was standing there while Dr. Mensah explained why she didn't want to rent me as part of the bond guarantee agreement, she had called the increase in intelligence a "hellish compromise." This ship was not my responsibility and there were no human clients aboard that I had to keep anything from hurting, or keep from hurting themselves, or keep from hurting each other. But this was a nice ship with surprisingly little security, and I wondered why the owners didn't leave a few humans aboard to keep an eye on it. Like most bot-driven transports, the schematics said there were drones onboard to make repairs, but still.

I kept patrolling until I felt the rumble and clunk through the deck that meant the ship had just decoupled itself from the ring and started to move. The tension that had kept me down to 96 percent capacity eased; a murderbot's life is stressful in general, but it would be a long time before I got used to moving through human spaces with no armor, no way to hide my face.

I found a crew meeting area below the control deck and planted myself in one of the padded chairs. Repair cubicles and transport boxes don't have padding, so traveling in comfort was still a novelty. I started sorting through the new media I'd downloaded on the transit ring. It had some entertainment channels that weren't available on the company's portion of Port FreeCommerce, and they included a lot of new dramas and action series.

I'd never really had long periods of unobserved free time before. The leisure to sort through everything and get it organized, and give it my full attention, without having to monitor multiple systems and the clients' feeds, was still something I was getting used to. Before this, I'd either been on duty, on call, or stuck in a cubicle on standby waiting to be activated for a contract.

I chose a new serial that looked interesting (the tags promised extragalactic exploration, action, and mysteries) and started the first episode. I was ready to settle in until it was time to think about what I was going to do when I got to my destination, something I intended to put off until the last possible moment. Then, through my feed, something said, *You were lucky.*

I sat up. It was so unexpected, I had an adrenaline release from my organic parts.

Transports don't talk in words, even through the feed. They use images and strings of data to alert you to problems, but they're not designed for conversation. I was okay with that, because I wasn't designed for conversation, either. I had shared my stored media with the first transport, and it had given me access to its comm and feed streams so I could make sure no one knew where I was, and that had been the extent of our interaction.

I poked cautiously through the feed, wondering if I'd been fooled. I had the ability to scan, but without drones my range was limited, and with all the shielding and equipment around me I couldn't pick up anything but background readings from the ship's systems. Whoever owned the ship wanted to allow for proprietary research; the only security cameras were on the hatches, nothing in the crew areas. Or nothing I could access. But the presence in the feed was too big and diffuse for a human or augmented human, I could tell that much even through the feed walls protecting it. And it sounded like a bot. When humans speak in the feed, they have to subvocalize and their mental voice tends to sound like their physical voice. Even augmented humans with full interfaces do it.

Maybe it was trying to be friendly and was just awkward at communicating. I said aloud, "Why am I lucky?"

That no one realized what you were.

That was less than reassuring. I said, cautiously, "What do you think I am?" If it was hostile, I didn't have a lot of options. Transport bots don't have bodies, other than the ship. The equivalent of its brain would be above me, near the bridge where the human flight crew would be stationed. And it wasn't like I had anywhere to go; we were moving out from the ring and making leisurely progress toward the wormhole.

It said, *You're a rogue SecUnit, a bot/human construct, with a scrambled governor module.* It poked me through the feed and I flinched. It said, *Do not attempt to hack my systems,* and for .00001 of a second it dropped its wall.

It was enough time for me to get a vivid image of what I was dealing with. Part of its function was extragalactic astronomic analysis and now all that processing power sat idle while it hauled cargo, waiting for its next mission. It could have squashed me like a bug through the feed, pushed through my wall and other defenses and stripped my memory. Probably while also plotting its wormhole jump, estimating the nutrition needs of a full crew complement for the next 66,000 hours, performing multiple neural surgeries in the medical suite, and beating the captain at tavla. I had never directly interacted with anything this powerful before.

You made a mistake, Murderbot, a really bad mistake. How the hell was I supposed to know there were transports sentient enough to be mean? There were evil bots on the entertainment feed all the time, but that wasn't real, it was just a scary story, a fantasy.

I'd *thought* it was a fantasy.

I said, "Okay," shut down my feed, and huddled down into the chair.

I'm not normally afraid of things, the way humans are.

I've been shot hundreds of times, so many times I stopped keeping count, so many times the company stopped keeping count. I've been chewed on by hostile fauna, run over by heavy machinery, tortured by clients for amusement, memory purged, etc., etc. But the inside of my head had been my own for +33,000 hours and I was used to it now. I wanted to keep me the way I was.

The transport didn't respond. I tried to come up with countermeasures for all the different ways it could hurt me and how I could hurt it back. It was more like a SecUnit than a bot, so much so I wondered if it was a construct, if there was cloned organic brain tissue buried in its systems somewhere. I'd never tried to hack another SecUnit. It might be safest to go into standby for the duration of the trip, and trigger myself to wake when we reached my destination. Though that would leave me vulnerable to its drones.

I watched seconds click by, waiting to see if it reacted. I was glad I had noted the lack of cameras and not bothered trying to hack into the ship's security system. I understood now why the humans felt it didn't need additional protection. A bot with this complete control over its environment and the initiative and freedom to act could repel any attempt to board.

It had opened the hatch for me. It wanted me here. Uh-oh.

Then it said, *You can continue to play the media.* I just huddled there warily.

It added, *Don't sulk.*

I was afraid, but that made me irritated enough to show it that what it was doing to me was not exactly new. I sent through the feed, *SecUnits don't sulk. That would trigger punishment from the governor module,* and attached some brief recordings from my memory of what exactly that felt like.

Seconds added up to a minute, then another, then three

more. It doesn't sound like much to humans, but for a conversation between bots, or excuse me, between a bot/human construct and a bot, it was a long time.

Then it said, *I'm sorry I frightened you.*

Okay, well. If you think I trusted that apology, you don't know Murderbot. Most likely it was playing a game with me. I said, "I don't want anything from you. I just want to ride to your next destination." I'd explained that earlier, before it opened the hatch for me, but it was worth repeating.

I felt it withdraw back behind its wall. I waited, and let my circulatory system purge the fear-generated chemicals. More time crawled by, and I started to get bored. Sitting here like this was too much like waiting in a cubicle after I'd been activated, waiting for the new clients to take delivery, for the next boring contract. If it was going to destroy me, at least I could get some media in before that happened. I started the new show again, but I was still too upset to enjoy it, so I stopped it and started rewatching an old episode of *Rise and Fall of Sanctuary Moon.*

After three episodes, I was calmer and reluctantly beginning to see the transport's perspective. A SecUnit could cause it a lot of internal damage if it wasn't careful, and rogue SecUnits were not exactly known for lying low and avoiding trouble. I hadn't hurt the last transport I had taken a ride on, but it didn't know that. I didn't understand why it had let me aboard, if it really didn't want to hurt me. I wouldn't have trusted me, if I was a transport. Maybe it was like me, and it had taken an opportunity because it was there, not because it knew what it wanted.

It was still an asshole, though.

Six episodes later I felt the transport in the feed again, lurking. I ignored it, though it had to know I knew it was there. In human terms, it was like trying to ignore someone large and breathing heavily while they watched your personal display surface over your shoulder. While leaning on you.

• • •

I watched seven more episodes of *Sanctuary Moon* with it hanging around my feed. Then it pinged me, like I somehow might not know it had been in my feed all this time, and sent me a request to go back to the new adventure show I had started to watch when it had interrupted me.

(It was called *Worldhoppers*, and was about freelance explorers who extended the wormhole and ring networks into uninhabited star systems. It looked very unrealistic and inaccurate, which was exactly what I liked.)

"I gave you a copy of all my media when I came aboard," I said. I wasn't going to talk to it through the feed like it was my client. "Did you even look at it?"

I examined it for viral malware and other hazards.

And fuck you, I thought, and went back to Sanctuary Moon.

Two minutes later it repeated the ping and the request. I said, "Watch it yourself."

I tried. I can process the media more easily through your filter.

That made me stop. I didn't understand the problem. It explained, *When my crew plays media, I can't process the context. Human interactions and environments outside my hull are largely unfamiliar.*

Now I understood. It needed to read my reactions to the show to really understand what was happening. Humans used the feed in different ways than bots (and constructs) so when its crew played their media, their reactions didn't become part of the data.

I found it odd that the transport was less interested in *Sanctuary Moon*, which took place on a colony, than *World-hoppers*, which was about the crew of a large exploration ship. You'd think it would be too much like work—I avoided serials about survey teams and mining installations—but maybe familiar things were easier for it.

I was tempted to say no. But if it needed me to watch the show it wanted, then it couldn't get angry and destroy my brain. Also, I wanted to watch the show, too.

"It's not realistic," I told it. "It's not supposed to be realistic. It's a story, not a documentary. If you complain about that, I'll stop watching."

I will refrain from complaint, it said. (Imagine that in the most sarcastic tone you can, and you'll have some idea of how it sounded.)

So we watched *Worldhoppers*. It didn't complain about the lack of realism. After three episodes, it got agitated whenever a minor character was killed. When a major character died in the twentieth episode I had to pause seven minutes while it sat there in the feed doing the bot equivalent of staring at a wall, pretending that it had to run diagnostics. Then four episodes later the character came back to life and it was so relieved we had to watch that episode three times before it would go on.

At the climax of one of the main story lines, the plot suggested the ship might be catastrophically damaged and members of the crew killed or injured, and the transport was afraid to watch it. (That's obviously not how it phrased it, but yeah, it was afraid to watch it.) I was feeling a lot more charitable toward it by that point so was willing to let it ease into the episode by watching one to two minutes at a time.

After it was over, it just sat there, not even pretending to do diagnostics. It sat there for a full ten minutes, which is a lot of processing time for a bot that sophisticated. Then it said, *Again, please.*

So I started the first episode again.

•　•　•

After two more run-throughs of *Worldhoppers*, it wanted to see every other show I had about humans in ships. Though after we encountered one based on a true story, where the ship experienced a hull breach and decompression killed several members of the crew (permanently, this time), it got too upset and I had to create a content filter. To give it a break, I suggested *Sanctuary Moon*. It agreed.

After four episodes, it asked me, *There are no SecUnits in this story?*

It must have thought that *Sanctuary Moon* was my favorite for the same reason that it liked *Worldhoppers*. I said, "No. There aren't that many shows with SecUnits, and they're either villains or the villain's minions." The only SecUnits in entertainment media were rogues, out to kill all humans because they forgot who built the repair cubicles, I guess. In some of the worst shows, SecUnits would sometimes have sex with the human characters. This was weirdly inaccurate and also anatomically complicated. Constructs with intercourse-related human parts are sexbots, not SecUnits. Sexbots don't have interior weapon systems, so it isn't like it's easy to confuse them with SecUnits. (SecUnits also have less than null interest in human or any other kind of sex, trust me on that.)

Granted, it would have been hard to show realistic SecUnits in visual media, which would involve depicting hours of standing around in brain-numbing boredom, while your nervous clients tried to pretend you weren't there. But there weren't any depictions of SecUnits in books, either. I guess you can't tell a story from the point of view of something that you don't think has a point of view.

It said, *The depiction is unrealistic.*

(You know, just imagine everything it says in the most sarcastic tone possible.)

"There's unrealistic that takes you away from reality and

unrealistic that reminds you that everybody's afraid of you." In the entertainment feed, SecUnits were what the clients expected: heartless killing machines that could go rogue at any second, for no reason, despite the governor modules.

The transport thought that over for 1.6 seconds. In a less sarcastic tone, it said, *You dislike your function. I don't understand how that is possible.*

Its function was traveling through what it thought of as the endlessly fascinating sensation of space, and keeping all its human and otherwise passengers safe inside its metal body. Of course it didn't understand not wanting to perform your function. Its function was great.

"I like parts of my function." I liked protecting people and things. I liked figuring out smart ways to protect people and things. I liked being right.

Then why are you here? You are not a "free bot" looking for your guardian, who presumably cannot simply be sent a message via the public comm relay on the transit ring we recently departed.

The question caught me by surprise, because I hadn't thought it was interested in anything besides itself. I hesitated, but it already knew I was a SecUnit, and it already knew there was just no circumstance where it was legal and okay that I was here. It might as well know who I was. I sent my copy of the Port FreeCommerce newsburst into the feed. "That's me."

Dr. Mensah of PreservationAux purchased you and allowed you to leave?

"Yes. Do you want to watch *WorldHoppers* again?" I regretted the question an instant later. It knew that was an attempt at a distraction.

But it said, *I am not allowed to accept unauthorized passengers or cargo, and have had to alter my log to hide any evidence of your presence.* There was a hesitation. *So we both have a secret.*

I had no reason not to tell it, except fear of sounding stupid. "I left without permission. She offered me a home with her on Preservation, but she doesn't need me there. They don't need SecUnits there. And I . . . didn't know what I wanted, if I wanted to go to Preservation or not. If I want a human guardian, which is just a different word for owner. I knew it would be easier to escape from the station than it would from a planet. So I left. Why did you let me onboard?"

I thought maybe I could distract it by getting it to talk about itself. Wrong again. It said, *I was curious about you, and cargo runs are tedious without passengers. You left to travel to RaviHyral Mining Facility Q Station. Why?*

"I left to get of Port FreeCommerce, away from the company." It waited. "After I had a chance to think, I decided to go to RaviHyral. I need to research something, and that's the best place to do it."

I thought the mention of research might stop its questions, since it understood research. No, not so much. *There were public library feeds available on the transit ring, with information exchange to the planetary archives. Why not do the research there? My onboard archives are extensive. Why haven't you sought access to them?*

I didn't answer. It waited thirty whole seconds, then it said, *The systems of constructs are inherently inferior to advanced bots, but you aren't stupid.*

Yeah, well, fuck you, too, I thought, and initiated a shutdown sequence.

Excerpt from
The Calculating Stars

by Mary Robinette Kowal

One

PRESIDENT DEWEY CONGRATULATES
NACA ON SATELLITE LAUNCH

March 3, 1952—(AP)—The National Advisory Committee for Aeronautics successfully put its third satellite into orbit, this one with the capability of sending radio signals down to Earth and taking measurements of the radiation in space. The president denies that the satellite has any military purpose and says that its mission is one of scientific exploration.

Do you remember where you were when the Meteor hit? I've never understood why people phrase it as a question, because of course you remember. I was in the mountains with Nathaniel. He had inherited this cabin from his father and we used to go up there for stargazing. By which I mean: sex. Oh, don't pretend that you're shocked. Nathaniel and I were a healthy young married couple, so most of the stars I saw were painted across the inside of my eyelids.

If I had known how long the stars were going to be hidden, I would have spent a lot more time outside with the telescope.

We were lying in the bed with the covers in a tangled mess around us. The morning light filtered through silver snowfall and did nothing to warm the room. We'd been awake for hours, but hadn't gotten out of bed yet for obvious reasons. Nathaniel had his leg thrown over me and was snuggled up against my side, tracing a finger along my collarbone in time with the music on our little battery-powered transistor radio.

I stretched under his ministrations and patted his shoulder. "Well, well . . . my very own 'Sixty Minute Man.'"

He snorted, his warm breath tickling my neck. "Does that mean I get another fifteen minutes of kissing?"

"If you start a fire."

"I thought I already did." But he rolled up onto his elbow and got out of bed.

We were taking a much needed break after a long push to prepare for the National Advisory Committee for Aeronautics' launch. If I hadn't also been at NACA doing computations, I wouldn't have seen Nathaniel awake anytime during the past two months.

I pulled the covers up over myself and turned on my side to watch him. He was lean, and only his time in the Army during World War II kept him from being scrawny. I loved watching the muscles play under his skin as he pulled wood off the pile under the big picture window. The snow framed him beautifully, its silver light just catching in the strands of his blond hair.

And then the world outside lit up.

If you were anywhere within five hundred miles of Washington, D.C., at 9:53 a.m. on March 3rd, 1952, and facing a window, then you remember that light.

Briefly red, and then so violently white that it washed out even the shadows. Nathaniel straightened, the log still in his hands.

"Elma! Cover your eyes!"

I did. That light. It must be an A-bomb. The Russians had been none too happy with us since President Dewey took office. God. The blast center must have been D.C.

How long until it hit us? We'd both been at Trinity for the atom bomb tests, but all of the numbers had run out of my head. D.C. was far enough away that the heat wouldn't hit us, but it would kick off the war we had all been dreading.

As I sat there with my eyes squeezed shut, the light faded.

Nothing happened. The music on the radio continued to play. If the radio was playing, then there wasn't an electromagnetic pulse. I opened my eyes. "Right." I hooked a thumb at the radio. "Clearly not an A-bomb."

Nathaniel had spun away to get clear of the window, but he was still holding the log. He turned it over in his hands and glanced outside. "There hasn't been any sound yet. How long has it been?"

The radio continued to play and it was still "Sixty Minute Man." What had that light been? "I wasn't counting. A little over a minute?" I shivered as I did the speed-of-sound calculations and the seconds ticked by.

"Zero point two miles per second. So the center is at least twenty miles away?"

Nathaniel paused in the process of grabbing a sweater and the seconds continued to tick by. Thirty miles. Forty. Fifty. "That's . . . that's a big explosion to have been that bright."

Taking a slow breath, I shook my head, more out of desire for it not to be true than out of conviction. "It wasn't an A-bomb."

"I'm open to other theories." He hauled his sweater on, the wool turning his hair into a haystack of static.

The music changed to "Some Enchanted Evening." I got

out of bed and grabbed a bra and the trousers I'd taken off the day before. Outside, snow swirled past the window. "Well . . . they haven't interrupted the broadcast, so it has to be something fairly benign, or at least localized. It could be one of the munitions plants."

"Maybe a meteor."

"Ah!" That idea had some merit and would explain why the broadcast hadn't been interrupted. It was a localized thing. I let out a breath in relief. "And we could have been directly under the flight path. That would explain why there hasn't been an explosion, if what we were seeing was just it burning up. All light and fury, signifying nothing."

Nathaniel's fingers brushed mine and he took the ends of the bra out of my hand. He hooked the strap and then he ran his hands up my shoulder blades to rest on my upper arms. His hands were hot against my skin. I leaned back into his touch, but I couldn't quite stop thinking about that light. It had been *so* bright. He squeezed me a little, before releasing me. "Yes."

"Yes, it was a meteor?"

"Yes, we should go back."

I wanted to believe that it was just a fluke, but I had been able to see the light through my closed eyes. While we got dressed, the radio kept playing one cheerful tune after another. Maybe that was why I pulled on my hiking boots instead of loafers, because some part of my brain kept waiting for things to get worse. Neither of us commented on it, but every time a song ended, I looked at the radio, certain that this time someone would tell us what had happened.

The floor of the cabin shuddered.

At first I thought a heavy truck was rolling past, but we were in the middle of nowhere. The porcelain robin that sat on the bedside table danced along its surface and fell.

You would think that, as a physicist, I would recognize an

earthquake faster. But we were in the Poconos, which was geologically stable.

Nathaniel didn't worry about that as much and grabbed my hand, pulling me into the doorway. The floor bucked and rolled under us. We clung to each other like in some sort of drunken foxtrot. The walls twisted and then . . . then the whole place came down. I'm pretty sure that I hollered.

When the earth stopped moving, the radio was still playing.

It buzzed as if a speaker were damaged, but somehow the battery kept it going. Nathaniel and I were lying, pressed together, in the remnants of the doorframe. Cold air swirled around us. I brushed the dust from his face.

My hands were shaking. "Okay?"

"Terrified." His blue eyes were wide, but both pupils were the same size, so . . . that was good. "You?"

I paused before answering with the social "fine," took a breath, and did an inventory of my body. I was filled with adrenaline, but I hadn't wet myself. Wanted to, though. "I'll be sore tomorrow, but I don't think there's any damage. To me, I mean."

He nodded and craned his neck around, looking at the little cavity we were buried inside. Sunlight was visible through a gap where one of the plywood ceiling panels had fallen against the remnants of the doorframe. It took some doing, but we were able to push and pry the wreckage to crawl out of that space and clamber across the remains of the cabin.

If I had been alone . . . Well, if I had been alone, I wouldn't have gotten into the doorway in time. I wrapped my arms around myself and shivered despite my sweater.

Nathaniel saw me shiver and squinted at the wreckage. "Might be able to get a blanket out."

"Let's just go to the car." I turned, praying that nothing

had fallen on it. Partly because it was the only way to the airfield where our plane was, but also because the car was borrowed. Thank heavens, it was sitting undamaged in the small parking area. "There's no way we'll find my purse in that mess. I can hot-wire it."

"Four minutes?" He stumbled in the snow. "Between the flash and the quake."

"Something like that." I was running numbers and distances in my head, and I'm certain he was, too. My pulse was beating against all of my joints and I grabbed for the smooth certainty of mathematics. "So the explosion center is still in the three-hundred-mile range."

"The airblast will be what . . . half an hour later? Give or take." For all the calm in his words, Nathaniel's hands shook as he opened the passenger door for me. "Which means we have another . . . fifteen minutes before it hits?"

The air burned cold in my lungs. Fifteen minutes. All of those years doing computations for rocket tests came into terrifying clarity. I could calculate the blast radius of a V2 or the potential of rocket propellant. But this . . . this was not numbers on a page. And I didn't have enough information to make a solid calculation.

All I knew for certain was that, as long as the radio was playing, it wasn't an A-bomb. But whatever had exploded was huge.

"Let's try to get as far down the mountain as we can before the airblast hits." The light had come from the southeast. Thank God, we were on the western side of the mountain, but southeast of us was D.C. and Philly and Baltimore and hundreds of thousands of people.

Including my family.

I slid onto the cold vinyl seat and leaned across it to pull out wires from under the steering column. It was easier to focus on something concrete like hot-wiring a car than on what ever was happening.

Outside the car, the air hissed and crackled. Nathaniel leaned out the win dow. "Shit."

"What?" I pulled my head out from under the dashboard and looked up, through the window, past the trees and the snow, and into the sky. Flame and smoke left contrails in the air. A meteor would have done some damage, exploding over the Earth's surface. A meteorite, though? It had actually *hit* the Earth and ejected material through the hole it had torn in the atmosphere. Ejecta. We were seeing pieces of the planet raining back down on us as fire. My voice quavered, but I tried for a jaunty tone anyway. "Well . . . at least you were wrong about it being a *meteor*."

I got the car running, and Nathaniel pulled out and headed down the mountain. There was no way we would make it to our plane before the airblast hit, but I had to hope that it would be protected enough in the barn. As for us . . . the more of the mountain we had between us and the airblast, the better. An explosion that bright, from three hundred miles away . . . the blast was not going to be gentle when it hit.

I turned on the radio, half-expecting it to be nothing but silence, but music came on immediately. I scrolled through the dial looking for something, anything that would tell us what was happening. There was just relentless music. As we drove, the car warmed up, but I couldn't stop shaking.

Sliding across the seat, I snuggled up against Nathaniel. "I think I'm in shock."

"Will you be able to fly?"

"Depends on how much ejecta there is when we get to the airfield." I had flown under fairly strenuous conditions during the war, even though, officially, I had never flown combat. But that was only a technical specification to make the American public feel more secure about women in the military. Still, if I thought of ejecta as anti-aircraft fire, I at least had a frame of reference for what lay ahead of us. "I just need to keep my body temperature from dropping any more."

He wrapped one arm around me, pulled the car over to the wrong side of the road, and tucked it into the lee of a craggy overhang. Between it and the mountain, we'd be shielded from the worst of the airblast. "This is probably the best shelter we can hope for until the blast hits."

"Good thinking." It was hard not to tense, waiting for the airblast. I rested my head against the scratchy wool of Nathaniel's jacket. Panicking would do neither of us any good, and we might well be wrong about what was happening.

A song cut off abruptly. I don't remember what it was; I just remember the sudden silence and then, finally, the announcer. Why had it taken them nearly half an hour to report on what was happening?

I had never heard Edward R. Murrow sound so shaken.

"Ladies and gentlemen . . . Ladies and gentlemen, we interrupt this program to bring you some grave news. Shortly before ten this morning, what appears to have been a meteor entered the Earth's atmosphere. The meteor has struck the ocean just off the coast of Maryland, causing a massive ball of fire, earthquakes, and other devastation. Coastal residents along the entire Eastern Seaboard are advised to evacuate inland because additional tidal waves are expected. All other citizens are asked to remain inside, to allow emergency responders to work without interruption." He paused, and the static hiss of the radio seemed to reflect the collective nation holding our breath.

"We go now to our correspondent Phillip Williams from our affiliate WCBO of Philadelphia, who is at the scene."

Why would they have gone to a Philadelphia affiliate, instead of someone at the scene in D.C.? Or Baltimore?

At first, I thought the static had gotten worse, and then I realized that it was the sound of a massive fire. It took me a moment longer to understand. It had taken them this long to find a reporter who was still alive, and the closest one had been in Philadelphia.

"I am standing on the US-1, some seventy miles north of where the meteor struck. This is as close as we were able to get, even by plane, due to the tremendous heat. What lay under me as we flew was a scene of horrifying devastation.

It is as if a hand had scooped away the capital and taken with it all of the men and women who resided there. As of yet, the condition of the president is unknown, but—"

My heart clenched when his voice broke. I had listened to Williams report the Second World War without breaking stride. Later, when I saw where he had been standing, I was amazed that he was able to speak at all. "But of Washington itself, nothing remains."

Biographies

Kate Dollarhyde

Kate Dollarhyde is a Nebula Award-winning game designer and writer of speculative fiction. Her stories have been published in *Fireside Fiction*, *Lackington's*, *Beneath Ceaseless Skies*, and other magazines. Previously, she was the editor-in-chief of the short fiction magazine *Strange Horizons*. She is also a narrative designer at Obsidian Entertainment, where she's written for The Outer Worlds and the Pillars of Eternity series. She is represented by DongWon Song of Howard Morhaim Literary Agency. She lives in California.

Brandon O'Brien

Brandon O'Brien is a performance poet, science fiction and fantasy writer, media critic, teaching artist, and game designer living and working in Trinidad and Tobago. His short stories, essays and poetry has been published in in publications such as *Uncanny Magazine*, *Strange Horizons*, and sx salon, as well as anthologies such as *Sunvault, Ride The Star Wind,* and *New Worlds, Old Ways*.

His work is focused on using speculative lenses to reframe marginalized and Atlantic realities, imagine radical futures, and prescribe togetherness, awareness, and rebellion as forces for positive change leading into uncertain times.

P. Djèlí Clark

Phenderson Djéli Clark is the award winning and Hugo, Nebula, Sturgeon, and World Fantasy nominated author of the novellas *The Black God's Drums* and *The Haunting of Tram Car 015*. His stories have appeared in online venues such as

Tor.com, *Daily Science Fiction*, *Heroic Fantasy Quarterly*, *Apex*, *Lightspeed*, *Fireside Fiction*, *Beneath Ceaseless Skies*, and in print anthologies including, *Griots*, *Hidden Youth*, and *Clockwork Cairo*. He is a founding member of *FIYAH Literary Magazine* and an infrequent reviewer at *Strange Horizons*.

When not writing speculative fiction, P. Djèlí Clark works as an academic historian whose research spans comparative slavery and emancipation in the Atlantic World. At current time, he resides in a small Edwardian castle in New England with his wife, infant daughters, and pet dragon (who suspiciously resembles a Boston Terrier). When so inclined he rambles on issues of speculative fiction, politics, and diversity at his aptly named blog The Disgruntled Haradrim.

Rhett C. Bruno

Rhett C. Bruno is the *USA Today* Bestselling & Nebula Award nominated Sci-Fi/Fantasy Author of the *Circuit Series* (Diversion Books, Podium Audio), *Buried Goddess Saga* (Aethon Books, Audible Studios) and the *Children Of Titan Series* (Aethon Books, Audible Studios), and the Audible Original, *The Luna Missile Crisis*. He is also the co-owner and founder of Aethon Books, as well as the creator of the popular SF/F promotional platforms, Sci-Fi Bridge & Fantasy Bridge.

He's a full-time author and publisher living in Connecticut with his wife and dog Raven. Rhett also recently earned a Certificate in Screenwriting from the New School in NYC, in the hopes of one day writing for TV or video games. He is represented by Ethan Ellenberg of the Ethan Ellenberg Literary Agency.

A. T. Greenblatt

A.T. Greenblatt is a mechanical engineer by day and a writer by night. She lives in Philadelphia where she's known to frequently subject her friends to various cooking and home brewing experiments. She is a graduate of Viable Paradise XVI and Clarion West 2017. Her work has been nominated for Nebula Awards, has been in multiple Year's Best anthologies, and has appeared in *Clarkesworld, Beneath Ceaseless Skies,* and *Fireside*, as well as other fine publications. You can find her online at atgreenblatt.com and on Twitter at @AtGreenblatt.

Alix E. Harrow

Alix E. Harrow has been a student and a teacher, a farm-worker and a cashier, an ice-cream-scooper and a 9-to-5 office-dweller. She's lived in tents and cars, cramped city apartments and lonely cabins, and spent a summer in a really sweet '79 VW Vanagon. She has library cards in at least five states.

Now she's a full-time writer living with her husband and two semi-feral kids in Kentucky. Her short fiction has appeared in *Shimmer, Strange Horizons, Tor.com, Apex*, and other venues, and *The Ten Thousand Doors of January* is her debut novel. Find her wasting time and having opinions at @AlixEHarrow on Twitter.

Sarah Pinsker

Sarah Pinsker is the author of over fifty works of short fiction, including the novelette "Our Lady of the Open Road," winner of the Nebula Award in 2016. Her novelette "In Joy, Knowing the Abyss Behind," was the Sturgeon Award winner in 2014. Her fiction has been published in magazines including *Asimov's, Strange Horizons, Fantasy & Science Fiction, Lightspeed*, and *Uncanny* and in numerous anthologies and year's bests. Her stories have been translated into Chinese, Spanish, French, and Italian, among other languages, and have been nominated for the Nebula, Hugo,

Locus, Eugie, and World Fantasy Awards.

Sarah's first collection, *Sooner or Later Everything Falls Into the Sea: Stories* was published by Small Beer Press in March 2019, and her first novel, *A Song For A New Day*, was published by Penguin/Random House/Berkley in September 2019.

She is also a singer/songwriter with three albums on various independent labels (the third with her rock band, the Stalking Horses) and a fourth in the works. She lives in Baltimore, Maryland and can be found online at sarahpinsker.com and twitter.com/sarahpinsker.

Brooke Bolander

Brooke Bolander writes weird things of indeterminate genre, most of them leaning rather heavily towards fantasy or general all-around weirdness. She attended the University of Leicester 2004-2007 studying History and Archaeology and is an alum of the 2011 Clarion Writers' Workshop at UCSD. Her stories have been featured in *Lightspeed, Strange Horizons, Nightmare, Uncanny,* and various other fine purveyors of the fantastic. She has been a finalist for the Nebula, the Hugo, the Locus, the Theodore Sturgeon, and the World Fantasy awards, much to her unending bafflement. Her debut book with Tor.com Publishing, *The Only Harmless Great Thing*, was released in 2018. She is represented by Michael Curry at Donald Maass Literary Agency.

Tina Connolly

Tina Connolly is the author of the Ironskin trilogy from Tor Books, the Seriously Wicked series from Tor Teen, and the collection *On the Eyeball Floor and Other Stories* from Fairwood Press. Her stories have appeared in *The Magazine of Fantasy and Science Fiction, Tor.com, Analog, Lightspeed, Beneath Ceaseless Skies, Uncanny, Strange Horizons, Women*

Destroy SF and more. Her stories and novels have been finalists for the Hugo, Nebula, Norton, Locus, and World Fantasy awards. Her narrations have appeared in audiobooks and podcasts including *Podcastle, Pseudopod, Beneath Ceaseless Skies*, and more. She is one of the co-hosts of *Escape Pod*, and runs the Parsec-winning flash fiction podcast Toasted Cake. She is originally from Lawrence, Kansas, but she now lives with her family in Portland, Oregon.

Andy Duncan

Andy Duncan is a writer of fantasy, science fiction and horror. He's won a Nebula Award, a Theodore Sturgeon Memorial Award, and received three World Fantasy Awards. His 2000 debut collection *Beluthahatchie and Other Stories* was published by Golden Gryphon Press. His second collection is *The Pottawatomie Giant and Other Stories*, from PS Publishing in 2012. His other books include *Crossroads: Tales of the Southern Literary Fantastic* (co-edited with F. Brett Cox), and his stories also have appeared in such magazines as *Clarkesworld, Conjunctions, Light speed, Realms of Fantasy and Weird Tales*; in such original anthologies as *The Dragon Book, Mojo: Conjure Stories, Wizards and the Eclipse*, Polyphony and Starlight series; and in 14 year's-best volumes. He is a graduate of the creative writing programs at North Carolina State University and the University of Alabama and of the Clarion West writers' workshop in Seattle.

José Pablo Iriarte

José Pablo Iriarte is a Cuban-American writer and teacher who lives in Central Florida. José's fiction can be found in magazines such as *Lightspeed, Strange Horizons, Fireside Fiction,* and others, and has been featured in best-of lists compiled by *Tangent Online, Featured Futures, iO9*, and *Quick*

Sip Reviews, and on the SFWA Nebula Award Recommended Reading List. Jose's novelette, "The Substance of My Lives, the Accidents of Our Births," was a Nebula Award Finalist and was long-listed for the James Tiptree, Jr. Literary Award. Learn more at www.labyrinthrat.com, or follow José on Twitter @labyrinthrat.

Lawrence M. Schoen

Lawrence M. Schoen holds a Ph.D. in cognitive psychology, is a past Astounding, Hugo, and Nebula, nominee, twice won the Cóyotl award for best novel, founded the Klingon Language Institute, and occasionally does work as a hypnotherapist specializing in authors' issues.

His science fiction includes many light and humorous adventures of a space-faring stage hypnotist and his alien animal companion. Other works take a very different tone, exploring aspects of determinism and free will, generally redefining the continua between life and death. Sometimes he blurs the funny and the serious. Lawrence lives near Philadelphia, Pennsylvania with his wife and their dog.

Yudhanjaya Wijeratne and R.R. Virdi

Yudhanjaya Wijeratne is a Sri Lankan science fiction author (*Numbercaste, The Inhuman Race, The Slow Sad Suicide*) and data scientist. He is a senior researcher at the Data, Algorithms and Policy team at LIRNEasia, a nonprofit think tank. He co-founded Watchdog, a fact-checking organization, where he spends much of his time digging into misinformation. He is also a Nebula Award finalist with a five-book deal from HarperCollins. He built and operates OSUN, a set of literary experiments using OpenAI technology to test a human+AI collaboration in art.

R.R. Virdi is a two-time Dragon Award finalist and a Nebula Award finalist. He is the author of two urban fantasy series, The Grave Report and The Books of Winter; the LitRPG/portal fantasy series Monster Slayer Online; and the author of a space western/scifi series Shepherd of Light. He has worked in the automotive industry as a mechanic, in retail, and in the custom gaming computer world. He's an avid car nut with a special love for American classics.

Aliette de Bodard

Aliette de Bodard lives and works in Paris. She has won three Nebula Awards, a Locus Award, a British Fantasy Award and four British Science Fiction Association Awards, and was a double Hugo finalist for 2019 (Best Series and Best Novella). Her most recent book is *Of Dragons, Feasts and Murders*, a fantasy of manners and murders set in an alternate 19th Century Vietnamese court (upcoming July 7th from JABberwocky Literary Agency, Inc.). Her short story collection *Of Wars, and Memories, and Starlight* is out from Subterranean Press. She lives in Paris.

Jonathan P. Brazee

Jonathan P. Brazee is a retired Marine infantry colonel and now a full-time writer living in North Las Vegas, Nevada. His writing career started in 1978 with "Secession," a science fiction story published in Labyrinth Magazine, but as a Marine, he published non-fiction in a variety of subjects.

He wrote his first novel, *The Few*, while stationed in Iraq in 2006. Now, he is a hybrid writer with emphasis on self-published works and has over 55 fiction titles in military science fiction, military fiction, paranormal, and historical fiction.

Jonathan's undergraduate degree was earned at the U. S. Naval Academy (Class of 1979), and he attended graduate school at U. S. International University and the University of California, San Diego, earning a masters and doctorate. He is a member of the Disabled American Veterans, the Veterans of Foreign Wars, the US. Naval Academy Alumni Association, and the Science Fiction and Fantasy Writers of America.

Kate Heartfield

Kate Heartfield is the author of the historical fantasy novel *Armed in Her Fashion* (ChiZine 2018) and the Alice Payne time travel novellas (Tor.com Publishing 2018/2019). She also writes interactive fiction, including *The Road to Canterbury*, and *The Magician's Workshop*, published by Choice of Games. Her fiction has won or been shortlisted for the Nebula, Locus, Aurora and Crawford awards, and her journalism for a National Newspaper Award. Her novella "The Course of True Love" was published by Abaddon Books in 2016. Her short fiction has appeared in *Strange Horizons*, *Lackington's*, *Podcastle* and elsewhere. A former journalist, Kate lives in Ottawa, Canada.

Kelly Robson

Kelly Robson is a Canadian short fiction writer. Her novelette "A Human Stain" won the 2018 Nebula Award, and she has won both the 2019 and 2016 Aurora Awards for best Short Story. She has also been a finalist for the Hugo, Nebula, World Fantasy, Theodore Sturgeon, Locus, Astounding, Aurora, and Sunburst Awards. Kelly consults as a creative futurist for organizations such as UNICEF and the Suncor Energy Foundation. After twenty-two years in Vancouver, she and her wife, writer A. M. Dellamonica, now live in downtown Toronto.

Martha Wells

Martha Wells has written many fantasy novels, including *The Books of the Raksura* series (beginning with *The Cloud Roads*), the Ile-Rien series (including *The Death of the Necromancer*) as well as YA fantasy novels, short stories, media tie-ins (for *Star Wars* and *Stargate: Atlantis*), and non-fiction. Her most recent fantasy novel is *The Harbors of the Sun* in 2017, the final novel in *The Books of the Raksura* series. She has a new series, *The Murderbot Diaries*, published by Tor.com. She was also the lead writer for the story team of *Magic: the Gathering*'s Dominaria expansion in 2018. She has won a Nebula Award, two Hugo Awards, an ALA/YALSA Alex Award, two Locus Awards, and her work has appeared on the Philip K. Dick Award ballot, the BSFA Award ballot, the *USA Today* Bestseller List, and the *New York Times* Bestseller List. Her books have been published in sixteen languages.

Tomi Adeyemi

Tomi Adeyemi is the #1 Best-Selling and Hugo award-winning author of *Children Of Blood And Bone* and its sequel, *Children Of Virtue And Vengeance*. After graduating Harvard University with an honors degree in English literature, she received a fellowship to study West African mythology, religion, and culture in Salvador, Brazil. It was there that she discovered the inspiration for her debut novel, *Children Of Blood And Bone*. *Children Of Blood And Bone* has spent over two years on *The New York Times* Best Seller list and its film adaptation is currently in active development with Disney's Fox and Lucasfilms.

When Tomi's not working on her novels or watching *Seventeen* and BTS music videos, she can be found teaching creative writing on her website, through workshops, and through her online masterclass: **The Writer's Roadmap**.

She was recently named to the 2020 *Forbes* 30 Under 30 list, and her website has been named one of the 101 best websites for writers by *Writer's Digest*.

Mary Robinette Kowal

Mary Robinette Kowal is the author of *The Glamourist Histories* series, *Ghost Talkers,* and the Lady Astronaut series. She's the President of SFWA, part of the award-winning podcast *Writing Excuses* and has received the Astounding Award for Best New Writer, four Hugo awards, the Nebula and Locus awards. Her stories appear in *Asimov's*, *Uncanny*, and several Year's Best anthologies. Mary Robinette, a professional puppeteer, also performs as a voice actor (SAG/AFTRA), recording fiction for authors including Seanan McGuire, Cory Doctorow, and John Scalzi. She lives in Nashville with her husband Rob and over a dozen manual typewriters. Visit maryrobinettekowal.com.

About the Science Fiction and Fantasy Writers of America (SFWA)

Science Fiction and Fantasy Writers of America, Inc. (SFWA) was founded in 1965 by the American science fiction author Damon Knight and was originally named Science Fiction Writers of America. In 1991, the name of the organization was changed to Science Fiction and Fantasy Writers of America, although the acronym SFWA was not changed. In 2013, the members of the organization voted to reincorporate in California, effectively beginning a new 501(c)3 public charity. Activities of the old Massachusetts corporation officially merged into the new California corporation as of July 1st, 2014. Today, SFWA is home to over 2000 authors, artists, and allied professionals, and is widely recognized as one of the most effective non-profit writers' organizations in existence. Learn more about SFWA at sfwa.org; you can also follow SFWA on Facebook and on Twitter @sfwa.

About the Nebula Awards

The Nebula Awards, presented annually at the SFWA Nebula Conference, recognize the best works of science fiction and fantasy published in the United States as selected by members of the Science Fiction and Fantasy Writers of America. The first Nebula Awards were presented in 1966.

The Nebula Awards include four fiction awards, a game writing award, the Ray Bradbury Nebula Award for Outstanding Dramatic Presentation, and the Andre Norton Nebula Award for Middle Grade and Young Adult Fiction. SFWA also administers the Kate Wilhelm Solstice Award, the Kevin O'Donnell, Jr. Service to SFWA Award, and the Damon Knight Memorial Grand Master Award.

For more information, visit
nebulas.sfwa.org/nebula-conference.